NightShadow

Some Other Titles from Falcon Press

Joseph C. Lisiewski, Ph.D.
Ceremonial Magic and the Power of Evocation
Kabbalistic Cycles and the Mastery of Life
Kabbalistic Handbook for the Practicing Magician
Israel Regardie and the Philosopher's Stone
Howlings from the Pit
Geometries of the Mind

Christopher S. Hyatt, Ph.D.
Undoing Yourself with Energized Meditation and Other Devices
Techniques for Undoing Yourself (audios)
Energized Hypnosis (book, videos & audios)
To Lie Is Human: Not Getting Caught Is Divine
Secrets of Western Tantra: The Sexuality of the Middle Path
Hard Zen, Soft Heart

Christopher S. Hyatt, Ph.D. with contributions by
Wm. S. Burroughs, Timothy Leary, Robert Anton Wilson et al.
Rebels & Devils: The Psychology of Liberation

Christopher S. Hyatt, Ph.D. & Antero Alli
A Modern Shaman's Guide to a Pregnant Universe

S. Jason Black and Christopher S. Hyatt, Ph.D.
Pacts with the Devil: A Chronicle of Sex, Blasphemy & Liberation
Urban Voodoo: A Beginner's Guide to Afro-Caribbean Magic

Antero Alli
Angel Tech: A Modern Shaman's Guide to Reality Selection
The Eight-Circuit Brain

Peter J. Carroll
The Chaos Magick Audios
PsyberMagick

Phil Hine
Condensed Chaos: An Introduction to Chaos Magic
Prime Chaos: Adventures in Chaos Magic
The Pseudonomicon

Israel Regardie
The Complete Golden Dawn System of Magic
New Wings for Daedalus
The Golden Dawn Audios

Steven Heller
Monsters & Magical Sticks: There's No Such Thing as Hypnosis?

**For up-to-the-minute information on prices and availability,
please visit our website at
http://originalfalcon.com**

NightShadow

by
Joseph C. Lisiewski, Ph.D.

THE *Original* FALCON PRESS
TEMPE, ARIZONA, U.S.A.

International Standard Book Number: 978-1-61869-991-6
ISBN: 978-1-61869-992-3 (mobi)
ISBN: 978-1-61869-993-0 (ePub)
Library of Congress Control Number: 2021931359

First Edition 2007
First Falcon Edition 2021
First eBook Edition 2021

Front Cover by Gazink

Address all inquiries to:
The Original Falcon Press
1753 East Broadway Road #101-277
Tempe, AZ 85282 U.S.A.
(or)
PO Box 3540
Silver Springs NV 89429 U.S.A.
website: http://www.originalfalcon.com
email: info@originalfalcon.com

TABLE OF CONTENTS

CHAPTER ONE

▼

THE FIRST CORPSE

Gus Breach remained in a squatting position, his arms resting on his knees, hands locked together. On that bitterly cold day, January 12th, 1976, a man's breath would normally crystallize in front of him in a slow, steady stream. But not on that Monday. The Chief's breath froze in front of his face in short, even bursts, keeping pace with the pounding heart in his chest. As he stared down at the covered corpse lying on the mountaintop dirt road in front of him, he shook his head from side to side. The look of disgust sat heavy on his hard, cracked face, and he began to talk to himself.

"What could do a thing like this to a full grown man! Ten years on the Pittsburgh force and now twenty in this nothin' hick town. I expected to have it a lot easier than this near my retirement! This is for the big city boys with the detectives and resources needed to deal with insanity like this. This is why I left the city! Had my belly full of this kind of crap! It sure doesn't belong here in Kulpsville, Pennsylvania! Nothin' ever happens in the coal towns around here. Nothin' more than the usual drunks fightin' with their old ladies or with each other, or a punk or two breakin' a window at the Junior High, or maybe some son-of-a-gun rippin' off a vending machine in the Laundromat. Not this. Damn!

"I don't even know where to begin! It's been a long time since I handled anything even remotely like this. Things were a lot different then. Not like now. And murder like this one? Guess I'll have to call in the state boys down the road. Maybe they'll give me a quick refresher course in homicide investigation or offer some pointers. Maybe even help out with the investigation. Guess that's the best I can look for."

A loud shout hacked its way through the frozen winter air and finally reached Breach's ears. "Hey, Chief! I found somethin'! Better come and take a look!"

"What did you find, Barker?" Breach called back.

"I think you better come and take a look! I don't want to disturb any evidence!" the younger cop called back.

"Dave, how many times do I have to tell you? This isn't *Kojak*! What did you find?"

"Lots of weird footprints, Chief, and a...a...head!"

"What did you say?" Breach yelled back in excitement.

"A head. A human head. It's got to belong to the dead guy up there on the road with you! You'd better come and take a look!"

The Chief rose from his stooped position, walked over to a water-company cleared path, and joined Dave Barker in a hollow fifty yards away that paralleled the mountain road.

Barker had covered his find with an old rag he carried in his back pocket. He was new to the force, and still went by the book. He used the rag to keep his new, steel blue .38 Police Special polished, even while on the job. He would never be able to use the rag for that purpose again.

"Lift the rag up," Breach ordered. Let's see what you've got there, son."

Barker removed the soiled rag carefully. Staring up at the Chief of Police was a human head. Its eyes were frozen in place by the winter chill, but still they bulged from their sockets as if reeling in horror from the sight of some inhuman monstrosity, or perhaps from the realization of dying. The clear haze covering the pupils was frozen over by a more intense cold—one all men would know on a given day. The cold of death. Its curly graying blond hair lay in fixed, random loops on the top of its skull. Ice crystals had worked their way in from the outside, matting the strands after the body warmth had ebbed away. The ice sparkles on the skull reminded Breach of the head of Medusa.

The skin was an ashen gray, held tightly in place by contracted facial muscles. Its mouth was open, a blue-black tongue hanging out and lying over the left corner of the mouth. From the old cop's battlefield experience in World War II, the deep purple lips told him the man had been dead for less than twelve hours. Even cold doesn't turn a man's lips that color. Only death, and the time it came to him, did that. Breach began to clench his fists tightly. His black leather gloves made crackling sounds as he opened and closed his hands several times. He wanted to make sure the gloves were still on, and that he could feel through them. He didn't want to touch the thing with his bare flesh.

"Look at these footprints, Gus! I was born and raised around here just the others, and I've hunted these mountains since I was nine. I got to tell you, Chief, I've seen a lot of tracks over the years, but I've never seen anything like this! What do you make of them?"

Breach walked carefully around a set of tracks that were better preserved than the others. The vortex formed by the trees in the hollow caused the wind to roll around this particular set of prints, instead of covering them with blowing snow as it did to most of the others. He inspected them carefully, bending down to feel their curve and depth.

"Come here, I want you to learn. See here? Look at the heel. See how round it is at the back? Now look at it here, three inches down. You know what that slight arc is?"

"No," the young cop said. "That's what confused me. You can see the toes up at the front of the print clear enough, but a bare heel doesn't make a mark like that. It's flat near the arc, not round like at the base. So what could make a footprint like that?"

The Chief didn't answer the young man's question immediately. He had a linear way of teaching. Like putting one foot in front of the other to get from where he was to where he wanted to go. He didn't skip around like the young kids who were the patrolmen on his force.

"So why are you describing a bare human footprint?" the Chief asked, pulling the correct answers out of Barker by forcing him to order his mind.

"Well, because of the toes! Look at 'em! Those are human toes! Just look!"

"Yeah. But look at them again. When a man walks barefoot and upright, his toes lie out flat. So the toe prints would be long. That's not what we see. They're all bunched up, as though whatever made them pulled 'em up tight like a knuckle. Now look back at the heel, at the arc. The arc is pointing toward the toes, not back toward the heel. That shows the pressure of the stride was directed forward, not backward, as in a normal gait. What does that tell you?"

Dave thought for a few moments and then replied. "Well, if the toes are pulled back tight, and the arc is pointing toward them instead of back to the heel, then…" He stopped and worked his own right foot in his boots, trying to get the feel of the motion that could make the print.

"Then whoever made them was trying to balance himself because of the knuckled up toes!"

"Exactly!" Breach shot back proudly. "Now. Why would he have knuckled-up his toes in the first place?

"I can't figure that one out, Chief. It makes no sense," Barker replied sheepishly, as if he were a kid who just barely passed a geometry test.

"Sure you can," Breach insisted. "Just think and feel. Let your knowledge of hunting and tracking blend with your intuition. A cop's greatest asset isn't logic, Dave. That's his second most powerful tool. His intuition does him the most credit, and will solve cases logic can't touch. Rely solely only on logic, and you might as well quit the force now, because most of your case files will remain open."

"Well," Barker said slowly, trying to follow the Chief's instructions, "because he couldn't walk right and balance himself."

"Right again! And why couldn't he walk right?"

The young man thought and felt further. "Because something was breaking up his stride. So he balanced himself by knuckling up his toes so he could move."

"Correct. But you're still missing the point, the last point that will pull all of this together. Look at the print again. Try to put it together, but now go only on feeling. On your intuition. Throw logic completely out, because it has taken you as far as it can. Look again. Look at what you see, not what your logic tells you!" Breach encouraged.

"I'm sorry, Chief, I just can't see through it." Barker replied wearily. "I'm sorry to disappoint you."

"Don't worry, son. You didn't disappoint me. You did better than any of the other guys could have done. I mean it. Tom and Greg wouldn't have gotten this far. Let me explain.

"Everything you said is right on the money. The fact that ties it all together is completely illogical, and yet it's the answer. The something that was breaking up his stride was a shoe. Half a shoe, to be exact. The back of the shoe was intact. That's what made the heel mark. But the front of the shoe was missing. That half shoe broke up his stride, causing him to curl up his toes so he could balance himself and walk upright. He still couldn't walk right, but he could walk.

That's why we have the prints we do! And if you think about it, these are the same type of prints we found coming from the east leading to the spot where the man finally fell."

"But Chief. That's crazy! Who would be running around up here in the mountains with half a shoe in this bitter cold weather?"

"Now you've got the gist of it! It's crazy to you, because your logic fell apart completely. Because such a thing is so illogical, you didn't consider it. That's why I said you have to rely on your intuition first. Then bring in the logic. Now the logic comes into play, and gives us the question to ask. But the first question to be asked here is not why, but who made them. When we find out who, the why will take care of itself.

"And if you notice, the prints are exactly the same for each set. Now look at the stride. It's held back. How do I know that? Because there's more pressure on the curled toes than at the heel, which means he couldn't take the long strides his gait normally allows. He had to cut back on his stride-length in order to keep his balance. It tells us he limped off. Now take a good look at the thin streaks following behind each footprint. Something was hanging down over his shoes, being dragged along as he walked off. And from the looks of it, he headed south, toward Kulpsville!"

The young cop looked at old Breach with amazement and admiration. "Gus," he said softly, "I trust I'll get to be as good as you are as the years go by. I really mean it. I take my job seriously, sometimes maybe too seriously. I know, what with the town only having fifteen thousand people in it, and being such an out-of-the-way place and all, and still I get carried away with police work. I'll bet you were like me when you were a young detective back in Pittsburgh! But I figure, whatever a man is given to do in this life, he should do the best he can, wherever he finds himself. I'm sorry I couldn't put it all together, yet."

"Relax!" Breach said with a reassuring note in his voice. "You'll be all right. My smarts didn't come to me overnight. It took years, but all anyone ever sees is the result today. In five years or so, you'll no doubt be the next Chief. I'm sure of it. You have what it takes. Just remember what I said about logic and intuition. I learned those two sides of the same coin years ago. Well. You know the story. You've got the ability too. I'll continue to teach you as we go along. Just keep at it, and you'll be more than all right."

They continued to search the area for more clues. It was Breach who called out to Barker. "Come over here! I found something I want you to look at!"

Dave made his way through the snowdrifts crested among the trees.

"What did you find?"

Breach pointed to a frozen, dried red stain on the bark of a large white birch tree. "What does that look like to you?"

"Looks like a palm print. A bloody one."

"And what about those five fresh slashes in the tree bark? What do you make of them?"

"Well, they're up high, which means it was the hand of a big man. And they're smudged with blood too, so that means the hand that made the palm print made them as well. But that can't be, because it would mean the fingernails would have to be like some powerful claw to have made those gashes. I don't know what to think, Chief! Maybe they were made by a bear before the palm print landed near them?" Barker replied, again with a sheepish note in his voice.

"Look again. At the wood those slashes exposed. What do you see?"

"White, fresh wood."

"Feel it. Feel the bark. Now what does it do?" the Chief asked once more.

"It comes off in my fingers. It is fresh. Very fresh!"

"And what does that tell you, son?"

"If the wood had been ripped earlier, it would be frozen. It would snap like tinder because ice crystals would form in the sap, because the sap would have been exposed to the cold winter air for a longer period of time. But this wood is fresh and roll-able. That can only mean…the same hand that made the palm print made the gashes, as it pushed off from leaning against the tree?"

"Got it!" Breach approved. "That's right! The same hand made both, even though logic tells you a human hand couldn't have such claws. Yet when you allow your intuition to ask the right questions, you'll see the physical evidence—and your own personal world for that matter—as it exists. Not as your preconceived notions would tell you it should exist. Then the logical deductions will tell you the rest.

Just because it doesn't fit into normal experience is no reason to try and make it fit! Got that, son?"

"Yeah. Now I've got it, and I damn well wish I didn't!" Barker replied with disbelief in his voice. "What we have is a large, bloodied hand, obviously with fresh blood from the head. And that hand somehow has powerful claws attached to it. And logic tells me the owner of that hand didn't just handle the head. He was the murderer, because the wood is still fresh. So he had to kill the man up on the road, bring his head down here to the hollow for some reason, and then make his way back up to the mountain road. As he walked, he probably lost his balance because of his knuckled toes. And his crunched-up toes resulted from him having only half a shoe on one foot. The half exposing his toes was missing. Is that right?"

"Absolutely." Breach replied back, uneasy. "What we have here is something that doesn't fit into any normal murder. We have some type of demented psychopath on our hands. Or something that acts like one. That's how I read it."

"Did you say, something?"

"That's right. We exclude no possibilities. No matter how remote. I said possibilities, remember. Not probabilities. You might not understand this, but in time you will. It was best phrased by Shakespeare. Don't get me wrong. I'm no great literature authority. But I always loved the classics. And you don't have to be a college graduate to enjoy or learn from them. There's a lot of life in the great writings!

"There is one line in particular Shakespeare wrote that has haunted me all through the years, and played one hell of a role in a lot of my police work too. 'There are more things in heaven and earth, Horatio, than are dreamt of in your philosophies.' He was right. The bottom line of what he was saying is to keep an open mind, no matter what the pressures and status quo of society push you to believe. Because son, when it comes right down to it, life is about 90% belief of one type or another. Reality is the other 10%! And what you believe comes back to you as reality, one way or another."

"There doesn't seem to be any more evidence around here," Breach commented after the two spent another twenty minutes surveying the area. "If there's anything else of importance here, the snow drifted over it. We'd better get back to the body. I radioed

Trudy back at the office to send Frank Lewis up here. I expect him anytime. Oh, and Dave, bring the…head…with you. Keep it covered up. It's only right."

The two cops made their way back to the road. The last snowfall two days ago had dropped six more inches of new snow over the area. But in the mountains surrounding the town, it had combined with the foot of snow that had fallen since late December. The winds took care of the rest, bunching the white blanket up into two to three-foot drifts. Dave cop took no notice of his rapid heartbeat as he plowed through the obstacles. But Breach felt his heart pounding like a hammer, and noticed how winded he became.

As they neared the covered corpse, Breach stopped to catch his breath. "Dave, please put that down," he said, pointing to the rag-covered head the young man was holding.

Breach examined the tracks in front of him, and watched them lead right across the road. "Stand here near the body. I want to take a look at something. Wait here."

Barker did as instructed, and stood next to the body, flapping his arms around his sides, trying to stay warm. But the brutal winds continued to batter him, while Breach walked off alone down the road. He continued to the point where the thing that left the tracks in the hollow had emerged from the woods and crossed the mountain road.

"Damn," he said to himself. "I thought I might be wrong. I wanted that thing to head off down the road and maybe disappear into the deep mountains in the west. Looks like it didn't." He followed them leading into the next thicket of trees, and then straight toward the town. "I'd better tell the boys we'll have to set up night surveillance on the back streets, at least for a couple of nights. Maybe we'll get a break, and whatever it is will pass the town by, and just leave us with a murder case. God, I pray that's all that comes out of this!"

Breach felt very uneasy. His intuition told him he was wishing into the wind. Deep down inside, he felt whatever it was that committed this murder was not human. At least, not in the sense any normal person understood the word. The temperatures were just too extreme, even for a psychopath to go out and about killing, let alone to hang around the scene of his deed. His old experiences told him those types kill and then get out of the area fast. Not this one. After its slaughter, it made no attempt to get out of the mountains quickly. It hung around the kill site, and for some reason, took its victim's head down to the hollow. But why?

His mind went back to the decapitated head. It looked normal enough, but then it was badly frozen over and pretty well snow covered. Still, he had seen enough, and had no intentions of examining it further. That was Frank's job. Again and again the old cop's intuition lead him to the feeling something was terribly wrong with the entire situation. Something did not fit in with any homicide he had ever encountered. Breach carefully checked the footprints crossing the road. They were the same as in the hollow. A half-shoe and knuckled-up toes on the right foot, a full shoe on the left foot, and a drawn-back gait. And behind each set of tracks, long streaks of something narrow, being dragged along as the thing moved.

When he turned to walk back to the corpse, he noticed several faint stains in the snow. An inexperienced eye would have missed them, especially with the setting sun's rays glistening off the snow bed from ever-changing angles. Bending down to examine them, he found they were starburst patterns of fresh blood. These were patterns of the type made from liquid dripping several feet from a pointed object…like a claw.

"That tears it. Whatever made the tracks in the hollow and here, did kill that man. The blood of its kill was still fresh on its fingers, or claws, as it limped across the road. I was right. We have a real problem here."

After returning to the young cop guarding the body, Breach started to explain what he had found further up the road. But he was cut short seconds after he started by the sound of an engine making its way toward them. It was late, after four p.m. The frozen winter sun was starting to set in the west, the same direction the sound of the car engine came from.

"That's Frank Lewis. Maybe he can help us on this one. I know he was born and raised here, but has he been a mortician all of his life?"

"Sure has. He inherited the business from his old man the same way his old man inherited it from his father. That's how things are back here. From father-to-son, and on, and on, and on. He's good, too. That's why he's the only one in town. I remember when I was a kid. Another guy tried to come in, figuring to bring new cosmetic ways with him. You know, to make the stiffs look better when they're laid out. Couldn't even get a foothold here, although he tried like hell. Finally, after two years of trying, the newcomer gave up and left. No one ever tried to give Frank competition again. Besides, since he's a local guy, everyone in town knows him. It's weird too, because they like the guy. He's not like the usual undertaker. Never was. He parties a little, has a few friends over for poker, and takes an active interest in the town. Really a nice guy."

As Frank pulled his 1956 Chevy Classic behind Breach's patrol car on the narrow mountain road, he rolled the window down and called out.

"What's the matter, Gus! Don't you have enough problems in town? Have to come way up here for more excitement?"

Gus was severely concerned over the situation. But he was a man who never lost his sense of humor. Not even in the worst of times.

"Yeah, you know me, Frank," the Chief teased back. "Always looking for trouble! Hell, there's nothing to report now for the local police blotter in that fancy newspaper of ours! Got to dig something up!"

After Lewis joined the two men, they filled him in on how they found the body, and what they found in the hollow. Then they gave the head to him. The mortician bent down, lifted the sheet covering the body, and gave it an experienced once-over examination. Then he unwrapped Dave's former gun rag, and took a look.

"Any ideas?" Breach asked, holding his breath.

"Just a minute. My car's nice and warm. I'm going to put the head in the back seat. Let it thaw out, so to speak. I want a better look before I say anything. By the way, Gus, I couldn't bring the hearse up here, so I brought my own car instead. I'm afraid you and Dave will have to put the body in your patrol car and take it around back to my Preparation Room. I can't handle it myself."

The mortician took the head back to his car, returned to the two men and asked, "Before I say anything, what do the two of you think? I mean, not if you have any suspects or anything like that. What I'd like to know is do you have any idea as to how the man was killed?"

"I'm not certain," Breach replied, as Dave shook his head in agreement. "We're looking to you for more information."

"Doesn't it seem obvious?" Lewis answered, but in a probing way, as if concealing some deeper concerns. "He was decapitated, right?"

"Yes, but how? and where? Look for yourself. Turn the body over. There are no pools of blood near it or in the hollow, other than the bloody palm print I told you about, and a few large spots near the body. If I remember right, the human body has six or eight pints of blood in it. Those few spots certainly don't account for anywhere near that much. Fact is, this place should look like a slaughter-house…but it doesn't."

"Maybe he was killed somewhere else and dropped off here. Ever think of that?"

"Yeah," Barker intervened. "But if so, there would be blood all over that weird-looking tuxedo he's wearing, especially if he was stabbed or shot. There would have to be lots of blood all over it, but there isn't. The Chief couldn't find any such wounds on the corpse when he first took a look at it, either. And if he was strangled, we should see slide marks from the garrote moving around on his neck as he struggled. People don't just stand around and get murdered, you know. They fight like hell!

"Another thing, Frank," Barker said with authority. "If he was dumped here, where are the tire tracks? When we got here, there were none. The only ones here are ours, and now yours. And since the last snow fall was only two days ago, they would stick out like sore thumbs!"

"No tire tracks at all, Gus?" Lewis asked, as if he didn't believe the young cop's remarks.

"None. Nothing but the footprints I told you we found in the hollow, and those that come from the east. I sent Pelski out that way to investigate, and he hasn't reported back yet. Maybe he will turn some up. That would be a relief as far as I'm concerned, Frank, but I don't think it's going to happen. It doesn't explain some of the details of the other evidence we found. Two sets of tracks come out of the east and lead here. You can see them leading right up to the body. Look," Breach explained, as he pointed to the tracks emerging from a tiny path cutting through a patch of trees in the east.

"So maybe he was carried to this point by two men and left? I asked myself that," the Chief explained. "But why would they drop him here, in the middle of an old road? There are mine pits all over this area. If two men carried him out here, they could have dropped him into one of them, and we'd of never found him! But the idea of two men carrying him up here was very short lived.

"Look again at the tracks leading up to the corpse. You can clearly see the one set was made by our corpse. The other set is the same half-shoe print we also found in the hollow. Conclusion? One I don't like, but I feel in my guts it's the right one. This man was run down by someone or something and killed on the spot where he fell. How one man could have inflicted a severing deathblow cutting the head off another man, I don't know. But that's what I think happened. And when you examine the head more closely, I think you're going to confirm it. That's what my intuition tells me, if you want to know."

Dave Barker looked at the Chief, stunned, and did not say a word. To him, his boss was proposing something straight out of a horror novel. Something you read late at night before going to bed, so you can have dark, scary dreams.

But Frank Lewis spoke out. He had the same sixty years under his old belt Breach had. And at that age, men don't feel obliged to hold their tongues. They say what's on their minds.

"Are you crazy, Gus? Do you know what you're saying? You're telling me some psychotic, limping with one half-shoe and crunched up toes sticking out into this bitter cold and snow, ran an apparently healthy man of about fifty years down, overpowered him, drained his blood from him, and then cut his head off! Damn it, Chief, you must be nuts to even think of something like that!"

"Maybe," Breach snapped back. "But it fits the physical evidence we have so far. If I'm wrong, Frank, then give me your version of what you think happened here. I'm all ears!"

"Don't be an ass! That's your job! Mine is preparing them for the final peace! Nothing more!"

"Then don't have such a smart-ass attitude, Frank," the Chief replied back caustically. "If you can't advance an explanation more logical than mine and one that will cover all of the evidence we have, then this will have to do! Because one thing is for sure, whatever else we come up with isn't going to explain away the facts we have already. All right?"

"Sorry, Gus. It's just that…well…it's just this reminds me of something that happened a long time ago. Something I finally forgot and never wanted to be reminded of. Oh, never mind. I apologize for going off like that!"

"No problem. This has us all more than a little unnerved. We'll just have to take it a step at a time and keep our eyes and minds opened. If we close either one, I guarantee you, we'll draw to a bad hand, and will never know what happened here." The Chief took Frank by the arm and moved him to the side of the car, out Dave's hearing range.

"To be honest with you, I could live with never knowing what really happened here. Hell, I don't know who the body is, anyway! Don't even know if he's from around here! But my problem is, whatever killed him moved out of the hollow, crossed this road we're now standing on, and headed south. *In the direction of town.* This is my real problem! This corpse may not be our last one!"

"Goddamn it!" Lewis retorted, chills racing up his spine as he thought of more corpses like this one piled up in his Prep room. "Don't use those words 'whatever' killed him, and don't think of any more victims like him! I know you have to run down the son-of-a-bitch that did this, but I have to prepare them! It's hard enough dealing with one case like this, without you throwing up the prospect of more of the same!"

"Well, that's how I see it. Sorry if it upsets you. Doesn't do my stomach much good, either."

"OK. Tell you what. It's four-thirty now," Lewis said as his teeth chattered. "The sun's really heading toward the horizon fast. Where is your other deputy anyway? Pelski, you said, right? Here's what I suggest we do. You and Dave help me get the corpse into your patrol car, blow the horn to get Tom back here, and then all of us head back to town. We'll meet at my Prep Room, and maybe we can make some sense out of this. How does that sound? What with things as they are and the sun setting and all, it's getting damn scary on this mountaintop, and I don't want to be around here when it gets dark!" Now the quiver in his voice added to the noise being made by his teeth. Breach knew fear was causing his reactions, not the rapidly dropping temperature.

"Well," he replied in a sympathetic tone, "I'm afraid you're gonna have a passenger to take back with you. Tony Nigalo, the kid who found the corpse around noon. He's in the back of my patrol car now. Scared shitless. I think he's in shock, but he'll be all right."

"What was he doing up here in the dead of winter anyway?" Lewis asked, the tone in his voice suggesting that if the kid had remained in town where he belonged, none of this would have happened.

"He's just like his old man in some ways. He set a trap line for fox and weasel, and was checking it. Then he found this. I'll bet you a dime to a doughnut after this, he'll forget about trapping! Finding something like that would shake up a grown man, let alone a kid!"

"All right, Gus! Be happy to oblige you! I'll just have to put the head in the trunk. I was thinking it would thaw out enough in the car while we talked and it probably did. But I didn't see the kid in the car, and well, if it's all the same to you, let's examine it properly back at my place."

"That's fine by me. I was just nervous for a quick answer about what you thought caused the man's death. The decapitation is just too obvious, at least to me. That's why I pushed you when you got here."

"To be honest with you," Lewis finally confessed, the door to the secret room of his own mind now opening to the place where his own fears and horrors lived, locked safely away from the light of his everyday mind. "It's hard for me to think about a 'whatever' killing that man. But my first rough examination has me wondering. See, I noticed the lack of puncture wounds and absence of blood just like you both did. But I didn't know where it fit into my own experiences. Except for something my father showed me back in 1926.

"I was only ten years old, and he was already preparing me to take over the family business, since I was the only son. He had had a strange, special case. I was there to help him. I remember him saying I should see everything, the good and the bad, if I was to do my job right. I never repeated the incident to anyone. But now, after seeing the corpse, and after recalling the outfit that guy is wearing, well, I might have to tell you about that time. You see, the tuxedo he's wearing is not a tuxedo. It's a—"

Frank's words froze along with his breath, as another voice boomed out at the three men from a distance.

"Chief! Chief! You've got to come here! I found something! I can't believe it! Something really weird!" Tom Pelski called out from a point fifty yards away to the east. He was standing on a ridge, waving his arms this way and that, trying to attract further attention the way desperate men do.

"Found what?" Breach yelled back.

"No, you have to come and see this! I...I can't just explain it! You've got to see it! In the cemetery!"

"Just a minute, Tom. Stay where you are. Dave and I will be there in a few minutes," the old cop fired back.

"Frank. Please put the head in your trunk, and then take the Nigalo kid back to town with you. It's getting dark now, and there's no use you and him hanging around here any further. Dave and I will put the corpse in the back seat of the patrol car after you leave, and then see what has Tom so all-fired up. We'll head straight back to your place when we're done here. OK?"

"Sure. I'll start the procedures on the head. But no full autopsy on it or the body until I give you a chance to look at both of them after they thawed out a bit."

"Thanks. We'll see you in about an hour, maybe a little longer. The cemetery's two miles away, and with this snow, it'll probably hold us up some. That is, if we have to go trudging out there." Breach spoke with a wry smile on his face. "Well, at least it will hold me up a little. You know." He was referring to the mutual age they shared, along with its physical problems.

After Frank's car disappeared from sight down the road, Breach and Barker put the body in the car, and made their way to Tom Pelski on the ridge.

CHAPTER TWO

▼

THE SECOND CORPSE – MISSING

"What's the problem, Tom? Do we have to go to the cemetery? It's damn near dark now, and that's a bit of a jaunt. What is so important we have to see it tonight? Can't it wait until the morning?" the Chief asked. His devotion to duty began to wane, as the now frigid night air caused the rheumatism in his lower back to flare up. The sharp pains were starting to affect his stance and walk. He didn't know if he could make the two mile hike, but did not want to let the younger men know.

"Well, Chief," Pelski replied sarcastically, "unless you want what looks like pretty fresh evidence to freeze overnight, I suggest we get there before it gets really dark. Besides, we have our flashlights, and there is a full moon tonight. That will make travel and the investigation of what I found out there easy. The way through the woods between here and there is pretty clear. Not much snow on the path, because it's wide. The trees took the drifts."

"Look, Tom," Breach said in a condescending voice, "I make the decisions around here, and don't you forget it! You've gone off half-cocked before, and caused no end of needless work for the department, and wasted a lot of overtime money in the process! I caught heat from the town council, because I'm the boss! You've got to remember, there are only four of us for the whole town, and Trudy for dispatch. We can't waste what little resources we have on your excitable nature! Just because you're my nephew is no reason for you to think you can get away with shit! Now I mean it, keep screwing up and getting carried away with intrigues, and you're going to find yourself off the force! I'll personally sign your pink slip! Now what the hell did you find?"

Dave Barker felt embarrassed, not just for Tom, but for himself. Getting chewed out in private is bad enough. But a public display was something else. He knew the Chief had a fiery nature, and would unload on anyone as he saw fit. But the young cop often wondered about such tactics. He doubted their effectiveness, and thought them unprofessional. This instance was no different. To ease the strain for Tom, Barker looked down at the ground and began kicking the snow lazily, the way a kid would do on his way home from school. At the same time, he managed to slide away near the trees, putting some distance between himself and the scene unfolding in front of him.

"Uh, sorry Chief," Pelski replied. The young cop had a good instinct for career survival. He knew he had pushed Uncle Gus too far, and the older man was done covering up for him. His uncle was a tolerant man, but only up to a point. When pushed past that point, he had a temper second to none, and no fuse, as opposed to a short fuse.

"It's in the cemetery," Tom said quietly. "A grave has been dug up, and there are two sets of footprints around it. Just like the ones leading up to the body. One set is clear, the other is funny, and has long streaks behind it. Like the guy who made them had something hanging from his pants cuffs or somethin.' I don't exactly know what to make of it.

"And there's something else. There's a big circle right near the open grave. It was made in the snow. There are scuffmarks inside of it and on the outside. A lot of it's been worn away, as if the two men had one hell of a fight inside the circle, and then kept fighting outside of it. I figure that's why so much of it has been scuffed away. And there's more. I wish we had a camera with us! The circle is actually three circles. The larger one has a smaller one set inside of it, and then the smaller one has an even smaller one inside of it. There are markings of some kind in the spaces of all three. At least, what's left of them. And Chief…the strangest part of all of this…the body that was in the grave is gone!

"I mean it! I checked and checked the abandoned cemetery from one direction to the other, and all around its entire perimeter. That's why I was gone so long. And to add to my sense of intrigue," Pelski teased his uncle cautiously, "the old gate at the front of the cemetery is still pad-locked tighter than Fort Knox, and there are no tire tracks anywhere. Not even outside of the cemetery. I guess with the bad weather, people take the long way around by Route 16 to get to the Heights. Since that's the town nearest ours, I climbed over the cemetery fence and walked another mile to it. I checked the whole area out. It was just as I thought. All the traffic to the town took

Route 16. There were no tire tracks at all on the back road that goes past the cemetery to the Heights. So what do you make of all of this, Chief?"

Now Breach was proud of his nephew. But he knew he was younger than Barker, and that Dave was quicker to ferret out evidence and put it together. Dave was also much more intuitive, but still had to be taught how to use that gift more effectively. Gus wondered how he would tell his sister Dave would get the Chief of Police job when he retired. It was already set up that way with the mayor.

"I can't say, Tom," the uncle replied wearily. "But you're right. We've got to take a look at the situation tonight. The wind will kick up as usual about ten, and even across a flat lawn like the cemetery, it'll cover up the evidence without drifting. Well, let's get on with it!"

The three men turned their flashlights on and began to walk the two miles to Saint Alacious cemetery. But after a hundred yards they turned them off and replaced them in their field belts. The full moon shone brightly against the frigid blue winter sky, providing them will ample light to make their way along the long-abandoned mountain path. As they walked along in silence, the thick undergrowth and trees lining both side of the path caused their pulse rates to quicken.

Tom and Dave grew up in Kulpsville. Like generations of kids from before them, they had explored the mountains and woods surrounding the town throughout their childhood. Yet neither one of them saw their former playground the way it appeared to them this night. The mountains looked terribly forbidding when viewed against the background of a grave desecration and its missing corpse. They never noticed before how the trees bent over and sagged as if weary of their decades of mute silence, watching men and other things move along the forgotten mountain roads and secret paths they guarded. These silent witnesses seemed to have another life now, unknown to people. And in that unknown life, they hid the knowledge of dark and forbidding magical things mortal men should never know.

The stride of the two young men slowed. The fear of the unknown was weighing their legs down. Their bodies seemed heavier. After a quarter of a mile, they were moving slower than the old cop.

Breach felt the same way. After he moved to Kulpsville, he took to hunting in these same mountains throughout the years. But he never saw them like this before. Not this dark. Not this terrifying. Not this sick with age, trying desperately to hold back on the secret things they saw throughout their long lives of silence. But his years of just living life, combined with his police experience, taught him to effectively mask his inner emotions. He understood what was happening to his two deputies, but did not console them. He was grateful for their fear. Their faltering speed allowed him to take the lead, and look every bit the Chief of Police he was.

The hike had taken them longer than expected. The rapidly freezing snow surface and their fear slowed them down more than they realized. It was six-fifteen when the trio reached the small ravine that led into the back of the cemetery. Its sides were slick from the deep snow piled up by the winds, while the near zero temperature had frozen the surface into a hard, thick sheet of ice. Carefully they made their way down the side that emerged from the woods they just passed through, and then up the other side and into the cemetery. They paused to catch their breaths. Then Breach spoke.

"OK, Tom, where is it?"

"It's over there in the north end of the cemetery behind that clump of brush and trees."

"Over there? How the hell did you find it if it was hidden?"

"Well, uh, if you take a look at the ground, you'll see two sets of tracks coming out of them." Tom spoke shyly, trying not to upset his uncle's lack of thought in the matter. "But then, uh, it was daylight, and easy to spot. Not like now."

Breach smiled to him, knowing his nephew was covering up for his tired brain. It had been a long day, filled with more exercise and stress than he had experienced in a very long time.

As the trio made their way over to the thicket, Breach turned his flashlight on to examine the two sets of tracks coming from them. The open layout of the area allowed him to see details of the tracks the close mountain road had hid from his seasoned eyes. As they walked along, Breach stooped down every so often to feel the depth of the prints. Then he would stand up quickly and turn in a full circle, looking for a pattern of motion surrounding the tracks.

He observed the thin trail streaming behind the half-shoe of the right foot. But now he could clearly see that the left foot also had a thin, streaming trail behind it. As they stood at the edge of the thicket hiding the desecrated grave, the Chief stooped down once more, stood up quickly, swung around, and carefully eyed the pattern of prints that led away from the bushes and toward the back entrance of the cemetery. His rapid motions were his way of trying to get a moving picture of the action that led toward the west and the ravine. Now it was clear.

The first set of tracks with the two normal shoes were running away, sliding and falling a few times, as the victim tried to escape his pursuer. The half-shoe prints were directly behind the victim, and always displayed an unbalanced gait, yet still moving fast, very fast. Faster than was humanly possible for a man with half a shoe to normally move. He knew his original feelings were correct, as was the conclusion he deduced from his intuitive promptings. The victim had fled from behind the thicket of woods, ran across the cemetery grounds, through the ravine and across the two miles of woods, all the while being pursued by his assailant. As he suspected, the murder victim was literally run down by whatever, and butchered where he fell. Yet, he recalled there was no sign of massive blood loss at the murder spot, nor in the hollow.

Neither did the mountain road display signs of a fierce struggle. Nor did the victim's body show signs of a terrible fight. Now it seemed obvious the thing had run the man down from behind and killed him in some way the old cop did not understand. He counted on some evidence at the cemetery giving him a better idea of the modus operandi of the killer. That could lead to a motive and then possibly to the murderer's identity. But now, the Chief was left with a complete mystery. He had never encountered a homicide case that left him so confused. In the old days, after examining so much of the evidence, he always had a follow-up hunch. Some feeling that would point him in the right direction. Not this time. He could not fathom the method of the killing, or its motive.

"You two wait out here," he barked. "I want to take a look at the grave site myself. I don't want any more tracks scuffling up the area than is necessary. I'll call when I need you."

As he moved along the small path leading through the underbrush and small trees, he wondered why anyone would bury a person in such a remote location. Why not bury them like the others? Out in full view? Or maybe this guy was buried in this section when the cemetery first opened, his relatives died or moved away, and there was no one left to tend it? The bushes and small trees would have shot up around it in no time. But that didn't make any sense. There must be a lot of people planted here who have no kin, and yet their graves are perfectly tended. Perpetual care shot through his tired brain. Surely one of the other two churches in town would maintain the cemetery of the long-closed Saint Alacious parish. "It doesn't make sense," he finished thinking, as his head emerged into the open area hidden within the thicket.

The full moon lit the large concealed area. But he needed a close look at everything there was to see. After making the trip out there on that bitterly cold January night, he intended to justify it by gathering as much additional insight into the background of the case as he could. Removing his flashlight from his field belt, he flicked it on, and began to sweep the area slowly with its bright, wide beam. He noted the regular dimensions of the area. Even with the steadily invading underbrush, he could clearly see the open area was about twenty feet on each side.

The grave was almost exactly in the center of the square. A pick lay on a frozen mound of earth made when the grave was dug up. A shovel stood straight up, having been driven into the mound as if to punctuate the act of desecration. Off to the side, he saw the handle and head of a sledgehammer. As he stepped from the thicket path onto the open area, Breach saw the set of circles Tom reported. His deputy's description was accurate. Each was a circle drawn within a circle, traced deeply into the frozen snow cover. Between the spaces of each circle, unknown figures and words had been inscribed with a sharp object. He could not make out most of the symbols. They were smudged and smeared beyond recognition, as were the circles in different parts of their circumference. But he copied them down as best he could, along with one complete sentence from the innermost circle he was able to clearly read. Latin? Something inscribed in Latin?

Unconsciously, he placed the flashlight under his left arm, withdrew a small notebook from his back pocket, and wrote the words down.

Et verbum caro factum est, Jesus autem transiens per medium.

A chill, more frigid than the winter night air, knifed through the Chief's mind and body. He understood the religious implications of the word Jesus. He also jotted down a few of the symbols as best as he could, being sure to draw them in their proper positions in the three circles in his notebook. Old memories from Pittsburgh filtered back to him. Hushed-up reports. Word of strange occult practices passed quietly and quickly, even through the Homicide Department. It was in his eighth year on the force he recalled, not long after he reached the grade of Sergeant.

But now the old cop's mind refused the implications his intuitive machinery was drawing for him. He could not accept them. Not just yet. His rigorous mental self-discipline told him all of the facts were not in yet. Logic was needed at this point. To draw such a bizarre conclusion now could sidetrack the investigation and lead it far afield from more rational, everyday explanations. Yet his intuition continued to nag at the rim of his reason, telling him his suspicions were correct. Deep within him, he had his own circle of beliefs about the world. That circle was marked by age, experience, reason, and fear. And at the center stood his need to believe in the reality he could see and feel.

Beginning at the perimeter of the hidden area, he walked around slowly, clockwise, examining the ground and surrounding bushes. After his first pass over the site, Breach began moving in a circular pattern, tightening the circle on each pass, looking carefully at the evidence the beam of his flashlight revealed. It was as Tom reported. A horrific struggle ensued on the spot. Two men had fought and grappled with each other, wrestling this way and that in the frozen snow. Finally one of them, the one with both shoes intact—the victim—broke away from his attacker and darted out to the path, and out of the hidden area. But half-shoe dogged his victim mercilessly.

Breach's methodical circular motions finally brought him to the edge of the grave. The pile of earth was frozen, but not solid, indicating it had been dug up from the underground vault within the last twenty-four hours. Bare earth freezes quickly in the north and northeast, he thought. But it takes little more than a single day for it to get as dense as fully compacted earth. Someone dug this guy up last night all right, late. That would account for the earth still being so loose. He shined his flashlight down into the grave itself.

"Well," he muttered, "that's why the victim needed the sledge hammer. To break through the vault." The old cop caught his own last remark. He was thinking in the direction he didn't want to go, and so pushed the emerging thoughts out of his mind once more, forcefully.

As his light swept the interior of the grave, he saw several large pieces of the vault stacked up against the black-earth walls of the dead man's final resting place. The force of the sledgehammer had splintered the cement enclosure. Breach bent down to get a better look. After a few seconds he was able to make out the outline of the coffin in the bottom of the vault. It was made of wood. The condition of the sides of the coffin surprised him. They were in almost perfect condition. The lid had remained intact, forcing the desecrator to hack it apart. "Obviously used the pick to break through the frozen earth first, then to get through the coffin lid," Breach said to himself loudly. He jumped down into the six-foot hole, and stood on a piece of cement vault across the bottom part of the casket.

There wasn't any smell, but then the body had decomposed long ago. He felt better now that he was now thinking more rationally. Slowly, his flashlight beam scanned the interior of the open casket. Scraps of soiled, dark cloth and greenish-black pools of liquid filled the box. Breach put the blade of the pick down into the grave, and poked the scraps of cloth and liquid. It was apparent to him the bits of cloth were the remains of the suit the dead man was buried in. But the pools of liquid were thick, and dripped off of the pick blade slowly, like a putrid, green-black molasses. Breach suddenly realized the oozing substance was body fluids from the corpse that had coagulated from years in the grave. "Yuk! Time to get out of here!"

As the Chief of Police placed his hands on the edge of the grave and began to lift himself out of the hole, his hands touched something thick and wetter than the snow lining the opening. "Goddamn! This is some of that liquid shit from the coffin! Must have dripped off the corpse when that thing raised it up to the surface! I'll never get my hands clean now! Be lucky if I don't get some goddamn disease from it! Goddamn dead-man oozing pus!"

As he desperately wiped his hands against some clean snow, he caught sight of an image out of the corner of his eye. Collecting his wits, Breach picked up his flashlight and examined what he saw a few moments earlier. Directly across from him at the edge of the grave, were two sets of five, spike-like slashes that penetrated the snow and gouged out pieces of earth beneath them. The slashes were separated by a distance of about three feet—the span a big man's shoulders would make as he lifted himself up. Examining them in the light, he saw all ten slash marks were covered with the same green-black liquid as he found in the coffin. Breach froze in place. He realized his worst fears and suspicions were slowly breaking through the circle of his beliefs about reality. As if propelled by some burst of youthful energy, the old cop sprang out of the grave and hollered to the others outside of the thicket.

"Dave, Tom! Get in here, quick!" Breach was visibly shaken, and they could hear it in his voice. But the seasoned cop managed to hide his fear by the time his two assistants reached his side.

"What is it, Chief?" his nephew asked, being somewhat out of breath. "I thought you'd never call for us!"

"Tom, I want you to stay here! Dave and I are going back to the patrol car. I'll put in a call to Greg right away, and tell him to wake up old Henry, the guy who owns the sporting goods store in town. Greg will get as many of those plastic tarps and tent stakes as he can from Henry, and bring them up here. I want this entire area tarped over until morning. The plastic will keep the snow off, and the covered area shouldn't thaw out.

"Then I want everything photographed before the sun gets too high, including the prints leading out of here and across the cemetery grounds. I want it all on film, including the ten gashes you'll find over by the grave itself. I want those on close-up shots, good and goddamn clear! I'll make sure Greg brings the 35 mm camera with all of the lenses. He's a photography bug anyway, and should be able to do a good job. Do you understand? No slip-ups on this one, Tom, and I mean it! When Greg gets here, you're in charge. Make damn sure every one of my directions is carried out!

"And I want this entire cemetery roped off too. You and Greg put up *Crime scene. Do not cross this line.* yellow ribbons at every entrance to the cemetery—bar none—and make sure the two of you don't track this place up too much. Walk back and forth in your own tracks. Make as few new ones as possible. I want everything just like it is now.

"Dave and I will go straight to the mortuary. I've got to find out more about the corpse we found before sunrise. Because if what happened here is what I think happened, we have one hell of a problem on our hands none of us is going to want to believe."

Tom Pelski's voice flared up, several octaves higher than normal. "Are you out of your mind, Uncle Gus? I'll freeze up here! It must be damn near zero now, and the temperature's going to drop even further around ten when the winds start blowing! It'll take Greg at least a few hours to get back here with the tarps! I can't stay here like this! I'll get frostbite or somethin'!"

"You're young, Tom, you'll be all right. And don't exaggerate! Greg will be here in less than an hour and a half. Say around nine. We'll double-time it back to the patrol car, and I'll put the call in to Trudy immediately. She'll get him on the phone, pronto. Besides, he's no doubt at home now, as usual, just relaxing, getting ready for his eleven p.m. shift. It'll be no trouble to catch him and get him up here with the goods. So just hang tight.

"Oh, and Tom," Breach said, the sound of caring in his voice now replacing the warning tone of a few moments ago, "I don't want to scare you. But please! Be careful! We might have something on our hands here that makes no sense at all. If anything should happen…if you're threatened…fire a warning shot first. If that doesn't stop the threat, I don't want you to take any chances. On my orders—in front of Dave, here, as a witness—I am ordering you to level your weapon and fire at point blank range. No shooting to wound. Aim to kill, and don't stop firing until whatever it is either retreats or lays dead at your feet. Do you understand me?"

The younger man looked at his uncle in the pale moonlight. A grimace of total disbelief overtook his face. "Don't want to scare me? Don't want to scare me? Are you kidding? What are you talking about? I'll be shitting marbles in a minute! All colors! You're starting to scare the hell out of me with talk like that! What are you talking about?"

"I mean I'm probably wrong in what I really think caused this murder. I pray I am. And knowing the way the world is today, what with all of the crazies out there, well, it'll most likely turn out to be some psycho who escaped from the mental asylum, or someone who went over the edge. But at any rate, just do as I say. Don't take any chances! If you're threatened, I want you to shoot to kill! No warning shots beyond one round in the air. Got that?"

"You can be damn sure I got it! One round in the air, the other five into him! You can count on it!"

"Come on, Barker," Breach said. "Let's get out of here and back to the car as fast as we can."

Tom watched from the edge of the thicket as the other two made their way quickly across the cemetery grounds, and disappeared into the ravine. No sooner were they gone from sight than his nerves began to play with his thoughts. He stood against the backdrop of the silent trees. On the other side of the woods, a grave had been desecrated, and the corpse stolen. Two miles away, about twenty hours ago, a middle-aged man of strong build had been run down and savagely murdered. Now, here he was standing alone in a cemetery on a bitterly cold winter's night, guarding a grave, with who-knew-what running around loose in the mountains.

The young cop forgot about the cold chill in the air. Goose bumps raised over his entire body, replacing the winter cold with a deeper chill. This was the chill of fear turning into terror, created by the possibility of *something* lunging out of the bushes or shadows, and tearing him apart as it did the corpse they found on the mountain road. Tom loosened the safety strap on the hammer of his Police Special, and locked his right hand firmly around the stock. Without realizing it, his index finger curled around the trigger. He was ready for the threat to make its appearance.

The surface snow on the mountain road was now completely frozen over, making the trek back to the car very difficult. It took them about one and three-quarters of an hour, slipping and sliding the entire two miles. Gus grabbed the microphone of the two-way police radio as soon as they got back, and flicked a switch. With labored puffing, he radioed the station house.

"This is cruiser number 4 to base. Do you copy? Over."

"Yeah, Chief," a middle-aged female voice shot back through the speaker. "You're coming in fine. How did the murder investigation go? Do you have any leads?"

"Dammit, Trudy, how many times do I have to tell you to keep your mouth shut about what's going on when you're on the radio? You know how many CBs and police scanners there are out there?! Just keep to the script? Got it?"

Trudy was apologetic. "Sure Chief, I'm sorry. Just forgot myself, I guess. But what with the stories the Nigalo kid spread all over town, I guess I got carried away. I mean, everybody already knows about it anyway. Some guy with a missing head and all that. You know what I mean? So what's the big deal, anyway?"

"Look, Trudy," Breach sighed, realizing this was one of the disadvantages of being on a small town force. "Just never mind. I want you to call Greg at home. When you get him, tell him to come down to the station immediately. Tell him to dress warmly. And tell him not to lose one minute shaving or making sure his uniform is all neat and pretty. I want him down the station house in fifteen minutes from now, no matter what he's doing. Tell him if he isn't there by nine, he's fired. And Trudy, tell him I'm not goddamn kidding. Got it?"

The sound of anger and desperation in his voice cut through her carefree attitude. "Yes, Chief! I'll have him here in fifteen minutes, if not sooner. Then what?"

"Then patch the phone line through to my radio phone, and be damn sure to tell Tom to use the scramble switch before his calls me up. Oh. Another thing. When Greg walks in, you walk out. You're off for the night. I want you out of the station house when he calls me. Is that clear?"

"But Chief, I'm your dispatcher! I have a right to know—"

"Goddamn it, Trudy!" Gus shouted back. "The only rights you have are the ones I give you! Do you understand me? I'm tired of that big mouth of yours! More information leaks out of the office than Carter has liver pills, and I've known for a long time it's coming from you! Now do as I tell you, or I swear to God, I'll have you out of your job quicker than shit through a goose! Do you understand?"

"Yes, I understand," she cowered back, knowing her job was genuinely on the line this time. "It will be as you say, Chief. I'll take care of everything."

"Pretty hard on her, weren't you?" Dave asked cautiously. He knew Breach had a temper, and a legendary reputation for having 'no' fuse instead of a 'short' fuse. Not even a wife beater, or two drunks slugging it out at Pap's Bar, would tangle with him when he was in one of those moods of his, as people coined his furious outbursts behind his back.

"Not hard enough, and not soon enough! And it's my fault. All of this. The Department has gotten sloppy. All hick. And I'm to blame. I got fat and lazy these past twenty years, and let everything go to hell. No one has any self-discipline except for you. And professionalism? Hell, this force never had any! But you can't blame them. All my predecessors were local boys with no training. They had an excuse. I don't. Not after spending ten years on the Pittsburgh homicide squad.

"There are days…more than you know, or I want to admit to myself…that I regret coming here. But it got to me. So many bodies, mutilated and torn up eleven ways from Sunday by some hoodlum or gang. Trying to put the pieces together, finally succeeding after months of work, building a case, only to have some stinking mouth piece get the guilty bastard off on some technicality, or having him plea bargain down from murder in the first or some other nonsense.

"It just got to me, son, and so I took my sister's advice and came here. After she married Jim Pelski, they came back here to his hometown and settled. Normal. When the last Chief retired, she phoned me. It was right after an incident I don't want to remember, let alone talk about. But that last incident broke the camel's back, and I hotfooted it here, and before a half-hour of the interview was out, I had the job. I was so damned relieved not to have to face another dead body, that I put all of it out of my mind for all these years. Until today. But that's only the beginning.

"As the years wore on, I not only let pride in myself as a cop go to hell, I let pride in myself as a man take the same route. And our Department shows it. Everything from misplaced and unorganized files, to unsolved cases—even of child abuse, to Trudy the big mouth, to my nephew Tom who has about as much instinct for police work as I have talent for ballet, to Greg who acts like Barney Fife the Second. No, it's not right anymore. Never was. But I didn't care.

"Somehow though, the events of today brought everything back into focus. This day made me feel as if I was standing outside of myself, watching what I had become. And I have to tell you, Dave, I didn't like it. Not one bit. Want the truth? I'm ashamed of what I've become. I see my own reflection in the events of today. Something I've been avoiding for the past twenty years. Now it's all crystal clear, and laying at my doorstep.

"I'm going to tell you something so you won't be too surprised later on. Starting now, and I mean right now, this hick police force is going to become a real police force. No, I won't overcompensate and try to turn it into something it'll never be, or try to make people into something they're not. But by goddamn, the procedures of law enforcement and criminal investigation are going to be carried out according to the letter and spirit of good police work, no matter what. And to do that, I'm going to begin with myself. 'Teach by example' they taught us at the Police Academy years ago. I didn't forget that. I got too tired and lazy after the homicide years to care anymore. But that's over. As of this moment the worm has turned and with it, our police force. Are you with me?"

Young Dave Barker looked at the grim determination on the face of the Chief of Police. There was something different about his hardened features. Something Barker never saw before, as if an inner resolve that disappeared long ago had reemerged into his personality, carving itself in the furrows of his aging face. The young cop liked what he saw. He felt as if he truly had a superior who would help him learn his craft completely, and in expert fashion.

Dave smiled broadly. "You're darn right I'm with you, Gus! But I have to tell you, I always looked up to you as a man. You're too hard on yourself. I always knew there was one hell of a cop hidden in there somewhere. Now I know it! Just tell me what you want me to do. Kick my ass as hard as you have to as we go along, but for God's sake, Gus, teach me everything you know. I told you when I joined seven years ago, the way I figure it, it doesn't really matter what a man does in this life, as long as he does it the best he can. In the end, that's what it's really all about. Only that. Nothing else.

"The way I figure, the town's bound to grow up some over the years. There are new people moving in right now. Outsiders looking for a peaceful place to live or retire. Some of the problems they bring with them, we locals have no experience dealing with. I'm hoping after a few more years of learning from you, I'll make a good Chief of Police when you retire. Then you can set your mind at rest, because the show will still be run your way, since I'll be using what you taught me. So like I said, count me in!"

"You have a deal, son. And we're going to start by solving this damn case, and either getting the son-of-a-bitch who murdered the poor bastard behind bars where he belongs, or waste him in the field if we have to. But either way, this case is going to be solved."

"Back at the cemetery, you told Tom we might have something on our hands that makes no sense at all. What did you mean?"

"I'm not sure what killed that poor guy. My hunch, my intuition tells me the evidence points to a completely insane conclusion. What's worse is that the facts seem to support that conclusion. But I have seen good cops go off on tangents before, and waste months of time, energy, and resources. Bottom line—no results. Then the files would get closed, shoved in the back of a file cabinet, and that was the end of it.

"I'm not straddling the fence and trying to be noncommittal. I'm just trying to be cautious before drawing any conclusions. Whatever conclusion I finally come to will lead us down a path that will eat up the few resources and overtime hours we have in the budget for this year. It has already started. I had to call Greg in two hours before his shift starts. The Chief of Police has to think of all of that, too. It's a pain in the ass, but I have to take things like that into account before going off half-cocked. Especially with this case, and what seems to be an absolutely impossible conclusion."

"Cruiser number 4, come in. This is Officer Greg Dovrak reporting early for duty, Chief. Do you copy?" A loud, mid-thirty-something, military-sounding voice broke in through the speaker of the radio.

"I copy you, Greg," Breach replied. "Are you alone in the office? I told Trudy she was to check out as soon as you checked in. Is she gone?"

"Yes sir. She met me at the door, told me what you wanted, hooked up the phone on scramble, and asked me to wait until she got outside before making the call. What gives? You didn't lay into her again, did you?"

"Never mind," Breach replied surly. "Here's what I want you to do. Go to the sporting goods store and wake old Henry up. He goes to bed around seven and sleeps like a log, so you may have to pound on the door. But wake him up! Get as many plastic tarps as he has in stock. Not the canvas ones! Plastic! And get tent stakes. All that he has. Tell him my office will pay for them. Sign a sales slip if you have to. Oh, and take two good-sized hammers with you. Check the utility room at the station house. There are at least three of them there. And take the big crow bar with you too. You'll need it.

"Then take Route 16, bypass the Heights, and connect to the back road that runs past Saint Alacious cemetery. The gate is padlocked, so you'll have to use the crowbar to bust the lock. Drive up the cemetery road to the first knuckle. There's a thicket on the left. Tom is waiting for you. He's been there since seven-thirty, and I promised him you'd be there by about nine, so get there as fast as you can. He'll tell you what the two of you are to do when you get there. Do you copy?"

"Yes sir, I copy," replied the deputy in his super cop formal manner. "I take it Tom and I are to hold our position at the thicket until we hear from you. Over."

"Yeah, Dave and I will join the two of you as soon as we can. We're at the mountaintop road now. Actually, on the old coal road where we found the body. I guess you heard about it. Over."

"Yes sir, I did. It's all over town. But from the details I heard it's obvious the Nigalo kid is spreading false rumors. I suppose you haven't had time to correct his misinformation? Over."

"Don't be too sure what you heard are rumors. Not in this case. We have an extremely unusual situation on our hands. And no, I haven't had time to correct any misinformation. That will have to wait until later. We can't lose the evidence we have now. That's why I'm sending you up to the cemetery. If you and Tom do your jobs right, we may be able to put a lid on this thing faster than looks possible right now. That's why you have to get up there as soon as you can. Over."

"Understood. But I have to tell you the mayor called me, and so did several members of the town council. All of them are furious with you! They want an accounting of the situation, and they want it tonight, before you go any further. All of them, especially the mayor, insisted. I said I would intervene on their behalves when I report for duty this evening. Would you like me to take a few minutes to call the mayor before I leave, and communicate to him what you have to report thus far? Perhaps I should also set up a meeting with him later this evening, so you can at least fill him in on where we stand in this murder investigation? Over."

Dave smiled in the darkness of the cruiser, shook his head from side to side, and then looked at Breach. In light of the Chief's confession to him, Dave had a pretty good idea what was coming.

"Greg," Breach replied coolly, trying to hold his temper back. "I've had my bellyful of those tiny people with their tinier minds and big noses for news and gossip. If you run into any of them, I want you to tell them this for me, and in these words. Now listen carefully! Tell them, Gus said he runs the police department. Not the mayor, and not the town council! You tell them that from now on, my department is going to run the way a professional law enforcement organization should be run. One responsible to the citizens of the town, not to a bunch of old farts who don't have a goddamn better thing to do than to stick their noses in where they don't belong! Tell them they will receive news of the investigation when I determine such information is to be released, and not before.

"As to the mayor. You tell Bob Slab for me if I hear one more goddamn puffing about being elected by the people to look after their interests, I'm going to take this tin badge they gave me twenty years ago, and shove it down his throat until it comes out of his asshole!

"And Greg? I've had a bellyful of your attitude! You can drop the phony shit of being super cop from now on! Because that you ain't and you never will be! Your job is to take orders from me and from no one else. Your responsibility is to me and only me. Not to the mayor or the town council of nose pots and back stabbers. Do you understand me? You call no one. You just do as I ordered you to do. Wake up old Henry, get the supplies I told you to get, and get your ass up to the cemetery just as fast as you can! Over!"

A deafening silence shattered the two-way communication for some time. But Breach would not break it. He had given his commands to his subordinate, and fully expected Greg to adjust to his new Chief as fast as he could. Finally, Greg Dovrak ended the numbing silence.

"All right, Chief, it will be as you say. I'll get what we need and get up to Tom as fast as I can. Over and out."

"Sounds miffed to me," Barker said, wondering if Gus had gone too far this time.

"I don't give a rat's ass if he's miffed or not. He had it coming. He's my deputy. I'm not his. I've put up with all of the shit I'm going to from all of them as of today. The entire law enforcement situation in this town has gotten way out of hand thanks to me, and I'm the only one who can correct it. Molly-coddle them, be considerate of everyone's over-inflated opinions of themselves and of the so-called power they wield, and you'll never get a goddamn thing done. And in the end, your reluctance to take the bull by the horns will either get you fired for incompetence by the very ones you've cozied up to, or get you stuck behind some desk filling out accident reports until the day you retire.

"I've seen it happen. And to good cops too. Ones who got too understanding, or were afraid for their jobs, or ones like me who got too fat and lazy. But none of those scenarios are going to happen to me. At least not that way. If they want this badge back, they can have it anytime. That's what gives a man the edge in any fight, or in the world. And that's what gives me the edge in this matter. After today, I just don't care about what 'they' want. Only what's best for the law enforcement of this town. And what's best is what makes me act and feel like the professional I was in homicide."

Dave Barker listened attentively. He found a new level of respect for the old cop, and counted his blessings. He knew he had just found the best teacher he could possibly ask for.

"OK, Dave. Let's get out of here. We have an appointment with Frank Lewis."

Breach turned the heater of the cruiser up to high and started to drive down the treacherous mountain road in the darkness. After fifteen minutes of slow going, the police car turned off the dirt road and onto a coal-packed black road that had an outlet to Route 16.

"We better get there in a hurry, Chief. The corpse is beginning to thaw out, and boy does it smell bad!"

"Not as bad as the victim we dug out from under a discarded mattress in the woods. That was back in '50. He was stuffed under it for two weeks. I was the lucky one who discovered it. When I lifted that mattress, the smell almost took my head clean off. But you're right. We'd better get this guy to Frank's fast. Decomposition is starting to set in."

CHAPTER THREE

▼

FRANK'S PLACE

It was around nine-thirty when Police Cruiser number 4 finally pulled in behind the Lewis Funeral Home in Kulpsville. Breach parked in the area marked for Staff only. They emerged quickly and made their way to the back door of the Preparation Room. Breach knocked hard.

Frank opened the door and let them in. He was dressed in an immaculately clean, white laboratory coat, and was wearing transparent surgical gloves badly stained with fresh blood. The contrast between the pure white of his coat and the bright red liquid staining his gloves sickened the young cop for a few seconds. But he reminded himself this was as much a part of law enforcement as giving out parking tickets or directing traffic through town on busy weekends.

"We'd better get the body out of the back seat," Breach suggested. "It's starting to thaw out."

"Consider it done, Gus," Frank replied, as he motioned his two assistants standing next to the Preparation Table to carry out the Chief's order. While Gus and the mortician talked, Dave watched the assistants reverently handle the headless corpse, placing it gently on the table. Frank gave another wave of his hand to them and they went out through a side door.

"Here," Lewis said as he handed them a small jar of salve-like paste, "place a dab of this directly beneath each nostril. It should block all odors completely. It really helps with these tough cases."

As Breach and Barker applied the salve, Dave began to feel nauseous again. Looking around the clean, grim room filled with the necessary shining, stainless steel hand and electric tools, the impact of the finality of death hit him. Like many his age, he was usually absorbed in thoughts about the problems of life or about succeeding in the world. He had never seriously considered the reality of death and of dying. Now, as he looked around the antiseptic room and saw the large jars of clear and yellow embalming fluids standing next to oversized blending machines, thoughts of his own mortality began to fill his mind. The image of drawing his own last breath filled him with dread. The day of finality would eventually come to him too, as it must to all men. Dave shook slightly, while thoughts of a cold grave replaced the warmth of the room. He could only pray his final day was far off.

Breach and Lewis were not unsympathetic. They knew as men get older, the fear of death is replaced by an increased joy of life. The mind focuses on the happy times of the past, and the joys yet to come. Dave was unaware Frank and Gus were watching him as they talked about the case, reading his thoughts of apprehension and dread. They smiled briefly to each other, and Frank broke into Dave's private world of fear.

"Dave, please come here. I think you should be in on these discussions too. We need your input. After all, from what Gus told me, you're next in line for his job. So I want to be able to get to know you better and have you understand my work a little. If I have it right, Gus will be retiring in a few years. Then I'll be working with you directly. And after I hang up my lab coat my son will take over, and you'll be working with him. So it's best we start building bridges right now."

Frank turned his back to Dave and winked to Gus. The mortician played his hand well. By involving Dave in the details of the case, he would get the young cop's mind off the inevitable. In time, Breach thought, Barker would adjust to this part of police work. But both of the older men realized getting the young cop to that point began at this moment, especially with the use of a little kindness and understanding.

"OK, Frank," Breach said. "What did you find after examining the head?"

"Come and take a look for yourself, Chief," Lewis replied. "And you too, Dave. I need some corroboration here. Just to make sure my thinking isn't getting a bit bizarre." He led them over to a porcelain counter behind the large Prep table, where there was a large white cloth that seemed to be standing upright by itself. Frank lifted the cloth. Underneath it was the severed head. It had reached room temperature over the past several hours.

"Here, put these gloves on. I've dried it off and cleaned it up a little, making sure not to disturb anything looking like evidence."

Frank removed the cloth completely and handed the body part to Breach.

"Damn, it's heavy!" Gus replied, startled. "Why is it so heavy?"

"More like your hands are thawing out, Gus. The feeling is coming back into them, so you sense things better. Examine it carefully if you would, please."

Breach lifted it up to eye level and stared at it closely. As he took mental notes, he rotated the head first one way and then another, turned it upside down, examined the spinal cord hanging from the back of the neck, and then set it back down on the counter. After looking at the flesh carefully, he tilted it back into an upright position and ran his gloved fingers along the tip of the nose, the sides of the jaws, and the fleshy parts of the cheeks. As a final measure, he turned the head around, laid it face down, and examined the flesh at the back of the neck.

"I think I see what you're getting at. Now it's your turn Dave. Check it out thoroughly. Then the three of us will talk."

The young cop did as his Chief ordered, and imitated his superior's motions. After a few minutes he satisfied himself his analysis was complete, and he put the head back on the counter. Without thinking, he placed the white towel over it carefully, as if out of respect. Then he turned and nodded.

"What do you think, Frank?" Breach asked. "Let's have your analysis first. I may have spent a lot of years in homicide, but when it comes to handling murder victims at this level, you're the expert."

"Which is exactly why I want you to give me your views first. I don't want to prejudice either of your opinions. Go ahead, Gus. What do you make of it?"

"Well, it seems to be a clean kill. From the lack of expression on the poor guy's face, I'd say the deathblow came quickly. He didn't know what hit him. Shock set in first, freezing his blank expression in place. From the looks of the back of the head, I would say he was killed face down, and some type of coarse blade was used to hack his head off from behind. His neck was probably snapped clean first, though. That's what killed him. Otherwise, he would have an expression of pain if he was still alive when the decapitation began. No, he was killed first. Then he was decapitated.

"But it looks like his face was pushed down into the frozen ground from behind, prior to his neck being snapped. It would have caused his nose, cheeks, and jaws to get torn up as badly as they are. All gouged out. But the type of weapon used to decapitate him escapes me. It wasn't a saw or anything like that. It had to have large, widely spaced teeth to match the tear marks ridged around the flesh of the neck. Those ragged edges of tissue all around the neck suggests to me this was a bad cutting job. It seems the head slid from side to side as the killer severed it from the body."

Breach's matter-of-fact graphic analysis caused Dave to swoon, but the counter behind him broke his fall, and stunned him back to consciousness. His right hand caught the edge of the counter and he steadied himself instead of falling to the floor. The other men said nothing, pretending not to notice. Neither did they laugh. The atmosphere in the room was serious, and their lack of humorous response helped the young cop to re-center himself.

"Now, Dave, give me your opinion," Frank asked calmly.

"I...I think I agree with the Chief," he answered back weakly. "The killer had to kill him from behind after he ran him down. The guy was probably tackled from behind, and hit the ground, face first. Then the maniac pulled his head backward sharply and snapped it sideways with a very fast jerk, causing the neck to snap. That did the man in. And it's like Gus said. The victim hit his face against the ground hard after he was run down, busting it up badly. Then the psychotic used some kind of weapon to cut the head off. That's all I can make of it."

"Well," the mortician replied calmly, "I'm afraid both of you are completely wrong. But don't take it so hard. This is one for the books. I'm damned certain you never encountered anything like this before, Gus. Let me explain.

"Forensics is a hobby of mine, if you will. It has developed into a full-fledged science over the past ten years. It may still be in its infancy, but it's getting extremely complicated, and is as telling and accurate as a fingerprint. I have studied a number of bizarre cases throughout the years. Going on that knowledge and the experience I had with my father back in '26, but mainly from some physical evidence neither of you would be able to interpret without medical training, here's what I think we have. I'll show you."

They all moved closer to the head. Removing the cloth, Frank turned it upside down, and pointed to the spinal cord. "See this long, narrow fibrous band on each side of the spinal cord? It runs through–

out the entire length of the cord, and separates the anterior and posterior roots of the spinal nerves. Look at the outer part of it. It's made of a triangular, saw-tooth type piece of tissue used to support the cord in the spinal fluid surrounding the cord. There are twenty-one of them, all connected together by a continuous tissue. Take a close look at the last one where the head was severed from the spine. What do you see?"

"It's drawn down to a point," Breach said.

"Exactly. Now, let's take a look at the body." They moved over to the table where the assistants had placed it. "I haven't examined it yet, but evidence is evidence, and from the condition of the *Ligamentum Denticulatum*—the anatomical name of that narrow band of tissue—I already know what I'll find.

"Give me a hand to turn it over," Lewis asked. Then he examined the other end of the spinal cord to which the head had been attached in life. "Precisely as I expected. You both take a look, and tell me what you see at the end of the cord. What does it look like? I mean, what is the shape of the other half of the ligament?"

"Like a small cup," Breach replied.

"I agree," Dave added.

Frank walked over to a cupboard, and removed a box of modeling clay used for the cosmetic repair of damaged cadavers. He pulled a section off the block and rolled the clay into a long, thin cord-like shape. With his fingernails, he etched triangular shapes into in, simulating the triangular structures of the *Ligamentum Denticulatum*.

"Now," he continued, "this clay has the approximate diameter of the spinal cord. The indentations I made along its length correspond to the narrow band of fibers like the ones we saw at the base of the skull and the top of the spinal column of the corpse. Here Gus, take this clay cord. OK, now hold it straight up in front of yourself, parallel your body, and pull it up sharply."

Breach did as he asked. The clay cord made a popping sound as it separated.

"Take a look at the ends. What do you have?"

Breach looked down at the two ends in disbelief and did not say a word.

"Come on, Gus," Lewis encouraged. "What do you have?"

"A point at the top end of the fractured cord, and a cup at the bottom end."

"And what does it mean?" Lewis asked, as if giving a medical student the practical part of his examination.

"It means," Breach replied very quietly, "the ends are exactly the same on this clay cord as they are on the corpse and its severed head. It means," he said as if pulling the words out of his mouth, "the man's head was ripped off of his body. It wasn't severed by some tool. It was literally pulled off by an unbelievably powerful set of arms."

"You're quite correct," Frank replied in a matter-of-fact manner. "The truth is it was a clean kill, but he did not die from a snapped neck. The exposed vertebrae at the base of the neck would have shown indications of swelling at the point of fracture, and they didn't. And if his back was snapped further down, there would be a settling of spinal fluid at that point. That is, it would settle down near the base of the spine, creating an inflammation, or swelling there, which I don't see. No, the fluid is there, frozen around the cord. And if you notice, as the body is thawing out, the fluid is seeping out of the neck cavity." Indeed, a cloudy liquid was running into the porcelain drains around the table.

"Then what killed him?" Breach asked. "Look at the face. There's no expression. I've seen this look before and always from a clean, quick kill," he objected.

"Maybe I'm being overly technical, but I think it's important," Lewis replied dryly. "Bring the head over here. I want to line it up with the body."

Gus did as instructed, and the two men situated the head cleanly on top of the corpse's neck.

"Now look at the right side of his neck. See that gash in the skin?" He pointed to a deep wound on the right side of the corpse's throat. "Take a good look at it. I saw it immediately when the head thawed out. See what's missing? Part of the esophagus tube."

"I don't see what you're driving at," Breach said in a disgruntled tone of voice. "Do me a favor. No more lessons in Forensic Science. How about cutting straight through to the bone as it were. Get to the bottom line."

"OK, I will. You have some parts of the analysis right. But your conclusions are a bit wrong. As it turns out though, one of your speculations was correct. The man was run down from behind. His face hit the ground. But the ground was snow covered, so he didn't pick up those scrapes and gashes when he came in contact with the hard snow cover. No. After he was run down, whatever it was chewed through his carotid artery and the side of his esophagus tube, producing the gash on the right side of his neck. From the teeth marks, I say they were more like fangs. I examined the ridges of the gash. It was one, and only one powerful bite that ripped through the artery and the throat itself. That's what killed him, and that's what produced the expressionless look on his face. It is the look of pure shock. Pure horror. His mind could not accept the fact not just that his life was ending at that moment but ending in such a way.

"It's also the reason there is no significant blood spill at the kill site. All of this man's blood was drained from him, sucked out through the main artery in the neck as you originally speculated. Only a few spots overlapping the skin drained onto the snow.

"Now look at the edges of the skin along the neckline. See? Saw-tooth edges on both the upper parts of the neckline on the torso, and on the neck of the severed head. This confirms his head was literally ripped off his body. Now, please bring the head over here. I want both of you to take a close look at this. I did before you arrived. It's very interesting," Lewis commented.

This time Breach had the young cop bring the object over to a side counter where Frank was now standing. He switched on an oblong-shaped lamp producing a bluish-silver glow.

"This is a sodium vapor lamp. It allows us to pick up details ordinarily missed in regular fluorescent or white light. Look here," he said, as he pointed to the scrapes and gashes on the face. "The skin on the face is more fleshy and fatty. That's why the marks don't show up as well as on the neck. See them now? Those are teeth marks or, once again, fang marks, gentlemen. The man didn't scrape his face on the ground. His face was gnawed on immediately after the blood was drained from him, but before his head was ripped from his body.

"You asked me to put it all together? Well, this is it." The mortician spoke as though he were a detective who just solved an important case. "The man was run down from behind, and his face went into the snow. The murderer then tore out his victim's carotid artery and part of his throat with one bite from powerful fangs, sucked all of the blood out of him, and then started to gnaw on the face: the nice, soft, juicy parts. The cheeks and nose, where the deepest gash marks appear.

"But it was either surprised by something or as I suspect, just wanted to feed in peace without the threat of discovery. So the ghoul ripped the head off with a powerful yank, and then took it down into the hollow where Dave found it. That, officers, is my analysis. Why it didn't finish its meal in the hollow, we'll probably never know. But there you have it. Oh, don't worry. I'll run a complete autopsy. But from my experience, I am 100% certain my conclusions will be the same after the postmortem. What we have on our hands is some type of escaped lunatic, or…or…something else.

"And I can tell you more. What I didn't want to go into before. That corpse lying on the road brought back memories from when I was a kid and helped my dad on his special case back in 1926. I think it all ties in. Are you ready to hear it?"

Breach and Barker looked at the old funeral director in disbelief. What he was describing was something out of a badly written horror novel. Something that simply could not exist in the technological society of the later part of the twentieth century. Neither man replied.

"Very well," Lewis replied calmly, "I'll tell you anyway. My father had what he came to think of as an experience. He only referred to it three times after that, as I recall. I was only ten years old at the time, but dad asked me to assist him in this very room. It was Wednesday, January 13th, a night very much like this one. My dad got a phone call from the Chief of Police, Walt Garret, at about nine-thirty. The Chief had found a body in Saint Mary's Cemetery. You know, the old abandoned graveyard in the woods to the south, outside of town.

"That guy was dressed very much like this one. But here's the clincher. Your victim is not wearing a tuxedo. The outfit you see this corpse wearing is the same type of outfit the corpse back then had on. A three-quarter length black coat, black trousers, and underneath the coat, a pure white linen handmade shirt with a high collar. Over it was a medallion. An eight-sided gold medallion with strange characters and inscriptions on it. The inscriptions were written in Latin. Now, my dad was a language buff. He loved studying ancient Greek and classical Latin, and reading the classics in their own language.

"Anyway, I remember the translations he made of those Latin verses as clearly today as on the night I first heard him speak them.

'Protect me, O Lord, from the Terror that moves by night, and from the rage of he who is awakened from Eternal Night. Let him arise from his grave without fury. And by Thy mercy, let him answer me all I ask.'"

Chills went up and down the two cops arms and backs. Both of them began to shiver, as if the door to a meat freezer had suddenly been thrown open.

"There were three circles drawn in the snow, one inside of the other," Frank continued, "right next to the open grave. So what my dad and the Chief were confronted with were strange circles in the snow, in between each of which were more strange inscriptions. An opened grave and its corpse missing. The body of the man later brought to my dad for preparation was found next to the open grave. He was mauled terribly, gashes all over his body. But his head was not severed like this one's.

"There were also deep puncture wounds through his chest and back, unlike your victim over there, as if extremely sharp, thick, razor claws gouged him just for the pleasure of it. Yet my dad's case was killed by exactly the same modus operandi as we have here tonight. The right side of his throat and his carotid artery were torn open, and every last drop of his blood had been siphoned from his body. Aside from a few spots in the snow around the grave, just like the kill site of your victim, there was no other blood. My dad re-examined the murder site along with Chief Garret the next day. He saw everything firsthand and I did too.

"Unlike your victim, the man's face was not gnawed upon. However, his right arm was. It was stripped clean of flesh right down to the bone, leaving all of the sinew and tendons hanging off the remaining pieces of muscle. His entire arm from fingers to shoulder was stripped clean of flesh. At the surface of the bones were teeth marks or rather, fang marks, just like this victim here. There are a lot of similarities between these two cases, Gus, and I thought you should know about them."

"Who was the victim, anyway?" Breach asked.

"No one knew. He wasn't a local. My dad ran his photo in the town paper, and in the papers of Ashvale and Port Trenton. But no one came forward to identify him. Back in those days there were no federal fingerprint files, computers, or databases, so he was just cremated. It was the cheapest way. The state paid for it. Actually, dad shipped the body to Dannsville, the only place in the region with a crematorium. He was cremated there, and from what I understand, his ashes were scattered. I take it you didn't find a medallion on this man, as my dad found on the other body."

"No, but seeing this poor guy had his head ripped from his body, his medallion—if he had one—probably flew off in some direction and got buried in the snow. I doubt we'll ever find it. But you're absolutely sure the dress of both victims is similar?"

"No, Gus," the mortician replied softly. "They're identical. Aside from the missing medallion, there's virtually no difference in the dress. Now I have some more bad news for you. You're not going to like hearing this, either of you, but I have to say it. My dad told me the outfit was a ritual costume of some kind. Probably one used in Black Magic."

The two cops looked squarely at the mortician but did not say a word. Suddenly Dave started to smile, and quickly suppressed a laugh. But the old cop didn't. He recalled the hushed rumors that ran through the homicide squad years ago. Rumors of occult activities and Black Magic practices hounded the east side of Pittsburgh for two years.

The mortician gave a disapproving glance to the young cop and said coolly, "I know what the two of you are thinking. But my dad told me when he was a boy a lot of that sort of thing went on back in this area. The coal-mining immigrants brought it with them from the old country. Mostly Poles, Germans, Irish, and Italians. They all had their favorite spells and rituals. They went to church every Sunday like good Christians, but practiced their own special types of White and Black Magic privately."

"Well, Frank," the Chief replied, puffing from emotional exhaustion, "we also found three circles inscribed in the snow at the cemetery. They had strange inscriptions in them too, just as you described. We also found an open grave, and its corpse is missing. Looks like we have a repeat of the 1926 incident. But tell me. Can you remember anything of the investigation? Any of the details at all? Did Garret make a thorough follow-up exam of the site? Did he track the footprints? Did he find out where they led to? Anything at all?"

"Are you kidding? Chief Garret investigate anything? He was the laziest cop this town ever had! It took a severe wife beating or gun fire like when the miners would argue over a pay shortage or fight over gambling losses at one of the local beer halls, for him to leave the station. And then he always arranged to arrive on the scene after the fighting was over! 'Investigate?' Him? Never!

"But I remember one peculiar thing. It was the footprints. Not the man's who was murdered, because he was killed right at the open gravesite. But the other set of tracks. They had two very odd features about them. I pointed them out to Garret but he just laughed and pushed me away. My dad wasn't interested, either."

"Well, what the hell was so strange about the footprints?" Breach asked, his heart now pounding in his throat, fearing the mortician's information might corroborate his own findings.

"The shoes. They led away from the grave, toward the woods. But both of them were only half shoes. As though the front parts of them were cut off, and someone was walking with bare exposed toes. For the life of me, I couldn't figure out how anyone could run around in such bitter cold weather with half shoes. That's why I remember it so well. And there was something else. Behind each footprint were long streaks. Wisp-like trailings, as if the someone or something walking away from the grave was dragging something behind."

"And the tracks. They began at the gravesite, walked toward the woods, and ended there?"

"Yes, I'm certain of that too. I have to tell you, to this day I still think someone or something crawled out of the grave, walked over to the woods, and disappeared. But of course, such things can't happen. I mean, even with my dad's stories of Black Magic and ritual costumes, such things can't happen. Not really. Not today. Can they, Gus?" the mortician asked in a half-frightened, rhetorical way as if the impact of the same conclusions Gus was struggling to accept in his own mind, had finally hit him fifty years after the fact.

"You left out one part in your scenario," Gus replied grimly. "Whatever—not whoever—but whatever crawled out of the grave, killed the man your father worked on, and then made his way over to the woods and disappeared. You see, Frank, Dave and I found the same half shoe marks you observed fifty years ago, except our murderer had only one half shoe. And we found the same trailing behind the prints in the hollow, where it went to feed. It all adds up. I wish to God it didn't, but it does.

"I'm going out for a smoke," he announced.

As he walked toward the door, young Barker started after him. But Frank grabbed Dave by his forearm, shook his head, and held him back. He knew the old cop needed some private time. He had to reconcile the facts with an impossible conclusion, and then somehow emotionally accept the situation. Only then would he be able to do his job and begin the hunt for whatever it was now roaming loose in the mountains, or perhaps, even in town.

As his hand met the doorknob, a loud thud broke through from the other side. The short, military-like precision of the pounding startled him for a moment. Barker noticed the hesitation before his boss finally opened the door. He saw just how badly their situation unnerved the Chief, but admired the way Gus quickly regained his outer composure.

As the door swung open, Breach was confronted by the black outline of a human figure. It stood motionless, silhouetted against the darkness of the parking lot. Breach peered intently through the darkness, trying to identify the form. As he stared, the shadow took two slow steps toward the rays of light streaming through the door. Slowly, it broke the plane separating the darkness from the emerging light, and stared down at the somewhat shorter man. The old cop's mind refused to reconcile the identity of the figure with the condition of the image in front of him. It was Greg Dovrak.

Greg's face was expressionless, yet his facial muscles were drawn in hard, lending the well-proportioned features a taut, frigid appearance. His complexion was pure white, as if every drop of blood had been drained from his body, just as had been done to the corpse lying on the table. Tiny beads of frozen sweat and night dew glazed over his white skin and frosted his brown eyebrows, lending him the appearance of a man dying from frostbite. His lips were blue-black; indicating to the old cop either the man had been deprived of oxygen for a time, or else had suffered a terrible trauma, driving the blood to his lower extremities. The pupils of his eyes were dilated, and seemed to stare in zombie-like fashion through his boss, not at him.

For what seemed to be an eternity, the two figures stood facing each other in the doorway, both seemingly lifeless. Inside Breach's mind, the contradictions between his orders to join Tom at the cemetery and Greg now standing in front of him, began to vaporize.

Somehow, the death-like appearance of Barney Fife II aided the old cop's struggle for mental balance until he was finally able to ask, "What…what are you doing here?"

Greg Dovrak did not reply. The daydream-like mental state hidden behind his frozen, terrified appearance caused him to continue to stare through his boss. Alarms of panic began to break out in Gus' mind, sending his blood pressure soaring and his heart pounding violently in his throat. Yet Breach was able to force the same question once again past his own, now quivering, lips. Still Dovrak did not answer. Out of frustration and accelerating fear, Breach instinctively grabbed him by the lapels of his jacket, and smashed him up against the doorframe as he screamed into Greg's frozen face.

"Goddamn you, what are you doing here? Where's Tom?"

Dovrak remained mute. His eyes transfixed, his body, now limp in Breach's desperate, powerful grasp. Frank regained his senses and nudged Dave to follow his lead. Without question, Dave moved across the large room in step with the mortician until they were at Breach's side. Lewis was used to dealing with the depths of human emotion and the schizophrenic actions they produced in emotionally disturbed people. Consoling bereaved families was a part of his job he had learned and perfected throughout the years by reaching deep within his own soul, and accepting the finality and grief that came with the ending of life.

"Here, Gus," Frank said in an almost whispering voice, "let Dave and me help you get Greg into that chair over there. He'll be all right after a bit. He just needs to warm up first."

Without realizing another was controlling him, Breach did as directed, and helped move the shell-shocked officer into a chair behind a small desk in the corner. Without warning, Frank disappeared, and in a minute, reentered holding a large cup of steaming liquid.

"Gus, help me to get this down his throat, will you?"

"Strong coffee?"

"Stronger than that," Frank said with a wry smile. "It's a Black Russian. Three-quarters hard whiskey, one-quarter very strong black coffee. I've never known it to fail yet. It snaps a person out of hysterical states."

"But Greg's not hysterical," Dave advanced. "He's in shock! Anyone can see that! Are you sure you're not doing him more harm than good?"

The two older men looked at each other in a knowing way, their knowledge from years of experience passing between them in a single glance.

"No, Dave, what Frank's doing is right," Breach replied, his own self-control quickly returning. "Shock can be a form of hysteria. Hysteria doesn't necessarily mean a person goes running around screaming and throwing temper tantrums. That's one manifestation of it, yes. But there are others, such as this one. See, Greg's mind has turned inward to such a point, it can't relate to the outside world anymore. This is hysterics in the fact that this is a state of uncontrolled fear due to something he saw or did. The Greg we all know couldn't handle it, so he escaped by introverting. He could have done one of two things: fight or run. They call it the fight or flight response. It's the primitive reaction hard-wired in our brains from the days of the cave. It's how we react when confronted by the unknown. In this case Greg chose to run away deep within himself."

"Then shouldn't we call a doctor or something? I mean, if he's that bad off, what the hell are we doing trying to bring him out of it? Can't we do him some kind of damage? I've heard of that! Maybe I'd better call the hospital in Ashvale."

Breach grabbed the young cop as he moved toward the telephone, spun him around, and pushed his large face into Dave's smaller one.

"Now listen to me carefully!" Gus said in a raised voice. "Get a grip on yourself! I know this is all new to you, but it's part of the job, and you've got to learn it! You were the one who said outsiders will eventually be moving to this town and bringing their outsider problems with them! Problems we have no experience in handling! Well, consider this the beginning of those problems! Doctors and hospitals are fine, and they have their place, when there's time for them! But this is not that time! Do you understand that?"

"No! I don't understand! Nothing makes sense! We have this dead body and a head and a cop who doesn't know who he is! Sometimes I think you are just plain nuts Gus, and all that experience you keep telling me about is a lot of bullshit meant to cover up winging it as you go along! I'm calling the hospital, because Greg needs the right kind of medical care!"

Breach exploded. All the events leading up to this moment in time drove him over the edge of consideration. The thought of teaching the future Chief of Police 'the right way' flashed across his mind, telling him to give the young cop a crash course in emotional control in criminal investigation—something he thought he had forgotten. Instantly, he grabbed Barker by his coat collar, and screamed at him.

"Do you know what the field is, boy? Well, I'll tell you! It's having a body over there on the table killed by having its throat torn out and the blood sucked from its body, and then having its head ripped from it and half-eaten! It's having another cop standing guard at a desolate cemetery in the dead of night, at the sight of a grave desecration and who knows what else, waiting for another cop who's now sitting in a chair over there in a state of trauma, unable to talk to us! It's having something crawling around the mountains surrounding this town, or maybe even in the town itself by now, looking for more fresh kills! And the entire series of events are a near-perfect reflection of Frank's old man's case from 1926!

"You want the field boy? Well, wake up! This is it! And when you're in *this* field, you don't have time to do things the right way. All you have time for is doing what you think will work. At that moment! And one of the things you don't have the time for is explaining yourself every step of the way to anyone! Nor do you have the inclination to tit-feed a young snot-nose cop who talks a good fight about 'handling outsiders and the problems they'll bring,' but then bolts for the right way to do the job when the job explodes in his face! That, boy, is the field! And you, me, Dovrak over there, and that poor bastard of a nephew of mine up in the cemetery, are in it! Do you think you can get what I just said through that goddamn thick head of yours? Because if you can't, you're no use to me! So just give me your goddamn badge and sidearm right now, and get out of my sight! You're fired!"

The almost savage tone in Breach's words and the intense emotional delivery produced a type of trauma in Dave Barker's mind. The overload of information and rage sliced through the young cop's socially-induced sense of propriety like a hot knife through butter. As the Chief removed his hands from Barker's collar, the young cop dropped his shoulders and said in an exhausted voice, "I'm sorry, Gus. I don't know what came over me. First I had the thought of just getting some help for Greg, and the next thing I knew I was in a mindless state, desperately just wanting to make that phone call. I don't know what happened."

"Panic, Dave," Breach said in a milder tone of voice. "Panic. That's how it works. It first presents itself as a thought, and before you can count from one-to-two, it takes over. I didn't mean to be so rough on you, but it was the only way I knew to snap you out of it. Yeah, I had to vent my fears and frustration too, and you gave me the perfect opportunity to do it. I'm sorry, son. I really didn't mean every word I said, but I did mean the sum total of it. You've got to learn to evaluate a situation as it unfolds, and react to it the best you can when you're in the field. Because unless you're sitting behind a desk in the station house filling out forms or straightening out files, you are in the field every minute you're in the outside world. That's the only way I found a cop can function and maybe survive thirty or forty years on any force, and walk away with most of his sanity, and maybe all of his body parts intact. OK?"

"OK!" Dave said as he smiled back at the now smiling Chief of Police.

"If you two are done over there," Frank cut in jokingly, "I could use your help. Greg is coming out of it."

Dave looked at Gus sheepishly. He suddenly realized the two older men did know what they were doing after all. Their tactics worked. As the two cops walked over to the mortician and his ward, they heard Greg's voice. He began to cough violently, cursing and gagging in between the short, sharp noises of coughing, trying to clear his throat in the process.

"What...the...fuck is that...stuff, Frank? Don't...have...enough business? Trying...to...drum...up some more with that...filthy goddamn brew...of...yours?"

The others began to laugh in relief. Greg was coming around, and letting the military guard that normally defined his personality down.

"Gonna be OK, Greg?" Frank asked.

"Yeah, fine. Just take that liquid shit away from me. I never tasted anything so disgusting in my entire life. What the hell is it?"

"Another time," Breach broke in. "Tell me what happened. Where is Tom? You were supposed to go to the cemetery to help him out. Goddammit, son, it's eleven-o-five! He was right! He's probably frozen by now! Dammit, Greg, what the hell happened?"

Dovrak had regained his mental composure, although his body was still shaking uncontrollably. After his mind cleared a bit more, the events of the past hour-and-a-half slid back into his conscious-ness. As if each word had weight to it, Greg labored to speak.

"I did as you said. I took two hammers from the station, a ball-peen and a flat-head. The big ones. And the damn big crow bar we use to block the back door in the summer. Then I went over to Old Henry's. I was lucky. He wasn't in bed. Guess he couldn't sleep again. He was going over his inventory when I got to his store. Old Henry gave me every damn plastic tarp he had in the place. Ten of them, all fifteen-by-fifteen feet, and the last two-dozen tent stakes he had. I packed up the cruiser and headed to the cemetery by Route 16 just like you told me to, and got there at nine fifty-five sharp. I checked my watch. I busted the lock on the century gate, drove up to the first knuckle of the cemetery road, and parked across from the patch of woods you told me about. Hell, I knew that place from when I was a kid. That's where Martin Cavendish is buried. It's unconsecrated ground, you know. He was supposed to practice Black Magic and be in league with demons, or so the story goes. When he died—"

"Please, Greg," Breach broke in, "save the local history lesson and get to it! What the hell happened, and where is Tom?" His suspicions were growing black. He did not need his intuition to tell him what his reason was signaling. Something had happened to his nephew. His heart began to pound in his throat again as he bent down and stared directly into Dovrak's brown eyes. "I asked you where Tom is, Greg. Now cut the shit and get to it!"

"All right, all right!" Greg shot back. "I'm trying to follow good police procedures and do it as fast as I can, Chief! Cut me some slack here, will you?"

Breach said nothing more. He forced himself to refocus on the still fragile state his deputy was in, and listened intently for the young cop to resume his account of the events that brought him here.

"I turned my spotlight on the thicket, and walked toward it, calling for Tom as I walked. But there was no answer. As I approached, I suddenly thought I saw something out of the corner of my right eye, near the edge of the brush. Something like a patch of blackness against a dark background. I figured it was Tom trying to scare the hell out of me, because the bushes near it began to rustle. But then it stopped instantly, as if someone just threw a switch. All of a sudden the rustling started again. But this time, the patch of blackness disappeared. So I figured it was only the wind rustling some branches, because when it began this time, it kicked up something fierce. You know how windy it gets in the mountains.

"I didn't make anything out of it until I was nearly at the thicket. Then I heard it clearly. It was something in the underbrush. It made such a racket, I knew it couldn't be a rabbit or even a fox, and so I figured for sure, it was Tom lying in wait for me. I told him to quit the shit because it wasn't funny anymore, and I was getting nervous. But it continued. The rustling got louder and more frantic, if you know what I mean. At that point, I drew my service revolver and gave a warning. But the racket kept up, getting louder with each passing second. And somehow, Chief, it seemed more threatening.

"Then I thought of Tom again. I don't know what happened next. I think I panicked. All I could see was Tom in some kind of trouble on the other side of the thicket, next to the grave of Martin Cavendish. The next thing I knew, I was on the other side of the brush, standing in the opening. The noise in the bushes to my right escalated, as though the entire right hand corner of the thicket was going to be ripped out of the ground and thrown at me. I was going to back out when I saw the open grave. I didn't expect to see that. Either my mind went blank or I couldn't think clearly. I don't know.

"All I remember is calling out for Tom again and again, and automatically moving closer to the gravesite. But there was no answer from him. I kept sweeping the area with my flashlight as I came up on the grave. Finally my light caught a reflection of something. It was Tom's revolver. I picked it up and fumbled with it, because I think I was on the verge of complete panic. Even at an arm's length away, I could smell it had been fired. When I checked the cylinder, I found all six rounds were expended. That's when I dropped it to the ground and turned around to run back through the opening to the cemetery. I caught hold of myself momentarily and realized I had to get out of there and back here as fast as I could. Then I saw it."

"Saw what?" Barker screamed, his own anxiety now at a critical level.

"It came out of the thicket, on the right side where all that racket came from. I don't know what it was. It had the shape of a man, but also not. One thing I know for sure, it was no human being. It couldn't have been. It was all black and had points behind it, off to the right and left, behind its shoulders. I could see them clearly, because they had a silver glistening to them. I figure it was the way the light of the full moon reflected off of them. I'll never forget that sight! It was as though the night tore off a piece of itself, and hammered it into a shadow. That's it! A NightShadow! Something a part of the night, but yet has a life of its own! It made a wheezing sound as it moved from right to left. It was horrible. Like air escaping from a throat filled with something sickening. Or maybe, Chief…oh, that sound…maybe…maybe…like all of the sickness of mankind rolled up into one and stuck in that thing's throat!

"I don't know, Chief, I don't know what it was! It moved fast, but seemed to rock sideways as it moved. Like it was constantly trying to keep balance. The NightShadow tried to cut me off at the opening to the thicket, but I was faster and got there before it did. Just before I darted through the opening I stopped and emptied all six rounds into it at point blank range. I swear to you, it couldn't have been more than ten feet from me, and every round found its mark. I could hear them hit, you know, the dull 'floop' sound a bullet makes as it enters a man's body at high speed. But there was something else too. Something I don't understand. As each bullet hit, there was a streak of light coming off of it as if it ricocheted off, but there was no whizzing sound like when it happens. No, every bullet went through or into it. I'm sure. But why did the sparks come off as they found their target? I don't know.

"The impact of the rounds knocked it off balance for sure, because the blackness swayed, and fell sideways to the left. It didn't hit the ground, but just lost its balance. That gave me time to escape. When I got into the cruiser, I didn't even try to turn around. I knew whatever it was would be on me in seconds, so I put the gear in reverse, slammed the gas pedal to the floor, and barreled my way down the hill and right through the gate. I took half the fence away with me. Then I headed straight back here. I don't remember the drive. I think I got to Frank's parking lot and then I blacked out in the cruiser for a while."

Everyone stood quiet for a moment. Then Frank spoke softly.

"You didn't black out, son. You managed to get to the back door. You were in a bad way, but we helped you out of it. Just rest easy there for a few minutes. I want to talk to Gus."

Frank tilted his head in a motioning gesture, and the two men walked over to the table. Dave knew he wasn't needed or wanted at that point, so he stayed at Greg's side and began to rub his shoulders, trying to improve his circulation while helping him to relax.

"Gus," Frank said quietly, "I know this is your side of the street, but I'd like to give you some input if you don't mind."

"I'd be damn grateful for any help you can give," Breach spoke wearily. "This is not a good situation, none of it. And right now, I'm trying to adjust to the hardest part, for me personally. The idea that Tom is gone."

"You think so?" Lewis asked. But the politeness in his voice revealed he too was thinking the worst.

"Of course, Frank. He's been up there four hours. When Greg didn't show up, he could have hotfooted it back to town in two hours tops, through the snow and all. He's young.

"Now figure. He stayed there, waiting for Greg. I'm sure he waited past nine. Greg was nearly an hour late, but that's not the problem. Tom waited as ordered, all right. But I'm guessing he ran into trouble sometime between nine-thirty and when Greg finally arrived there. Otherwise we would have heard the report of his weapon. You know how sound echoes at night, and especially in the dead silence of the mountains. That would explain his not leaving for town around nine because Greg didn't show, as I promised him he would. So if he did head back to town, he'd have been back about a half hour ago and we'd have heard from him. I told him we were coming straight here.

"So the conclusion is he waited past nine for Greg. Between nine-thirty and nine fifty-five he had trouble. And during Greg's ordeal in the thicket, he found Tom's gun with all of the cartridges spent. It all fits. I have no idea how I'm going to explain this to Sally. He's my sister's only child. What a son-of-a-bitch of an uncle I turned out to be. A lazy, fat cop who ran from his duty for twenty years. And when I finally woke up, it was too late to save her only child and my only nephew. Goddamn it, Frank, I think I'm going to be sick to my stomach."

"Gus," the mortician replied in a strained voice ringing cold truth, "all of us make mistakes. Big ones. That's what life is all about, whether for good or bad. You can't blame yourself to this extent. You woke up as you say and in the nick of time—for yourself, and for this town. You've got to buffer your grief with that. It's the only way. It doesn't even sound like a good excuse now, but I'm telling you as a man who has dealt with more grief-stricken people than you'll ever see, in time it will make complete sense. Tom's loss will never go away. You know that. But your role in causing his death will. At least, you'll see it in the light of 'I didn't know,' or 'those are the dangerous odds of police work.' It won't be much, but it will be enough to reconcile his loss within yourself. And you will go on. Everyone does.

"There's something else," Lewis continued. "We're giving Tom up for dead. Maybe you're right. Maybe he is. But then again, as you said, he's young. Maybe the odds fell in his favor. Maybe he escaped into the brush and hid after emptying his weapon. Don't forget. If you're right, he was attacked between nine-thirty when you and Dave got down off the mountain, and nine fifty-five when Greg swears he got to the cemetery. That's only twenty-five minutes give-or-take. If he was killed, there would be some kind of evidence, and Greg didn't find any. I mean, whatever it is wouldn't have had enough time to…uh, you know. So you might be getting all upset over something that didn't happen. I say we should get our asses up there right now and take a good look all around. The full moon is with us, and we have your cruisers' floodlights, and more than enough flashlights to go around. Hell, we don't have to wait for morning! All we need is more manpower, and I think I have the answer!"

Gus looked at his friend and smiled. The cop's mood started to improve. Maybe Frank was right. Maybe Tom did manage to get away from his attacker, and was hiding, freezing, in some clump of underbrush or in one of the old coalholes dotting the mountainous area. It was possible. There was no evidence of blood at the gravesite, not even some spilled during a brutal murder. Greg would have picked that up for sure even though he was frightened, and his senses were not at their sharpest. Of course. He would pick that up no matter what. After all, he was the super cop, whether his boss wanted to accept it or not.

"You may be right," Breach finally replied after a short silence filled with internal self-dialogue. "OK, Frank, what's your solution for increasing our manpower? There's no time to round up a posse and deputize anyone. Besides, I want to be out of here and headed back to the mountaintop by midnight."

"Well," Frank replied energetically, "We have the two of us and Dave. Greg can't go. Look at him, he's still shaking. It'll take him at least until the morning before he's any good, even to himself. But I have my two assistants, Mike and Pete. They're good men. They work as orderlies at the Ashvale hospital and moonlight with me. You saw the size of them. No one in their right mind would want to tangle with two brutes like them. They've got to have at least five hundred pounds between them, and they're built like brick walls. Besides, both of them were Marines in Vietnam and had plenty of combat experience. Pete even won the Silver Star for bravery in the face of overwhelming enemy odds. If my son Brian wasn't vacationing with his wife and my four year-old grandson in Miami, I'd ask him to go too."

Gus heard the sigh of relief in Frank's words. The mortician did not want to lose his own son any more than the old cop wanted to find his nephew torn to shreds by the 'something' that attacked Greg. But his gesture was well meant, and Breach appreciated it.

"So what do you say, Gus? I'm sure I can get Mike and Pete to go with us, if you'll arm them. How about it?"

"Get 'em, Frank!" Breach said, the sound of hanging on to Tom still being alive was heavy in his voice. "I'll do better than just arm them. I'll deputize them! That will make whatever actions they take under my command legal. Period. No questions asked. Not in my command, and especially not in the situation we're in! I'll go over and explain our plans to Dave and Greg."

Frank disappeared behind the door leading to a storage area, as Gus pulled up a chair and began talking to the two younger cops.

"Dave, Frank and his two assistants are coming with us. We're going back to the cemetery. We've got to look for Tom, no matter how bad it looks for him right now. He's—"

"Please, Gus!" Greg shouted as he tried to lift his quivering body from the chair. "Please don't go back there unless you have more men and plenty of fire power! You don't know what you're up against! Five of you are no match for it! I'm telling you! Wait for morning at least and raise a posse!"

Breach steadied him and helped him back into his chair. He said calmly, "And what about Tom, Greg? What do we do? Leave him up there all night in this freezing weather? What if he got away and is hiding somewhere, maybe wounded, trying to hold out, knowing we'll come for him? What do we do, Greg?"

"But don't you see," Greg snapped back quickly, "if he did get away, he would have hollered out to me! Or he would have tried to get my attention somehow so I could help him and the both of us could get out of there before the NightShadow attacked me! But he didn't! Please, Gus, I know how hard it must be for you, but you have to accept the fact Tom's gone! And if you take more men up there tonight, without the numbers and the firepower you'll need, you're gonna lose more! Maybe none of you will come back! Then what does that do for the town, or that matter, for all of you?"

Greg's words fell hard on Gus' emotions. Most of his experience told him the reasoning of the terrified man sitting in front of him was correct. Tom had fallen to whatever it was killed the stranger they had found earlier that afternoon. But the possibility Frank suggested might be valid too. Tom could still be alive, unconscious, lying in some underbrush, passed out from sheer terror and maybe loss of blood if he tangled with his attacker. In that case he wouldn't have been able to cry out to Greg, or attract his attention. It could be the case. Deep down, he felt he owed it to his sister and her only child to at least try while it was still night.

"You could be right, but there are some other possibilities and I have to check them out. That's my job. Remember, if it was you missing, I'd still make the same decision, and we would be on our way to look for you."

Super cop did not reply. He lowered his head, and began to cry bitterly.

Gus put his hand on his shoulder and said compassionately, "Greg, I'm ordering you to stay here. You've been through enough for one night. You'd make any Commanding Officer proud the way you handled yourself in battle. Now you've got to rest. I'll have Trudy come by and take you home. She's a good sport, you know, and she'll stay with you through the night. It gets toughest near dawn, just as the sun breaks over the horizon. Memories darken the night before they get pitch black. You'll need her to get you through first light. I'll come by to see you tomorrow. Until further notice, you're on medical leave."

Greg Dovrak did not reply. But Gus could read his deputy's relief at having been relieved of duty, by the sudden drooping of his shoulders, as though the weight of the world had been lifted from them. Yet, he could also see a hidden sadness in the younger cop's eyes. Half of him wanted to join the upcoming fight, while the other half wanted to stay safe in that room. That terrible room devoted to Death.

Gus and Dave made certain their revolvers were fully loaded, and counted the additional rounds in their holster belts. Thirty extra rounds each of high velocity .38 caliber specials rounded their belts.

"Dave, these weapons aren't good enough. We're going to swing around to the station house on our way back to the cemetery. We'll get rid of these .38s, and replace them with .45 caliber pistols. As to the ammo, I want you to break into our cache and load up your belt and pistol with blunt-head rounds. I will too. Those damn things are the deadliest shells I ever saw. When they hit a target, the lead buttercup casing around the solid shell expands outward into its target and literally explodes from inside its victim. Makes a hell of a mess. That's what I want to do to that bastard whenever we encounter him. Because count on it. We will encounter him!

"I want you to see Frank and his two assistants get the same side arms we'll be carrying, and the same ammunition. Each of us is to have thirty-nine rounds of blunt-heads, total. Seven rounds in the pistol magazine, and thirty-two around the belt. I also want each of us to carry a sawed-off 12-gauge scatter gun with six rounds of double-aught buckshot. You probably know those shells are called dead man shells, but you might not know why. That's because in the old days they were used for hunting men. One round is enough to tear a man in two at ten-to-twenty feet. I'll also call Trudy and make sure she comes down here to take care of Greg. Then we'll be off to the cemetery.

"We'll take both cruisers. Frank and I will be in the lead. You bring up the rear with Frank's two assistants. I think he said their names are Pete and Mike. I want them to feel official by having a cop with them. Lucky for us they have plenty of experience handling themselves and weapons too. Frank told me they both have combat experience from Vietnam, so at least we're not going in with newbies."

Dave smiled slightly at the reference to men untried in battle. He began to realize just how extensive the Chief's WWII experience had on the older man's way of thinking.

"When we get there," Breach continued, "I'll swing my cruiser around so the lights are pointing at the thicket hiding the grave. That will be in the east. I'll turn my spotlights on so they're flooding the south and north. I want you to park directly behind me at a hundred-and-thirty-five degree angle so your cruiser lights are showing up the southwest. Then train your spotlights so they're lighting up the southeast and the west. That will blanket the area with light, and we'll be able to pick up any motion.

"When we deploy, Frank and I will take the thicket. I want you, Pete, and Mike to flank the perimeter of the thicket at a distance of fifty feet. I want one man in the west, one in the south, and one in the southeast. The man in the southeast will be able to cover the open area behind the thicket in the east as well. Frank and I will take care of the north from inside the bush. If we flush anything out, the fifty-foot distance and the underbrush will shield us from the buck-shot, because if anything does come out—walking or running—I want all three of you to open up on it. And Dave, shoot to kill. Wait till it gets about twenty-to-thirty feet from you, and then open up with your scattergun. Whoever gets the action, be sure the other two know to give him support immediately. After that, go for your .45s. If the fucker's not finished, then finish him off. Tell Pete and Mike about this on your way up to the cemetery. I'll tell Frank. I want us to be ready and fully mobile so we can go into action as soon as our feet hit the cemetery ground. No delays of any kind. Do you understand?"

The five men assembled quickly. In less than a minute, the Chief of Police deputized his three new volunteers. As they walked out the back door, Gus bent down and whispered to Greg, "Son, can I have your keys to your patrol car? We're gonna need it and mine tonight."

Without replying or lifting his head up, the distraught cop handed him the car keys, and continued to sob. Breach patted him on the shoulder as he turned and walked out to join the others waiting in the parking lot.

Greg Dovrak sat motionless, staring at the white tile floor. He could feel the coldness of the cement beneath it, despite the warm air in the room. His mind convoluted deeper and deeper within itself, as his eyes stared at the white tiles, locked in a dazed, daydream state.

At first, his mind was an empty, black shell, devoid of all thought, all reason. Every feeling of love, joy, and hate had abandoned him. He felt relief, glad for the peace of nothingness. Then they came. Small, seeping streams of images played the events of his ordeal at the cemetery, over and over again on the screen of his mind. At first they were tiny images without meaning. But then they grew into pictures of overwhelming proportions, in which he saw himself as a coward. He had prided himself on being a perfect, professional officer, even if it was in the tiny town of Kulpsville.

Who cared if people laughed behind his back over his efforts at professionalism? Who cared if they nicknamed him Barney Fife II? Who cared if his Chief had enough of his phony shit of being a super cop.? Who cared if he wouldn't get the Chief's job when the old man retired? Hell, everyone expected Dave to get it anyway. Who cared?…He cared. Gregory Milton Dovrak cared. But his caring didn't matter. It never did. And after the events of this night, everyone would know what he really was. A coward. A spineless worm running from danger when a fellow officer was down. How could he protect the public? He was unworthy to hold the public trust. The last vestige of respect his uniform and he commanded would be torn from him, as he had torn down part of the cemetery fence during his cowardly act of running. He was worthless. No one would trust him. No other cop would ever ride with him again. No other law enforcement officer would ever turn their back to him, uncertain whether their back was being protected.

Everyone would laugh now. Adults, kids, strangers. Even his own family. His father would be the most disappointed of all. He was on Walt Garret's force for twenty-seven years, and retired with accolades. Hell, that's what a gold pocket watch meant in those days, and with a big retirement party at the VFW hall to boot! As his mind sank into ever widening and deepening pools of blackness, Greg was unaware his right hand slid around to his holster and withdrew his .38 Police Special.

And then there was Chief Breach to consider. Only minutes ago, his cowardly words to wait until morning, told his boss all he needed to know about the worm still shaking from his experience at the gravesite. The blackness in his mind now blended with thick, dark green swirls, as his left hand removed a cartridge from his belt, and slid it into the chamber of his emptied revolver, another reminder of his cowardice. His weapon had fired its bullets at NightShadow as he fled back to his police cruiser. Breach's understanding a few moments ago would fade as fast as the last wisps of darkness evaporate in the first rays of the morning sun. Then the Chief would not wait for his resignation. He would demand it by noon. "No cowards on my force!" he would tell him. "You're fired! Turn in your shield and revolver! You're a disgrace to your uniform, and to yourself! You're worthless! Get out of my sight before I remove you myself!"

The black-green miasma of his mind flowed out of his eyes, toward his hands. He looked at the weapon. Its bore was pointed upward toward his face. Somewhere in the cascading waves of sickness ebbing through his brain, his thoughts twisted and turned inside out. The pain of life was replaced by the joy of death. It was all so simple. Why hadn't he seen the answer before? Of course! The noble answer. The Roman answer. The only answer. Without hesitation, he moved his revolver from its resting place between his knees, and put the barrel into his gratefully awaiting mouth.

Cruisers 2 and 4 were rounding the corner of the block behind the mortuary, their newly deputized occupants being filled in by Dave and the Chief as to the battle plan they would launch when they got to the cemetery. They did not hear the muffled sound of the single gunshot that poked through the heavy, still night air outside of the Preparation room. Greg Dovrak had finally found the peace he inwardly longed for all of his life.

▼

CHAPTER FOUR

BODY COUNT

The two cruisers stopped at the station house only long enough for Gus and Dave to arm the three deputies, and for the Chief to call Trudy. She liked Greg. They were both unmarried, and in their mid-thirties. Secretly, she wished he would make a move. But it never came. This was her chance, maybe her only chance. Her one golden opportunity to show him how much she cared about him. He needed mothering now. Or better yet, wiving, to show him how much of life he was missing without her. With these thoughts, she assured the Chief he had nothing to worry about. "Consider me already there," she said merrily as she hung up the phone.

As she raced down the steps of her small home at the end of Scott Street, she could see her and the Law Enforcement Officer she admired and respected, standing in front of the priest of Saint Joseph's parish, taking their wedding vows. A new era was dawning in her life. Some great Good was coming out of the death and destruction that had fallen on their small, backward town. She said a prayer of Thanksgiving as she jumped into her car and drove toward the mortuary.

Breach's lead vehicle stopped fifty yards short of where the cemetery gate once stood. Dave pulled up behind. "One hell of a mess Greg made of the gate and fence," Breach radioed to Barker. "Guess he was damn scared when he tore through them. Are you men ready?"

"Yeah. We're ready."

"All right, we're moving in. Remember my instructions! Deploy as ordered, as soon as your feet hit the ground!"

In an instant, Breach's lead cruiser was rolling up the cemetery road to the first knuckle, followed by Barker. The Chief swung his cruiser around to the east, his tires screeching as they dug through the snow covered cemetery lawn, his headlights lighting up the thicket. In seconds, his spotlights were flooding the south and the north ends of Saint Alacious Cemetery. Dave's cruiser slid into a hundred-and-thirty-five degree angle behind him, headlights turning the darkness of the southwest part of the lawn into daylight. A moment later, Barker's flood lamps lit up the southeast and west.

Their assault on the cemetery was taking place with military precision. The doors of both vehicles swung open. Frank and Gus stormed the thicket, as Dave, Pete and Mike ran to their positions. Dave flanked the thicket from the southeast at a distance of fifty yards. Mike took up his position in the south and hunched down, while Pete blocked off the west. Once inside the concealed grave area, Gus shouted out to his men.

"All clear! Everyone in position?"

"All clear here too, Gus," Barker yelled back. "We're all in position! Our weapons are locked and loaded!"

"Stand ready! We're going to circle round and get caught up on the hook!"

He was referring to a military sweeping motion that begins at the center of the sight of an assault, and works its way outward in ever expanding circles. Such a move was designed to leave no piece of ground unchecked for enemy presence or activity. Gus and Frank began at the gravesite, sweeping the area with their flashlights. As they expanded their search in a circular fashion and moved to the edges of the thicket, they saw Tom's service revolver. Gus picked it up and examined it.

"Greg was right," he said to Frank, almost in a whisper. "It's been fired recently. The entire cylinder is empty. Look here, Frank. More signs of struggle. Fresh scuffle marks. The entire circle has been almost completely destroyed. Looks like Tom fought hand-to-hand with his attacker.

"There!" the Chief shouted. "There, Frank! Look at those marks! Something was drug into the brush toward the east! And behind it, a whole shoe and half of a shoe! And look! Directly behind the footprints, long wisps just like at the grave and in the hollow where we found the head! Goddamn, the bastard didn't head to town! He was probably hiding in the woods, watching us when we were examining the body at the mountaintop! Goddamn, goddamn!

"He followed us out here, and we didn't hear a thing! The son-of-a-bitch must have watched all of our moves! When he saw Tom was alone, he waited until we left and then attacked! I'll never forgive myself for this! I should have known better! What was wrong with me! My only nephew! Oh, Frank! What have I done? I should have never left him here alone! I was so worried about having the site photographed and collecting as much evidence as I could! Yet I knew, I knew, Frank, deep in my gut we weren't facing an ordinary murderer! My intuition told me what my logic couldn't accept. And now this! What have I done?"

Frank had seen so many versions of grief and misery in his business he immediately knew what to say. "Gus, you followed good police procedure, the kind you learned back in the city. You didn't know. You couldn't have. If you jumped to some cockeyed conclusion, then you would be at fault. You didn't have enough evidence, and you know it. Remember, if that thing did follow the three of you out here from the mountaintop road, not one of you heard it. The three of you are not only cops, you're all hunters, with a lot of experience in the woods. One of you should have picked up something. But none of you did. Whatever this monster is, it can reason. That makes it one of the deadliest of animals, as deadly as any man. Plus it has such strength and stealth, such superhuman powers, it makes it deadlier than anything you or any of us has ever known. It takes the blame right off your shoulders. There is no way you could have known, and nothing else you could have done. Listen to me—"

Frank's reassurances broke off in mid-sentence as the loud sound of frozen underbrush being crushed broke through the thicket in front of them. Immediately the two men threw their beams in the direction of the sound. As their lights fell in the general direction of the sudden noise, they saw a tall, wide clump of brush swaying furiously against the moonlit backdrop.

"On me!" Gus cried out loudly, even though Frank was standing next to him.

The rush of combat began pounding hard through the Chief's veins, just as it had in war. Frank's body began shaking. His own combat experience was in the Navy during the war. It was extensive, but limited to the action of Midway, with the enemy always at a distance. Never this close. Not thirty feet away, preparing to break into the open ground they held.

"Don't fire till we see it, Frank!"

"Dave, Pete, Mike," he screamed, "we have engagement! Hold your positions! Ready yourselves!

"This is Chief Breach of the Kulpsville Police Department!" Gus yelled at the shaking brush. "Put your hands on your head and walk out slowly! This will be your only warning! There's nowhere for you to go! We have the area surrounded! Surrender yourself peacefully!"

Breach's ultimatum was answered with a louder rattling of the brush. As the sound of undergrowth being violently trampled continued, Breach knew the unseen enemy was moving out from the thicket and into the open area of the gravesite. It was approaching them. His heart pounded fiercely in his throat, matching the wildly beating rhythm of Frank's. Suddenly, the last few large saplings crashed to the ground in front of them as the thing emerged.

For what seemed to be an eternity of time trapped in the schizophrenic unreality of a horrendous nightmare, Gus and Frank looked on at their enemy. Their reason told them such a thing could not exist. Not in this world. Not in any world on this side of the grave. Maybe not even in hell. But it stood not twenty feet in front of them, swaying, moving different parts of its cloak of blackness in various directions at the same time. Greg's description of it raced through Breach's mind. "It was as though the night tore off a piece of itself, and hammered it into a shadow. That's it! A NightShadow! Something a part of the night, but with a life of its own!"

As the onyx-blackness of the shadow stood out against the darkness of the night, it started to make a wheezing sound as though air was escaping from a throat filled with some kind of sickness. Or as Greg told his Chief less than an hour ago, "...maybe all of the sickness of mankind was rolled into one..." and caught in the thing's throat. The spell over them was shattered by a hideous guttural roar that quickly replaced the wheezing sound issuing from the shadow concealing something within. With lightning speed it raced across the final twenty feet of snow-covered ground toward its prey.

"Fire!" Gus screamed to Frank, as he leveled his shotgun to his right hip and squeezed off both rounds of deadly buckshot. The command had not fully fallen on Frank's numb brain before he realized he too had emptied his two rounds into the advancing shadow. The force of the blasts halted the shadow's progress. It fell backward, but did not collapse to the ground. As it regained its stance, its roar changed to a low, fierce, loud growl as it readied itself to resume its attack.

"No time to reload, Frank! Use your .45! Empty it into the bastard!" Breach screamed, as he drew his pistol and began firing at near point-blank range into the shadow now nearly on top of them.

"It's no good, Gus! Nothing will stop it! Run!" Frank cried back, his reason now being overtaken completely by terror as he raced past Gus and out of the thicket.

But Breach held his position. He sidestepped a slicing motion the shadow made at him, and rolled to the ground. As he jumped back up, he reached into his jacket and withdrew a long, red cylinder, uncapped it, and struck it against the side of its cap. Instantly, a bright red, hot flame shot out of the cylinder's end.

"Bullets won't kill you, huh!" Breach screamed, as the blood lust of hand-to-hand combat over took his reasoning mind. Blind fury ran through him in this life-or-death close-quarters struggle. "Then eat this!" he raged, as he threw the burning road flare into the darkness of the approaching shadow. To his amazement, the flare disappeared into the shadow's darkness, as though it had fallen into a pool of black—so empty of light its darkness swallowed up even the flare's hot, burning brilliance.

Breach stood motionless, spellbound. Somewhere between now and then, the flare began to glow inside the darkness of the shadow. As the flame reared up, changing from red to a pale pink light, they exposed an agonized face of something that could have once been a man. The features were riddled with black pits and yellowing strips of loose, hanging flesh. The eyes were some unknown color, the opening that served as a mouth stained with a still dripping, red-black liquid the color of fresh blood covering old, clotted blood. As it tossed its head from side to side in apparent pain, Breach could see its throat was strained, gasping for breath of the greater darkness it had suddenly been deprived of.

The assault stopped, as if the secret of its destruction lay in exposing its identity. The growls changed to long, sharp, baleful moans of agony tearing through the electrified night air. Breach was frozen in place. Caught between the horror of the sight before him and the emptiness of his weapons, he was at the mercy of NightShadow. Suddenly, the monstrosity pushed past him, knocking him to the ground as it tore its way through the thicket leading out into the south side of the cemetery. Somehow Breach managed to scream out a warning as he struggled to come to his senses.

"Dave! Pete! Mike! It's coming your way! Get out of its path! Let it pass! Bullets are no good! Get out of the way!"

But his warnings were muffled amidst the crashing sounds Night-Shadow made as it broke through the underbrush.

"There it is!" Barker yelled. "It's coming toward me! Pete, Mike, bring up your flanks! Give me support! We have to cut it off while we can!"

The report of weapons discharging cracked through to Breach on the other side of the thicket.

"Pete! Watch out! Mike! Get down, get down!" Barker's voice roared out over the volleys. "Frank!" The young cop continued to scream. "Reload! Reload! Give the fucker all you've got!"

Once more Breach screamed out, "No! Leave it go! You can't kill it with bullets! Leave it—" His words caught in his throat as he realized the gunfire was drowning out his desperate cautions. Again and again he heard shooting as he ran through the opening of the thicket to join the fight. As soon as he emerged into the open area, Breach pulled his last remaining flare from his jacket, and struck it hard against its cap as he raced to the south end. Rounding the edge of the thicket, he stopped. Memories of intense battle from the war seized his mind, as his eyes focused on the scene in front of him.

Pete was on his knees, both hands on his throat. Even in the faint, silver light of the full moon, Breach could see the young man was trying to stop the flow of blood gushing from his torn throat. His last few gurgles before he fell face down into the snow told him the young man had just given up his life. Still entranced, Breach looked further up the lawn where his remaining troops were in the heat of battle. His eyes no sooner focused on the three remaining men, than he saw the still-glowing NightShadow within the blackness cloaking it. In a single motion it picked Mike up like a rag doll, slammed him to the ground, and grabbed him by his feet. But Frank struck at the now-glowing shadow with the butt of his empty shotgun.

Instinctively, the thing sliced at him with a part of his darkness that took the shape of an arm. The blow caught the mortician on the side of the head, and knocked him to the ground senseless. With blinding speed, the shadow grabbed Mike's two feet again, and swung him around, smashing the young man's head against an eight-foot tall granite cross. The impact severed Mike's head from his body instantly, leaving his quivering corpse wiggling on the ground. This horrible sight snapped Breach out of his trance-like state.

Screaming and cursing, the old cop ran toward NightShadow as it turned its attention to the last defender. Barker put two more rounds in his shotgun and fired. The blasts knocked the attacker backwards a few feet, buying enough time for Breach to attack the shadow from his right flank. The insanity and uncoordinated actions of every battlefield reached the combatants in the cemetery. Even Night-Shadow was caught off guard when it realized this new assailant with another dreaded burning light was nearly on top of it. As the thing abandoned its assault on Barker to face Breach, the cop hurled his last flare into the now pinkish glowing darkness concealing the tortured body within its blackness. The new flare burned hot and bright, once again exposing the horror hidden within the shadow. Barker was unable to move as he looked on in awe at the occupant of the darkness. Once more, long, baleful moans of agony escaped and the horror ran at breakneck speed toward the far end of the cemetery lawn, jumped over a small embankment, and disappeared into the surrounding woods.

The surreal events put the two in a state of shock. Breach struggled to pull himself out of it. He knew if he didn't snap Dave and himself out of shock quickly, they could sink into deeper levels of shock that could immobilize them for hours or days. They could freeze to death from the frigid winter night air, or become easy prey for NightShadow if it returned. Grabbing Dave by his jacket collar, Gus shook him violently while screaming into his ears, "Wake up! Goddamn you, Barker, snap out of it! This is no time to go simple on me! Wake up!"

Slowly Dave focused on Breach's face. His pupils were still dilated. Breach bent down, grabbed a handful of frozen snow, and pushed it into Barker's expressionless face as he continued to scream and shake him. As though waking from a sleep he was not aware he was in, Dave started to struggle. "What are you trying to do to me? Gus! Goddamn it! I'm all right! What the hell's the matter with you?"

"Never mind son. Are you going be all right? Can you pull yourself together, or do you need more help from me?" The veiled threat in those last words brought him around quickly.

"Yeah, I'm Ok, Gus. I'll manage," Barker replied quietly.

"All right. Breathe deeply for a few minutes and get a grip. After that, we have to take a body count, and that means looking for Tom. I have to tell you, this is one of the worst days of my life. Maybe *the* worst. Unless he got away by some miracle, I'm afraid we're going to find him dead, too."

"Don't talk like that! Tom was always resourceful even when he was a kid! I was older than him, yeah, but I still knew him. He's got more inside him than you give him credit for sometimes. I'll bet you a dime to a doughnut…"

Dave's words trailed off in the night air as a moaning sound reared up from the snow-blanketed ground.

"Uhhhhh, uhhhhh."

"Quick, it's Frank! He alive! Help me get him to his feet!" Breach yelled.

They picked him up, and seated him on a nearby gravestone.

"I thought the hit in the head you took finished you," Gus said in a surprised, but happy voice. "Damn it, Frank, we don't want to lose you too! Are you OK?"

"No, I'm not, but I will be as soon as my head clears. What happened?"

As he asked for an update of the situation, he looked around. His question was answered when he caught sight of Pete's blood-soaked body, and Mike's headless corpse in the distance.

"Oh, no!" He bent his head down in despair and disgust. "Not them too! What are we dealing with here? What hell kind of an animal are we dealing with?"

Breach put his hand on his friend's shoulder and replied softly, "No animal, Frank. We all know what we're dealing with. We just don't want to admit it to ourselves. But I finally did. We're up against something that can't exist. Yet it does. Something from beyond the grave.

"No human being could withstand the attack we hit it with. At least a dozen shotgun blasts at point-blank range, and who knows how many rounds of blunt-heads. Whatever it is, it came from the other side of the grave. From some world no living man knows, but which every religion professes to know all about. It couldn't come from anywhere else. That's the only explanation that would account for all we've been through this night, and especially the unworldly appearance of NightShadow.

"Our real problem is going to be convincing other people just what we're up against. Can you imagine the Town Council's reaction if we tell them what really happened here, and what we saw? And can you imagine what the State Police down the road will think if I tell them the truth and then request more manpower? They'll think we're crazy! Or worse yet, they'll figure we did the killings and we're trying to cover up! I don't know what the hell to do. I can't think clearly right now."

"No one could," Frank reassured. "I have to tell you, your explanation is the only one that makes sense. I saw it too. How anything could be wearing a cloak of blackness around it and hide inside that darkness, is something unreal, like the fiction in a horror movie. But all of us saw it. And there are two more bodies over there to account for it as well. I'll never forget how that flare of yours lit up the inside of the shadow and exposed the thing hiding in it.

"No, Gus, you're right. But one thing's for sure," Frank continued, the pain in his head lessening, "we'd better get our story straight among the three of us before we head back to town. Otherwise, unless I'm mistaken, they won't just disbelieve us. It'll be like you said. They're bound to call for an investigation. The mayor will call in the State Troopers, and we'll be the ones under suspicion. They'll cook up some kind of conspiracy involving me, too. And seeing only the three of us know what the thing really is, they'll never believe it. We'd be arrested for murder, tried, sentenced, and never be cleared. We've got to think about that!"

Gus went as white in the face as the snow surrounding him. He never thought of these implications. But Frank was right. No one would ever accept their story, and they would be suspect. He suddenly realized the double problem they faced: finding and destroying NightShadow, while explaining the murders in terms other people could understand.

"Look. We're going to have to think this through before we return to town. But first I have to find Tom, as hard as it is to face."

Frank shook his head from side to side but said nothing. Dave turned around so he didn't have to face them.

"Remember those drag marks in the thicket, Frank? And the crushed down section of brush? I said it looked like something was drug into it from the scene of the fight at the gravesite. You know what I'm thinking."

"Yeah…I know what you're thinking. I guess we'd better check it out."

They returned to the entrance of the thicket. On their way, they stopped at the car and took the last six road flares from the trunk. Each man took two of them and they stuffed them into their jackets.

"These are our only weapons as far as I'm concerned," Gus said heavily. "In case that son-of-a-bitch comes back, he'll get more of the same. Who knows? Enough of them all at one time might destroy him. Dave, please stay outside the thicket. I want you out here in the open. Keep sweeping it from east to west, and for all of our sakes, keep an eye out for it. After getting burned as it did, he probably won't attack us again tonight, but we can't be sure. Frank and I will go inside the thicket to look for Tom."

Dave did as asked. There were no words left to say between them concerning Tom. Only the grim search for what the three men knew they would eventually find. In less than a minute Breach and Frank were standing at the gravesite on the other side of the woods-enclosed small thicket, their flashlights pointed toward the crushed section of brush the drag marks led to. Slowly and cautiously they approached that section of brush, and made their way inside. The full moon's light could not penetrate the dense undergrowth. Instead, it rested on the tops of branches, giving the scene an eerie effect. As they searched, they saw the mangled brush extended inward for ten yards. All of the underbrush was crushed flat, as though a struggle occurred along its entire length. Finally, Frank's light caught a reflection from something glistening in the shadows.

"Gus," he said, trying to suppress the panic in his voice. "Do me a favor and get out of here, will you?"

"What did you find?" Breach replied heavily. "Just tell me, Frank."

"Do as I ask, will you? For once in your stubborn, goddamn life, just do what someone else asks you to do, will you? Please?"

"Can't Frank. You might prepare people for their final rest, but I have to understand what sent them there."

Together they walked over to the glistening object. It was the badge from Tom's jacket. A few feet from the badge, lying face down, was Tom Pelski. Frank turned the body over. His throat had been torn out, exposing his spinal column, and his face had been gnawed upon. His nose was gone, and his left cheek had been cleanly eaten away. As with the stranger on the mountaintop, there were no massive pools of blood coloring the snow. Only a few spots near the body. Tom's left eye was also missing, probably gouged out and consumed as well.

"Let's go, Gus," Frank whispered. "I think I'm going to be sick." Gus stood a few moments over the body after Frank walked away. He was recalling Tom as a boy, and the fun they had together. Never married and childless, the old cop had looked upon his nephew almost like a son. Throughout the years, he spent as much time with the young man as he could, just living the life and excitement of as-close-to-a-real-father as he would ever come. After all, Jim Pelski's sudden death left the boy without a male figure in his life. So Gus gladly took the role.

Baseball games, trips to the entertainment park, rough-housing together, hunting these same mountains now the scene of so much death and tragedy, and the thrills he received watching his nephew open Christmas and birthday gifts—all this returned to his mind without mercy. So many scenes of happy days floated across his mind. Then the realization of a lost future together sank in. So much he would never see, good times and bad. The Chief lowered his head, and began to cry bitterly.

Ten minutes later he emerged from the thicket. As he walked toward them, the other two realized something had happened to the Chief. His nephew's murder had reached the depth of his soul, transforming grief into hate and blind rage he could control by will, but which still showed, nevertheless. Breach's stride was solid, his bearing direct and strong. The young cop had seen him like this only once before, when he pulled a car over for speeding, and three drunks rolled out in force and tried to assault him. He recalled what the three fully-grown men looked like when the Chief dragged them into the station house.

"Frank," he whispered, "whatever you do, listen to him carefully and go along with what he says whether you agree or not."

"Dave, Frank, we have to talk." Breach said loudly.

The sound in his voice was one of total command. Dave was right. He was not going to ask for ideas or opinions. He was in a violent state, ready to erupt at any moment.

"We have a dead stranger at Frank's Place, and three bodies here. That's four murders in about twenty-four hours. What's more, we know what it is. Something was resurrected from the grave. Somehow, my gut tells me the stranger must have used some kind of Black Magic to call up the life, or soul, or whatever you want to call it, back from the dead. I remember plots from Dennis Wheatley horror books and rumors back in Pittsburgh about reanimation of the dead. There were similar incidents back there, but the Commissioner hushed everything up damn quickly. Bad press for the city and its growing economy. These things aren't impossible. Hell, we all saw what we saw tonight. Things like this just aren't publicized for the average Joe who couldn't give a damn less about anything he can't see, feel, or taste. So there you have it. No more logic. Only intuition from now on.

"Now, here's what we have to do. Dave, I want you to go back to town. Frank will ride with me. I have to talk to him about some things. Maybe he already knows more than he thinks he does about the mess we have on our hands, because I have a sneaking feeling he does." Frank kept a blank expression. "But before you start back, I want you to radio the station house. Maybe someone will be there. There shouldn't be, because Trudy's with Greg taking care of him. Still, with the Nigalo kid spreading the word around about what happened today, and Greg saying the mayor and his town council want some answers, there just might be one of those ass holes down there waiting for us. In the meantime—"

"Hello? Hello? Gus, are you out there? Is anyone out there? Come on, come on, one of you guys have got to be there! Pick up! What the hell are we paying you for? To sleep on duty? This is Mayor Slab calling! I need to talk to the Chief!"

The sound of a voice coming over their cruiser communication systems jarred the three men momentarily.

"Come on, Breach! Pick up the mike! I gotta talk to you! It's important! Goddamn it, Breach, if you're off somewhere while you're supposed to be on duty, I tell you, your ass will be grass when you get back here! Now pick up!"

Barker and Frank looked at each other. Bob Slab, the town mayor, had no idea what the three men had just passed through. He wouldn't believe it if he knew. All he knew was his grossly exaggerated sense of self-importance. Breach picked up the microphone.

"This is Cruiser No. 4 to base. Breach, here," he said coldly. "What are you doing in my station house, Slab? No, never mind! I can guess! Now listen to me carefully! There are FCC regulations governing the use of police bands, and you're breaking all of them. Either put the mike down now, or get someone else on it who can help me! We're coming in. We're at Saint Alacious Cemetery. We've had trouble. Lots of it. I want the town council assembled in my office by the time I get there."

The tone in Breach's voice rang an alarm in the mayor's deepest instincts. He knew Breach had a highly controlled but violent nature. Somewhere in the few words the old cop just spoke, fury was communicated to Slab.

"Oh, and Bob? Most of all, I want you to be there when we get in!"

"Now, Chief, don't get upset. I'll have everyone on the council here by the time you get back. I called to tell you whatever trouble you had up there, well, we had some here too about an hour ago. Trudy went to Frank's place to take care of Greg like you asked. But Gus, when she got there, she, she…" Long pause, then very softly, "Greg put his gun in his mouth and pulled the trigger. Blew the top of his head right off. That's how she found him. What the hell is happening here, Gus? Why would a good cop like Greg kill himself? Dammit, Gus, we want answers, and we want them now!" Bob Slab's anger overrode his instinct for self-preservation.

"You've run this police department for the past twenty years like you own the thing! Well, you don't, you bastard! You're accountable to the council, and to me, and through us, to the entire town. And you'd better get that through your head, because we're tired of putting up with your shit! From now on, we tell you how to run this department! You won't be telling us! Now get your ass down here as fast as you can!

"Oh. You can add one more casualty to the way you've been running this department! Trudy had to be taken to the psychiatric ward of the Ashvale hospital! She was beyond hysterical, 'Chief!' There's something else you can be proud of!"

The anger in Slab's voice grew with each word. His own sense of helplessness in dealing with the events of the past twenty-four hours overcame his reason. It blinded him to Breach's temper and professional police work ethic the politician did not understand, causing him to shoot past the years of fear he had of the old cop.

The three men stood in the cemetery dumbfounded. Greg's suicide hit Gus almost as hard as his nephew's murder. His voice melded into a strange tone fusing rage with further shock, as he finally found the words to reply.

"Bob, we'll be right there. Please have everyone assembled. I want you to call the State Police Barracks in Port Trenton. Tell them the Chief of Police and you are requesting as many officers as they can cut loose. Tell them we now have *four* murders on our hands, and that doesn't include Greg. Tell them we are about to declare martial law unless we get the troopers we need. And we're gonna need a hell of a lot of them. You tell them, Mr. Mayor," the fury now surpassing the shock in Breach's voice as he continued to speak, "my nephew Tom, and Frank's two assistants, Pete and Mike, are dead, just like the stranger the Nigalo kid found this afternoon. You got that mayor?

"And you be sure to add Pete and Mike—two Vietnam combat veterans—were butchered right in front of our eyes as we fought some insane psychotic who attacks out of nowhere, and strikes without warning. You tell them after he kills his victims, he proceeds to mutilate the bodies, drain all of their blood so only a few spots are left on the ground next to the corpses, and then hacks away at their flesh! You tell them unless I get the goddamn backup I need and get it fast, I'll personally call the Governor of this goddamn state, and report I had no option but to call his office for help after being refused the assistance I need by the local State Police. And you tell them if I have to do that, I guarantee that little prick of a Watch Commander from the Port Trenton Barracks who turns us down will have his name right at the top of my list when I talk to the Governor's office. That, Mr. Mayor, is what you tell the State cops! And goddamn you, Slab, get on the phone right now, and do as I say, or there'll be a fifth killing when I get back. Do you copy Mr. Mayor?"

The dead air of the open channel between Breach and Bob Slab shattered the already taut situation. Finally, the Mayor replied.

"Gus, I, I had no idea. I'm so sorry. Not Tom, too. Oh, Gus! What's happening here? Our town is falling apart! This is insanity! Look. It'll be as you ask. I'll get on the phone to the State Police now, and tell them what you told me. I'll demand immediate action! And if they don't or can't give us the help we need, I swear to you,

I'll call the Governor's Office myself, tonight, and get you the help you need! OK, Chief?"

Somewhere in a fleeting instant of time, amidst the horror of the dilemma they found themselves in, the mayor and the Chief of Police managed to lay aside their loathing of each other and became friends. Both of them knew it. It reminded the old cop of similar situations on the battlefront. Situations he prayed he would never experience or cross his mind again, but ones dredged up by the events of this unholy night.

"OK, Bob." Gus replied in a calm, friendly voice. "Please do all you can before we get back there. There's nothing else the three of us can do here tonight. And there's no evidence left for my department to worry about. Not after what we saw and went through. Besides, we now know what the bastard looks like, I mean, how he appears. That's what we have to concentrate on now. Finding him, and dealing with him.

"I have to tell you too, Bob, I have a real bad feeling. Unless we get that psychotic fast, we're going to have more bodies on our hands. This maniac kills for the pure pleasure of killing. I mean it. I never saw anything like this before. Not even back in the big city. It has me scared, Bob, scared real bad. Not for me, but for the town. That's why I need you to do all you can before we get back. There's no time to lose. Over."

"I'm on it now, Chief, over and out."

"All right," Breach said flatly, realizing fully their dilemma. "We have the beginnings of our cover story. It should help to get the dangerousness of the situation across without making us look like fools or worse. Dave, Dave..."

Dave Barker's eyes were transfixed on the thicket some thirty yards away. He hadn't heard a word of the Chief's argument with the mayor. Three times within a single day, he had been hit with the reality of life's end. This time, a fellow cop he did not really care for. But somewhere between his dislike for Greg Dovrak and his almost daily interactions with him, the realness of the patrolman's life now brought his death even closer to a personal reality.

"Dave," Breach nudged gently, "are you with us?"

"Hum?" Barker sighed back. "Uh, yeah. I'm here."

"You have to bury what you're feeling, son," Breach cautioned gently. "Now's no time to get caught up in the fear of death and dying. That alone can cost you your own life in a fight. And before we're done, we'll probably have a few more of them to make our way through. I need your attention, Dave, and I need all of it."

Barker's body shook violently, almost automatically, while his deepest fears worked their way through his skin, chilling him from the bone outward. "I'm with you. Go ahead."

"I think the best scenario for us to paint is as follows. If I forget anything, or if it doesn't sound believable to either of you, let me finish first, and then give me your input. We have to be careful here. I don't want to mess this up.

"We'll tell them after the Nigalo kid informed us about the body on the mountain road, the three of us—Dave, Tom, and I—came up to investigate. Then I radioed Trudy to send Frank and Greg up here. So far, the story's true. Now come the lies. Trudy is in no condition to contradict us. Besides, when she finally does recuperate, she won't be able to trust her own memory. That's what I'm counting on.

"Frank got to the murder site first, and waited for Greg. When he arrived, the two of them took the body and the Nigalo kid back to town. Greg was hit hard by the viciousness of the murder, and we had to snap him out of it. He looked all right after that.

"In the meantime, Tom found tracks leading to Saint Alacious cemetery, so Dave and I went back with him to see if they could possibly be connected to the murder. We searched the cemetery for hours, returning to our patrol car every so often to warm up. Don't forget. It's too cold to think we spent all that time in the open air without some relief. After Frank and Greg took the body back, I wanted Greg to wait around and get a preliminary report from Frank as to the real cause of the stranger's death.

"Greg was supposed to drive back to help us with the search. But Frank called on the Greg's radio and told me my deputy wasn't doing so well. 'It's getting to him bad,' he said. I asked Frank for his help, and if he could get some others if possible, and for him to bring the reinforcements up to the cemetery in Greg's cruiser. He agreed, and brought his two assistants with him. Together, the six of us continued the search. Remember, I insisted we search for tracks immediately, before the winds and dropping temperatures scattered them or froze them over.

"That's when we were attacked. Tom was killed first. We didn't know it, because our search party was spread out. Then Pete was killed. But when the attacker jumped Frank and Mike together, Dave and I heard the fight and joined in. Mike was killed next, and Frank was downed. Make no mention of our scatterguns! Just say it all happened so fast, Dave and I only got a few rounds off from our side arms. What with the darkness and the fury of the fight, we don't think we scored any hits. But we finally drove the assailant off. He jumped over the small embankment at the south end of the cemetery and headed south toward town. That will give us the reason for beefing up town security, and if necessary, imposing martial law."

"What about old Henry? He'll remember Greg going to him for the tarps and tent stakes," Dave reminded him.

"Not a problem. It's really a side issue. Henry can't remember what day of the week it is. It won't come up. And if it does, I'll say Greg got them for the next day's investigation after he dropped Frank and the body off. I insisted he get them from Henry before returning to the cemetery. Whether the prints got snowed or frozen over or not overnight, I'll say I still wanted a full investigation at first light. Then he returned to Frank's place for the preliminary report. But that's when he went off the deep end.

"As to our attacker. He's a big man who dresses in some kind of black outfit, complete with black ski mask. You know, the kind that covers the entire head and face. He's very powerful, and wields either a machete or a razor-sharp, small sword. That will explain Pete's slashed throat and the decapitated stranger. As to eating flesh, we won't disclose that. No one will want to see the bodies. We'll say when the bastard has time he mutilates his victims after he kills them. Luckily I caught myself when I went off on Bob, and didn't tell him the whole truth.

"And as to my telling Bob about their blood being drained, yeah, I made a mistake there. I lost it for a few moments, and talked without thinking. But it can help us if we play it right. Essentially, we use his blood-drinking as the reason we think he's an escaped psychotic from the Dannsville State Hospital, or one of our locals who just went nuts for whatever reason. That'll do it. It will make him sound like some insane, powerful, unbelievably vicious, almost invisible lunatic who could strike anytime, anywhere. And for all we know, he can. Even in the daylight. It also covers his modus operandi, in case we wind up with more bodies in the same condition. This way, no one will be surprised. They'll know what to expect. What do you think, fellas?"

"I think it's pretty foolproof, Gus," Frank replied. "It covers everything."

"I do too," Dave said. "It explains everything."

"It does something even more important," Gus added. "It doesn't let the facts interfere with the truth. Because what we have here is a truth no one would believe. And yet, we can still provide them with facts to allow us to do what we have to do, keep the Town Council and the mayor off our backs, and protect them and the town at the same time."

Gus had each of the two men repeat the story to make sure they understood the lie well, and then said, "Dave, I want you to take my car and go back to the station house. Give Bob a hand getting the council assembled in my office. I want them there as soon as possible. The State Troopers should be arriving in about an hour. I'd like you to coordinate their arrival with the council people showing up. There's gonna be a lot of jabbering and speculating going on, so please help Bob put it down. You weren't paying attention at the time, but he and I had one hell of a fall-out over the radio a few minutes back. I see his point now, and he sees mine. I think we're going to be able to work together now, the way it should have been all along. But when you put two ass holes like us together in the same small town, there'll be trouble for a while. I think that time is past, and we can look forward to his help. One thing's for sure. He can look forward to mine."

Gus' apologetic and understanding attitude stunned the younger cop, but not Lewis. He knew the way of life, age, and men, and saw this same situation many times throughout his own life. Barker spoke out.

"OK, Chief, if that's the way you want it, consider it done! I'll treat the mayor the way you said. Maybe if he does work with us from now on, it'll be a lot easier for all of us! I'll head back now. But what should I tell them about you and Frank? When will you be along?"

"Frank and I have some hard duty yet," Breach wheezed out. "We're going to use the tarps in the back of Greg's vehicle to cover the bodies. It's nearly two a.m., and the temperature is still dropping.

We have to give the men the respect they deserve. Besides, I don't want any animals getting at them. It's the least we can do. I guess tomorrow Frank will make arrangements to get their bodies, and start the long process of dealing with the families. I don't envy him at all!"

Frank signed. "It's going to be a very bad time for sure, but it's part of the business. What I'm sorry about Gus is you having to tell your sister about Tom."

"She already knows, Frank. I'm sure of it. Remember, I said Tom was one of the men killed. There were a couple of voices in the background, probably a couple of the council members there with him. At any rate, you know how word travels in a small town. Someone called her. It doesn't make my job facing her any easier, but at least her initial reaction will have run its course. That's the best I can look for."

While the cruiser rolled down the cemetery road, the old cop and the mortician began their grim duty covering the bodies. After nearly an hour of silent working, the last tent stake was driven through the tarp ring and into the ground, covering Mike's body. His severed head was laid next to it, positioned gently by his right arm. The two men then walked slowly back to their car, the despair in their hearts driving out the frigid temperature of the surrounding night. Neither man could feel anything else.

After settling into their seats, Frank stopped Gus from starting the engine. "Before we go, I have to know something. What did you mean when you said NightShadow could strike at any time, even in the daylight? Don't you think the darkness of the night helped hide him too, and maybe he really is only a psychotic, killing with a machete or something like that? Because if that's the case, Gus, he's going to need the night before he can strike again. I mean, maybe our imaginations and the heat of battle added to our fears, and our murderer is more human than inhuman after all. Wouldn't that give us the edge?"

"No. This thing is not human. It's from the other side of the grave, brought back from the dead. You said it yourself. The dead guy lying on your table is wearing a ritual outfit. And no, Night-Shadow wore the darkness like a cloak. It wasn't our imagination. It was as real as the night itself. When I threw the first flare into it, it swallowed it up as though it didn't exist. Only seconds later did it slowly begin to light up the thing hiding within it. This thing can strike anytime, even in broad daylight. All some future victim would see at first would be something black that doesn't make any sense. Before he could figure it out or come to his senses, the shadow would be all over him and we'd have another mutilated corpse to deal with. Now's not the time for your reason to interfere with your intuition, Frank. You and I both know what we saw…what we fought. And what it is.

"We'd just better accept it and learn to deal with it if we're going to find a way to destroy it or get rid of it. I doubt we'll succeed in destroying it in some chance encounter. But maybe we can devise a way to get it out of this area permanently. Because if we're left with no other choice, maybe we can drive it off just like the one that simply disappeared for your dad. Who knows what happened to that thing? As I see it, the best we can hope for is for the shadow to vanish like the other one did back in '26. The middle of the road solution is we'll be able to make contact with it again, soon, but on our terms. Maybe lay a trap and somehow destroy it. If not, if we can't manage any of these solutions and it stays around and continues to kill, we'll wind up with an empty town.

"It's happened before. People will just move out overnight. That's what happened in one case in Pittsburgh back in the 1940's, I'm told. There were some real bizarre murders that occurred in a small town about 60 miles southeast from the city. About a dozen people were brutally murdered over the course of two weeks. Most of the population of two thousand just packed up, left their homes, and moved away. Later, after the killings stopped, they put their homes on the market, sold them to newcomers, and never returned. The town came back to life, but only over time, and with a whole new population. And to be honest with you, I have no intentions of pulling up my roots now, and starting again somewhere else. I'm just too old to do shit like that anymore."

"OK," the mortician said dryly. "I was just wishing for the best. But I guess you're right. We'd just better learn to deal with it."

"Now you can answer me one. What's the low-down on the guy missing from his grave? What was the name, Martin Cavendish? Do you know anything about him? We know it must be him out there running around killing. But maybe something from his life history might help us in some way so we can track him down. Anything might help, Frank. I'm damned desperate now, so think hard!"

"There's no need to think hard! I know all about him! Hell, all of the locals around here do! He's one of the legends passed down over the last fifty years! Let me tell you about him." Frank stopped suddenly and became quiet. Then he said, "Wait here. I'm going back into the thicket for a look at the gravestone. I want to see something."

"Not alone you don't. I'm going with you. What gives, anyway?"

"Just stay put. This will only take a minute. I still have my flares. Anyway, I want you here with the motor running just in case we have to make a quick get-away. I'll be right back."

In a few minutes Frank got back into the car.

"What were you looking for?" Gus asked.

"With everything that went on today, I didn't connect it all up. I can't believe I didn't add two-plus-two. Now I'm convinced you're right. Let me explain bit-by-bit, and see if I can put it all together out loud. Sometimes it makes a difference. If I'm right, we might really have something to go on. But if I'm on the money, then we have a very special problem on our hands. I went back to check the marker. The date on it is January 14, 1926."

"So? What does that have to do with anything?"

"If you recall, my dad's case occurred on January 13th. Coincidentally or not, the infamous Martin Cavendish died the next day. My dad prepared him. He was supposed to have died of a coronary, but we didn't know for sure. He had all of the signs of having had one. But the laws for burial were different back then. Autopsies were only done at the discretion of the attending physician, and Cavendish never had a family doctor. There was another reason a postmortem wasn't conducted. His Will stated he was to be buried within twenty-four hours, without an autopsy, and without embalming. All those things considered, my dad complied, even though Cavendish's hands were terribly scarred, his fingernails nearly gone, and his arms bloodied all the way past his wrists and his skin badly bruised. And the bruises were fresh. No more than a day old. My dad made those comments to me when I assisted him.

"I remember another strange thing too. Cavendish had a requirement for his burial. He was very emphatic about it in his Will. It said he was to be buried in a cement vault, but his casket must be made of Black Oak. This made no sense to me. Even then I knew wood would rot, so why the cement vault? But that's what he insisted upon.

"And there was another reason his last requests were carried out. His Will stated the conditions of burial had to be met in order for the town to inherit his wealth. We found out he had over $3,000,000 stashed away in two banks in Philadelphia. That was one hell of a sum back in those days! Needless to say, Jim Brodie, the mayor back then, positively demanded the four conditions of the Will be met. And they were. The town got the money, or Brodie and the council members did, and that was that. Cavendish was laid to rest, and no one thought anymore about him. Not until tonight."

"But if they were so careful to carry out his last wishes, why bury him in the thicket? Or did it just grow up around the grave because no one cared for it? With all of that money, surely they provided for perpetual care like the other residents up here?"

"Do you remember Greg's remarks? He said Cavendish was buried in unconsecrated ground because he was supposed to have practiced Black Magic and be in league with demons. Remember?"

"Of course I do," Breach replied. "What are you getting at?"

"Well," Frank answered, "the fourth condition in his Will was that he was to be buried in Saint Alacious cemetery, but in unconsecrated ground. You know, ground the church doesn't bless. It's actually a way the Christian church has of punishing people who don't tow the spiritual line during their life the way the church demands. It's supposed to bring perpetual shame and be a sign of the person's eternal damnation. Years ago, suicides and people who dropped away from the church were treated that way after they died. It's still practiced today, but to a much lesser extent than it was fifty years ago. But in Cavendish's case, he demanded it! That was the fourth condition in his Will. And so everyone, including the catholic priests in the town, happily obliged him. That thicket didn't just grow up around him. As a kid, I remember they had to cut the inner section out of the bush so they could bury him there!"

"Pardon me," Breach snapped, his patience running out, "Where is all this getting us?"

"Just hold on, Gus. I'm trying to see if my two-plus-two addition is still going to get me four. A lot depends on this." Breach sighed and leaned back into the seat, waiting for his friend to continue.

"When I went back to the grave a few minutes ago, I took a good look around this time. I noticed the casket is in remarkable shape. It shouldn't be for having spent fifty years in the ground, even in a cement vault. And I noticed something else. Those ten slash marks at the edge of the grave, and the wisps behind the half-shoe and full-shoe prints. They're just like the ones I saw back then when my dad and I went with Garret to the other murder scene, the day Cavendish died of a heart attack. It's starting to come together now.

"You see, those trailings behind the footprints are the remnants of trousers dragging behind the corpse's shoes. I've seen marks like that hundreds of times before at the sight of winter interments. The long hassock the priest or minister wears would trail behind him in the snow. The back edge of the pleat of the garment left a "v" impression as it drug behind the priest. I wondered about those marks all of these years. But when my dad and I accompanied Garret to the open gave, the snow had blown and frozen them over. They weren't as clear as the ones I saw a few minutes ago. That's why it didn't click in my head until now. I can tell you emphatically, the marks at the gravesite behind the thicket, and the ones I saw fifty years ago are definitely the same.

"And the gashes next to the open grave were made by a powerful set of razor-sharp claws. Somehow by some force no mortal man understands, Cavendish was preserved in the Black Oak casket for these past fifty years. While in the ground, he not only underwent some type of diabolical preservation, but a metamorphosis as well. Then he was resurrected from the dead, as you suspected. But there is more to it. Much more.

"Something went wrong with the unholy business of resurrection. Very wrong. Just as it did back on that terrible night in '26. I'm positive now the two events spanning the past fifty years are connected. Exactly how, I don't know. Cavendish must have crawled out of his grave and slaughtered the poor bastard who called him back into his body. And the metamorphosis made him even more powerful than when he was a man. Let me tell you, Gus, he was a giant of a man in life. I remember him very well. The sight of him struck fear into everyone. Six-foot-six, about two hundred and eighty pounds, and all of it solid muscle. Even with your height and build, Gus, he'd tower over you. He was huge for the times, even for a coal mining area.

"He never married, and kept to himself. He lived in the mansion at the end of Routelage Street, in the south of town. The dilapidated one. They say he slept during the day mostly, and I can personally vouch for the fact his lights burned all through the night. But there was something else about him. An air about him like pure evil. It was as though there was a malevolence inside of him growing every day, becoming more powerful, more sinister. Even visiting strangers who happened to run into him made the same comments about him the locals did. He wouldn't say a word to them as he passed. But the coldness in those steel blue eyes of his and the aura that seemed to surround him, conveyed the same feelings to everyone. In those days, it earned him the reputation of being evil, probably in league with demons or a pact with the devil, even though he never harmed a soul we know about.

"Now it's clear to me Cavendish deserved his reputation. Why? Because the resurrection conducted in '26 was done by two men, not one. I say this because of a remark my dad made to Garret at the scene of the crime. I forgot it until a few minutes ago. My dad told Garret even though the prints were badly snowed over, there were two sets, not one. Garret dismissed it, because he didn't want to get involved in an investigation. Prep 'em, plant 'em, and forget 'em, was his policy. I'm assuming something went wrong during the ritual back then, just as it did in this one. The stranger was killed at the site of the ritual, and Cavendish, who either assisted the stranger or was assisted by the stranger, died the next day, probably only hours after their hideous business blew up in their faces. That would explain the heart attack. What Cavendish witnessed when the dead body actually climbed out of its grave, finally took its toll. It was a delayed coronary. I've seen dozens of them throughout the years. It ended his life, but only in this world.

"I said I'm assuming something went wrong back then but I don't really know. It could be in some sick way it's part of it. I mean, maybe an offering is required after the dead man is re-animated. Maybe Cavendish knew this, and let the corpse kill his partner. Or maybe something just went amiss, and his friend was killed because the ritual went wrong.

"Either way, from what we've put together from this crime scene, and comparing it to the one fifty years ago, it's safe to say Cavendish was preparing for his own resurrection. How can I be so certain of all of this? Because of the conditions of his Will. What we have today was paralleled in the old case. That casket was made of wood and in a cement vault. And the man was buried on unconsecrated ground. Again, just like Cavendish."

"I know what I've been saying all along," Breach interjected. "But Frank, I don't think I really believed it. This is insane! How can anything like this happen in the twentieth century? Maybe you're right. Maybe our imaginations played tricks on us during the fight. It was dark. Maybe…" Breach was struggling between his intuition and reason. His rational faculty was sternly rejecting his own impossible conclusions.

"Gus, Gus, do I have to remind you of what you yourself just said a while ago? Now's not the time to let reason interfere with intuition. You and I both know what we saw, what we fought. The point-blank-shotgun blasts it took. We both know what it is. We have to accept this and learn to deal with it if we're going to find a way to destroy it, or get it out of this area permanently."

"I guess this nightmare is getting to me," the Chief answered. "You're right, of course. Keep going, you're remembering and connecting all the details. I of all people should know this is all part of police work. Just look at what you dredged up from your memory. Now, let's try again and see if you can come up with any more facts to fill in this picture for us. I have a few more questions."

"Go ahead," Lewis replied with a broad smile.

"When I think about what you said, it seems to me this resurrection thing is some kind of dark spiritual conspiracy. Look at it this way. There's one guy dug up in 1926 who obviously planned for his comeback. Now we have a second one who did the same thing, fifty years later. So let's see. To this day, you don't know the identity of the man who was killed at the gravesite. Right?"

"Right."

"And who was the guy they dug up back then? Do you remember anything about him?"

"Yes, a few things. He was buried for forty years at the time. He was interred in 1886. Kulpsville was just starting up as a town back then. There were no official records of any kind, not even church records. And since my family didn't get here until 1910, we're now talking ninety years ago. Any real knowledge about him is long gone. Even in the 1920s, coal-mining families were still arriving. Irish grouped with Irish, Germans with Germans, and so on. One group didn't fraternize with another, except at the mines, which wasn't much, I'm told. Pretty much the way it is today."

"What was the resurrected man's name?"

"Seaton Stannish."

Gus clutched his hands around the steering wheel tightly, looked straight ahead at the thicket still lit up by his headlights. "How old was Cavendish when he died? Did you notice on his marker?"

"Sure did. He was fifty-seven years old. Born 1869, died 1926."

"And did Cavendish live here all of his life?"

"As far as I know, yes. Even at the age of ten, I remember the stories about him, and seeing him walk the streets at night."

"Now I have a big question for you, Frank. I doubt you'll have the answer, but you can always check your dad's old records for the information. But I'll ask anyway. How old was Stannish when he died?"

Frank's face blushed in the low level light of the cruiser's interior. He had a fascination with death beyond the norm, even for those in his profession. He knew there was something dark and unhealthy about his fascination, and he kept it to himself. Not even his own father knew of his private mental compiling of dark statistics. He rationalized his memorization of the dates of birth and death of everyone he or his father prepared, the same way some people memorize baseball or football statistics. But he knew better, and so kept his hobby to himself.

"Hum," Lewis replied squeamishly, "I couldn't forget something like that! Not after helping my dad with the mutilated body and seeing the actual scene of the crime at the tender age of ten! He was born 1818, died 1886. Age 68."

"That means," Gus mumbled, "Cavendish was seventeen when Stannish died. I guess you wouldn't know if there was any connection between them, would you?"

"As I said, nothing is known about Stannish. What are you driving at?"

"The connection you mentioned earlier, the one that ties the two cases spanning the years between 1926 and 1976. What I'm thinking is Stannish was passing his Black Magic practices onto someone. There's just too much coincidence for both of those two odd balls to be in this town together at the same time, and for them not to have known each other. And then for Cavendish to have died within hours after the first body was found at Stannish's grave. I'm thinking young Cavendish was a student, if you will, of Stannish. Cavendish would have known him while he was growing up here. They were two-of-a-kind, and in a small town like this, they would have hooked up fast.

"If this is true, and Cavendish resurrected his old teacher in 1926, then the shock of the experience did him in. And I'll wager you Cavendish had a student of his own who was trained to do the same for him when the time came. Can you remember if anyone ever visited Cavendish? Maybe some young guy or even a young kid who was an odd ball in this town?"

"Goddamn it!" the mortician screamed as he sat straight up in his seat, and snapped his fingers hard. "Goddamn it, Gus! I completely forgot! I can't believe it, but I completely forgot! That explains it! That's the missing piece! That's where I saw the guy before!"

"What? What did you forget?!!"

"There were two such kids in town back then, older than me maybe by six or seven years. Probably in their late teens. They were two really strange kids. Timothy Shannon and Abraham ben Yakov. They had a very strange relationship. A Catholic kid and a Jewish kid, pals in a town like this, filled with suspicion of anyone from another ethnic group, let alone a Catholic kid taking up with a kid from the only Jewish family in town. Yet these two became fast friends. I remember the talk about them. No one could understand why they were so close, and always by themselves. They behaved strangely, at least that's how the town viewed them. For one thing, they'd frequently go up into the mountains at night, and wouldn't return until around midnight or later. No one knew what they were up to, and didn't want to, either.

"And the missing piece, Gus, is that they were suspected of visiting Cavendish at his spooky old house, only at night, though. Late. The one neighbor across from Cavendish's mansion told some people my parents and I were with at a church picnic, she saw the two of them go into Cavendish's place one night about eight o'clock, and not come out until well after eleven. She said they'd go see him two or three times a week, every week. This supposedly went on for a couple of years.

"The kids' families didn't care, either. Shannon's father was a simple miner with more mouths to feed than he could count, and the Jewish kid's family felt so ostracized from the rest of the community, they didn't want to make any waves by inquiring. That's something else. No one knew why the Jewish family moved to the town in the first place, which if I remember right, was around 1920. Besides, they had a slew of kids too. But Ben, as he was called, was the last of the litter. The others were grown and on their own by the time the family came to Kulpsville. So Ben was like an only child, if you know what I mean. I remember hearing that from my dad.

"And the connection between the two events spanning these fifty years, Gus," Frank blurted out in an extremely anxious state, "is that now I recognize the corpse lying on the table in Preparation Room. It's Timothy Shannon!"

"Whhaatt?" Breach screamed out. "Are you sure of those names? Are you sure it's Tim Shannon?"

"Yes, I'm positive. Faces may change over the years, but there's always an element of the person as you knew him, no matter how many years have passed. When the head thawed out a few hours ago, I knew I saw him somewhere before. I just knew it. But I couldn't quite place him. It's been bothering me all night. Then when you started prodding me with your questions, the wondering surfaced again, but I couldn't see how it figured in. Now I do. And that's the connection. The stranger is one of those two weird kids who was raised here fifty years ago.

"But there's more to it. It's all coming back now. Ben and Tim had a rift not long after Cavendish died. They stopped seeing each other. I also know both of them left the town about three years later, around the onset of the big Depression in '29. They were probably about eighteen years old. Neither one ever came back, not even to see their families. No one knows why. But I remember hearing about twenty years ago Ben became a psychiatrist and had a very lucrative practice in New York City. I only heard one piece of news about Shannon. He was rumored to have made his way to Wales where he disappeared in some backwater town. That was about thirty years ago."

"That tears it," Breach responded heavily. "After fifty years, Cavendish's old pupil, Tim Shannon, came back to resurrect his former teacher. And now I have a shock for you, Frank. About six weeks ago, my sister Sally told me she finally unloaded an old house abandoned years ago. It became town property because of back taxes. Some kin of the family who originally owned it retired from the city and bought it. She said in all of her years as a realtor she never had a client like him. He didn't haggle, just asked her the price, once. Being a good businesswoman, she inflated it. She put it completely out of sight, just to maneuver him into a reasonable price range so he might buy it. She told him it was going for $60,000. A worn-down old house selling for sixty-grand in a town like this? Hell, she told me she would have jumped at an offer of $10,000!

"But when she told him it was sixty-grand, he simply took out his checkbook and wrote her a check for the sum on the spot, and took possession immediately. The next day, he had Stieff's Construction come in, and five days later they began restoration. That's why I was so surprised and asked you if you were sure about the names.

"You see, the man who bought the house is Abraham ben Yakov! I think we'd better get back to town. Fast."

▼

CHAPTER FIVE

KILLING SPREE

Cruiser No. 4 rolled into Kulpsville from the south at 3:40 a.m. This end of town was the least populated. As Gus drove in, he scanned the deserted entrance and said to his passenger, "I'll be glad to get to the station house and see how Dave handled Bob Slab and the State Police. If he was as smooth with them as he was with others I saw him handle, they should be waiting for us, lined up like little dolls in a row. You know, Frank, that kid is going to make a fine predecessor for me. He has what it takes. Brains, finesse, eagerness, intuition, and a balanced personality. I think he's just the ticket for this town.

"What the hell!" Breach yelled, as he turned a corner and pulled onto the main street. "What's going on? Half the town must be here!"

"More like everyone!" Frank replied. "Word traveled fast! I thought with nighttime and bitter temperatures, we'd get a break! Some loud mouth in your office with the mayor when the two of you went at it over the phones! Didn't take them long to start a panic, did it?"

Maple Street was jammed. Women wearing heavy coats overnight robes, men with parkas carrying rifles and wearing side arms, and kids running through the crowds blocked them from getting any further.

Breach switched on his rotating red and blue lights and the megaphone system. "This is Police Chief Gus Breach! Clear the streets! You're obstructing a homicide investigation! Everyone! Disperse peacefully and go back to your homes! There's nothing you can do here!"

Rick Sadaleski, one of the few town troublemakers Breach had to contend with every so often, stepped in front of the immobile cruiser and began pounding on the engine hood with the butt of the high powered rifle he was carrying.

"What the hell good are you going to do for us, Breach? We hear tell there were four murders tonight! If you're so good, you should have stopped it after the first one! Now you want us to go home like good little sheep so we can be slaughtered in our beds while you play cop? Nothin' doing! We'll form search teams and go after the scum who did the killings! He's got to be roaming the woods or the back streets of town, and we mean to find him and do what the law won't! We'll string him up on the spot, and there's nothing you and the one pissant deputy you have left can do to stop us! And if you think those Staties who came here are gonna slow us down any, you're nuts! There's a couple of thousands of us here, and that makes *us* the law, not the likes of you!"

Angry shouts and screams of support for Rick went up from the crowd swarming over the sidewalks and the thoroughfare of Maple Street. Several husky, drunken men dressed in fluorescent orange hunting coats and field boots converged on the sides of the police cruiser, and began smashing the windows with their rifle butts, while others began rocking the vehicle from side to side. Normal law-abiding, self-respecting residents had become a raging mob driven by sheer terror and hysteria.

"They're going to turn us over in a minute!" Frank yelled, as he threw his left arm across his face to deflect the flying glass while holding on to the door handle with his right hand. He was desperately trying to keep his car door from being pried open by two men outside. "Goddamn, Gus, they're completely out of control! They'll kill us if they get us out of here!"

Breach grabbed the microphone of his two-way radio. "Dave! Dave! Come in! We got problems down here! We're at the nine hundred block of Maple! We're under attack! The townspeople have gone crazy! We need support! We heard State Troopers were sent to assist us! Get their asses up here as fast as you can! Dave! Dave! Do you copy? They'll be on us in a few seconds, if they don't overturn the cruiser first!"

"No good, Frank!" Breach yelled, trying to shout above the screams of the crowd and the pounding being inflicted on the car. "We're cut off! They don't hear us! Only one thing to do! You stay here! And listen! If they break through, use your forty-five. Start killing! I mean that! That's what they would do to you if they drag you out!"

As Breach shouted, he reached into the back seat and grabbed his twelve-gauge scattergun, slid two rounds into its chambers, and forced his car door open. As he struggled to get out, John Federoski

and Jim March, two well-respected members of the community, tried
to drag him from the vehicle. Pushing and pulling, Breach tried to
get to his feet. As he finally stood up, John directed a heavy blow
with a tire iron at the Chief's head. Breach deflected the blow with
the barrel of his shotgun, and with a twisting motion of his powerful
right arm, brought the butt of the weapon up into Federoski's jaw,
sending him crashing back into the crowd unconscious.

Jim March grabbed Breach around his throat from the back, and
began to strangle him with the stock of the rifle he was carrying.
Blood red in the attacker's eyes reflected the madness overtaking the
entire town. All of Gus' previous combat experiences and police
training stood him in good stead. Throwing his hips to the left, he
raised his shotgun up in front of his body, and thrust it backward as
fast and as forcefully as he could. The butt smashed into Jim's groin.
The sound of a baleful moan of agony shot through the frenzied
crowd. March doubled up and fell to the macadam road.

Breach raised his weapon once more, and fired a double-volley
into the night sky. The thundering roars of the sawed-off gun were
further magnified by the closeness of the buildings. The air pressure
from the blasts increased so greatly during the double volley, the
sounds registering on the crowds' eardrums caused intense pain,
snapping them out of their frenzy. In what seemed like an instant,
Breach slid two more rounds of buckshot "High Brass" shells into the
chambers, and discharged them in rapid succession, this time just
above the heads of the crowd. The mob quieted instantly. Reason
reentered their minds.

The people of Kulpsville began to realize what they had done.
The Chief was within his rights to level his weapon and discharge his
third volley directly into their ranks. As the daydream-like stares
vanished from their eyes, they knew they were in a standoff. There
were thousands of them against one man, but that one man was the
Law. The very embodiment of the law they all lived by. Fear of legal
reprisals ran through every mind at that moment, as the expressions
of stark insanity and terror faded from their faces. A cold silence fell
like a black curtain over the nine hundred block of Maple Street.

Frank Lewis forced his car door open and stepped out, brandishing his pistol. As he stood up, the townspeople lowered their heads in
shame and stepped back, allowing him clearance to make his way
around to Breach's side. The old cop knew he had the crowd where

he wanted them. But he also knew the situation could revert back to a state of mindless frenzy unless he punctuated his momentary upper hand with a dramatic act to permanently solidify his position.

"Frank," he shouted as Lewis made his way to him, "I deputized you earlier tonight. If anyone lifts a weapon, or attacks you or me, I'm ordering you to open fire. Kill on the spot. I'm declaring martial law on this town as of now. Under martial law, you must do as I order. Is that clear?"

"Yeah!" Lewis yelled loudly. "That's perfectly clear Chief! I'll do as ordered!"

Instantly, the sound of metal rifle and shotgun barrels were heard scrapping the street as their owners laid them down. The crowd stepped further back as Breach walked slowly over to Rick Sadaleski. In a few moments, he stood directly in front of the town trouble-maker and handed his own shotgun to a bystander.

"Sadaleski, you're under arrest for inciting to riot, destroying public property, vandalism, obstructing a police investigation, assaulting a police officer, and resisting arrest. Turn around and put your hands behind your back!"

Sadaleski turned his head from side-to-side, desperately looking for support and failing to find it. Nervously, he threw his rifle up across his body, its muzzle pointing upward and to his left. This defensive posture was meant to warn Breach the next move would see the muzzle in the Chief's face. As Sadaleski stood defiantly brandishing his rifle, the old cop's brain was calculating the situation at blinding speed. Breach knew the unwritten rules men live by dictate he must end the confrontation instantly, humiliating his foe once and for all, and be the final punctuation of his ultimate control in all matters of law enforcement. Before Sadaleski's feet took a firmer stance, he acted.

With blinding speed, Chief of Police Gus Breach threw his right arm backward, and with a clenched fist, delivered a decisive blow to the face of the armed enemy in front of him. Sadaleski's rifle dropped from his tightened hands as he fell to the ground. The Chief grabbed the semi-conscious man by his collar, pulled him to his feet, dragged him over to the cruiser and smashed him into the hood face down. Blood shot out in all directions, as the crack of a nose breaking echoed through the hushed, stunned crowd. After handcuffing the dazed man, he spun him around and pinned him against the hood once more. He screamed at him.

"If you ever get in my way again you little prick, you'll curse the day you were born! Do you understand?"

Unable to speak, Rick slid down onto the ground. Breach picked up his bloodied, former foe off the road and threw him into the backseat. He grabbed his shotgun from the bystander, reloaded it, and addressed the crowd through the megaphone. He knew he was now in complete and permanent control of the situation.

"Listen to me! All of you! Disperse immediately, and return to your homes! There's nothing any of you can do here now! If I need a posse, I'll call for one! In the meantime, do as I say! Return to your homes and stay there! We have a crisis, yes. But your interference won't help us, or yourselves! This town is under martial law, and the rules of procedure will be obeyed. Turn your radios to 1480—the radio station in Port Trenton—and listen for announcements! The conditions of martial law will be announced by sun up, and all residents will have to comply! Now everyone! Please! Return to your homes peacefully!"

As the crowd began to disperse quietly, Breach put John Federoski and Jim March in the back of his squad car as well. "You two," Breach snapped, "are under arrest for aiding and abetting incitement to riot, obstruction of justice, and assaulting a police officer. You're looking at three-to-five years in the county jail as it is, so just keep your mouths shut! Your rights will be read to you at the station house. Oh, while I have you two as witnesses, I want to say this to Sadaleski, so listen good! Rick, you're looking at ten-to-twenty in the state pen for your acts tonight. Keep your mouth shut until you get your rights read to you at the station house!"

As they drove Frank said softly, "That was scary! I'm glad you knew how to handle it."

"I had a similar experience about twenty-five years ago in an outlying district of Pittsburgh. It wasn't as bad as this one, but it was bad enough. Lucky for us it gave me some ideas on how to handle the mess we were in."

"You know," Frank said with a sigh of relief as he settled back into his seat, "we never really knew each other until today. Even in a small town like this, it's amazing how you can see people all your life and never get to know them. Really know them. I'm glad I had this chance. I think by the time this is all over, we're actually going to be friends."

"'By the time this is all over? Hell, as far as I'm concerned, after the firefight in the cemetery, we already are friends, Frank. In fact, I'm going to impose on our friendship further, if I can. I'd like you to stay with me through this. We have to pay a visit to Yakov, to try to find out all we can. I know you never knew him per se, but you're the closest link I have to him and the clouded past of this town. Are you game?"

"I was going to ask you the same thing! I'm in too deep. I've got to find out too. I'd like to close the book on all of this for myself. The past has always haunted me, and it haunted my dad until the day he died. I want to know why. It's as though he knew or suspected more than he ever let on, and I've got to resolve things if I can."

"That's great." Breach stretched his right arm out in the darkness and patted Frank on the shoulder. "Glad to have you aboard!"

"Another thing. I'd like to turn the matter of the autopsies and preparation of Mike, Pete, your nephew, Tom, and uh, Greg's body as well, over to the Dubbner funeral home in Port Trenton. He's a good man, very skilled. Frankly, because I knew the victims so well, I wouldn't want to handle it. This will free me up to stay with you on the case. OK?"

"Sounds only right." The sadness in his voice over the loss of his only nephew and the other men was obvious. His words hung heavy in the air as they pulled in front of the police station. "Let's see how Dave fared through all this," Breach mumbled. "He probably had trouble too. That's why we couldn't get in touch with him before."

As they rounded the corner from Maple Street to Willow Lane, Breach slammed on his brakes. The sudden jolt threw them forward.

"What the hell?"

A faded yellow light from the front office was streaming into the street through the single entrance. The door guarding any access was lying on the sidewalk, splintered. Two large, barred windows next to it were smashed, sending out tiny reflected points of light. Official police papers and "Wanted" posters were scattered across Willow Lane, blowing listlessly here and there, as if the rising and falling gusts of frigid air were frantically attempting to sweep them aside. Breach pulled up to the curb and shot out of the car, leaving Frank to follow at his own pace. As he walked into the remains of his office, the old cop kicked a chair away blocking his path, all the while eyeing the damage.

"I didn't think they'd go this far, Dave. Are you all right, son?"

"I'm fine," Barker replied in a tired voice, as he finished wrapping a white gauze bandage across his forehead. "One of our darling town residences caught me right in the head with a two-by-four. Damn, Gus, there were so many of them in here! I never knew this room could hold so many people! It happened right after the state cops got here. They got here a little after three. Said they saw people gathering along Maple Street as they pulled into town. I figured word just leaked out, and everyone was curious. The next thing we knew, the door flew open, and in they came.

"They went wild! They didn't even demand to know anything! They just started smashing and destroying everything in sight! They even tried to tear the bars out of the cells, but they couldn't and that infuriated them even more. It all happened so fast, we didn't even get a chance to stop them. They just lit into us with whatever they could find. Chair legs, rifle butts, fists, you name it. I guess I should have known better. Maybe I should have done something when the troopers told me about the crowd. But who would have thought? Goddamn it, I saw faces here tonight I see every day of my life! Faces that always smile and give me the time of day! People I grew up with and knew since I was a kid! Then this! I'll never be able to trust any of them again! Never! Not after this!"

"Frank and I had a scaled-down incident of our own when we rolled into town," Breach said with disgust. "When you get a minute, you'll find three of them in the back of the cruiser. Rick Sadaleski, John Federoski, and Jim March. I'll file charges against them myself as soon as I get some time. Meanwhile, read them their rights, and throw them in jail. Make sure you take one of the state cops with you as a witness. I don't want them getting off on any goddamn technicality. Sadaleski is in trouble big-time. John and Jim are close behind. This goddamn nightmare is tearing the town apart." Gus felt a hand grab his left shoulder.

"Chief." Bob Slab was exhausted. "We've got to do something fast. I never thought our people could do anything like this! They burst in here and went wild like they were on some kind of feeding frenzy. We didn't even get the council meeting off the ground, because I wanted to wait until the state got here. Dave started to fill the council and the cops in on what happened in the mountains, and the next thing we knew, the townspeople were all over us! Even two councilwomen got beat up! Look at them! They're going to have shiners for weeks!"

"Bob," Gus replied quietly. "It's like this. The situation is clouded because we're all panicked right now. All of us are exhausted, and no one is thinking clearly. We've got to get a grip on ourselves. Here's where we stand. First of all, I declared martial law back in the street a few minutes ago. I had to. Things could erupt again and we can't trust anyone in town until everything is resolved. Fear will drive the sanest and mildest of men and women to the most desperate acts, and we can't take that chance. Are you with me on declaring this state of emergency?"

"You're damn right I am. More troopers or no, we've got to have order. OK. Martial law is now in effect, and I'll alert the Governor's office right away."

"Good! Next, Frank and I have to get some rest. It's four-thirty. I think we'll go over to my house and sack out and be back here at eleven. What with Greg's suicide, I don't think Frank should go back to his place tonight. You and Dave should quiet everyone here. Dave, I want you to fill everyone in on what happened at the mountaintop yesterday, and at the cemetery this morning.

"After Dave briefs you I want you to call the radio station in Port Trenton and tell them to announce we have imposed martial law. Give them the rules of citizen conduct under this state of emergency. Tell them by law, they must announce it during their next newscast, and must follow up with a new announcement every half hour for twenty-four hours. Bob, be damn sure to get the first announcement out for six a.m. The entire town should be listening by then.

"Then call the governor and explain to him exactly what Dave tells you happened. Be sure to stress the rioting and the destruction done to the station house by our normally law-abiding citizens. You've got to impress upon him how dangerous and desperate our situation is. Insist on more troopers when you tell him about martial law. Tell him we need at least another twelve troopers with riot gear, and we need them here before noon. If that doesn't work, tell him we're going to ask for military force. Dave will be here to help you explain the details.

"The Governor has got to understand we need manpower. Trained and fully equipped State Troopers—at least for now. Not some goddamn townspeople going off into the woods half-cocked on some kind of manhunt. You be sure to get across to him if that happens, if the townspeople get out of control again, we'll have more of a body count on our hands than we know what to do with. And nudge him with a reminder such a catastrophe won't help his administration any when election time comes around. You tell him the press are going to have a field day with what's happening here anyway he slices it, and it's up to him to pave the way for his own reelection!

"Then, Dave, I want you to get the oldest and most experienced trooper here and put him in charge until I get back. Have him set one of their patrol cruisers for each roadblock, two troopers per cruiser, and block off all four entrances to the town. After you're done, I want you to get some rest. We'll see you back here sometime this afternoon. Agreed?"

Bob and Dave nodded their heads in agreement. As Frank and he moved toward the door, Gus pulled Dave over to the side and spoke to him quietly.

"Listen! I don't want those state cops going out there unarmed. Stick to the cover story we made up at the cemetery, yes, but add that we used road flares to finally drive him off. Tell them we didn't think we scored any hits when we fired on him with our side arms. But now we're not sure. Tell them for all we know, he might be wearing some kind of bulletproof vest or something. Just tell them all we're certain of is that he's terrified of fire, especially the kind of hot fire our road flares produce. And since he's so damned dangerous, they're to resort to them first if they engage him. Stress this over and over to them, Dave. They've got to understand their weapons won't do a thing against him!"

"Sounds damn crazy to me, Gus. I don't think they're going to buy it. I wouldn't!"

"Can't be helped and you know it. Besides, it's no crazier than him killing two young, powerful men right in front of our eyes. Make it convincing! We've got to do all we can to try to keep the body count from going up!

"See you at eleven," were his parting words as he and Frank made their way through the shambles that was once the Kulpsville Police Station.

§§§

Old Henry couldn't sleep. He usually retired at seven sharp every evening, but that ritual had been shattered over the past several weeks. At seventy-nine years of age, time had caught up with him. Sleep was no longer important. Neither was his life. Fifty years as the owner of *Henry's Hunting and Tackle Shop* had netted him only deep debt, a wife who left him thirty years earlier, and two sons he didn't speak to. He wondered where they were now—his former wife and two boys—as he logged the last two hunting rifles into his inventory journal and closed it quietly.

"Guess there's no cryin' over shades of the past." Henry muttered to himself as he turned toward the only door of his small shop. "Got to get some air," he thought. "The cold should help clear my head and send thoughts about Donna and the boys to the back of my mind where they belong. They abandoned me. I didn't leave them. It's been no kind of a life, but it's been mine, and that's about all I can say."

As he stepped through the door and onto Maple Street, he tucked a Bowie knife into his belt. "Some kind a lunatic running around here killing people in this damn town is all we needed! Sure ain't like it was years ago I guess. Not even in little burgs like this. Well, one thing's fer sure. If some wacko tries to jump Old Henry, the son-of-a-bitch will have his ribs spread wide before the spit hits the ground! Maybe I'm not all that much in this damn world and don't mean nothin' to anyone. Not even to myself most times, but I'm all I got. And I ain't gonna be practice meat for no butcher!"

As Old Henry moved down Maple Street in the opposite direction from the Police Station, sounds of car doors slamming faded in the distance, and quiet settled over the east end of town. As the sounds died away, so did the old man's thoughts of his shattered personal life. Peace came over him and a smile of contentment broke out over the hard, wrinkled lines of his face. Then suddenly, a loud sound shattered his quiet state.

"Hey, Henry! Didn't you hear about the murders? If I were you I'd be locking my doors and staying inside, which is what I'm going to do right now! Better not be prowling around with that killer on the loose! You could be next!" Jake Munsion shouted at him from across the street.

"Thanks for the advice, Jake!" Old Henry called back through the thick, frozen night air that seemed to hang on him like a second coat. "I'll be all right. Got my favorite Bowie knife tucked away under this here topcoat! Any crazy give me trouble and I'll give him what-fer! Don't worry 'bout me! Jest get home and lock those doors of yers! Martha will be worried sick about now, what with you not bein' back yet! See ya tomorra'!"

"Have it your own way Henry! Just be careful!" were Jake's last words as he turned the bend and raced down Poplar Street toward his house.

Old Henry watched as Jake disappeared into the darkness. Then he turned the corner onto Chestnut. "Might as well walk up to Pine and circle back down the Heights hill to get home. Got to be careful though, that street borders the field and right beyond that, the woods. Maybe that crazy is hidin' out back there!"

As Old Henry walked slowly up the side street, the temperature of the air began to drop even lower.

"Damn, it's gettin' cold! Always does a couple a hours before the crack of dawn though. Always during the darkest part of the winter nights," he said to himself as he pulled the lapels of his topcoat up tighter against his throat. "Maybe this isn't such a good idea after all. Maybe I should jest turn around half way up and git back home as Jake said. Hell, all I need is pneumonia or somethin' like that! That'd do me in fer sure! Those sons a mine will get everything I own someday, but no use givin' it ta them any sooner than I haf'ta!"

The old man's self-dialogue was cut short as he noticed something on the other side of Chestnut. A large, black patch, infinitely blacker than the surrounding night, seemed to be standing between several huge, new sewer pipes, scheduled to replace two of the town's older lines in the spring. Old Henry rubbed his eyes and tried to re-focus on the area of darkness. As he did, the patch moved slowly and took a position near the front of the pipe closest to him.

"What the hell is goin' on?" he mumbled to himself as he unbuttoned his topcoat and withdrew the knife from its sheath. "I shoulda brought a flashlight with me. But who woulda thought—"

His words were snapped off by a frigid gale of night air that worked its way past him. Old Henry stared at the blackness across the street and rubbed his eyes once more. The blackness seemed to stare back at him, displaying tiny points of twinkling white light coming from behind and above its own darkness. He pulled his large knife up sharply, displaying it in front of his body, slicing through the air in random motions as a warning sign to whatever he was approaching as he crossed to the other side of the street. He was determined to solve the mystery. As he approached the huge sewer pipe, he saw the darkness standing in front it, motionless. Old Henry was sweating hard as he began to close the last few feet separating him from the blackness.

Closer now, he heard a wheezing sound coming out of the blackness standing directly in front of him. The white points of lights stood out clearly, twinkling some eight feet or so above the blackness beneath them. He watched in amazement as the lights began to move inward and outward above the blackness, as though they served as markers, outlining raised peaks on some massive set of moving black wings connected to a wavering, black patch. As Old Henry watched, his eyes grew heavy.

A gentle, soothing warmth coursed through his brain. A feeling of utter peace led into a sleep-like state he had not known since his childhood. As his sad, tired eyes closed, the knife fell from his hand to the snow-covered earth. Henry Dickers did not realize the blacker-than-night patch of darkness closing in on him had placed him in a hypnotic state. He was defenseless. With shadow speed, the darkness converged upon the old man, and swallowed him up. Old Henry disappeared from the world of Kulpsville and all he knew.

He entered into the strange and fantastic world existing within the blackness. This was a separate world no human being outside of the darkness could have known existed within its shadow-cover. Slowly, the old man's eyes cleared. He did not know where he was. Only a jet-black emptiness surrounded him. Everywhere he looked, his eyes found the same impenetrable emptiness of light. As his mind cleared from the state of near-sleep, he turned to run. He ran through the emptiness as fast as he could, but there was no exit. There was no way out. The blackness hidden within the shadow was infinite, closing in upon itself from a million different directions, always bringing him back to the place where he was. Old Henry cried out in terror, only to have his screams and pleas for help swallowed up by the same absence-of-light pressing in on him from all directions, and yet from no direction.

Without warning, a yellowish form appeared in the distant emptiness. Its size grew quickly as it raced toward the old man. The black silence surrounding him suddenly became filled with a sickening wheezing sound. Between the blinks of an eye, the form converged upon Old Henry.

His mind was unable to withstand the horror of what his eyes beheld. The rotted clothing hanging from the huge human-like form, the stench of decaying flesh swirling in yellow vapors, the madness of the few remaining hairs on its head squirming like small snakes with a life of their own, and the agonized face of a man who had crawled out of his own grave after fifty years, sent the old man's mind into a darkness greater than the one engulfing his body. As the enormous face of black pits and yellowing strips of loose, hanging flesh opened its mouth, two rows of fangs jutted out. Somehow, the blackness of its insane inner world flashed off of them, and reflected into the old man's eyes.

But Henry Dickers was unaware of what was happening. His mind had turned deep within itself, never to emerge again. He could not see the madness from beyond the grave shining through Night-Shadow's blanched, lurid eyes. Nor could he witness its mouth-like opening stained with the red-black liquid of old clotted blood. The nightmare that was once Martin Cavendish stretched out its right arm to the motionless old man, and grabbed him by his neck. It tossed its head from side to side wildly as its strained throat rippled in spasms, awaiting the nourishment of salty, thick, warm, human blood.

NightShadow's wheezing changed to low, guttural growls absorbed by the blackness of its world, as it fangs tore unmercifully tore through Old Henry's throat. As it drank, a sucking sound, broken only by a noise like someone sipping the last drops of a liquid through a straw, filled the blackness before being absorbed by it. Only a few spots of the old man's blood would be found on the white-earth covering now occupied by NightShadow's world. The thing that had once been Martin Cavendish left the lifeless corpse of

Henry Dickers slip from its grasp, and fall into the darkness. Bending down, the fiend hunched over the body and began to eat. Quick, ravenous chewing and swallowing sounds crackled through the black emptiness momentarily, before they too were quelled by the darkness.

As it ate parts of the old man's head and throat, the black pits on its face began to fade. Waves of human nourishment began replacing the swollen yellow skin with healthy pink flesh. Its eyes faded in and out between their colorless state and the steel blue they had been in life. NightShadow stood up. Power surged throughout its rotting body. Once-human senses were returning, magnified beyond all conception. A deadliness from a place beyond Death filled its massive carcass with an evil more loathsome than any serial killer could ever dream of matching. Instantly, the black patch disappeared from its killing ground, leaving Old Henry's mutilated body on the frozen earth. In a man-measured second, it covered the distance between sewer pipes and Maple Street, and was charging down Poplar Street in the direction Jake Munsion had taken only minutes earlier. Martin Cavendish was regenerating.

§§§

Crazy Mary was a harmless old woman who lived in the basement of a small two-story home passed down to her from her parents. She hated steps of any kind. "An invention of the devil!" she would say to anyone or no one every time she stepped out of the back door of her basement flat onto Maple Street. Besides, the easy access to the town's main street saved her from the searing pain of a birth defect she lived with throughout her sixty-odd years. This pain rose from her body's bent toward the left, while a neck dislocation cocked her head permanently toward the right. Her off balance walk, combined with her long gray straggly hair, small stature, and a narrow face with a pointed nose and missing teeth, gave her the appearance of an old hag. She was a living portrait of wretchedness, incurring the cruelty of generations of children who taunted her with calls of "Witch! Witch!"

But Crazy Mary never heard them. In her mind, she and her only sibling Claire was all that mattered. She and her sister would spend the day quietly in her small basement world, talking of the days of their childhood, and laughing over their memories of those happy times. Each morning before sunrise, she would take a small bouquet of freshly picked flowers from her garden, and walk the four miles through the woods and mountains to Saint Alacious cemetery. At every sunrise, she would place the fresh treasure on top of Claire's grave, and polish her sister's marker. As she polished the marble headstone with the end of her tattered dress, she would tell Claire she would be back home shortly, and they could sit down and talk once more.

She didn't see the Claire living in her house as an apparition living only in her mind. When she returned home, they would once again re-enter their past of sunshine, and plans for their futures, and talk of having children and enjoying the bounties of the lives they looked forward to. When she returned daily to the gravesite and her hands would swirl over the cold marble, somehow her eyes would not catch the words carved in the stone. "Claire Janoski. Born 1908. Died 1922. Late victim of the influenza epidemic."

The early morning of January 13, 1976, was no different than any other for her. As she closed the basement door behind her and stepped out into the early morning darkness of Maple Street, she smiled back at the image of Claire in her mind, and told her younger sister she wouldn't be long. "Jest 'nough time ta put these pretty flowers on yer grave, honey! Then I'll be back!" As the old woman made her way up Barnes Street and past Pine, she smelled the flowers and stroked them as if they were tiny children. "My dears, I'm takin' you to see my lovely sister Claire! Oh, she'll be so happy to play with you today! She loves little ones like you so much!"

Without realizing it, she entered the woods. Her crooked feet did not need the light of the full moon to light their way. They knowingly walked each step of the black dirt road they had traveled each day for the past fifty-four years as they made their way through the mountains to the cemetery. Stroking her flowers and talking to them softly, the old woman did not see the patch of blackness standing motionless across the narrow mountain road in front of her. Neither did she hear the wheezing sound welling up from inside its blackness. Nor did she see the mesmerizing points of white light on the patch's huge wings unfolding above and behind it. Looking down and smiling at her small colorful treasure, and laughing as they answered her, Crazy Mary walked into the blackness. In a few moments, she and her beloved sister, Claire, would be together again.

§§§

Corporal Bart Stoker and Sergeant Sam Goreman pulled their Pennsylvania State Police patrol car across the narrow street entrance into Kulpsville at 5:25 a.m., blocking all traffic from entering or leaving the town from the south. After setting up large flashing red warning lights next to their vehicle, they took up their positions in the car, and waited in silence for some time. Finally Stoker broke the quiet.

"Man, I'll tell ya, this damn duty is gonna kill me yet! I don't mind stakeouts, Sam, but what the hell are we staking out this time? And what's this nonsense about using road flares against some kind of psychotic? I think the real psychotics are those two idiot cops! That so called Police Chief of this stinking burg and that lunatic of a cop who works for him! Four men dead in one day, and all killed by some guy wearing all black, that bullets don't stop but road flares scare off? I tell ya Sam, there's more to that cock-and-bull story than meets the eye! Somethin' doesn't smell right here!

"We're not being told everything! That's what has me scared. We don't know what we're up against! I tell ya, either those two hick cops are hidin' somethin', or they're just goddamn hysterical, cause there can't be anything the likes of what that young cop told us about! Screw him and his road flares! If I see some son-of-a-bitch roamin' round here or comin' after us, I got to tell ya, I'll use my .357 magnum here to blow the fucker from here to hell! I ain't takin' no chances with no half-assed road flares, and I don't care who tells me to use 'em, least of all some so-called cops who don't know their asses from a hole in the ground, or who are stringin' us along hidin' something."

Sam, the older state trooper, could feel his partner's intense fear hiding behind all the curses and rationalizing. He knew he had to calm Bart down, but at the same time, he knew he also had to straighten him out on some bad points the younger man was known for. Twenty-two years as a trooper had taught Goreman respect for the chain of command and for any badge, whether federal, state, or local. Orders were orders, and had to be followed, not questioned.

Looking straight ahead, he grasped the steering wheel and replied calmly to his partner.

"Well, Bart, it might be as you said. Maybe we haven't been told everything. Maybe that's because the Chief and his deputy don't know everything yet, either. Ever think of that? But in my opinion, one thing's for sure. The young cop told us all he knows that's important for us to know, especially about what worked to drive the killer off. Remember, they saw two former Nam vets cut down right in front of their eyes. Sure, there was gunfire, plenty of it, and maybe some of it hit the mark. Or maybe, in the heat of the fight, all of their rounds missed him. But one thing's for certain, and you'd better think this through real carefully. They saw plenty of action, and they know what works. Period. We can hem and haw and speculate until the sun comes up, but that won't replace what they went through.

"I got to tell you Bart, for having eight years on the Force, you're still a little wild. Better get that in check quick, trooper! Because when orders come down, you act on them. Otherwise, you not only put yourself in danger, you put your partner in danger too. And tonight, young fella, that happens to be me!

"And I'll tell you something else you should know, seeing you're feeling the way you do. Before we left the Port Trenton Barracks, I talked to the Watch Commander tonight. He knows the Chief of Police of this 'burg' as you call it. His name is Gus Breach. Yeah, he's been the Chief here for about twenty years. But did you know he was decorated twice in WWII for valor in the face of overwhelming enemy odds? Did you know he spent ten years on the Pittsburgh Police Force, in homicide no less, before coming here? Bet you didn't know too, he came to this burg because his sister lost her husband when their only son was just a baby. She was stuck here, because this was her husband's home. When he died, she had nothing. No insurance, not even enough money to bury him.

"So Breach took it upon his own shoulders to give up a career in Pittsburgh and come here to keep the family together, because it was too expensive trying to raise a family in the city on a cop's salary. Even on a Sergeant's salary. Oh, he puts it off and says he gave up the city job because he was getting tired of it and all that, and I'm sure it's true, up to a point. But Lukek told me Dan Dares, the state trooper who retired from our barracks last month after thirty-five years on the Force, knows Breach pretty well. Years ago, when

Breach and he had a little too much to drink one night, Breach told him about his sister and the real reason he came back here. So all things considered, Bart, you'd better hold your tongue and do what you're told. In this case, we've been told to hold this road until sun up or until we get relieved. And if we come across the killer, *use the road flares*. Have I made my point?"

"Yeah," Stoker replied casually. "You have. But I don't buy any of this shit about road flares. I'll trust my .357 any day. Don't worry. I'll back you up in case anything happens. I don't want to see your twenty-two years go down the drain by you bein' killed or anything like that. Hell, you've only got three more years to go before retirement. Then you and Julie can sit and watch the grass grow, while us young snips keep the law and order for you!"

The callousness and disrespect in his reply infuriated Sam. But he knew further explanations and reprimands were useless. Turning to the younger trooper, Sam grabbed him by the collar and said, "Just make sure you do your job, Stoker, or you won't have to worry about some psychotic killer tearing you apart. I'll do it myself!"

A long silence fell between them. Each peered out of their side window facing the road in both directions, since it was parked horizontally to block the street off. Finally, Stoker spoke.

"Sam, I'm getting a bad crick in my neck! I got to get some air. It's too stuffy in here with the heater running, and I want to stretch my legs. Coming?"

Goreman's anger had subsided in the past half hour since their talk. After a long pause he replied.

"Yeah, I think you're right. Might as well stretch our legs. It's 6:05 now. We have about another hour and a half before daybreak, so we'd better make the most of it. And Stoker, take two road flares with you. That's an order, Corporal!"

The two troopers walked around their patrol car and stretched. The biting cold, enhanced by intermittent gusts of wind, tore through their heavy-duty jackets. In a few minutes, they were chilled through to the bone.

"Enough fresh air," Goreman said between chattering teeth. "Let's get back into the car. It seems to be getting darker too. I don't understand it. Not with a full moon, and not this close to daybreak."

"Ah, come on, Sam, you've heard the old saying! It's always dark-est right before the dawn!" Bart said with a wry smile and flushed face. "What's the matter? Goin' soft on me? Don't do that, Sam! I'm gettin' the willies as it is! I was thinkin' about—"

"Sssh! Quiet! Look over there by that stop sign. What is that?"

"Goddamn it, Sam, stop the shit! You're startin' ta scare the piss out'a me now!"

"Damn you, Stoker, look over there! What the hell is that? That section of darkness! Look at it!"

"Look at what?" Bart sputtered, tiny drops of saliva flying out of his mouth and freezing before they hit the ground. "I don't see nothin' 'cept a stop sign!"

"No, No." Goreman was puffing from an adrenaline rush. "You can see the top of the sign from the reflected streetlight over there, but that's all! The bottom part of the sign—the metal frame the sign sits on top of—isn't there. Where are your powers of observation anyway, boy? Dammit, look closely! See the light from the street lamp? It should be lighting up the whole sign, metal frame and all, but it isn't!"

As Stoker peered at the image, the stop sign suddenly began to disappear. It was as if something black was slowly standing up in front of it, hiding both the sign and its frame. He finally understood what the Sergeant was talking about. Without a moment's hesitation, he drew his revolver, and pointed it directly at the blackness.

"It's about thirty feet away, Sam! We got time! Draw your piece and let's flank it!"

"Don't be a fool, kid. You know the orders. Strike up your flares! Then we flank it and see what happens!"

"Fuck you, Goreman! I ain't gonna be another casualty from some half-assed advice that hick Chief's been spoutin'! I'll handle this myself if you're too scared to!"

Before Sam could grab his partner, Bart broke out from his position behind the car and advanced rapidly on the darkness, his weapon leveled at it.

"Get the hell back here!" Goreman shouted. "That's an order!"

Stoker did not reply, but steadily moved toward the motionless black patch. As he closed in, the patch seemed to shift somehow. Not in position, but in size. Slowly, two enormous wing-like extensions of darkness unfolded above and behind it.

"Look at that!" Stoker screamed out. "It just sprouted two giant wings! The goddamn things looks like bat wings! I'm goin' after it!"

Before Goreman could reply, white twinkling points of light began glistening off the wings' peaks. Their flickering, alternating display caught the younger cop's eyes. A gentle feeling of warmth started to course through his brain, as thoughts of a peaceful child-like sleep began to overtake him. His arms lowered, and his weapon dropped to the ground.

"Snap out of it!" Sam screamed, as he struck his two road flares against their caps. "I'll flank it from the right! Get your flares out and get them burning Bart! Dammit, snap out of it!"

Somewhere between his partner's shouts and the sound of his weapon hitting the frozen snow-covered ground, the young cop found the last thread of his own will. After slapping himself hard in the face several times, he started to regain consciousness. With blinding speed, Bart picked up his revolver, leveled it at the darkness, and without giving a warning, fired two volleys directly into the blackness. Sam ran around the car and up the right flank, his two road flares burning hot red and pink.

"Hold your position, Bart! Don't advance anymore! The damn thing's only about ten feet away now as it is! Get your flares burning! Then we'll close in on it from both flanks and give it a taste of burning phosphorus!"

But Sam's orders fell on deaf ears. Bart was in his own state of battle fury. He advanced toward the darkness slowly, firing round after round as he approached. When he was within three feet of the darkness, he heard the 'click, click' of the revolver's hammer. The cylinder was empty. Frantically, he began reloading rounds of fresh ammunition from his belt. As he struggled to get the shells into the chamber, the darkness moved at a speed the older cop couldn't believe. One moment it was concealing the sign, and before another second passed, it slid over to his partner, and engulfed him.

In another split second, the darkness moved away from Bart's position and raced toward him. As he threw the first flare at it, he saw the mutilated, blood-drained, partially eaten body of his partner. Sam ran toward the patrol car. Fear overtook him as his mind lost its balance. He couldn't understand the horror he had just witnessed. How could his partner have been torn to shreds in less than a second? What was this blackness? Nothing made sense. Teetering towards insanity, he reached the car. Pulling the door open wildly, he grabbed the microphone of the two-way radio, and screamed into it.

"Chuck! Chuck! This is Sam over at the south entrance! Bart's dead! There's something here! A moving shadow of some kind! The kid emptied his revolver into it, but nothing happened! It tore him to shreds! I threw a flare at it but missed! I—"

Like Sam, Sergeant Chuck Betters was an older man, a trooper eight months longer than Sam. It was a chance occurrence that put him in charge of the situation, and one that would save his life.

"Come in, Sam!" Betters yelled into his microphone at the Kulpsville station house. "Come in! You're breaking up!"

Before Sam could finish his sentence, the darkness moved closer. As if playing with its prey before the kill, it slowed its advance while the cop raced toward his vehicle. It hovered in the air silently, less than five feet from the panic-stricken man. NightShadow was enjoying the terror it created in this next victim.

Goreman threw the last of his two flares at his enemy. The second one found its mark and disappeared into the floating darkness. In seconds, the interior of the blackness began to glow. As the flame reared up, the ever-changing, red-to-pale pink light revealed a human face in agony. Yet its facial features were distinct. Sam Goreman had no way of knowing the horror hidden within the emptiness had transformed. No longer was its skin riddled with black pits and yellowing strips of loose, hanging flesh. Only small dark boils remained on its cheeks and forehead, while the skin projected a healthy color through the light of the flare. The once colorless eyes now gleamed with cold steel blue radiance, and the body stood strong and powerful. Martin Cavendish was regenerating. His recent feast on the blood and flesh of his latest victims was bringing him back to life. Human life, or rather, to something beyond human life that could walk in the world of men.

Sam grabbed the microphone again. "Chuck! Chuck! In the blackness! It's the black that hides it! It's not some guy wearing a black outfit! It's a man! At least it looks like a man! I threw my last flare into it…into the blackness! It uses it like some kind of cloak! Stoker emptied a full cylinder into it, but bullets don't stop it! Only flares seem to hurt it somehow and slow it down! He…"

The old cop broke his report off and stood spellbound, as Night-Shadow darted from a hovering position in midair, and blanketed him with its emptiness.

Sergeant Betters screamed into his microphone. "Can you hold on, Sam! I'll send another car over! It'll be there in minutes! Sam! Sam! Do you copy?"

Sam's microphone hung dangling outside of his patrol car. Next to it, his mutilated body was sprawled in the snow, his lifeless eyes staring up at a full moon slowly traveling across a scene from hell.

§§§

Gus Breach stormed into the station house at 11:10 a.m., with Frank Lewis right behind him. "What the hell is going on in my town?" he yelled, directing his comments to a red-eyed, tired Chuck Betters. The state trooper Sergeant was sitting in a chair against a wall, while an army Corporal was manning the station house two-way radio. "Dammit Betters, I haven't seen so many military in one place since the war! There are armed troops everywhere! Who's in charge now, anyway? I want some answers, and I want them fast!"

Bob Slab appeared from the back room of the station house and grabbed Breach by the arm. Pulling him to the side, he motioned downward with his hands.

"Keep it down, Gus! Let me explain before you go off half-cocked!"

Breach composed himself and folded his arms across his chest, awaiting Slab's explanation. Frank discretely joined them, listening intently to what the mayor had to say.

"Gus, listen to me," Slab said in a lowered voice. "Things have gotten way out of hand here. While you and Frank slept, we had more trouble. Old Henry, Crazy Mary, Jake Munsion, and the two state cops who blocked off the south entrance to town were all murdered. Only a few spots of fresh blood were found near the bodies. Just like the guy you found on the mountain road, Gus, they were literally drained of blood, and savagely mutilated. Especially their faces. As if…as if someone actually ate parts of them.

"Now add those to the four murders from yesterday, and that brings the count up to nine in less than twenty-four hours. What's worse is that four of those killed were heavily armed men. What we have here is something that makes no sense. The murderer doesn't just attack ordinary people. He kills whenever and whomever he likes, whether they're armed or not. That is not the mark of a serial killer, and you know it.

"From the report the state cop radioed in before he met his end early this morning, we have something more than maybe an escaped mental patient. And it sure in the hell doesn't look like a psychotic running loose either. Here. Sergeant Betters had the training and good sense to tape all incoming reports from his men last night. I want you to listen to the last words of Sergeant Goreman. He and trooper Stoker were the two cops sealing off the south entrance. I think his final call will help explain the rest."

As Bob Slab and the two confederates walked over to the two-way radio, Breach looked directly at Frank. They now knew everyone had the details about the killer and its victims. A sigh of relief passed instantly through each man. Their worst fears would not be realized. Neither they nor Dave would be accused of the crimes, or of any conspiracy. Yet the relief was short lived. Both of them loved the town and its people. But now they must acknowledge the truth. Somehow, an evil dead man had been brought back to life, escaped from his grave, and threatened the entire town. The three options they discussed earlier were the only ones left. The evil had to be destroyed outright in a chance encounter, driven from the area permanently, or lured into a trap and then somehow destroyed. The first option was clearly out of the question after the events of the past night. Both men were aware of that. But how could either of the remaining two possibilities be accomplished? This was the uppermost thought that tore through their minds in a fleeting instant of time.

"Listen to Sergeant Goreman's last message," Slab said quietly, as he turned on the tape recorder wired into the station house two-way radio set. The three men listened carefully. Then Breach asked for a replay two more times.

"As you can hear, Gus, we have an extraordinary situation on our hands if that trooper was right. If he wasn't hallucinating, then something no one understands is happening here. I played that recording this morning for the people at the Governor's office. When they heard it, and were told how many people have been killed so far, they handed the whole matter over to the military. The Governor sent two hundred army troops from Fort Indian Gap Post. They got here around ten-thirty, and began deploying throughout the town immediately. At any rate, the state police will be pulled out of here in about an hour. They're just turning command over to the military right now.

"But there's more. The Governor's office also told me we're to keep our mouths shut. I've got to tell you, Gus, they meant business. They put it to me this way. The Liaison Officer to the Governor told me society today doesn't want anything it can't understand. It wants no part of anything otherworldly, no matter what. So to make sure a tight lid is kept on the situation, they sent the army in. After they heard the recording, they brought in flamethrowers, along with some heavy weapons. They figure between the two, they'll be able to destroy whatever it is behind this killing spree. At least that's what Major Puffner over there told me.

"He's a real hard-boiled case. He's running the whole show now. About a half hour ago he strutted into this station house as if he owned it, after he had already begun deploying his men throughout the town. I can tell you something else too. There's no talking to him. I get the feeling he's acting under some kind of covert orders. They want to keep a tight lid on this, and make sure the story that finally gets out after all this is over, is one of their own convenient design. Go ahead and talk to him if you want, but I'm telling you, you won't get anywhere.

"Another thing, Gus," Slab continued, "not only is the town blocked off from anyone entering it, but no one is allowed to leave it or their homes. It's the damnedest hard-core martial law I ever saw. The radio station made the announcements at six as you ordered, and since then the entire town has been sealed up."

"Bob, you've done a hell of a job," Breach replied, gratitude and admiration replacing all contempt he held for the mayor over the past twenty years. "I guess it's out of our hands now, at least, directly. Frank, Dave, and I are going to pursue some other leads on our own. So I guess I might as well introduce myself to the major, and let him know. Martial law or not, I'm still the Chief of Police, and he can't interfere with me doing my job as long as I don't interfere with him doing his."

"Well, take it easy, Gus," the mayor answered cautiously. "He's really hard-nosed."

Gus walked over to the major while Frank stayed by Bob's side. The mayor and mortician watched in silence to see what would come from a meeting between two hotheads.

"Major Puffner," Breach said in a strong, sure voice, "I'm Chief of Police, Gus Breach. Nice to meet you."

Puffner's cold eyes told the old cop he was about to have his hands full. With a sarcastic smile, Puffner replied.

"Yeah, right. Now listen Breach, and listen good! I'm in charge here, and I won't put up with any crap from some local sheriff or chief, or whatever title they gave you. This is my show, and I'm going to run it the way I choose. If you really want to be of help, just go off and secure yourself in your home. Keep your doors and windows locked, and your weapon at the ready all the time. That's all I've got to say to you. I'm too busy to play host to some small time cop."

As the major turned his back as if to walk away, Gus grabbed him by his left shoulder and spun him around like a child spinning a top. Breach towered over the smaller, slender man. The Chief's broad, powerfully build frame, years of experience, and his deep, strong voice drove home the points he wanted to make.

"Let's understand each other real good!" Breach said in a normal volume. He intended the others present to hear what he had to say. He knew word of their confrontation would spread through the ranks of the troops quickly. The old cop did not intend to put the major in his place for some egotistical reason, but rather to clearly declare his own position in the matter. He and his two allies would need freedom of movement during this state of emergency, and to insure that, he had to have command over their personal situation. He could not afford to have the cock-sure little major dictate their actions and movements to them.

"It's like this. You may be in charge of the general situation. But I am still the Chief of Police of this town. Long after you and your toy soldiers are gone, I'm going to be the one who's responsible for answering all of the questions the locals will have. Now, I couldn't give a damn less about all your fancy psychological tactics they taught you in that ninety-day wonder school you went to, or the ass kissing you did since then to get your oak leaves! From your ignorant talk and your stupid attitude, it's clear to me you were never in charge of men in a combat situation. Not even in Vietnam, which I doubt you ever saw except maybe read about in *Stars and Stripes*!

"And I don't give a rat's ass about the bullshit they've pushed into that empty head of yours about dealing with some local sheriff or chief or whatever. But I'm going to tell you one thing, and I'm only going to say it once. You do your job and stay out of my way, and I'll be good enough to return the courtesy. You got that son? Now that's all I got to say!"

As Breach turned from the stunned Puffner, muffled laughs from his own troops cracked out through the intensely quiet station house air. The old cop knew he had accomplished his goal. But he also knew he had to punctuate the effect he created to end any of Puffner's possible objections.

Stopping in his stride as he returned where Frank and Bob were standing near the door, Breach turned casually and added loudly, "Oh! Major! One more thing! Make sure you and your 'troops' don't screw up anything in this office, and that includes my files! You can make this your Command Post, yes. But aside from that, keep your goddamn fingers off property that doesn't belong to you! And yes, 'Major,' " Breach continued, stressing the rank as more honorary than earned, "my men and I will be back in here as often as we like. Have a problem with that, and I'll be on the phone with your CO before the spit hits the ground!"

The embarrassed officer did not reply. He hadn't missed the inferred remark about the old cop's own military experience during the war, or the correct reference to Puffner being a product of a ninety-day Officer Candidate School.

Breach faced Bob, who was smiling.

"I'll see you later, if that's all right with you. I'll keep you posted on what we find. You were right all along. I am responsible to you and the town council, and through you, to the people of this town. I've been running this office like it was my own. You were right. This office is not my own, and it never was. But I can tell you there will be a lot of changes around here now that you and I understand each other. And I've got to tell you that personally, I'm looking forward to them." As he finished speaking, a huge smile broke out over the old cop's face.

"Dammit, Gus, I'm sure glad we see eye to eye! Judging from what I just heard, it's good we're on the same side now!" The three men started laughing as Breach motioned to Lewis, and the two men walked out the door.

"What next, Gus?"

"There's only one answer to that, my friend. We've got to drop in on the one man who we're sure can fill in the missing gaps. We've got to pay a visit to Abraham ben Yakov."

Chapter Six

▼

Abraham ben Yakov

As Breach and Lewis walked toward the parking lot, Frank remarked about the heavy, dark gray snow clouds that had moved in and now blanketed the entire valley. "Judging from those clouds, Gus, I think we're in for another good snowfall," he added, as the two of them got into the cruiser. Their defiant strides told any onlooker they were on a mission. They both knew this was one time they dare not fail.

"It won't matter much," Breach replied in a matter-of-fact way, "that thing will keep on killing no matter what the weather does. It seems as if nothing natural has any effect on it. That's because it's unnatural, as we well know. And that means we'll have to do whatever it takes to either destroy it or get it the hell out of the area permanently. A heavy snow will make it tougher on us, yeah, but we'll just have to do the job that fell to us.

"Absolutely," Frank replied grimly. "But I have to tell you, I'm looking forward to the time I can get back resuming my quiet business! My nerves are shot!"

"You're not alone!" Breach replied smiling. "I'm going to need some R&R...uh...vacation time after all of this is over."

As they drove up Willow Lane, Lewis asked, "Where is ben Yakov's house anyway?"

"Ironically, he lives only two blocks away from me. On the six hundred block of Pine Street," Breach replied in a matter-of-fact way.

"It figures," Frank said dryly. "The last block in the north part of town bordering the woods. But at least it has that big empty field between it and the woods. That's where I fear trouble coming from."

"It could come from anywhere." Breach turned right onto Pine. "We can't assume anything now. I still think Cavendish will strike in broad daylight. That is, if you can call the light of this gray-soaked day, daylight. But why? What is his purpose in just killing and drinking his victim's blood? He can't be a vampire, the script is all wrong! I mean, being brought back to life by Shannon by some type of Black Magic, being hidden in some darkness moving with him, and eating some of the flesh of his victim. That doesn't describe any vampire I ever heard of! Not even the Hollywood type! What could his motive be? Just to kill? None of it makes any sense!"

"I don't understand it either, Gus. There is something wrong. Something hidden. Something we don't understand. And I'll bet you a dime to a doughnut that something has the key to NightShadow's destruction hidden deep within it. I can't shake the feeling that whatever the secret is, it's going to be something that can be reasoned out or assumed, contained in some knowledge that's been lost to the everyday light of human understanding. That's what I think we're going to find out eventually, if not from Yakov, then from someone or something else."

Lewis gazed through the windshield with a faraway look in his eyes. Gus wondered if his newly made friend was not in some type of trance, the words of his prediction floating up from some obscure recess within his mind.

"We'll find out soon enough," Breach answered as the cruiser rolled to a stop in front of a large, single three-story house. "This is it. 622 Pine Street. This is the family homestead Yakov bought back from my sister. Let's see what kind of reception we get."

The two men passed over a short four-foot sidewalk to a white picket fence, opened the gate, and walked up a long cement walk running along the east side foundation of the house. "I don't like going in the front door," Breach explained as they rounded the edge of the walkway and made their way up seven steps to the back porch. "It's an old habit. Somehow, people are always knocked off balance when they have to answer their back door. Maybe they only expect bad news to come through the front door, while backdoors are for family and 'good' conversations and activities. People, huh? Go figure."

While Gus directed the final part of his explanation to a blank-faced Lewis, he rapped hard six times on the back door. Minutes passed, but there was no answer.

"Maybe he's out?" Lewis offered. "It's noon. Maybe he went out for lunch?"

"Not likely. Did you see that new Audi we parked behind? No one in this town has a car like that. Only some rich shrink who could afford to pay sixty grand for this old house could afford a car like that. No, he's home all right. Just a matter of getting his attention. Maybe—"

Breach's words ended on his lips when the white and green back door suddenly flew open as if the person on the other side wanted to confront the intruders who were trying to gain access through the wrong door. A tall, heavy-set man of sixty-five years of age stood in the doorway. His receding hairline of white mixed with remaining strands of auburn, deep set hazel eyes and high forehead, balanced his long, tightly drawn face. In a deep, resonant voice bearing a strange note of gentle reassurance, the man looked squarely at his uninvited visitors.

"Yes? Can I help you?"

Instead of Yakov being caught off guard, it was Breach and Lewis who were stunned at the rapid appearance and air of command the man in the doorway projected. Breach quickly regained his composure. He replied calmly and in a forced, deep voice.

"My name is Gus Breach. I'm the Chief of Police of this town. And this man is my, uh, deputy, Frank Lewis. I'm looking for the man who purchased this house about six weeks ago. I'm told his name is Dr. Abraham ben Yakov."

"And you were told right," came the response from the stranger who now displayed two rows of large white teeth through a huge smile. "I'm Abraham ben Yakov!"

"Doctor, I'm sorry to intrude upon you like this. I know you just returned home after being away, oh, what's it been now? About forty-seven years? But I'm afraid I have to speak with you. As you probably know, the town is under martial law at this moment, and it's imperative we find out all we can from you about what we believe to be the cause of the problem that drove us to this desperate measure. I have reason to think you have at least some of the answers we need."

Breach's directness and assumptions, coupled with the old cop's method of telling the psychiatrist the law had some level of investigative interest in his past, was quickly interpreted by the analyst. Yakov immediately separated Breach's statement of the known facts from the Chief's veiled accusation. The psychiatrist knew the cop's accusation that he had answers to their problem was meant to strike fear, a tactic many of his patients used to try to intimidate him to act in a way their neuroses saw as safe. After a brief pause, Yakov replied candidly.

"Well, I can see it's going to be one of those days, or is it interrogations, Chief Breach? You're either a very excitable man by nature, or else your current state of anxiety and unsubstantiated assumptions are being produced by some extraordinary condition that has this town in the grip of fear. Some unusual state of affairs your everyday police work can't seem to touch, much less handle effectively, wouldn't you say?"

Breach felt the psychiatrist had just thrown a bucketful of ice water into his psychological-face. He let his interrogation style drop. He quickly realized he would have to be completely honest with the man if he was to obtain his help.

The old cop laughed as he replied, "Well, Doctor, I guess that put me in my place! Try to understand, a cop has to rely on his experience when it comes to what works and what doesn't. And in my business, knocking the other guy off his proverbial psychological feet gets the job done nine times out of ten. Problem is my past thirty years of experience in police work doesn't include working on shrinks, let alone, one who had a very prestigious and lucrative practice in New York City. OK?"

Yakov stared at the Chief for a few moments, and then returned the good-natured laugh. "That's a pretty good attempt at a soothing compliment mixed with a confession to gain approval, Chief Breach! Maybe you're not a 'shrink,' but your police experience has made you quick on your feet! I have to admit, that comeback was an effective attempt to allay my suspicions! Come on in gentlemen! We can talk."

After making their way through a moderately sized kitchen and living room, he led them into a large parlor and motioned for them to be seated.

As he sat in a huge rocker-recliner, he said, "Please forgive the mess, gentlemen! But it's been all of forty-seven years as you said, and this old house has fallen into considerable disrepair! The construction company is working as hard and fast as they can to make it homey again, but I'm afraid it's going to take time. And certainly, your martial law isn't helping their schedule any! Now really, how can I be of service to the law enforcement agency of my old hometown?"

Breach sensed a sudden, quickly passing uneasiness in Yakov as he squirmed in his seat, trying to find a comfortable position. The Chief was not a psychiatrist, but his years of police work had made him something of an amateur psychologist, and a good one. He didn't know the theory behind his observations of suspects, but he could read them very clearly. He had seen similar behavior many times before in murder interrogations, movements made by suspects trying to find or make a psychological way of escape out of being caught in a lie and exposed.

Breach had immediately seized upon Yakov's self-violation of his cautious attitude, and launched into his promised honesty with the stranger. But now the stranger's body movements told him he would have to be brutally honest with him if he was going to gain the psychiatrist's complete and unconditional support. And he would have to execute brutal honesty in such a way so that the only conclusion left for any logical mind was to admit to the past. He had to get Yakov to admit to his past with Shannon and Cavendish. If necessary, the old cop knew he would have to intimidate the psychiatrist into complete cooperation.

"Well Doctor, it all began yesterday in the early afternoon when a local kid came running into the station house screaming he had found a dead body on the old mountaintop road. Maybe you know the place, seeing you spent your childhood here. It's the old coal road through the woods to the north."

Breach watched the analyst's reactions carefully, but he gave no indication of astonishment or disinterest. A look of mild curiosity overtook him as his eyes rolled, searching his memory for answer.

"Yes, I think I remember it. Please go on."

"Anyway, when we investigated, we found the body of a stranger, someone unknown to these parts. At least, that's how it started out. And yes, it was a murder. The first one this town has seen in fifty years I'm told by Frank here. In fact, the last murder occurred at an old abandoned cemetery to the south, outside of town. Frank was only ten years old at the time, but he remembers it well. Why? Because his father was the only mortician in town, and handled the case. He had Frank tag along to learn the family business, which he runs to this day. You see he's just assisting me with this case because of the extraordinary events I'm about to relate.

"The last murder that occurred here was back in 1926, also a stranger. His identity was never discovered. We were fortunate this time, however, as we now know who the murder victim is. But more about that later."

Breach kept his eyes fixed on Yakov. He was laying a blatantly obvious trap. But the psychiatrist gave no indication of any knowledge about the matter. He stared back, maintaining detached, polite interest. Frank watched the Chief closely from his chair across the room, wondering how he would weave the tale in order to force the analyst into admission and cooperation.

"To make a long story short, one of my deputies—my only nephew to be exact—found something in a cemetery a few miles from the murder scene. That was early last night. When we investigated, we found an open grave. Beside it was a series of large circles with strange inscriptions traced in the snow. *The corpse was missing.* But that's not all. There was nothing to connect the murder of the stranger with the cemetery scene, at first. That is, not until my men and I were attacked. Our attacker was no ordinary man." Breach moved forward in his chair, as if preparing to rise out of it suddenly, his fixed gaze upon Yakov turned into a piercing stare.

"My one deputy described it best. 'It was as though the night tore off a piece of itself, and hammered it into a shadow. Something a part of the night, but yet has a life of its own!' He called it a 'Night-Shadow' and we did too, until we learned more about it! As it attacked us, it made a hideous wheezing sound. 'Like air escaping from a throat filled with something sickening. Like all of the sickness of mankind was rolled up into one and stuck in that thing's throat.' as the deputy put it."

Breach's portrait of an unimaginable terror from the other side of grave and the conclusions he was drawing proved to be too much for Yakov. Jumping to his feet, he said in a loud, angry voice, "I've had enough of this backwoods nonsense! I'm a man of science, Breach! Not one of your locals given to hysteria and superstition induced by fear, shadows in the night, and sounds that could be explained away by simple, natural phenomena. You have nothing more to say to me, and I have no more time for you! Now please, take your medieval mind and leave through the same door you entered!"

Gus rose rapidly from his chair to meet the verbal assault from his host. In a strong, commanding voice he replied, "Sit down! I haven't even started yet! From what I have on you, I could haul you in this minute for obstructing a police investigation. And if the killings continue, I'll have you up on charges as an accomplice to murder! At the very least, the DA can build a damn solid case against you for conspiracy in a murder cover-up! And that, Yakov, carries a twenty-year stretch in the state pen. Do I make myself clear? Now sit down and keep your mouth shut, or we'll go down to the station house and continue this there. I'm telling you now, you're my number one suspect in aiding and abetting the killer!"

"How could I be a suspect if you said it was no ordinary man that attacked you? How could I aid such a fiend?" Yakov fired back hostilely, losing his composure.

"Just sit down, Doctor, and hear me out, or I'll put the cuffs on you now and take you in!" Breach was deadly serious.

Yakov backed up and sat down, his gaze fixed on the carpet in front of him. Breach remained standing, staring at the psychiatrist as if his eyes could bore a hole through his skull. His ploy had worked. His years of practical psychology told him he was right. Yakov was involved, as he and Lewis had reasoned. All that remained now was for the former Pittsburgh murder squad Sergeant to resurrect his intensive interrogation tactics to force the analyst to cooperate.

"The thing—the NightShadow—that attacked us in the cemetery, was literally wrapped in black, a darkness moving with it. No, it wasn't a cloak or black outfit, but an actual darkness hiding something within. That 'something' withstood round after round of 12-gauge shotgun blasts and .45 caliber bullets fired into its cloak of darkness by both my men and myself. 'Something' that kills by tearing out the throat of its victims, and then drains all of their the blood, leaving only a few spots of bright red blood in the snow next to the body. 'Something' that then proceeds to eat parts of their flesh. 'Something' that cut down two full-grown men in front of my eyes, and butchered my nephew.

"You see, my nephew's body exhibited the exact same manner of death as did the stranger we found hours earlier on the road. That's how we know the murdered stranger is connected to the butchery Frank and I witnessed in the cemetery. And that 'Doctor' Yakov," Breach said with disgust, "is the same 'something' that early this morning slaughtered five more people in this town. Two fully armed state troopers who were brought in to help, and three residents who never harmed a soul in their lives.

"And how do we know it's the same 'something' that did these latest killings? Because their mutilated bodies bore the same signs of violation. That's how we know all nine murders are connected. Plus a suicide! A deputy of mine who did his best when he encountered NightShadow, blamed himself for my nephew's death, and took his own life. That makes ten people dead in not quite twenty-four hours. All from this nightmare!

"Now, let me tell you what we found out about the something that's concealed within the darkness it wears like an overcoat," Breach continued, his stare still fixed hard upon the psychiatrist.

Yakov was frozen in place, his gaze still fixed on some point on the carpet. His right index finger began to move, tapping rapidly, as if sending a Morse code plea for help to some unknown rescuer. Breach noticed the tapping, a sign his suspect's defenses were falling apart. The old cop ruthlessly continued.

"When my men and I were attacked in the cemetery, that something nearly got me too. For some reason I don't understand myself, I took two road flares with me. After my shotgun and pistol proved worthless, I struck one of the flares, and threw it at the blackness. Know what happened, Doctor? The flare disappeared inside of the emptiness, swallowed up by the darkness. In a few seconds, the flare began to light up the interior of that piece of the night. And in its darkness, I saw a figure all of my reason and life experience told me could not exist. It was the figure of something that could have once been a man.

"Its face, if that's what you could call it, was riddled with black pits and yellowing strips of loose, hanging flesh. Its eyes were some color I can't describe, and the mouth was stained with dripping, red-black liquid like fresh blood covering old clotted blood. It tossed its head from side to sign in pain, as it strained its throat as if to breathe. Maybe, breathe more darkness the flare's light was depriving it of. Or maybe, maybe it was afraid the light would expose its identity, and somehow I'd learn the secret of its destruction.

"Then it started to growl, but not for long. The growls turned into long, sharp, hideous moans of agony ripping through the night air. It raced past me and out into the open. Then it began to kill. Two men—Frank's assistants, Pete and Mike—cut down brutally right in front of my eyes. Only after the firefight was over did we find the body of my nephew, Tom. Mutilated, exactly as the stranger's body we found only hours before. Except for one difference. The stranger's head was torn from his body. Frank, here, made the examination. For what it's worth my nephew's body was spared that violence. But like the headless stranger, his throat was torn out, and his face gnawed upon.

"Now, Doctor Yakov," Breach continued, rage filling his voice, "why did I say the something that appeared to be a man of sorts, ran out into the open? Well, I'll tell you, sir! Because its grave…that's right…its grave was hidden in a thicket of trees guarding and marking off the only piece of unconsecrated ground in the entire cemetery. The same piece of ground one man insisted on being buried in. The one man whom this entire town feared, many long years ago. The one man who insisted four special conditions of his will be fulfilled before the town fathers got all of the money he left behind after his death. That he be buried in a black oak coffin, in a cement vault, on unconsecrated ground, and without embalming. The one man who died on January 14, 1926, the day after the other desecrated grave was found in the old cemetery south of town. The same grave with another butchered body next to it, pretty much in the same condition as the stranger we found yesterday, but with his head intact, just as my nephew's was.

"The one man whose name is scrawled on the headstone of the now empty grave in Saint Alacious cemetery and who has been killing and devouring the living flesh of its victims. The one man you and Tim Shannon would visit almost every night when you and he were only fifteen years old who taught you both his secret, forbidden knowledge, and who told the two of you about his teacher Seaton Stannish. The one man who resurrected Stannish on the night of January 13, 1926 and either offered his assistant up to Stannish as a sacrifice of some kind, or who cut and run when Stannish attacked that stranger.

"The one man who left his assistant's body to be found back then by the open grave by the Chief of Police and Frank's father. The one man whose heart couldn't take the strain of the black reality he and his assistant created when they brought Stannish back to life and died of a heart attack the next day after accomplishing his insane, dark purpose of resurrection. The one man who caused you and Shannon to go your separate ways immediately after his death. The same man who now, fifty years later, crawled out of the grave as his teacher, Seaton Stannish did before him, brought back by the rites of Black Magic he taught you and Shannon. The same man who now occupies a cloak of darkness. The man whose name is Martin Cavendish, who we call NightShadow."

Yakov's index finger ceased its relentless tapping. He stood up from his chair slowly and walked over to Gus Breach. In a calm voice he replied, "Breach, you've got nothing! Can you imagine taking those 'facts' to the District Attorney? I can. He'd laugh you out of his office. I realize being trapped in a small, backward town like this has softened your brain, and with it, your views of reality and the outside world. You see, Breach, they don't indict or arrest people these days for what amounts to charges of witchcraft or Black Magic. Nor can prosecutors build a case on evidence suggesting a man was brought back to life from the dead and has been killing people and devouring their flesh.

"Can you imagine what they will do with you for declaring a state of martial law, when the time for accounting comes? The Governor's office will require a full disclosure of the facts and your interpretation of them. Do you know what will happen to you, Breach? You'll be placed under psychiatric observation at the very least, or stripped of your position as Chief of Police, or both. I imagine it will be both, and in that order. You'll have to be proven unfit for the job first, and a psychiatric evaluation will certainly do that!

"What you've said here today is nothing but conjecture, Chief," Yakov continued, the contempt in his voice now sounded shaky to Breach, as if it was mixed with fear. "Nothing but conjecture combined with circumstantial evidence! And all of it tied together by the threads of what must be a witness's statement. Someone who fifty years ago said they saw some other kid at the time—Tim Shannon, I think you said his name was—and me go to see some old man at night. Some old, probably lonely man this hysterical town was afraid of for who knows what reason. And somehow you 'just know' he taught this Shannon person and me, his Black Magic, after which this Cavendish brought some poor dead bastard, a Seaton Stannish, back to life.

"At the very, very least, your threads are pure hearsay, and are not admissible in a court of law, much less in a court hearing felony charges of conspiracy and accomplice to murder. No, Chief," the psychiatrist said, signs of contempt and growing fear still weighing down his words, "you've got nothing, and you, that poor dupe of yours over there, and I, know it!"

Breach moved closer to Yakov until he stood directly in front of him. Looking straight into his eyes, and with a strength in his voice that communicated he still held the upper hand he said, "I'll tell you what I do have, Yakov! I have a small backward town here in Pennsylvania with an equally small backward District Attorney's office, manned by DAs who grew up right here and who know its history. What's more, they're people who understand the so-called 'hysterical' nature of this area, and who don't dismiss it out of hand.

"As to hearsay evidence? Police work is not your field, Doctor. What you know about it comes from the television shows you watch, and from general hearsay about law enforcement. Let me tell you something! More cases are solved from taking hearsay seriously than most civilians think! Why? Because hearsay is only a wrapping for an observation here, an overheard conversation there, or an experience somewhere else. As to small town hearsay, I've got news for you that your years in the big city blindsided you to. There are no secrets in small towns, Yakov. Memories run long and deep. Their wrappings don't change all that much over time, and the facts they conceal never do!

"And you want to know something else? Facts are facts, depending on how you look at them. From my ten years of experience on the Pittsburgh homicide squad, I can also tell you something you're going to find absolutely amazing about the treatment of facts!"

Yakov looked at Breach with a blank expression. He assumed the cop standing in front of him was a local man who was given the job, and whose only police experience was confined to dealing with small town problems. The news of his professional background stunned the psychiatrist. He was beginning to lose his mental control, while beginning to rapidly recalculate the situation.

"Facts are viewed differently by courts in different parts of the country! Did you know that? It's incredibly remarkable how facts can be twisted one way and turned another so the essence of them comes out. Did you ever hear the saying, 'Never let the truth get in the way of the facts?' Nowhere is that applied more often than in what they call the Process of Law. And the ones who are so good at doing all the twisting and turning are called lawyers!

"I have to tell you, sometimes—oh, not often maybe—but sometimes those facts can be used by a clever prosecutor who wants to climb the ladder of success right out of this hysterical area. You know what he does? He begins to build a case on purely circumstantial evidence by twisting and turning the facts. Then, and this is really clever, then he ties them together with threads of hearsay handed to him, and his own skillfully woven threads called interpretation." Breach's voice was condescending and intimidating. Yakov's face grew pale and then red. He was near his breaking point, just where Breach wanted him.

"I'll tell you what else these DAs or assistant DAs who want to get out of such hysterical, backward towns need in order to make their ascent to legal stardom. They need to get the word out. They need publicity! Especially on strange cases that attract public attention. And do you know how they get that, Doctor? They get the newspapers involved! Oh, and not just the ones from their own state. No, a couple of years ago I heard one DA say, 'Local press is no press. You've got to have more than that!' They can get out-of-state presses involved if one of the players in the case happens to be someone either famous or well known. Someone like a retired shrink from New York. Why, you'd be amazed at how fast word like that spreads! You know what happens then? Even a cop whose brain's been softened by twenty years in a backward town can put it together!

"First, the famous man is arrested on suspicion. Then he has to get lawyers of his own, but certainly not any local ones. He has to hire some big city talkers, say from Pittsburgh or Philadelphia. They can use all of the good press they can get for their practices too, so they get newspapers from those cities involved! Yes, sir! Especially when the case is bizarre. The public goes wild over that! Now, the newspapers play it up even more, adding insinuation to innuendo, heaping speculation upon speculation, rolling it all together, and presenting it as facts to their readership, so they can sell more newspapers! Then other papers pick it up because they want to get in on the action too! Pretty soon, the wire services get hold of it, and in a heartbeat after that, it's on the national news! Before you know it, all of that 'conjecture' becomes 'facts' to everyone. Even to future jury members. Now I'm not saying the law is unfair. I'm just saying it's human, like the newspaper readers. And of course, Doctor, you know all about human, and the forces that drive the human mind, don't you?

"But there's another side to all of this. One I bet you never considered. That pragmatic, daily occurring, human need for greed called medical malpractice! Can you imagine what some of your former patients would think if they read about you being embroiled in a mass murder scandal? Being indicted on charges of conspiracy or as an accomplice to murder? You'd have more lawsuits on your hands than you'd know what to do with! Because unless I'm mistaken, before you could practice psychiatry, you had to become a medical doctor. You had to become a physician of the body, before you could become one of the mind. Am I right? That means you're subject to malpractice even years down the line. Still carry that big-ticket insurance to save your ass? Bet you don't! Not after retiring!

"But maybe I'm wrong. Maybe you had the foresight to keep it. If only for a few years. Just in case. The question is, do you think it'll cover the number of suits your patients of the past will file against you? You know, the ones you 'cured.' Or did you? You know what happens then 'Doctor' Yakov? After the malpractice insurance that you so wisely kept gets fed up with the number of litigations pending against you? It'll settle just so many, and then cut you loose. It will cancel your protection.

"Then…then 'Doctor,' " Breach's disgust rising against the stubbornness of the man standing in front of him, "your personal assets, all of your savings, will be drained dry. If not in payoffs to those former patients of yours who you 'helped,' then to the team of lawyers you'll need to save what's left of a former perfect, professional reputation! Those, sir, are some of the possible scenarios I see waiting for you. All as a result of keeping your mouth shut, and playing coy with us.

"You're involved in this nightmare up to your teeth, Yakov, and you know it! And you'd better start talking now, because I'm goddamn tired of trying to show you what's behind the reality of this situation if you don't come clean. If you don't throw your weight behind this investigation and do whatever is necessary to help us solve these crimes and either destroy NightShadow or drive it out of the area permanently, I swear to you, I'll do everything in my power to destroy you just as completely and as fast as I can! Because now I have a personal vendetta against you! Against you and the terror stalking my people! And I'm going to make it my business to take that vendetta all the way! Not just because of my slaughtered nephew or the other butchered innocents, but because I know you're holding out, ready to let more people die horribly, just to save your own ass and remain anonymous throughout the entire ordeal!

"I've seen your kind before, Yakov, in Pittsburgh and on the battlefield. I made it my personal business to take out each and every one of your kind of vermin legally when I could, or by other means as I had to. You know the TV shit about cops not getting personally involved in their cases? I have news for you, every cop gets personally involved with his cases. It's the emotional fuel that drives us to solve them! And I am *very* personally involved in this one. Have I made myself clear?"

Breach knew he had used up all of his psychological ammunition. He had pushed past the law blindly, attempting to commit blackmail, rewriting the definition of psychological intimidation, and carrying out outright assault. He knew he had no hard evidence on him. Nothing that would stand up in a court of law, but could cause Yakov a great deal of personal trouble if he used it skillfully against him. Folding his arms across his chest and staring directly at him, Breach asked, "Well, what will it be? Help us, or go to the hell I have planned for you?"

Yakov's heart was pounding fiercely, the right side of his throat pulsating visibly. His breathing was labored, his eyes dilated. Tiny beads of sweat worked their way through his skin, making his hair wet and oily-looking. Breach saw the telltale signs of a man falling apart.

Yakov struggled to regain his reason and then replied in hoarse voice, "You still have nothing on me, Breach. Your scare tactics are working, I'll admit, but still you have nothing you can arrest me for. You can take me in for questioning, but even then you can only hold me for a day or so. Then you must either charge me or let me go. You can't hold me on suspicion and you know it. Try to damage my reputation or press false charges against me by any of your illegal moves, and I'll sue you and this town for slander, defamation of character, violation of my civil rights, false arrest, and harassment. That's all I have to say to you. Now leave."

Breach was a master of the unwritten rules of psychological battle. He had maneuvered the psychiatrist to squeak out his weak and obvious empty defense.

"Come on, Frank," Breach said as he turned toward the kitchen, preparing to leave. "We can do no more here. This man has just ended whatever prospects he had for a peaceful retirement."

As they started to walk toward the backdoor, Breach stopped suddenly, clicked his middle finger against his thumb, turned back and added, "Oh! I almost forgot! We do have one piece of heavy duty circumstantial evidence tying you to these murders. It's going to be damn hard for you to explain why you and Tim Shannon returned to this town within weeks of each other after a forty-seven year absence, and just before the killings started. The DA's office and the newspapers will have a field day with that one!"

Yakov froze. "What do you mean Tim Shannon returned to town? What are you talking about?"

"Didn't I tell you, Doctor? The dead man we found on the mountaintop road. Frank identified him. And when I run his prints through the FBI, I'm sure they'll confirm it. It's Tim Shannon! The man who resurrected Cavendish and was then run down by the thing he called back from the grave in Saint Alacious cemetery in the early morning hours of January 12th! That's the Tim Shannon I'm talking about! He was our first murder victim! That's how I know you and he are somehow connected in all of this!"

Yakov swooned and fell forward. Breach dashed toward him and caught him before he fell to the floor. Then he and Frank helped him back to his chair in the parlor. After a few seconds, Yakov spoke.

"Please be seated, gentlemen. We have much to discuss."

Breach and Lewis leaned back in their chairs, burning with excitement. They sensed the paled man sitting across from them held the solution to the terror that had befallen them. Neither spoke, waiting for Yakov to continue.

"Chief Breach, Mr. Lewis, it's not what you think. I am not heartless. I do care about this tiny town and the people who live here. That's why I came back here to retire. Actually, I own property in the south of France, a lovely little villa. I have enjoyed going there for a getaway for many years. But when it came time to settle down in the last years of my life, I returned to my roots. And my roots lie here in Kulpsville. It may sound strange in light of the villa, but that's the way it is.

"However that is not the only reason I returned. I came back to stop the horror that has unfortunately already begun. All through the years I knew I would have to face my past, a terrible past, beginning when I was a child. Oh, I learned to deal with it mentally and prepare for it slowly, until the reality of those early years could be addressed in the here and now. By and by I succeeded. My coming here, prepared to do whatever is necessary to stop the evil from growing, is proof of that. But now I see I was too late. If only I had found the moral courage sooner. Maybe I would have been in time. But…" Yakov's words fell hard on the still air, as if he was no longer aware of his guests, spiraling into a black pit full of regret. Suddenly he caught himself, shook his head violently from side to side and continued.

"You see, Shannon and I kept a secret for fifty years. A secret he finally acted on. He carried out this diabolical work and called Cavendish back from the grave. But he did so before the dark of the moon, before the last phase of Luna, as the ancient Magical texts call it. I knew he would be back this month to perform the black work and bring his Master back to life, so I came here six weeks earlier to buy this house and nose around as best as I could, waiting for some sign of his coming. But I had none.

"I tried talking to the locals, but they have always had a basic mistrust of strangers or anyone new. Even though word got around to those who didn't know that I grew up here, well, nearly fifty years is a long time to be gone. People die, move away, new ones come, and attitudes change. I was treated as if I was a stranger in my own hometown. Nevertheless, I questioned the men from Stieff's Construction cautiously about the town, visitors, strangers passing through, all on the ploy I was expecting an old friend to pay me a surprise visit and wanted to surprise him instead. But no one had heard or seen anything. At least, that's what they said.

"Then when I heard martial law had been declared this morning and about the killings, I didn't know what to think. The news announcement gave no facts. Since I didn't go out of the house yesterday and the contractor's men were out getting more building material, I had no contact with anyone, so I didn't hear that a local kid found Shannon's body. For all I knew, the state of emergency could have been declared for any number of reasons. A biker gang could have come into town terrorizing and killing people, some local could have gone berserk and went on a killing spree, or any number of events could have escalated out of control requiring martial law. I never, never suspected it was due to what we now know to be the cause."

"Hold on," Breach cut in, the hostility in his voice replaced with curiosity. "Then as insane as my conclusions about the killer are, they're correct? Frank, my other deputy, Dave Barker, and I have not lost our senses or are completely misinterpreting the situation? Because I have to tell you, even though Frank and I figured this thing out, I still don't think either of us truly believe it. I mean, deep down. Maybe secretly inside somewhere we doubt our own sanity."

"No, Chief, you and your collaborators are not insane. Only three very sane men could have had the mental courage and endurance to face this mad and incredible situation, and still be able to reach the only conclusion possible. And the three of you did just that. Nor have you misinterpreted the cause behind the events. The analysis you gave me during our argument a few minutes ago is frighteningly and astonishingly correct. Honestly, I would have never believed anyone other than Shannon and myself would ever be able to entertain such fantastic reasoning.

"But you, Mr. Lewis, and that deputy of yours, succeeded. I have to compliment you for those conclusions and the cold, analytical insights that enabled you to reach them. I don't know Dave Barker. But I can tell you both you would have made fine psychiatrists! You see, most people fail to understand reality is only what their minds make of it. It's as real or unreal only so far as our minds are capable of intellectually comprehending and emotionally accepting what they see and experience. But that's another matter."

The old cop waited anxiously for Yakov to finish his lecture, and then interrupted once more. "Then why the hell didn't you just level with us when I was giving you the third degree? I told you what we figured out! You see, we reasoned purely from circumstantial evidence, conjecture and old gossip, the scenario behind the events I gave you. You knew we had no hard evidence against you. But you held fast to your ignorance of the matter! You could have come clean, and saved us all a lot of trouble! What was your reason for that? As a cop, I've got to know!"

"It's really very simple. There are three unknowns in this equation. First, I don't know you very well. But what I have seen tells me you are, uh, shall we say, very reactionary? If I had admitted your analysis was right, for all I know you could have gone off, beefed up your martial law with more military, and risked even more lives than are at risk this very moment. Second, you could have locked me up as an accessory. Or at the very least, you could have taken me completely out of the picture. I believe the word is protective custody.

"That leads to the third unknown, which you know nothing about. Only I can destroy Cavendish. No one else possesses the knowledge or the means of destroying him utterly, forever ending his reign of terror. But I only have a seven-day window to accomplish this. Seven days after the resurrection and seven days only in which to destroy the man once known as Martin Cavendish. If I was being held by you, that window would close forever. Then there would be no way to stop him. For those reasons, I had to deny you confirmation of your conclusions. If I admitted to even one, I would have had to admit to all of them, because that's how you structured your questioning, and you know it. You're as professional in your work as I am in mine.

"I'm aware my lack of cooperation drove you to dig deep into your bag of techniques in order to try to intimidate me. I'm sorry I drove you to it, and I'm sorry for the bad time I gave you. I had no other choice. But when you finally told me you knew the identity of the first murdered man, I realized you did have enough circumstantial evidence to arrest me. You could hold me long enough to destroy my mission. At the end of it all, really, we both know you have no concrete evidence against me. Given the number and violence of the murders and the real nature of the killer, you would have had to drop all charges and release me. But not before more people were killed, Cavendish escaped, and I fancy, not before this town of ours became a ghost town."

"What do you mean by escaped?" Breach asked quickly.

"But how can something dead be destroyed?" Frank asked, making his first contribution to the discussion by cutting across Breach's question.

"Not so fast, gentlemen. We have to approach this matter in an orderly way, or we might miss something that could be important later. Allow me to go on.

"Actually, Mr. Lewis," Yakov replied, answering Frank's question first, "your mind is contradicting what it already knows. That happens when reality clashes with beliefs. You know Cavendish died, but you also know he's out there killing. At odd moments, your mind can't reconcile these two fantastic facts, and so denial arises. Let me explain so your mind can finally declare peace in the war it has declared on itself.

"Cavendish was dead, as dead as anyone can be. But the life force that was Martin Cavendish still existed. Where, who know? That's the province of religions. But it continued to exist after the death of his physical body. Why? Because as I see it, life is energy, and the laws of physics tell us matter and energy cannot be created nor destroyed, only transformed. That's what death does. It brings about transformation. Usually, of course, the body decays, and the life force goes wherever.

"But not in the darkest and most dreaded of all Black Magic practices. Not in the ritual of Infernal Necromancy. In that dark quarter, the life force of the individual can be brought back to inhabit its body. But only for a while, an hour or so at best. According to the old Magical Grimoires, meaning grammars of Magic, it is brought back only to answer questions the Necromancer demands it to answer. After that, the life force is left to escape again, and the body returns to its grave to resume its decomposition. So you see, something dead has been destroyed again. There in a nutshell, is the root cause of all of this trouble. Infernal Necromancy, and the process by which Cavendish was brought back to life."

"But," Frank asked, "you said a body could only be brought back to life for about an hour, and had to be returned to the grave after that? What happened with Cavendish?"

"Now here," Yakov replied with a wry smile, "is where the Chief could arrest me and put me away for good. That is, if anyone would believe him and if the courts would admit the reality of Infernal Necromancy. This is where I am guilty. But that guilt goes back a long time, gentlemen, to a time of childhood innocence. So maybe a law admitting such an impossibility would not find me guilty.

"You see, when Shannon and I were boys, we were different from the other kids. Who knows why? Their lives were pretty much cut-and-dried, and their futures laid out for them. Back in those days, a coal miner's son became a coal miner himself, as his father did before him. The son of a clerk became a clerk. In other words, he had the same mental set of pleasures and problems as his parents did. Marriage, kids, a job, and pretty much what most people still hold to as the good life even today. Except back then, here in this little town, the definition and expectations of the good life were much, much narrower. Seeing you're not from the town as I gleaned from your earlier comments, Chief, and since Mr. Lewis has lived here all of his life as you mentioned, I'm sure he can bear me out on this. It's only background, but I think it is important for you to understand the complete picture. It will make it more real for you, and could make the difference in your later thinking about what we will have to do."

"*We* will have to do?" Breach questioned. "I thought you said only you can destroy him! How did this thing become *we*?"

"I'll get to that in a minute," Yakov replied softly. "Please allow me to continue. As I said Shannon and I were different, in exactly one way. Neither he nor I could understand, much less accept the definition and expectations of the good life as defined by our parents and the other kids. He and I were always off together, up in the mountains looking for adventure. It was anything and everything. From looking for strange animals no one ever saw before, to searching for monsters like we read about in our ten-cent horror books. As a psychiatrist, I know we were looking to escape a dull life neither of us related to, and so we fled into a fantasy world of our own design. That is, until we met Martin Cavendish.

"We were thirteen years old at the time, and had just started our seventh grade school year. I remember it was in late September of 1924. School had just begun, and one night Shannon and I decided to explore the woods in the south, just outside of town. Our way led us down Routelage Street. As we walked toward the end of the street, we saw Cavendish's mansion. It intrigued us of course, what with all of the sinister comments made about him by the townspeople, including our parents.

"We didn't have the courage to bother him of course, but it was still a nice juicy mystery to whet our appetites for more of our own self-designed adventures, nevertheless. I remember we were talking about him as we rounded the bend next to his house. The woods were only a few hundred yards away, and being kids, we changed the subject in mid-sentence, discussing our plan of action to look for monsters once we got there. That's when it happened."

"What happened?" Frank blurted out, like a young boy sitting round a campfire, anxiously waiting for the next line in a ghost story.

"Cavendish stepped out from the shadows," Yakov continued, "and scared the living daylights out of us! He was a big man! His stature was imposing enough. Everyone in town feared him, even the hard-working, hard-drinking miners. Everyone. But that night when he stepped out of the darkness, dressed all in black, with his shocking silver hair and cold, steel-blue eyes, an image was created in my mind I'll never forget. And his voice! As imposing and terrifying as his figure and reputation was, oddly, his voice was very melodic. Almost musical. It was so soft and gentle that he lulled us into a strange, physical quiet. As though all of our misgivings and fears melted and flowed out of our pores, like some kind of invisible vapor.

"He asked us what we were up to, and we told him. There was no lying to that man. We knew instinctively not to, not out of fear, but rather because of a curious need we felt to share our strangeness with him. When Shannon and I told him where we were going and what we intended to do, he didn't laugh. He just smiled. There was a streetlight not far away from where the three of us were standing. It barely lit up the place where we stood, but it reflected sharply in his eyes. The look in his eyes spoke of hidden things, of a secret, dark, resplendent world filled with fantastic realities our imaginations could never invent.

"He invited us in to talk. 'There's a coming chill in the late night air, boys,' he said in a voice almost narcotic. 'Let's go inside where there's warmth, hot food, and quiet to open your souls to the realms of real adventure that you seek! You see, I have heard of you two, and know that like myself, you are outcasts in this town. We are of a kind, young fellows, and our kind must stick together!'

"We went with him," the psychiatrist continued, "not as if our minds had been hypnotized, but our souls were. Somewhere in both of us existed a seedbed for the fantastic. We were born with it. We were born with a driving need to explore and understand what the rest of the world called unreal, yet we felt, we somehow knew, was every bit as real, if not more so, than their humdrum world of everyday 'reality.' Both of us knew this man was the Keeper of the Gates of that world. We wanted to enter it. And we did.

"Everywhere in the huge home, there was darkness, but not the kind you can't see in. It was a blackness producing a cold light of its own. I tell you gentlemen, I can't remember seeing any table lamps or overhead lights whatsoever throughout the long halls we walked down leading to the kitchen. Yet there was a grayish glow every-where that allowed us to see. He served us a hot roast beef meal, and then we went to a room he called his study, and talked of worlds concealed within the study and practice of Magic.

"The four walls of that big room were lined with enormous black bookcases extending from floor to ceiling. Everywhere we looked were books and ancient manuscripts on Magic and the Occult. Later on we would find out they covered both forms of Magic: White and Black. But as our Teacher told us—because that's what he became from that night onward—only the dark world of Black Magic offered the way to the power all men desire to wield in this world, and to fulfillment no church or religion can dare attempt to even hint at. We didn't leave his house that night until two a.m., as I recall to this day.

"From that night onward, three or four night a week, Shannon and I would steal away to his house. We would be there for hours on end. In the study, he taught us the theory and basis of Black Magic, things no one would believe. Not even you two gentlemen would be able to accept them, even though you have been through so much already. And the magnificent and terrible events he created in another room adjacent to his study, his Temple, as he called it, are beyond the understanding of any mortal mind that has not experienced them for itself.

"Curiously, through Cavendish's teachings I came to fully appreciate the depth and power of the human mind. In time, that appreciation drove me to learn all I could about it. Then, for some reason, my growing awareness of the power of the human mind caused me to take a turn away from the immediate idea of Magic. After a year of studying with Cavendish, I began to feel ordered, scientific study of the mind was necessary before Magic could be worked properly. Eventually, I became a psychiatrist because of the promptings to study the mind. Make no mistake, I fully intended to continue with Magic even then, but only after I became adept in the ways of psychiatry. Yet Cavendish's hold on me was so strong, that even realizing what I did, I persisted to study with him."

"Did you go back to studying and practicing Magic after you took your psychiatric license?" Breach interrupted. Yakov made no reply, but gave the Chief a piercing sideway glance and resumed his explanation.

"Shannon and I continued to study with Cavendish through the autumn of 1925. It was mid-October when our Teacher abruptly shifted our attention from the topic in the Black Arts we were studying to what he referred to as the darkest and most powerful ritual of them all, Infernal Necromancy. He explained the few grammars of Magic on the subject are incomplete by design. The ancient Magicians knew if the real purpose behind Infernal Necromancy was divulged in the Grimoires, the greatest secret of all time would be revealed. Unlike other branches of Magic—that are the invocation of divine beings and evocation of the fallen angels, and can be achieved more or less successfully by anyone—if the revelation behind Infernal Necromancy was ever given to the world, it would change the entire course of human history forever.

"Yet as Cavendish explained," Yakov said as he stared off into space, "the old Magicians did not want this darkest corner of Magic to be lost to humankind. So they disguised it carefully, and set it down in their Magical tracts in such a way that it appears to be just a curious ritual to this day. One everyone avoids.

"And their ploy worked! I mean, after all, what is so important to know that someone would go through all the trouble to dig up a dead body and then ritualistically summon back the life force inhabiting it while it was alive? There are countless methods of Divination offering information on virtually any subject. Information not available through normal means, if you get what I mean."

"Hold on a minute," Breach interrupted. "Just what did you mean when you said this Necromancy would change the entire course of human history forever? What are you saying?"

"We finally get down to the brass tacks of the matter," Yakov replied. "I mean, as our Teacher told us, the purpose of the ritual of Infernal Necromancy is actually meant to confer physical immortality. As fantastic as it sounds, that's what it's meant to do. Cavendish went on to explain when the life force—the spirit if you will—of a dead body is brought back from some world beyond the grave and made to re-inhabit its decomposing body, there is a secret set of ritual conjurations that reinvest it in that body permanently. After that, the Magician who resurrects the corpse uses what is called the Dark Command, by which he empowers the re-animated body to begin the process of its complete regeneration, a process by which the decay is replaced by new, vibrant, living tissue. That process involves the consumption of the blood and flesh of living human beings.

"That's why NightShadow is killing! Not to destroy, but to live! To gain the physical immortality he craves beyond all else! After completing the regeneration, such a person will now live forever. Nothing can stop him! No force of man. Not bullets, not bombs, not a toppling building, nothing can destroy him. He would be prater human, beyond human. But that's not all. There is no force in nature that could end his reign either, because he would be beyond Nature! No sickness, no disease, no aging. He would be whole and complete unto himself.

"Along with his body's regeneration, all the mental faculties the resurrected corpse possessed during life would return to him. All of his knowledge, cunning, shrewdness, and intuition. They all return.

But he now possesses more. The theory behind the act of Infernal Necromancy states that in the world beyond death, the spirit learns knowledge hidden from mankind before the beginning of the world itself. Knowledge meant to be beyond man's reach while yet in his earthly life. But the re-animated corpse can bring that occult knowledge back with him, and has it to use as he pleases in the world of living men. This, coupled with a new strength superseding any known to mortal man, and his physical immortality, enables him to do whatever he chooses.

"Imagine what he could do! Over time he could maneuver himself into any position he cared to, because he literally has all the time in the world. Can you imagine the impact he could have on history and on the lives of individuals and nations? He could work and weave himself into any of society's fabrics. He could become the CEO of some newly emerging corporation affecting national or world economies. Or he could become a scientist whose work turns the course of human history in some frightening new way. He might become a venture capitalist, directing his money into development of new inventions aimed at making individuals even more docile than they are now, or for making more beads and baubles to contribute to the further mental deterioration of the masses. Perhaps he could become a big time player in the stock markets of the world, and control more wealth than any one man before him has in the history of the world.

"Can you visualize what a man with such power could do? He could determine who lives and who dies, all based on his personal whims. He could become the leader of some fantastic new religion or cult that would seductively degrade the spiritual lives of individuals and even nations. And who knows where that action would lead? Or, perhaps the most deadly of all, he could become a political figure. Someone who could topple the governments of other nations, or even this nation, or begin another war. A final war designed to destroy the greatest part of mankind, and hurl those left into a new Age of suffering, despotism, and mental darkness. I can tell you one thing for certain. Any individual who would plot and plan something as fantastic as his own resurrection, would not be driven by holy and noble desires. No. He would have to be an egomaniac of the worst kind. Some 'thing' not even conceived of in the annals of psychiatry.

"That's why I put your question off about his escaping, Chief. I wanted to explain the basis of this madness first. You see, after he has completed his regeneration, after he has consumed enough human flesh and blood, he would appear again as an ordinary-looking man and be able to escape from this area. After that, he would be free to pursue any of the possibilities I just mentioned. Or who knows? Perhaps another possibility he had planned, and which he took to his grave with him, awaiting for resurrection.

"There is one thing I know for certain about Cavendish. One thing fits my analysis of the personality type that dares to believe and plan for his own resurrection. His direction is totally directed toward self-fulfillment, at any cost. He is the prototype egomaniac, consumed by pure psychoses. He could care less about others. He is a devoted Servant of the Powers of Darkness, which is what Cavendish told Shannon and me pointedly on that October night in 1925, right before he told us the rest of his story, and what he wanted us to do for him when he died."

Gus and Frank sat motionless. Both men were stunned over the details and speculations of Yakov's story, unable to fully accept what they were hearing. Gus gave a sideways look to Frank, communicating his disbelief. The mortician returned the facial gesture. They were wondering if the man sitting across from them was insane. Yakov took notice of their exchange, but brushed it aside and resumed talking.

"I can't remember the exact date, but it was late October. The leaves had taken on their autumn colors and were beginning to fall. It was probably about two weeks after our Teacher began to instruct us in the subject of Infernal Necromancy. That night, Cavendish told us he and a friend were going to bring his Teacher back from the grave. That Teacher was a man named Seaton Stannish who died in 1886, and who was buried in the old cemetery south of town. Cavendish told us a friend from Hungary, whom Stannish had also personally instructed in Infernal Necromancy, was coming here to help out with the ritual. Together, the two would raise their Teacher, this Seaton Stannish, from the dead. As Cavendish stressed, it took at least two Operators to perform the ritual correctly. He explained the ritual would take place in a few months, but he did not disclose the exact date.

"Cavendish went on to instruct us in the rite, as Stannish had done for him and the Hungarian fellow years earlier. That is, he explained each section of it so we would clearly understand what he was about to do, plus he added oral instructions not included in the written text. I thought it curious he was going into so much detail. But then he satisfied my curiosity. He stood up from the big black velvet chair he would sit in during our periods of instruction, walked over to one of the great bookcases, and withdrew two Staffs."

Yakov caught the bewildered look Gus and Frank exchanged before they returned their attention to back to him.

"I can only imagine what you're thinking, gentlemen, but that's what happened. Each of us received a seven-foot long, three inch thick Staff made out of highly polished, black ebony. They were beautiful. He told us to guard them well. We were to always keep them concealed, and at no time was anyone other than us to handle them. Then he explained the reason he had given us the Staffs and had gone into such detail of the ritual. He was preparing us to do for him what he was about to do for his Teacher. When his time came, after he was buried according to certain instructions he would leave behind, we were to resurrect him exactly fifty years later, in the month of his death.

"You see, we were so deeply caught in his web of Black Magic and other worldliness, his demand seemed completely in keeping with our situation. Already, the practices he taught were producing fruits for us. Money came to us seemingly out of nowhere, and our mental abilities improved dramatically. Our poor performance in school changed dramatically. In a matter of months, the C's and D's we were bringing home on our report cards turned into straight A's, all without slaving over books. Shannon and I would read our homework assignments once, and it just stuck. And tests? We raced through them as if we knew all the correct answers, which we did, somehow. So all in all, benefits were flowing to us from dedication to our new world, and from the few basic rituals we were taught would bring us the things we wanted most. We owed it all to our Teacher, Martin Cavendish. Now he asked us a favor, and we willingly agreed to it. What could be more fair than this?

"You might be wondering how a man could count on two teen-age boys to carry out a request fifty years later. That's easy to answer. Our being different from the other kids gave us the mark, he said. It

was the mark of our kind, the kind who fulfill the Magical requirement, 'The true Magician is brought forth from his mother's womb.'
He told us we would never to be able to completely abandon Magic,
and he was right. I suppose, Chief, that answers your other question
concerning my continued involvement in the Secret Science,"
Yakov said with a broad smile.

"It does," Breach replied coolly. "Please go on."

"Cavendish told us his Staff of Resurrection or Return, as he said
it was properly called, was the means by which he would bring his
Teacher back. And indeed, our Staffs were the same means by which
we would bring him back at some future time. He also stated it was
the only means by which the re-animated corpse could be returned,
meaning destroyed, before it completed its regeneration. But he
never went into any detail or the method on how to send it back, at
least, not with me.

"He went on to explain there are Words of Power of the Final
Summoning, and of the Final Return of the spirit. The first words are
used to resurrect the spirit and allow it to re-animate its rotting
corpse. It is also called the Dark Command. The latter words force it
to return to the world beyond the grave. But the Words of the Final
Summoning and the Final Return are divided into two parts. The
rite of Infernal Necromancy gives the Magician the first part of each.
But the second part of the Words were never written down. Only
the Staff knows them. They are in some tongue unknown to
mankind, but one believed to be the language of the angels themselves. The Staff must utter them at the right time to bring the corpse
back to life, and later, if the Magician chooses, to send it back. And
those Words which only the Staff knows were never committed to
paper by the Magicians because they are said to be too terrible. As
Cavendish told us of this, a faraway look overtook him, as if he were
seeing into another world when he said 'To hear them causes great
terror in man, and brings about strange manifestations. Nature herself
becomes horrified and revolts,' whatever that means.

"That's why, Chief, I told you earlier I could not admit to your
conclusions about NightShadow. If you remember, I said only I
possess the means by which NightShadow can be destroyed. I
couldn't risk you arresting me on whatever charge and taking me out
of the picture. I meant that in the literal sense. The means of destruction is through the use of the Staff of Resurrection or Return."

"What do you mean, he never went into the method of using the Staff to destroy the re-animated corpse, at least not with you?" Frank asked.

"Because," Yakov replied, "that was the last night I saw Cavendish alive. After he gave us the Staffs and we left his house, he called Shannon back. When I asked him why, he said he had to discuss something extra with him. He told me to go home, hide my Staff, and dismissed me. I felt humiliated and rejected. I didn't like it. On the way home, I had time to think. Maybe for the first time in the year or so I was with my Teacher. A dismissal from him was very hard. It was more than a reprimand. The way he said it, and the look in his eyes when he told me to go, all communicated a warning to my deeper mind.

"But it was something I didn't understand. All I knew…all I felt…was that I was in some terrible type of danger. Something every now and then I felt had been lurking around the corners of Cavendish's words throughout the entire year, and which were aimed directly at me, not at Shannon. Sometimes, a few times during the year's training, I also got the very distinct and uneasy feeling Shannon was his favorite, and I was only a necessary attachment, an addition to their relationship that nevertheless had some very important but frightening role to play in what we were doing. I got within a block of my parent's house, hid the Staff under a grapevine in the alley, and went home, determined never to see Cavendish again.

"The next day, Shannon approached me in school as usual, but there was something decidedly different about him. His mannerisms and his voice concealed something, but very poorly. He was always bad at hiding secrets. It didn't take much to realize he and Cavendish had something planned for me. I felt as if it was time for the genie in the bottle to escape, and when I looked into his eyes, out it came. That look was the same as in our Teacher's, only younger. It had the same mad violence, the same animalistic quality, the same hunger. I caught myself before he started to weave his own spell over me, and told him I was through with Cavendish and would never return to his home.

"Tim Shannon, my former friend, exploded. He said if I didn't go back with him that night, something terrible would happen to me and to my entire family. But I felt my own survival was at stake then and there, and so threw caution and fear to the wind, hit him in the mouth as hard as I could, and down he went. We never spoke again. I did hear he continued to visit Cavendish at night. Less than two months later, as you gentlemen know, the former police chief and your father, Frank, had the rifled grave and missing corpse of Seaton Stannish to contend with, plus the murdered and mutilated body of Cavendish's friend from Hungary. The one your father could never identify, Mr. Lewis.

"A day later, your father had to contend with another burial. Martin Cavendish, who died of a delayed heart attack, not to mention his four very unusual burial requests. Even though I was only fifteen at the time, I knew all about them. You see, Cavendish went over them with Shannon and me during our instructions. Curiously, three years later, in 1929, Shannon and I left this town separately and never returned. That is, not until now. There you have my story. Any questions, gentlemen?"

"So you and Shannon broke up prior to Cavendish's death. I thought it was afterward, as I told the Chief earlier while we were trying to figure this thing out."

"No," Yakov replied. "As I said, I broke with him before Cavendish's death. There was a change in my friend during the year we were with Cavendish. Shannon was no longer just a boy. Malevolence grew in him daily, and I sensed it. But I dismissed it because I wanted the gain and profit our black studies were bringing to us. Such gain and profit was incredibly paltry now that I look back. But back in 1925, in this economically depressed area, the gain and profit was good enough. And as Shannon and I were promised, it portended greater wealth to come from growing deeper into Black Magic. It was as simple as that."

"Do you still have the Staff?" Breach pointedly asked, "and if so, what good is it going to be to you? You said Cavendish did not explain how to use it to destroy a raised corpse?"

"Yes I do. I saved it all of these years. As to its use to return the spirit to the world beyond the grave, that's another matter. Let me explain.

"For twenty years after I left Kulpsville, I put the matter out of my mind. That is to say, uh, as completely as I could. I went through college, medical school, and two different psychiatric colleges. I had more on my plate every day than I could handle, so I was able to avoid the subject, except for some passing thoughts about it. I did wonder about Shannon and Stannish, and what happened to them. In fact, they occupied more of my mental time than did thoughts about the Staff. After more years passed though, I all but forgot about the matter.

"But when I went into private practice at the age of thirty-eight, some of my patients reported dreams which triggered my memory. Not only of Shannon and Stannish, but also of Cavendish, and what he wanted us to do for him after he died. Those recollections brought back the memories of the Staff. Being older, I was able to see just how central that piece of wood now was to the entire situation, and began to research the subject of Infernal Necromancy. It was as Cavendish said. There is very little written of it in the Grimoires, and what is there is a blind.

"As time passed, I became more interested in the matter primarily because resurfaced feelings made me think I would have played the role of dupe for Cavendish and Shannon in the unholy business they concocted behind my back that night our Teacher called him back. My yearly vacations to my villa in France found me in Paris at the Bibliotique de la Arsenal, the vast French repository and research library. It contains millions of manuscripts and books on virtually any subject you can imagine, all from different centuries. Some date back to 100 A.D. Between it and the British Museum in London, I was able to find pieces of information about the process of Infernal Necromancy. Not as is given in the standard reprinted Grimoires bought today at many of the New Age bookstores. After twenty years of searching these libraries, studying, copying, and piecing the information together, I was satisfied my labors had produced the missing pieces of this Black Art Cavendish must have taught Shannon after I dropped out of the picture. It boils down to this.

"Number one, the Staffs were consecrated by Cavendish prior to his giving them to us. I found the consecration. It is terrible. It involves the blood of an innocent in its baptism, among other hideous acts. In short, Cavendish had to have taken the lives of two innocents in order to consecrate our Staffs to the Powers of Darkness. Put bluntly, he had to slay two children in order to properly conse-crate these tools of the devil.

"Number two, Cavendish's consecration was only the first part of the Staff's preparation for being called to life. The Second Consecration had to be conducted by each of the Operators who would perform the resurrection. But this final consecration has a built-in failsafe device. As the Staff is coming to life, the Operator tells it, during this Second Consecration mind you, if he should decide to reverse the process during the actual ritual, or even afterwards during the seven day window of the corpse's regeneration, he can will the Staff to utter the second set of the Words of Power of the Final Return, which will accomplish his will immediately, and send the corpse back to its grave. I discovered pieces of this Return part of the ritual, and have reconstructed it to the best of my ability. I think it will work."

"Come on, Doctor!" Frank interjected. "You mean to tell me that piece of wood can be brought to life? You've got to be kidding! This is the Twentieth Century, not the Middle Ages! You're supposed to be a man of science, yet here you are talking absolute rubbish! Such a thing couldn't possibly happen! Not in a million years!"

Breach did not support his friend's objections. He folded his hands together, rested his elbows on the arms of his chair, and dropped his chin on his fists. He was recalling the comment he made to young Dave Barker in the hollow only the day before, when they were examining the head of the stranger. "When it comes right down to it, life is about 90% belief of one type or another. Reality is the other 10%, and what you believe comes back to you as reality, one way or another."

"Well, Mr. Lewis," Yakov countered with a smile, "remember what I said a few minutes ago? You're illustrating my point. What most people fail to understand is that reality is only what their minds make of it. It's as real or unreal only so far as our minds are capable of intellectually comprehending and emotionally accepting what they see and experience. What each of us calls reality is only a personal interpretation of the events in our daily lives. Extend experience, and the unreal, the unknown, becomes the known, and becomes part of our new reality. I have seen enough in my fifty years of personal Magical practice to convince me of this. In fact, if you think about it, you'll find something else to be true. Something paralleling my view of reality to make it more believable, more acceptable. Reality is made from the inside out. Not from the outside in."

Frank's eyes rolled upward, an unconscious gesture made by a person searching his memory for forgotten facts or experiences. "All right," he said softly. "I'm trying my best to understand you. Please go on."

"Number three. I found out my instincts were right. I was to play the role of dupe in Cavendish's and Shannon's little game. You see, the reason at least two Operators are needed to perform the Ritual of Resurrection is because one of the Operators must be sacrificed to him. The Second Operator, the assistant Operator if you will, must be thrown from the Circle of Protection by the Principle Operator to the awaiting re-animated corpse. He serves as its first meal. If there was any humor to this horrible business, it would be sort of like starting the day right with a good breakfast. That first flesh and blood begins the process of regeneration, and gives him the strength to go after his next victim. That's what my former friend Tim Shannon and our Teacher had planned for me. I was to be Cavendish's first meal.

"The more flesh and blood the regenerating corpse consumes, and the quicker he does so, the stronger he becomes and the faster he regenerates, until he looks like an ordinary man. Then he is free to roam the world of men again, except now he is immortal, incredibly strong, and possesses knowledge no mortal man is aware of.

"And finally, number four. There is a catch to all of it. There always is in everything. He must completely regenerate in seven days. If not, and if he is not returned to the grave, he will remain as some kind of grotesque, partially rotting corpse, but with a man's mind, until the day comes when his body will die once more. In the meantime, he will be confined to living in the deep woods, getting along as best as he can on the flesh and blood of small animals, forever ostracized from the world of men and the power he craved to rule that world. Do you see the blind and dreadful justice in all of this? Can you imagine an existence like that? That's why he needs to regenerate, and quickly. Otherwise, he faces an absolute hell on this earth, for who knows how long. This is the window I mentioned earlier. It is during this seven-day period when we have the one and only opportunity to utterly and totally destroy him forever.

"To do this, we need to bring the Staff of Resurrection or Return to life because only it possesses the last verses of the terrible Words of Power of the Final Return. But there is something more to it. Something I didn't mention. The Staff also possesses what is called a

Spiritual Light and Fire. Together, the Words of Power of the Final Return, along with this particular light and fire the Staff will produce, are needed to destroy the monstrosity."

"I thought it was the heat of my flares that caused it pain and could possibly destroy it," Breach commented. "But you say a spiritual light. What do you mean?"

"Your flares gave off heat and fire, yes, but could not affect NightShadow, at least not severely. You must remember it is a thing caught between two worlds, our world and another world existing beyond the grave. Yet at the same time, it's trying to make a transition from its world to ours. Ordinary heat, fire, bullets—all have no effect upon it, as you found out. But should any invade its darkness, such as the flares you forced into its cloak of blackness, such are symbols of the Spiritual Light and Fire that can destroy it. Light and fire, whether of this world of any other, are kindred. As such, in Cavendish's case, they are his enemy. But only one type can utterly destroy him.

"But be warned. The Words of Power of the Final Return, this part I understand. But I must confess, gentlemen, I have no idea how light and fire will be produced by the Staff. All I know is it will be produced somehow during our attempt to send him back."

Frank felt panicky. "An important piece is missing! I don't like any of this to start with, and a critical part isn't known! Attempting to send NightShadow back is starting to sound like sheer madness! Are you sure we should attempt this?"

"What would you have us do, Mr. Lewis?" Yakov replied in a harsh, sharp tone. "Spend the seven days we have trying to find out how the Spiritual Light and Fire is produced, here in Kulpsville, when over twenty years of searching the greatest libraries in the world didn't give me the answer? Is that what you're about sir? Worry over your own hide? Because if it is, you're of no use to the Chief and me! That is if he's still game!"

"I'm with you," Breach answered quickly. "This thing has got to be stopped!"

Frank composed himself and continued. "What if he completely regenerates early? I mean, before the seven days are up? Does that mean he can't be destroyed? Can he kill in the daylight?"

"The number seven is a holy number in Magic. It's the length of time in which the Divine created the world. Remember your Bible?

The Divine created the world in seven days. As such it is an active metaphor, meaning it has practical application in Magic. If the world was created in seven days, then that window of creation was also the window of destruction. Because as we are taught in Magic, the Divine could have reversed itself and un-created what It began. In other words, Divinity could have destroyed or uncreated what it had created. Because of this active metaphor, NightShadow can most definitely be destroyed in seven days, whether he regenerates completely or not. After that, he will be invincible.

"As to his being able to kill in the daylight, yes, most definitely. The light of day cannot invade his cloak of darkness. Not now. Not after all of his night killing. His darkness and strength have grown much too strong. He is regenerating very rapidly."

"Then we're helpless," Breach said as he looked at Frank. "We can't stop his rampage of murder until Ben here can activate his Staff. Uh, do you mind my calling you Ben, Doctor?"

"You're right, Gus, we can't stop the slaughter until then," Yakov replied. "And yes, I think we'd better dispense with the formalities. The one thing we don't need is any artificial walls between us. Not now, and not ever."

"You're right about the formalities," Breach replied as Frank gave Yakov a smile. "But I see another problem. How do we find him so we can destroy him once the Staff is brought to life?"

"At least that is not a problem. After the Staff is activated, as you put it, we reconstruct the Circle of Resurrection at his empty grave. I know the first verses of the Words of Power of the Final Return, which will summon him to the spot. After that, if all goes well, the Staff will deliver the last verses of the Words, generate the Spiritual Light and Fire needed to rob him of his power, and return him to his grave for all time."

"You talk about what the Staff will say and do, but you don't really know how the whole process will work together, the mechanics of it, I mean. It's all so iffy. I wish I knew more about this Magic business in general. Maybe then I'd feel a little more sure about things and what part Frank and I need to play when the time comes."

"I'm afraid there's far too much you would have to know about the Secret Science before you would feel more at ease. You'll just have to trust me and go on my directions for the mechanics when the time comes. And depending on how the situation goes, both of you will also just have to play it by ear."

"Don't get me wrong, but that's a lot of trust you're asking for," Breach said.

"I know it is. But you have a lot of trouble on your hands. Kind of balances out, doesn't it," the psychiatrist answered with wry smile.

"I understand we have to help in the actual ritual," Frank said nervously, "but you also said 'we' when it comes to this Second Consecration to bring the Staff to life. How did what sounded like an individual effort of me, the Operator, become we, the Operators?"

"It's simple," came the calm reply. "Fate brought the three of us together. While I will be the Operator who actually performs the Second Consecration and the one who will wield the Staff when we attempt to send Cavendish back to his grave, the two of you will assist me. It's clear to me both of you are destined to have some input in the entire process. That's how Magic works. In my profession it is synchronicity. Commonly it is Fate. So in a very real sense, there will be three Operators. Two assistants and me."

"I have another question," Breach said. "Actually, two. You said at least two Operators were needed to perform the ritual correctly. Are you suggesting Shannon attempted the Operation by himself, knowing a first meal was needed to get the corpse going? That would have been insanity! Sure he was a lot of things! But do you think he was insane?"

"Not at all," Yakov replied. "I doubt very seriously he was clinically insane. I can't prove this, but knowing the way Shannon was as a kid, after his personality and character bases were already formed, leads me to think he was blind-sided into believing he could perform the ritual by himself if he had to. Here's how I figure it.

"Cavendish had a bad feeling about Shannon, in the end. Our Teacher was no fool. He knew I walked out on him. That left his favorite to obediently resurrect him after fifty years had passed. But he knew Shannon's weak character and ever-growing aberrant personality. It's a psychological fact the character base established during the first few years of life is pretty much set in stone. It can be modified and even controlled to a large measure through psychiatric therapy and mental techniques. But massive changes to the basic foundations of self are rarely achieved. Cavendish knew this. He suspected Shannon would never be able to find an assistant to serve as the sacrifice.

"So he played a deadly game with his remaining student. He lied to him. No doubt, he stroked the young man's ego sufficiently, and in some way convinced him if he had to, he would be able to bring his Teacher back by himself. A sacrifice would not even be needed. He would have guaranteed Shannon. It would be a gentlemen's agreement, made on this side of the grave. Shannon fell for it, hook, line, and sinker. Once he resurrected his Teacher, Cavendish turned on him as he had planned to all along. It was Cavendish's failsafe device to make sure he was resurrected. Remember what I told you about Cavendish's personality. His direction was totally directed toward self-fulfillment at any cost. He could care less about others. I mean every word of it."

"Dammit." Breach was disgusted and angry. "What a betrayal! Cavendish would turn on someone who devoted his entire life to him?!"

"I'm afraid this was Martin Cavendish. Psychiatry teaches many fascinating and glorious aspects of the human mind. But it also teaches some very disturbing ones. One of those darker aspects applies here. The fact is, Gus and Frank, there is a Martin Cavendish within the psyche of each of us. We keep him repressed, but he's there. Ever lurking. Ever watching. Ever waiting for an avenue of escape, or at the very least, for a way to express himself in our lives so we can destroy others. Because the Martin Cavendish within us cares nothing for anyone other than himself. He is a miniature version of the monstrosity out there now, butchering at will. Make no mistake about it. Given any chance whatsoever, our own Martin Cavendish will destroy as surely and quickly as NightShadow will, but usually, on a smaller scale. Otherwise, we call them serial killers, and the like. Now, what was your second question?"

Gus Breach shook his head from side to side, grasping the full impact of those words, but quieted his mind and continued. "If the Staff could have been used during the Operation to send the thing back to its grave, why didn't Shannon use it when Cavendish attacked him? From the evidence we found at the gravesite, it was clear Shannon was first attacked there, and then ran through the woods, with Cavendish hot on his heels. What do you think happened?"

"I figure Shannon trusted Cavendish so much, after the resurrection, Cavendish crawled out of his grave, approached the Circle of Resurrection, and either found a way to break through the circle, or somehow lured his old student out of it. When he did, I suspect he took the Staff away from Shannon, broke it in two, and then attacked his former student. You didn't find any trace of a Staff at the gravesite, did you?"

"None," Breach replied. "I figure he probably flung the pieces of it into the woods. It'll never be found."

"So then the mutilated body of the Hungarian my father discovered in '26," Frank interjected, "was Cavendish's sacrifice to his Teacher, Seaton Stannish. Lord, what a horrible way to die!"

"Yes," Yakov confirmed. "That poor fellow was simply thrown from the Circle by Cavendish into Stannish's waiting grasp, as is supposed to happen to the second Operator. Once the resurrected corpse had him, he slaughtered him. Then he had the energy to continue on."

"Then the entire Ritual or Infernal Necromancy is based on a diabolical deception from the very start," Frank continued. "No wonder it's called Black Magic!"

Neither Breach nor Yakov replied. Both men knew the mortician was talking out loud to himself, trying to grasp the depths to which human beings can descend. Silence filled the parlor as Frank stared off into space, struggling with his moral dilemma.

"Do you have any idea what happened to Stannish?" Gus asked, breaking the silence. "Do you think he made it out of the area? No trace of him was ever found, and the body of the Hungarian was the only casualty this town ever had from the incident. I'm thinking he didn't complete the regeneration in the seven days, and took to the deep woods. I figure he lived out the pathetic existence you described, and simply died a second time."

"I was coming to that," Yakov answered in a sullen voice. "Neither of you are going to like the answer. Stannish's whereabouts bothered me for years. Don't forget, I knew what happened while the entire town was speculating. At that time, I didn't know about the sacrifice. I just figured something went wrong. Cavendish's death the next day stunned me. It didn't make sense. He was not a weak man physically or psychically, not by any stretch of the imagination. Years later however, when I found out about the conditions of regeneration from my research, I figured Cavendish died of delayed shock from the horror he witnessed. I also surmised that Stannish didn't regenerate in time, and went off to the woods, and eventually died again.

"But about twenty-odd years ago I heard rumors from some friends of mine who visited family members living in Wales. They told me an American named Shannon something-or-other was living in an isolated village, deep in the mountains of north Wales. The thing that stood out about him was that he had taken up with another American who came to the village many years earlier. An older man who kept to himself, but who was pleasant enough to anyone in the village he chanced upon. Since it is rare to find even one American taking up residence in that rugged country, let alone two, and both of them in the same backward village, the gossip started. You know how it is. But I didn't put two-and two together, because at that point, there was nothing to add up as far as I was concerned.

"But in 1956 during one of my research trips to the British Museum, I recalled the gossip of the two Americans. So I decided to investigate the claims. I would say my unconscious made a connection, prompting me to investigate by arousing my curiosity. I drove to northern Wales. After much difficulty, I finally found the village they were supposed to be living in, and cautiously checked into one of the two small rooms in the local pub. I can tell you, eyebrows went up and silence fell like a lead curtain when a third American walked through the doors of the inn! No one spoke to me except as was needed to order food, and I spoke only when absolutely necessary. Above all, I asked no questions about any other Americans.

"I was there two days before I saw them. I was having a quiet dinner, sitting alone in a booth off from the center of the pub's drinking area. In walked two men. I recognized the one immediately, even though he was twenty-seven years older. It was Tim Shannon! The same man who planned to sacrifice me to his Master, Martin Cavendish. With him was a powerfully built, intense-looking older man. I quickly positioned myself into the shadows of the booth, and tried to make out their conversation while making sure they didn't see me. It was Friday night, and very noisy in the pub, so I couldn't hear the flow of their words. But I did catch one word

several times. Shannon called him Seaton. And the innkeeper clearly
referred to the older man several times as Mr. Stannish.

"It was all crystal clear. Then and there I decided I had to stop
Shannon. Obviously, Cavendish made immediate arrangements for
Shannon to take up with Stannish when I broke off. I figure it was
Cavendish's way of insuring his student with the weak character and
highly neurotic personality would be prevented from giving up his
task, while being protected from the world and the responsibility of
developing a life for himself. No doubt, Cavendish sweetened the pot
for Shannon by assuring him Stannish would train him further in the
Black Arts. Cavendish's old Teacher would thus guarantee their
young student the power he needed to take his place in their dark
spiritual conspiracy—"

"A dark spiritual conspiracy? What are you talking about, Ben?"
Breach asked.

"Exactly that. As unbelievable as it sounds, I think Stannish and
Cavendish planned their return so they could join forces as immor-
tals, after nearly a century passed. Remember, Stannish died in 1886.
Cavendish brought him back in 1926. He died the day after. And
here we are, fifty years later, Shannon having succeeded in bringing
him back. There are too many parallels and details I see adding up to
some kind of Black arrangement between them. Some kind of power
play they slated for a later time, maybe a time they had seen into
through divination. A time of more materialism and spiritual darkness, such as we have growing today. A time that allows them to
move about freely, over many years, without attracting suspicion. A
time when no one in their right mind would believe in Magic, let
alone in people being brought back from the dead by its methods.
Maybe a time like now, gentlemen. If one man gained physical
immortality and knowledge no mortal man ever suspected could
change the course of human events as I theorized earlier, can you
imagine the reign of power two such men could hold if they joined
up together?"

Frank jumped up from his chair. "This is fantastic! Do you know
what you're saying? Such a thing can't be! We're going off the deep
end, we're losing our ability to think rationally! I'll admit it looks like
a man was raised from the dead, and is out on a killing spree. OK.
But we've gone too far afield now. The only conclusion possible
from your diatribe, 'Doctor' Yakov, is if we don't break up this dark

collaboration, the world and all of its people will suffer, somehow, someday! You've turned this from the problem of a small coal-mining town into a do-or-die situation of global proportions! The military will find a way to stop him! They've got to!

"Maybe you're just plain deluded 'Doctor!' You say ordinary weapons won't have any effect upon him! Well, all we found out for sure is the weapons we used had no effect on him! Maybe there are others who will! And this rubbish about some spiritual light and fire! Pure rubbish! If one of those army boys trains a goddamn heavy-duty flame thrower on some moving patch of blackness and opens up on it, I'll bet you a sawbuck whatever it is will go up like the Hindenburg, and that will be that! The problem will end for good. But no! You've got to go on about some Staff supposed to be brought to life and have some 'Words of Power' to destroy whatever it is. This is plain nuts, and so are you, Yakov! You have no proof to back up anything except what we saw when we fought it in the cemetery! I say we get the hell out of this asylum Gus, get back to the station house and help the military all we can! I've got to tell you my friend, unless we start looking at this more realistically, count me out! No more hocus pocus!"

Static, followed by an unseen voice, broke into Frank's ravings. "This is Major Puffner, Commanding Field Officer of Kulpsville. Come in, Chief Breach. Do you read me? Over."

Gus took his walkie-talkie out of its slipcase attached to his belt and replied. "This is Breach, Major. I read you, over." He caught the shaking in Puffner's voice, and knew the news was bad.

"Chief," Puffner began, "there have been more killings, and all in broad daylight. We now know what it looks like. Six of my men were killed over the last hour in three separate incidents. Badly mutilated, yet no signs of blood at the scenes, except for a few drops here and there. We probably wouldn't even have spotted them if there wasn't snow on the ground. Doesn't make sense. The seventh man from the third attack got away though. He said the thing is not someone dressed in a black outfit. And he sure in the hell isn't wielding some machete or sword or the like.

"Whatever it is, it looks like a black blotch about eight feet high, eight feet wide and maybe ten feet thick. It either pulls its victims into it or just covers over them, and in a second or two it leaves what's left of them on the ground and moves on…just floats away in the air like some gigantic black balloon from hell. Looks like it doesn't care about sneaking up on its victims, just comes out of the woods or from behind a building and attacks with lightning speed. The last three men hit it with everything they had, including a heavy weapon Browning automatic rifle, and a flame thrower. Did no good. The bullets just disappeared into it, and the flames seemed to flow around it. But the corporal remembered the orders and got a flare inside the damn blackness. For some reason it slowed it down enough for him to get away, even though the flame thrower had no effect! That's what he reported.

"I don't know what the hell we have on our hands, Breach, but I've called for more troops. Three hundred more will be here before nightfall. We've got to have them, because if it's as fearless and powerful as my corporal reported, and with the night coming, we're going to have a hell of a lot more problems on our hands than any of us could have imagined. Are you and the other guy OK? Over."

"Yeah, Lewis and I are fine. Over." Gus replied.

"What are the two of you up to, anyway? Shouldn't you be down here helping us deal with this situation? It is your town you know! Over." Puffner said nervously.

"That's right, young man, it is my town," Breach replied caustically. "You're in temporary charge. That's all, and don't you forget it! And because it is my town, Lewis and I are out here pursuing some leads on our own, without all the firepower of yours that doesn't do a damn bit of good! We'd only be getting underfoot if we returned. Look, Puffner, let's face it. You and I don't mesh well together, and the military command is yours, not mine. Besides, it's better we open two fronts anyway. You fight on yours, and we'll fight on ours. The only thing I suggest is that you arm all of your men with road flares. As many as each man can carry, and tell them to keep them at the ready. Screw the standard weapons! They'll only increase the body count. Do you copy? Over."

"Yeah, Breach, I copy," Puffner replied, frustration hanging heavy in his voice. "I've already ordered the incoming troops to bring cases of the damn things with them! But I got to tell you, I don' know how well a ridiculous order to carry road flares is going to sit with HQ! I'll likely draw a general court for ordering them to carry them instead of their weapons! Over."

"Tell you what, young man, I guarantee you will draw a court martial if you don't drive the order into them! It's the only thing that will slow it down and allow them to escape. Your corporal will back you up if it comes to that. Add a few more men saved because of that ridiculous order, and instead of drawing a general court, they'll wind up pinning a medal on you! You're in too deep now Major! You'd better stick to it! Over."

"Yeah," Puffner said heavily. "Yeah, you're right. Better not lose my nerve now. Is there anything I can do for you on this end? Over."

Breach heard the first attempt at civility in the major's last sentence and responded in kind. "Sure is, son. When my other deputy Dave Barker comes in, please have him contact me on the talkie. Over."

"Keeping everything secret, uh Chief? Hell, I don't blame you! The way you and I started off, sure. I'll tell him to radio you as soon as he gets here. Over and out."

Breach turned to Frank and said dryly, "Well, any more objections to Ben's analysis of the situation and his proposed solution?"

"No, none. It's just that I'm scared out of my wits. I can't fathom any of this. I tried. Believe me, I tried. It's just so unreal and unbelievable. Yet I know Ben is right. I'm OK now. I'm in this 'til the end, too. Guess I just got a bit unnerved when Ben started talking about a dark spiritual conspiracy."

"Nothing to be ashamed of, Frank," Yakov said gently. "Most people have a hard time realizing reality is only what their minds make of it. That reality is as real or unreal only to the extent their minds can comprehend and their emotions can accept what they see, experience, and hear. What each of person calls reality is only a personal interpretation of the events of their daily lives. Extend the line of experience and the unreal, the unknown, becomes the known, and becomes part of our new reality. Somewhere in your mind, Frank, you've finally made the leap over that line, and reconciled our situation mentally and emotionally. That's how it works."

"But how? How could Cavendish convince Shannon the Ritual of Resurrection could be performed by one only Operator," Frank asked, "if the old texts say it takes at least two Magicians to perform it? I'm trying to understand all of this as best as I can. You gave some ideas earlier, Ben, but I think there's more here."

"Perhaps by sheer force of will," Yakov immediately replied. "A man of powerful will can make another person, or many other people for that matter, feel as though his will is their sole reason for living. History is filled with such examples. They're called dictators. Their goals become the driving forces of others' lives. Cavendish is one such dictator. Previously, he dictated on a small scale. He bent two young boys to his will. Who knows? He might have simply told Shannon it was all right to resurrect him solo because he knew a secret way not written down, but I doubt it. You see, in cases of blind trust, unless the other person is just plain dim-witted, he usually holds some reservations about the new driving force of his life. These reservations could change him at the critical moment and he could let his master down. I can tell you one thing. Shannon wasn't dim-witted.

"In my opinion, his master had to use some ploy to convince him. I thought this when I learned Shannon was under Stannish's protection. It was clear to me it was far too dangerous for Stannish to recruit a third Operator for Shannon. The people in Wales are far too close to the soil, as it were. Many still hold to the old ways, and practice pagan ideas and modest rituals informally in their daily lives. Oh, nothing that isn't practiced here in the States, such as Halloween, hanging horseshoes on the walls pointing upward, using hex signs in their homes, things along that line. But there life is fuller, and they take the meaning behind such actions much more seriously than we do here. There, people read books instead of sitting in front of the television for hours on end. And they know their history from day one, not like the average American who forgot most of what he was ever taught in school about his country's past.

"Those people work the earth even if they only have the tiniest of gardens, and they take time to socialize without trying to push some personal agenda. It's amazing! They'll go to the mountains just to think, and take time to help others without expecting any reward. All of those attitudes and actions produce a clearer and more balanced view of life. It also lends to some pretty good intuition when something doesn't smell right. And if Stannish or Shannon would have made a move to get some kid involved with them, especially in a tiny village, alarms would have gone off in every Welsh head in the region.

"No, Cavendish had to use some gimmick or ruse to get Shannon to agree to be the sole Operator and spring it on him when it was clear to them I bowed out for good. It was easy then for Stannish to confirm the plot and reassure Shannon throughout the years. I wonder…you didn't have a chance to photograph the Circle of Resurrection, did you, Gus?"

"We never got that far. But I did sketch it, and wrote down the figures and words inside the series of circles as best as I could."

"Excellent! Can I see what you have?"

Breach reached into his shirt pocket and pulled out a small, worn, dark brown spiral notebook. "Here," he said as he opened it to the sketches and handed them to Yakov, "but I don't see how this is going to help us."

"It might seem like I'm trying to answer some academic question regarding the ploy Cavendish used on Shannon. I am, yes, but there's more to it than that. Let me take a look at what you've sketched out."

"Here, look at this." Yakov was intense. "You see this inscription in the innermost circle? '*Et verbum caro factum est, Jesus autem transiens per medium,*' which translates as "And the Word is made flesh in Jesus, and made to dwell among us." This appears in Magical circles used in other rituals designed to summon demons of one sort or another. It is meant to terrify them to remain outside the circle, and obey the Magician."

"How's it supposed to do that?" Franks asked.

"According to Christian theology, Jesus was the living Son of the Father. When he took on human form and became part of mankind, the act sanctified all of mankind, and placed a spark of the Divine Essence in each human being. According to this idea, no matter how good or bad the individual may be, there is still a spark of the Divine within him. Thus, when a demon is summoned to the circle by a Magician—whether a Black or White Magician—and he sees such inscriptions, he is forced to remember that in a way he is dealing with the Father of All Creation Himself, and must obey all commands given to him. In Magic it's called 'The Divine Charge, or Remembering.'

"Now look at the inner circle you sketched, Gus. What do you see inscribed in there?"

"Nothing," Breach replied dryly.

"And you're sure these drawings are accurate?"

"Absolutely. I sketched whatever was there as best as I could, even though the circles were badly messed up from the fight when Cavendish attacked his old student," Gus answered firmly.

"Then I was right! This is how Cavendish tricked Shannon into believing he could perform the Operation by himself, and then used him as the sacrifice. Stannish nurtured this lie all through the years Shannon was with him in Wales. Look here. You see? There is nothing written in the middle circle. A Latin verse should be inscribed in it reading, 'You whom I have called back from the grave, pass not beyond this circle by the Names of the Most Holy One, IHVH, ADONAI, EHEIEH, and AGLA.' They're the holiest names in Hebrew of the Divinity. They are meant to create an impenetrable wall against invasion from the newly resurrected corpse, but they're missing.

"In short, gentlemen, poor Shannon had no defense against NightShadow. The monster simply crossed over the circles, and Shannon's terror began. I suspect the gimmick Cavendish used to deceive Shannon was that the Words of Power in the middle circle would hinder the process between a Teacher and student if only one Operator was present. Or he might have convinced him the Words in the middle circle were only meant for the type of Infernal Necromancy written about in the standard Grimoires, which is the type meant to call back the spirit of a corpse to answer questions, just a blind for the real Ritual of Resurrection.

"But your sketches tell me more than the nature of the ruse, Gus. They tell me I was right to think there is some type of dark conspiracy between Stannish and Cavendish, and they were willing to wait ninety years to complete it, no matter what the cost. Whatever it is, can you imagine the devastating effects it would have on the world in one way or another? Who knows how many lives it would affect or outright destroy? I never knew Stannish. But I did know Cavendish. It is said in Magic the Teacher always knows more than the pupil and is thus more powerful. Cavendish was the pupil of Stannish. If NightShadow went to these extremes to be resurrected, and his Teacher is more powerful and ruthless than he is, I can't even imagine the power they would control together.

"We know Cavendish is regenerating at a fantastic rate. The military man said there were six more murders today. That makes fifteen people killed in twenty-four hours. My hunch is Cavendish intends to kill as fast as possible to complete the regeneration as quickly as he can, and then go into hiding until the seventh day ends. After that, he will just be another face who no one here knows. Then he will simply leave and rejoin Stannish. We don't have much time."

"But you said you could destroy him anytime within the seven day window," Breach asked, "even if he regenerated completely. This is only start of the second day. I don't want to see any more killings, yes, but our real goal is to destroy Cavendish. We have six days left if we count today. Why all the urgency? Can't you just bring the Staff to life, the three of us go back to his grave, you summon him on any day within the window, and have the Staff destroy him?"

"There are two reasons for my increased urgency. First of all, the Staff can only be brought to life fully in this world, on the day ruled by Saturn, during the hour ruled by Mars. Why? Because the ritual is for resurrection or return, remember? By doing the Second Consecration of the Staff during that day and hour, the Magician has the option of using the Staff to destroy what he has resurrected. Magically, those are special times ruling both resurrection and destruction, which means the Staff is allowed to do both or either. Cavendish was brought back yesterday, in the early morning hours of Monday. Today is Tuesday, January 13th, the beginning of the second day. But we have to wait for Friday midnight to perform the Second Consecration. Why? Because that's the first hour of Saturn on the sixth day. Astrologically, it's also the hour ruled by Mars. There you have both conditions for the Second Consecration met.

"There is more. NightShadow cannot be destroyed on Sunday, the day of the Lord in the Christian religion. It is a day of Life. Since all medieval Magic is based on Christian Magic, those rules apply, which shows just how diabolical Cavendish was in having his student resurrect him on a Monday. He thought all of this out a half century ago. He knew all of these conditions, and boxed them in for whenever he died. He wanted as little interference as possible if anyone would ever uncover the actual ritual. The bottom line? We only have Saturday to destroy him, and he must be destroyed before the final stroke of midnight, because after the final stroke of the clock, the Lord's Day begins. If we don't send him back by then, he will be free. No one can touch him."

"Goddamn!" Breach screamed, as his frustration reached its breaking point. He smashed his fist hard against the chair's arm. "That's next to no time! So many things could go wrong! We have no back up at all, time wise! What are we to do? I thought we'd have all these days to do the Second Consecration and lure him back to his grave! Goddamn, Ben, what are we to do?"

"Calm down, Gus," Yakov replied in a quiet, soothing voice. "That is plenty of time, if we have our facts right. What is really bothering me is the second point I was about to make.

"Earlier you wanted to know how everything works together to destroy NightShadow. I said I didn't know how the Staff will generate the light and fire. I also said you'd have to trust me and go on my directions when the time comes, because there was too much you don't understand. I also told you I pieced the entire ritual together as best as I could from my research, and was satisfied with the results. Each part seems to bear out the part before it.

"But I'm not sure! This is where my anxiety comes in! Like any theory, it will have to be tested in the laboratory, which in this case is in the cemetery. A lot could go wrong, very wrong for the three of us. That's why this Operation has become we instead of an individual effort. Fate threw us together to stop this madness. If one of us gets killed in the attempt, the other two will have to try. That's what I meant when I said you would have to play it by ear. You two know nothing of Magic. And yet, how many times throughout the hidden history of the Great Art has someone from the outside played a vital role in it? The answer is, many times. And it may happen this time, too. That's all we've got."

Yakov paused. A cold, grim silence fell among the three comrades.

"Well, Gus? Frank? Are you with me?"

They turned to each other. The silence passing between them was as hard and frigid as the winter air. Each man understood the wheel of Fate had turned. With one motion they swung around and fixed their attention on Yakov. Breach finally spoke.

"Yes, Ben. We're with you all the way, no matter what the outcome."

"Then so be it! Follow me. I have something to show you."

CHAPTER EIGHT

THE STAFF OF RESURRECTION OR RETURN

"Keep your minds open," Yakov admonished sternly as he led Breach and Lewis toward a door set off from the main living area by a small alcove. After descending a short flight of stairs leading to the basement, Yakov spoke again.

"As you can see, there's a lot of repair to do down here, too. But I took care of the most important room myself as soon as I arrived. It's time to show it to you."

The basement was divided into three rooms. Two heavy doors walled off the end rooms from the central area. The psychiatrist directed them toward the room in the north quarter of the basement beneath the kitchen. Producing a key from his pocket he inserted it in the lock.

As the latches clicked open he warned, "No one but the Magician who constructed and consecrated the Temple is allowed to enter it. During certain rites, any assistants he may have are permitted entry, but only to prepare themselves for assisting him and helping him carry out the work he intends to do. That's why I'm showing it to you now. It's your preparation, so to speak. I want you to get a feel for it so you won't be ill at ease when the time comes for the Second Consecration."

After opening the door, he blocked their entrance. "I don't know if either of you have any religious convictions. But I ask you to try to evoke as reverent an attitude as possible before entering. This room is a miniature House of Worship. Not like a traditional synagogue or church, I'll grant you. It does not bear the style or decor of such places. But it is a place of worship nevertheless. In fact, because the energy contained within it consists of one frequency only—mine—it is much more pure than the houses of worship either of you might be used to.

"To sanctify this House of Worship, I recently purified it by ancient Magical techniques. Because of this purification, no evil can enter it unbidden by me. You should also know it is vital such a Magical Temple be maintained in this state of absolute purity after it has been ritualistically purified." Yakov's tone grew more serious, as if he were about to deliver a warning to the two men who were placing their lives on the line to help him destroy the monster created by the very Magic he was defending.

"So if either of you bear any malice in your hearts toward me for whatever reason, please leave it outside of the room we are about to enter. If not, you will pay for it. We are dealing with primeval forces, gentlemen, with entities and beings existing eons before the first human-like creature raised its eyes to the heavens. Their intelligence and power is as far above man, as man's is above the most primitive one-celled organism. They are helpful or harmful according to their individual natures. But all hold to certain rules. Even the fallen angels require the Magician, or Operator as he is generally called, to be pure of body and mind before he summons them. Likewise, these beings require that the Place of Working—the Temple—be pure and clean. Knowing this I now ask, are you ready to enter under the conditions I have stated?"

"I hold no malice toward you in any way, Abraham ben Yakov, neither in my mind nor in my heart. I am clean."

Breach was stunned to hear the melody of archaic prose flow from his lips. In his mind, he saw swirls of light and darkness. A pageantry of moving shapes and colors soothed his spirit and calmed his emotions, as they pulled him into their secret world. The old cop could feel something streaming out from the darkness of the room in front of him, preparing him to enter a hidden reality beyond the one he knew: one somehow contained within the space of four earthly walls.

"My hands and heart are open and clean," Frank replied in amazement to himself and to Breach. "In the name of Purity of Purpose it is my will to enter the Temple."

"Then let your actions be according to the nature of your hearts and the strength of your wills!" Yakov shouted out, as if in a state of ecstasy. "Remove your shoes and socks, leave them here, and Enter!"

After the three men removed their footwear, they entered the awaiting darkness. Yakov closed the door behind them. In a moment a yellowish light flooded the room. It seemed to stream out from every corner, even though only a single light bulb burned weakly in the middle of the twelve-foot high vaulted ceiling.

"That light bulb is pure white," Breach whispered. "Why is the room so yellow?'

"It's a Magical effect of purification. It is the Light of the Spiritual Sun of Tiphareth, an energy and consciousness stemming from the central part of the Tree of Life. It's one of the ten emanations of the Divine. It's all part of a doctrine of philosophy called Qabalah, which underlies the Western System of Magic."

"I take it this philosophy of yours is a part of the Jewish religion?" Breach asked.

"In reality," Yakov replied, "the western Qabalah is an application of the Jewish mystical doctrine of Kabbalah. While they are pronounced the same, ancient Jewish doctrine is spelled with a K, the westernized version uses a Q to distinguish between the two. You might say western Qabalah is adaptation of Hebrew Kabbalah which produces a practical Kabbalah or practical Magic, and you'd be right!"

"Do we have to learn either or both of those doctrines to help you?" Frank asked innocently.

"No, my friend! Learning those highly related seed philosophies takes many, many years, and even extends over many lifetimes. Uh, if you accept the idea of reincarnation, that is. It will be enough if you do as I ask. Believe me, that will require more mental fortitude than you could possibly suspect at this moment!"

Gus and Frank looked around the large room. It was empty except for a large nine foot circle painted in white on the cement floor, inside of which were two smaller circles, the spaces between filled with Hebrew characters and Latin words, and strange line drawings. In the center of the circle stood a flat black, waist-high, cube-like structure, two feet on each side.

"What is that?" Breach asked.

"That's the Altar." Yakov replied softly.

"A black altar? Why black?" Breach asked suspiciously.

"Hollywood and organized religions have done more to destroy the credibility and beauty of Magic, Gus, than all of the witch hunts in history could have hoped to accomplish," Yakov replied sadly.

"Western Qabalah gives the reason for the altar's color. You see, we live here on this earth plane, the plane of existence we identify with daily. It is the place of our normal existence. In the Temple, this plane is represented by the Altar. Qabalistically, its color is black, a symbolic statement that our world is the heaviest and densest of all the planes throughout Creation. Just as we are bathing now in the Light of the Sun of Tiphareth, so too does the black, earthly Altar remind us of the emanation of the Divine which created this world, the world of Malkuth.

"Actually, The Tree of Life uses four colors to represent this world. Olive, russet, citrine, and black. Black is chosen for the Altar's color to remind us of the severity of the world, and of the limitations we must overcome to reach upwards to the Light. But the altar also has a practical ritual purpose. It is used to hold the Weapons of the Art. They are certain Magical tools used to invoke, project, and control different Magical energy. Each tool governs a specific type of energy, and each is used to manipulate worlds behind the material. The Altar completes this set of tools, as it were."

"You said reach upwards to the Light. To the Light of Tiphareth?" Frank asked.

"No, to a Light much, much higher than that, to the top most emanation of the Tree of Life itself. To Kether, the Divinity and Creator of All Things. I told you the Latin phrase in the Circle was meant to keep the horror outside of it by reminding it that when Jesus took human flesh, the Divinity Itself was made incarnate in every human being from that point onward in history. In other words, from that point onward, all people possess a spark of the Divine, making them intrinsically like It. Thus, when the Magician commands a demon, it is actually The Divinity Itself commanding that entity. Hence the obedience the spirit shows to the Operator by accomplishing the Operator's will, because in so doing, it is obeying the will of The Divine. That's the operational theory behind Magic."

"You sure you're not a Christian after all?" Breach asked seriously.

"I'm quite sure, Gus. Nor do I practice the Jewish religion. You might call me a practicing Kabbalist instead. You should know the essential idea of the One Divinity did not arise from Judaism or Christianity, even though their theologians try to take credit for it. Thirteen hundred years before Christianity, and three hundred years before the historical beginnings of Judaism, an Egyptian Pharaoh, Akhenaton, uttered the words that there was only one Deity, not the many his world knew at the time. It was also the beginning of the idea that a spark of the Divinity resided in each human being.

"But his new religion failed after thirty years, and the priesthood of Egypt brought back the plural world of many deities. My people, the Jews, resurrected the concept of the deity of the One, and over a thousand years the concept was developed further. It was a logical step for Christianity to assert that a spark of The Divinity resided within each human being. But the Jewish religion sees a Deity of Severity, which is also represented in the right-hand side of the Tree of Life. It's called The Pillar of Severity. The Christ stressed the other aspect of the same One, The Deity of Mercy. That's also represented on the Tree by the emanations of the left-hand side of the Tree. That side of the Tree is called The Pillar of Mercy.

"Christ's apostles passed these mystical concepts on to their students, who finally carried it to the pagan clans of the world over time. So today, we have a Judeo-Christian culture. One culture stresses the Divinity of Severity, while the other, the Divinity of Mercy. Yet both are from the same One Divinity, a glowing ember hidden within the nature of every human being. In reality, the ancient religion of Egypt, Judaism, and Christianity are all connected at the root level. What we call Western Magic, which rose only during the late nineteenth century, is actually composed of a contemporary set of rituals with underlying principles and philosophies extending back from the time of ancient Egypt."

"Are you saying Western Magical practices are based upon the Pillar of Mercy?" Frank asked with a pointed intensity.

"Not at all. Practical Qabalah, the basis of Western Magical tradition, employs the Magic of both Pillars, although it seeks to combine them into the third pillar of the Tree—the Middle Pillar: a synthesis of the Pillar of Mercy and the Pillar of Severity."

"I'd like to learn more if we get through this, Ben. I'm very serious," Frank replied.

"We can get to it if and when we succeed," Yakov replied slowly, as if hesitating. "Right now, there's hard work to do. Both of you, please step into the circle and remain there."

As Gus and Frank moved into the circle, the Magician walked over to the north wall and pressed against its seamless surface. A thin crack appearing out of nowhere gave way to a tall, narrow panel, which suddenly sprang open.

"My mother used this hidden space to age pickles," Yakov said with a smile. "I find it useful as a closet."

Frank and Gus strained to look into the small compartment from where they stood. But all they could see were several long robes of different colors, and some odd looking equipment they could not identify. Yakov emerged holding a long, thin black velvet cloth concealing some object. After crossing into the circle painted on the floor, he turned toward the east. With the index finger of his right hand, he traced a five-pointed star in the air at the edge of the circle. Moving clockwise around the circle on the floor, he repeated his action in each direction while vibrating one of the four Names of the Divinity from the verse Shannon was duped into deleting from the Circle of Resurrection.

After completing his movements, he turned to Frank and Gus. "Whatever you do gentlemen do not leave this circle before me. I have just set up an astral circle. If you had the ability, you would see it suspended in the air, directly above the one on the floor. There are negative influences, malignant entities, lurking about in the area outside of the Temple. They watch such activities as ours, and may try to interfere. This circle will blind and deafen them to what we do.

"This is why we are here," he explained, as he held the long, black cloth vertically.

Yakov's aged fingers nimbly untied several black cords securing the single opening of the cloth. He withdrew the object from its case.

"This is the Staff of Resurrection or Return. Under no circumstances touch it!" he said to the two spellbound men. "You would discharge its power through yourself rendering it useless, and bring great harm to yourself at the same time."

"What…what is that horrible thing on top of it?" Frank asked nervously as he stared at a large head with a facial carving sitting upon the top of the Staff. "It's the most hideous face I've ever seen!"

"It is called the Face of Death or the Second Death. You see it now as the Face of Death, because Cavendish consecrated it to the Spirit of Death, the Shade that comes to all men in time. Look at it carefully. Notice the protruding fangs, hollow cheeks, and open mouth, as if it were screaming in terror. Look at it carefully. See the fury in its bulging eyes, and the madness of the wooden hair streaming out in all directions."

Waves of panic rippled through the two men.

"In the ancient texts," Yakov continued, "the expression it is wearing is also referred to as the Trance of Resurrection because of the violence the returning spirit feels when it reenters its own rotting corpse. If I would perform the Second Consecration on the Staff, and use it to help resurrect and regenerate the corpse the way the ritual is actually designed, this face would become even more grotesque, because as the second Operator, I would be sacrificed to it.

"But the texts also say if after performing the Second Consecrations of their Staffs, the Operators lose heart and decide to invoke the Return of the spirit after it reentered its former body, this hideous face would remain as horrible as you see here. In that case however, it would be called The Face of the Second Death.

"You might ask why, if the spirit is safely retuned to the grave, would it still bear these hideous features? Because it is symbolic of the event of death. That is, whether it's a spirit resurrected by Infernal Necromancy or the spirit of any man's natural death, after it leaves its physical body at the time of death, it undergoes an agonizing trauma. It is ripped from the body and the world it knew, cast into a darkness it knows not. The terror of the experience is so violent, the spirit loses all memory of the life it had upon the earth, sometimes instantly. At other times, it takes minutes, years, or even centuries for the spirit to be able to accept its own death and finally move on to the other world. That is the root of the ghost stories you hear. You see, the event of Death is always a violent action.

"Now, in the case of Infernal Necromancy, to resurrect a spirit produces another such experience. But it is one of such unimaginable violence that even though the two Operators would send it back immediately to the world beyond this one, their Staffs would only mirror the horror of the experience of Death. But now that Death is a two-fold death experienced by the same spirit, hence the term Second Death. Such a thing is unthinkable to the human mind, yet endured by the returning, and then returned spirit."

Breach and Lewis stared at the face, unable to speak. They were thinking of their own deaths, and the violence of the experience awaiting them. A chill of helpless fear froze their bones.

"I wish he hadn't told us," Frank whispered. "It would have been better not to know."

"I didn't need to know either," Breach whispered back, "but it's too late now."

They continued to look at the Staff closely, their sight eventually falling away from the face.

"It seems to shine with a light of its own," Gus commented. "A black light."

"You're right," Yakov replied. "The Staff does shine with its own black light. It is radiating black power. Remember, it was consecrated by Cavendish to serve his purpose of resurrection. And it was baptized, if you will, with the blood of two innocent children. If I had performed the Second Consecration along with Shannon, both of our Staffs would have radiated such an intense black light, the human eye would not have been able to withstand it even for a second. It's the opposite of the Light of Tiphareth, which radiates the Light of Life, Liberty, and Love."

"What are those strange figures carved on it?" Frank asked. "I become very still inside if I stare at them, and my eyes get sleepy."

"They are properly called the Characters of the Alphabet, but the alphabet is from a dead language of long ago. They are the letters of the Theban Alphabet, and possess great energy. They are like capacitors storing electrical energy, except these characters have stored another type of energy. A more intense Magical energy, which can be either destructive or constructive according how it is used.

"This energy is more powerful than electrical energy could ever be. The Hebrew and Greek alphabets possess the same characteristic. Over millennia, priests have transferred the energy of their intent into them by employing them in sacred writings and ritual practices. After centuries of such use, that energy gave them a life of their own so that today, they give power to whatever object they are inscribed upon, or to whatever ritual they are spoken in. They also attract power from other spiritual realms, with such power corresponding to their own individual natures.

"Each character has a specific sound and meaning assigned to it. When they are written together to produce a word, the combination of their individual energies combines to form a power that is the sum of their individual energies, which in turn produces a different effect than the individual letters could by themselves.

"Now, gentlemen, watch as I stand the Staff upright."

Yakov placed the Staff vertically on the cement floor and removed his hand. The black shaft stood erect without any visible support.

"How can it stand without support?" Frank asked.

"It is not governed by the laws of our universe. There is no place in its nature for gravity to take hold. While it is made of black ebony, it appears to be weightless. As in so many other branches of Magic, here, Nature is defeated. This staff represents the energy of chaos: the chaos of the grave."

Without warning the Staff began to vibrate slowly. After a few seconds, the slight vibrations grew into a low, guttural howl that rippled along its great length.

"My God, what is that?" Breach cried out. "It sounds like someone in torment!"

"That is the life, or death, force of the Staff. When it pulsates, it cries out in torment from something no man can understand, because it belongs to another world, the world of death, and 'life' beyond the grave. As long as it is trapped in our world, a party to the horrific business of Infernal Necromancy, it is not just suffering. It is in unimaginable agony. That's why it cries out! It wants release!"

"Please!" Frank screamed. "Please, Ben, make it stop! Put it away!"

Without further explanation, Yakov placed his right hand over the eyes of the Face of Death or the Second Death, leaned toward it, and whispered some unintelligible words into its blindness. Immediately, the howls and pulsations stopped. The psychiatrist grabbed the black cloth case, slipped it over the staff, and held it upright in his right hand. As fear slipped from Frank's mind, he framed the image of Yakov standing there with his veiled monstrosity as a mental picture of an evil Moses who might be leading them into a land of inconceivable suffering and torment, instead of a paradise of milk and honey.

"I'm sorry to have startled you, my friends, but I felt it was necessary. Even though you have been through so much already, what we must yet pass through will be all the more incomprehensible and horrifying. So I wanted to acquaint you with the nature of the terror awaiting us. Are you all right?"

"I've never been so terrified in all of my life," Gus stuttered. "I don't know if I have the guts to continue, Ben. I feel like I'm hallucinating, and have no control over reality. I may be coming unhinged."

"My feelings exactly," Frank said in a shaking voice. "We won't be any good to you like this. Maybe we—"

"Enough!" Yakov screamed. The strength in his voice was a command to be obeyed. "This is part of expanding one's reality. As I told you before, reality is based upon experience, and the acceptance of that experience! What you have seen doesn't fit what you are used to. The world as you knew it has just been turned inside out, just as it was in the cemetery last night! They are your experiences now. Take time to accept them, but you can and will eventually accept them, both intellectually and emotionally! When you achieve acceptance, then your new reality will stabilize, making you much more human, and at the same time, more spiritual. There is no way out of this for any of us, other than what we have planned. I suggest you get a grip on yourselves, and contain your emotions as best as you can!"

The tension filling the circle where the three men stood began to ease. Yakov's scolding had shamed the Chief. At the same time, it appealed to the surfacing spiritual desire in Frank. Neither man answered.

"Are we ready to move on?"

They nodded in agreement as the psychiatrist continued.

"You've had enough for one day. Let's return to the parlor. We have to wrap this up so we can begin our preparations."

Without further comment, Abraham ben Yakov walked through the astral circle, breaking it, and returned the Staff to the closet. After withdrawing some papers, he motioned for his two new friends to follow him back upstairs.

They entered the parlor. "Please take your seats again. I will be right back."

Returning, he handed each of them a set of stapled papers.

"You will have to study these documents over the next three days. I want you to be familiar with the ritual of Infernal Necromancy, or more exactly, the real Ritual of Resurrection or Return that lies behind it. I want each of you to understand it from the point of the Second Consecration of the Staff onwards. I deleted the first consecration that Cavendish performed since that would serve us no useful end.

"By studying these papers, you will understand the secrets I have uncovered during my years of research. It might be necessary to know just how NightShadow was called back into his rotting corpse, the process of the initial sacrifice, and the process of the Final Return. It's not as complicated as it sounds. Putting it all together was the hard part.

"You have today, Wednesday, and Thursday to get it down. We must meet back here on Friday at noon to begin our final preparations. Then we begin the Second Consecration at midnight, the first hour of Saturday, the hour ruled by Mars. According to ancient astrology, Mars is The God of War, bloodshed, and slaughter. He will oversee the consecration and add his force to our effort. Then, the Staff will be brought fully to life in our world."

"Is there any astrological meaning attached to the day of Saturday?" Frank asked.

"Saturday," Yakov said in a monotone voice, "is the day of Death. It is the day ruling all evolutionary changes and transformations. It represents finality and the finality of the grave. It is the only chink in his armor. So you see, we must not only give the Staff its Second Consecration on that day, but we must also destroy him before the final stroke of midnight. Otherwise, he will be free for all time. He and Stannish will team up, and together they will bring inconceivable chaos into the world.

"I must tell you something I haven't mentioned yet for certain reasons. I speculated as to what Stannish and Cavendish might do. But now, now I think I have to tell you what I really believe they are planning. It would take too long to explain why I hold this view. Nevertheless, it is my belief, my considered opinion they intend to plunge the entire world into the Pit, into a new Age of Darkness.

"Mankind would no longer rule this world. Instead, the world they plan on creating would be a madman's dream of a Black Utopia. Humans would have to share this world with abominations from the other side of the grave, and with unspeakable things from Hell itself. These things would mate with humans, producing a new Hell, the mirror image of the kind existing on the other side of the grave for those who have earned such a place during their lives on this earth.

"This New World would be everlasting torment and perpetual grief to what is now called humankind. Evil, the Principle of Evil itself would win out and destroy the Principle of Good for all time,

in all places. Its malignancy would spread throughout the universe by
the foothold it gains here on earth, and the laws of all Creation
would be reversed. God Itself would lose the greatest gift It ever
bestowed upon its highest creation, Man. The gift of Free Will. Now
you know why I must do this thing. Cavendish must be returned to
the grave at all costs. Do you understand?"

Gus' eyes glazed over. His spine froze to the inside of his skin and
his mind was numb. Frank began to quiver at first, and then he shook
violently like an alcoholic coming down from a drinking binge.

Gus' lips quivered as he forced his words out. "Whatever…what-
ever it takes, Ben. Whatever it takes. No sane man would believe
such a thing was possible. But after what we've seen over the last two
days, yes. I now know anything is possible. Don't worry. We'll
succeed. We've got to! Even if it means death for all of us. Right,
Frank?"

Through his violent shaking, the mortician blurted out, "I'll die
first before I see my son and his family living in the world you just
described. Yes, Ben, we'll stop Cavendish. We must! We can't fail!"

From his position across the room, Yakov made a series of circular
gestures in the air with his hands. As he did, warmth and peace filled
his visitors.

"Quiet," the psychiatrist whispered calmly. "Accept the peace and
stillness which I now give to both of you. It will help you over the
next several days, and prepare you to do what must be done."

As both men relaxed back into their chairs, Yakov continued.

"Know this also, gentlemen. Both of these forces, the Principle of
Good and the Principle of Evil, are as conscious as you and I. But
unlike us, they are eternal and as nebulous as is all of Creation itself.
Each has enormous, raw force at its command. A force of such
magnitude and power no human mind can imagine, let alone
comprehend. This is a force to create…or destroy.

"Each principle has many, many legions of followers. Some are
flesh and blood as we are. But others of these great hosts have no
physical bodies. They are made of pure spirit or energy if you will,
but energy that can think and direct its own force into activities that
serve the lord it pays homage to. Hence the eternal struggle between
the two, with humankind caught in the middle. It is important you
know this. We are not simply fighting NightShadow. He is an
advanced guard going forth to bring its lord the great prize the Evil

has yearned for since the day of Creation itself: to have all of existence under its direct and complete control. NightShadow is its vanguard; the one it has been waiting for all through the eons of time. Remember this!"

Breach and Lewis remained speechless as the psychiatrist continued.

"Also, over the next three days, both of you must fast. No meat of any kind. It's an ancient requirement in these things. Eat very lightly. Only enough to sustain your physical strength and the clarity of mind."

"Why this requirement?" Frank finally squeaked out, the uneasiness in his voice betraying the mingled peace and fear he was experiencing.

"To weaken your physical self—your body—so your spiritual nature becomes strong. That's how it works. The two bodies are always at odds with each other. Strengthen one, the other becomes weak. Since this is a Magical ritual, our spiritual bodies must be as strong as possible. The power to destroy NightShadow comes through our spiritual natures, not from our physical strength. As you've both seen, physical forces have no effect on something caught between two worlds. But the force of our spiritual natures *can* affect it."

Suddenly Yakov stood up, a signal to Gus and Frank it was time for them to leave and begin their work.

"We will be back here noon Friday," Breach said strongly as he and Frank walked toward the back door. "Is there anything else you want us to do?"

"Nothing, except as I instructed. Everything hinges on the three of us being on the same page in this work. Oh. There is a side issue, Gus. That deputy of yours, Dave Barker. For some reason, Fate has dealt him out of this matter. We'll never know why. I know he is your responsibility, but I suggest you somehow divert him away from any involvement with the three of us. Will you do that?"

"My thoughts exactly. I want him to survive this nightmare and take over for me in case I'm killed. It's not much of a town, but it is our town, and it will be growing, that is, if we stop this infernal conspiracy. And if we do and the town grows, it will need a good Chief of Police. He's the only one to fill the bill. Don't worry. I'll handle him. See you on Friday."

As Frank and Gus walked down the pavement, Frank spoke up. "What are you going to do about Dave anyway? I know how attached he is to you! He's going to want to see this thing through!"

"It can't be helped," Breach replied in a heavy voice. "We're in this up to our ears now. We couldn't explain what happened here and what Ben told us and showed us even if he would believe it! No, the shrink is right. Dave is out of it."

"There's something more to it too, isn't there?" Frank asked cryptically.

"I guess you probably figured it. Dave could be the son I never had. It's just I don't want him getting killed too. And there's no need. If the three of us can't destroy Cavendish, Dave sure won't do it by himself. He's better off staying out of it."

A voice broke through on the cruiser's walkie-talkie as they got in.

"Chief! This is Dave Barker. Do you copy?"

"Breach here. I copy you. Go ahead."

"I'm sorry I didn't call you sooner, Gus, but I just got in a few minutes ago. I didn't mean to sleep until two! What the hell is happening here? There are military troops everywhere! And who is this Major Puffner? Acts like he's running the show! Where are you anyway? I just want to get out of here and join you."

"Calm down, Dave," Breach replied in a soothing voice. "It's all right. Puffner is in charge. He's not all that bad once you get to know him a little. Don't forget, he's as confused by what's happening right now as much as we were yesterday. Frank is with me. Just stay put. We're coming in."

"OK," Barker replied gruffly. "But I don't see what good it's gonna do. Everything is in complete confusion. There were more murders besides the six soldiers. They found Old Henry—or what was left of him—and Jake Munsion. Puffner figured they were killed early this morning. And Crazy Mary too. They found her body on the old coal road leading up to the cemetery. That brings the number of killings to eighteen. The ones we know about, that is."

"Just hold on, Dave," Breach replied somberly. "We're coming in. Over and out."

When they entered the station, they caught sight of the major leaning against the cell doors, arms folded across his chest, his eyes staring straight through them as if they weren't there. Barker rushed over to Breach's side while nodding a greeting to Frank.

"Puffner is no good to us anymore, Gus" Barker whispered. "Look at him! He's lost it! This is one situation they didn't cover in his army field manual! He doesn't know what to do!"

"Which is why I'm ordering you to stay here and help him deal with it. It's our town. We have to be responsible for it even though we're no longer in command of what happens here. Unless we have someone here who can guide him and who knows these people and the town layout, more people will die, and you're elected!"

"Are you kidding me, Chief?" Barker snapped back angrily. "I'm no good to that ass! He won't listen to me or anyone else! My place is with you and Frank, trying to help us get rid of NightShadow! Not here! No way! Not with him! I won't do it! I'll resign first!"

"Then resign now, Barker," Breach fired back coldly, "if that's all you're good for, disobeying a direct order after I explain why to you, then you're no good to me or to this town. Turn in your badge. You're finished!"

Something in the way Breach spoke told the young cop his boss was not only earnest when he gave his ultimatum, but also concealing something. His stern words and the steel coldness in the older man's eyes shocked Barker back to reality.

"OK, Chief," Barker wheezed out. "If that's the way you want it. Maybe I can help him out, if he'll let me. I guess having one of us here in indirect command so to speak, is better than no input at all. You win."

"It's not a matter of winning, Dave," Breach replied unemotionally. "It's a matter of doing our job, and doing it right. I'll talk to Puffner, then Frank and I are leaving. You won't see us until Sunday, I fancy. We're on a lead of our own, and it will take time to develop it."

Before Barker could ask any questions, Breach walked over to Puffner and snapped him out of his daze.

"Major, I'd like to speak with you!" he said pointedly.

"Hmm?" Puffner replied as if coming out of a dream. "Uh, yes. What can I do for you, Chief?"

"It's not what you can do for me," Breach replied with a wry smile. "It's what I'm going to do for you. Listen! I know you're suffering some kind of shell shock. That's understandable. None of this is covered in the army regs. Which is why I'm leaving my deputy, Dave Barker, with you. He's a good man, Major. He can help you a lot. He knows the people, the town, the mountains, back roads, everything it will take your men time to find out, and most probably cost more lives in the process. If you give him a chance, we'll all benefit. What do you say?"

Puffner stared at Breach for minute, as if looking at him down a long, narrow tube. Finally he spoke. "You're right, Breach! I need help here. Sure. I'd be glad to add your finest to my command. I've been watching the kid since he came in an hour ago. Takes charge right away. Hell, even my Sergeant took orders from him! OK, you've got a deal! By the way, what are you going to be doing? Following up those leads you told me about?"

"That's right. Like I said before, opening up two fronts is better than all of us fighting on one. Besides, sometimes a small squad can do what a company of men can't. Just think of Frank and me as the smallest squad you ever heard of!"

Puffner laughed loudly, breaking the remaining ice between them. "OK, Chief, I surrender! But it sounds like this lead is going to take you out of the action."

"You catch on fast," Breach replied through a warm smile. "I just told Dave we probably won't surface until Sunday sometime. Got lots to do!"

"If that's the way you want it, it's all right by me. Just one thing. I suggest you tell Barker he's got to take orders from me. Agreed?"

"No, I don't agree. This situation is going to require a division of authority at the top. Barker knows everything there is to know about this town and the surrounding areas. Before this is all over, you and he will have to compare notes and cross hurdles together. No one man at the top. It's got to be the two of you giving orders, not one! In other words, I'm asking you to tell your men to take orders from Barker as if they came from you. It's got to be that way. You can't afford any breakdown in communication, because if that happens, more will die."

Puffner eyed the old cop carefully.

"OK, Breach. Damn it all, I suppose I have to agree with you. As you said when you stormed in here before, this is your town, and the local law enforcement should be directly involved. It will be as you say." He extended his arm and they shook hands.

Breach grinned. "You know, son, there's hope for you yet! See you on Sunday!"

Without further comment, Breach turned away and motioned to Frank to follow him as he passed by a speechless Dave Barker on his way out.

"What do we do now," Lewis asked as they stood outside. The temperature was dropping rapidly, with water crystals forming on their eyebrows and around the corners of their mouths. Their breath hung in white puffs of frozen steam in front of their faces.

"Go back home, Frank" Breach replied, rubbing his gloved hands together. "Get some clothes, and meet me at my house. I suggest we stay together over the next three days so we can be sure we have this whole ugly business nailed down. We can't take any unnecessary chances. And forget about bringing any food unless you have a special diet. There's plenty at my place. Besides, we have to go on a fast, but I doubt we'll have much of an appetite anyway.

"Did you notice the title on the first page of the documents Ben gave us? 'The Infernal Rite.' There weren't many pages in it, but I'll bet you a dime to a doughnut it's going to take time to get through them. Not so much to understand as to believe. Fasting will be the easy part. Tell you what. I'll drop you off at your place. When you're ready, come up to my house, and we'll begin. Ok?"

"Sounds fine. I'll be there in a couple of hours."

Light snow began to fall as they made their way from Willow Lane toward Maple Street.

"Dammit!" Frank shouted. "That's all we need! Another snowfall! Not now! If it's another big one, Route 16 will be closed, and if it's closed, you know damn well the back road will be impassable, and those are the only two ways to drive to the cemetery. You know what that means Gus? We'll have to trek four miles through the mountains to get to it! We're too old for that!"

"We can't change the weather," Breach replied with a tone of resignation. "We'll have to take what comes and do whatever it takes to stop Cavendish. We can't allow him to regenerate completely. If he does, Hell will come down on the world, including this tiny town."

Breach dropped his friend off at the Lewis Funeral Home and turned his vehicle toward his home at 834 Pine Street. As the cruiser felt its way through what was now heavy falling snow, the old cop whispered his deep-seated misgivings to himself.

"The three of us must succeed in destroying NightShadow. But I have a very bad feeling not all of us are going to get out of this alive....Maybe none of us."

▼

CHAPTER NINE

THE INFERNAL RITE

It was 7:30 p.m. when Breach heard his front doorbell ringing.

"I'm sorry it took so long, Gus," Frank said, "but I wanted to clean up my house and the Prep room a bit. A lot went on there over the last day or so."

"Come in, Frank!" Breach replied cordially. "I figured it was something like that. Are you ready to begin, or should we have dinner first?"

"I'd just as soon begin if you don't mind. I'm very nervous about all the unknowns facing us in this 'rite' thing."

"OK. I have a small study upstairs. It's bright and pretty comfortable. I've spent many happy hours there enjoying the classics. Maybe the atmosphere will help us get through what we're facing."

Breach led Lewis up a long flight of stairs to the second floor, through a guest room, and into the back room over the kitchen. As Gus turned on the single overhead light, Frank took a long look around. He handled some of the volumes on the bookcases lining all four walls.

"Boy, I had no idea! Look at these books! There must be a thousand of them! Some of them look like First Editions! Others certainly are Collector's Editions! Small towns, uh, Gus? You never know what or who you'll find in them!"

"Well," Gus replied humbly, "as I told Dave, I love the classics. There's so much a person can learn from them. Here, take a seat. We'd better get started."

As the hours passed, they lost awareness of each other as each man's mind spiraled into the fantastic world of Magic and The Infernal Rite. The only sound that echoed in the small room was pages being turned and rustled. Finally, a high-pitched creaking noise broke through their concentration.

"What's that?" Frank asked, as Gus peered out over Yakov's documents.

"Oh, no!" Breach shouted. "Oh no!"

The old cop threw the documents on the table next to him, jumped up and raced over to the single window in the study's north wall. After drawing the curtains aside and flipping a switch concealed behind them, he stared out into the night.

"Better come here, Frank," he said in disgust while shaking his head from side to side. "We're in for a very rough time of it, just as you expected this afternoon."

Frank joined him at the window and peered out. As he looked, he rubbed his eyes several times. "What the…?"

"That's the second story back porch I'm afraid," Gus answered. "Look at the snow! The entire porch is covered halfway up the window! That creaking we heard is coming from the porch's support beams. It only did that once before, back in the blizzard of '63. Remember that one? Goddamn it, we've got another one just like it on our hands now! Just what we didn't need! I know I said we have to take what comes, but dammit all anyway! This is more than I expected! It's as though the Principle of Evil Ben spoke about is trying to stop us, or at least slow us down, because I've got to tell you, this puts the worst possible spin on things!"

"At least a blizzard explains it," Frank replied in relief. "For a moment, I thought the snow was suspended in midair! Or worse, the house was nearly buried in it! With all of the bizarre events of the past couple of days, I'm beginning to lose hold on what's possible and what's not anymore! Lord, Gus, things are so bad in my reality right now, that the sight of this blizzard is actually a relief, no matter what it means for us later on! But you're right. If your second story porch is covered, what will the ground be like?"

"I'm afraid," Breach wheezed out slowly, "we're looking at a good five feet of the fresh white shit, without the drifts. It'll take the town a week to dig out. We just don't have the heavy equipment to get out any sooner. That means Route 16 will be closed shut for at least that long. And the back road running past the cemetery? It will be closed till spring! You were right. Looks like we're going to have to hike the four miles through the woods when the time comes. At our ages, the three of us will be lucky if we don't die of heart attacks trying! I just hope Yakov is in good shape…"

The telephone was ringing on the first floor. Breach raced out of the room and down the stairs.

"Hello. This is Chief Breach."

"Gus! This is Ben. I take it Frank is with you? I had a feeling he would be, and that the two of you were still up, so I called."

"Oh, hello, Ben! Yes, he's here. We're going to stay together until Friday to make sure we understand this Infernal Rite business as best we can. We were just going over the documents you gave us earlier today."

"Better make that yesterday. It's 4:20 a.m., Wednesday morning. Did you look out your windows lately?" the Magician asked.

"Yeah, Ben. In fact, just a few minutes before you called. I still don't believe it. Frank speculated we might be in for more snow, uh, yesterday afternoon, and he thought we might wind up hiking the four miles through the mountains to get to the cemetery. I didn't take his worry seriously at the time. But now, I'm sure he's right. We're going to have a hell of a time getting there. Are you in good enough shape to make the trek?"

"Don't worry about me, Gus. I've had medical training and have taken good care of myself throughout my life. I'll be just fine."

"We'll count on it, Ben," Breach replied with a sigh of relief. "We need you, remember that! The most Frank and I can do is help. If anything happens to you, all is lost, because what I have read so far tonight will take me at least until Friday to try and understand. Do you get my point?"

"Understood. We'll be all right. The reason I called at this hour was to alert you to the snow and to see if Frank was with you. But my real reason was to tell you I will be incommunicado until noon Friday, just in case either of you wanted to get in touch with me. I didn't think it would be necessary, but with the recent developments, I have to go into isolation to prepare for what is to come. You could call it a state of intense practical Magic. I will have to marshal all of my powers so we can get the job done. I'll begin in a few hours, and it will put me completely out of contact with everyone."

"What do you mean by recent developments?" Breach asked cautiously.

"I listened to the radio and television earlier tonight. This blizzard is completely unexpected," Yakov replied calmly. "The weather people are confused. They said this storm front formed out of nowhere over north central Pennsylvania, and now it is stationary. Which means they don't know how long the blizzard will last. One weatherman speculated it will drop eighty inches or more of snow within seventy-two hours. That's from today, Wednesday, right through Friday. If that happens, we won't even be able to march the four miles through the woods. Cavendish will win. I can't allow that!"

"Calm down, Ben," Breach cut in nervously. "What do you expect to do about it?"

"A development like this—with so much at stake—tells me the Principle of Evil is aiding Cavendish. It wants to overthrow the Principle of Good throughout the universe once It gets a foothold here on earth. That's what this storm front formed out of nowhere tells me. There is no synchronicity or coincidence involved in a matter of this magnitude. Not when we know what we know. I—"

The old cop anxiously cut Yakov off a second time. "That's just what I said to Frank only minutes before you called! Do you mean I'm right after all?"

"Yes. But it also means more than you being right. It means your intuitive faculties are operating at one hundred percent. Good! We'll need them! It always works like this. When Evil throws up some barrier or what seems like an insurmountable obstacle, Good counters with a move of its own, usually in some strange way, such as your intuition kicking into high gear. That's how the eternal struggle between Good and Evil has always worked to maintain the universal balance throughout all of Creation. One wins one time, the other the next time.

"But here, here, the struggle has been brought to a head by the blackest of spiritual conspiracies formed on both sides of the grave. This conflict is different, Gus. This one is for all of the marbles, and we're smack dab in the middle of it. Everything hinges on what we do and don't do within the next seventy-two hours.

"So what I am going to do is fight back Magically. Since this situation is a product of Black Magic, my Magic can be used to try and turn the tide. I have it in my power to affect the weather. If we get the massive snowfall we expect, I'm going to raise the temperature of the air so the snow turns to rain, but not until Thursday evening. I don't want to give the Principle of Evil time to counter my move. The rain will melt most of the snow. The rest it will pack down tight.

"Then, on Thursday night, right through Saturday, I am going to bring on a near sub-zero degree freeze. The snow will pack solid, and we'll be able move across its surface to hike to the cemetery. At least we won't sink down too deeply. It'll be rough going, but we can do it. It's our only chance. Frankly, Gus, I see no other way around the problem. It may sound strange, but certainly no stranger than the events of the past days."

"So besides facing death trying to destroy NightShadow, after making our way through a blizzard snowfall, we might freeze to death just getting there. Is that what you're telling me?"

"That's about the size of it. Do you have any better ideas? Because if you do, I'm all ears!"

Breach remained silent for a few moments and then replied. "I guess that's that then. I just hope you're right and the freeze will work so we can get there. Anything else?"

"No," Yakov answered. "That's why I'll be incommunicado. I'll be working my 'weather magic' you might call it. See the two of you here at my house at noon on Friday."

"See you then, Ben. Good luck!"

As Breach put the telephone back on its hook, he turned around slowly. His mind was desperately trying to frame their new dilemma in terms it could grasp. But a voice that seemed to boom through the old cop's trance snapped him back to the moment.

"Well, Gus?" Frank asked. "Are you going to tell me everything, or do I have to put the pieces of what I heard together for myself."

"Uh, no," Breach replied slowly. "Here's the story."

After explaining Ben's idea and tactics to the mortician, he smiled as a man might who knew his time on this earth was short. "It's quarter-to-five. I suggest we get some sleep and begin again around noon. You take the guest room upstairs. I'm going to sack out on the couch down here after I get my thoughts straight.

Frank Lewis had no illusions. He knew the recent developments may have signed their death warrants. They were aging men, with more physically bad days than good. Taken together, their situation would overtax the youngest and strongest of men. With a smile of acceptance that mimicked Gus' smile of a moment before, he said good night, and walked up the stairs to the guest room.

§§§

At 11:45 a.m. Gus heard the pounding of heavy-soled shoes racing down the stairs.

"Gus!" Frank cried out in panic. "Did you look out the window yet? Did you see?"

He sliced through his friend's panic attack quickly. "Yes, I've seen it. I've been up since ten. Couldn't sleep much. We have trouble for sure now. Even with Ben's weather magic, the going will be tough, very tough. But there's nothing we can do about it. It's all up to Ben. We might as well have a light meal and get back to our work."

"Just like that?" Frank blurted out.

"Just like that!"

"Gus, there's got to be a good five feet out there already! We'll never make those four miles, never! We'll drop dead long before we get to Saint Alacious! Then what? I say we leave now, right now, and bed down up there somehow, and wait for Friday night and..."

"And do what?" Breach countered angrily. "How is Ben going to do the Second Consecration of the Staff to bring it to life! What are we going to do? Drag everything he needs with us? And what about his Temple thing! He needs somewhere sacred to do the consecration so none of those evil spirits can get at him while he's doing it, remember? The ones supposed to be hanging around outside of his Temple? And how the hell would he do the consecration in this blizzard, anyway?

"So what if the snow stops before Friday and we somehow manage to survive through today and tomorrow, hunkered down in the cemetery? What are we to do? Dig down through seven or eight feet of snow on Friday so Ben can draw a circle on the ground and have him try the consecration with God-knows-what crawling around trying to stop him? Remember, if he's right—and I damn well bet he is—the Principle of Evil is trying to stop us!

"No, there's no other way. You've got to get a grip on yourself! The way you're acting now, maybe the Principle of Evil is working on you, so you become the monkey wrench in our plans! Is that what you want? To be Its pawn, and wind up helping It destroy Good once and for all? Is that the legacy you want to leave your son and his family? Do you want to turn them over to the kind of world Cavendish and Stannish have planned for them and the whole human race? Is that what this panic attack of yours is all about?"

Breach's words cut through the mortician's runaway emotions like a hot knife through butter. Inside, Frank's lifelong fascination with death took on a new dimension, forcing him to face the dawning fact that leaving this world might only be a couple of days away. His mind tilted sideways, allowing thoughts of the love and devotion he had for his son and his family to filter into the blackness of the terror he was facing.

"You're right. You're right," he replied thoughtfully. "No, I'll never be a pawn for any evil, no matter what the final outcome. All of us need our wits about us now like never before, and that includes me. Let's have that meal and get back to work."

As the day wore into evening, both of them were drawn once more into the images of Magic and madness the process of Infernal Necromancy painted. Throughout the night and into the early hours of the morning, the only sounds heard in the small study were pages being turned. Finally, Breach broke the long hours of silence.

"Well, what do you think? It's two-forty in the morning. So far we've had pretty near two days going over this material. Are we ready yet?"

"Personally," Frank replied softly, "I think we should spend today going over this together. No doubt we each have our own slant on the ritual. It would be best if we shared our understanding of this stuff, just to make sure we don't botch it. I say we get to bed soon for a little rest, and then spend the day comparing notes."

"I think you're right. We can't screw this up! Besides, today is our last day. On Friday we've got to go back to Ben's place. And I don't think it's too intuitive on my part to say from that point on our tension levels will be off the scale. Sleep will be something we only remember, and the few remaining holds on reality will go by the wayside. But before we hit the sack, we'd better take a look outside."

Breach pulled the curtain drawstrings and turned on the hidden switch to the second story back porch light as he did the night before.

"I can't see a damn thing, can you?" he asked, the disgust in his voice seemed to trap his words in a cage of resurfaced fear. He opened the door to the porch, and stepped out.

"Come here, Frank," he said wearily. "You've got to see this!"

As Lewis stared out over the old cop's shoulder he wheezed, "What the! There's got to be at least six feet of snow down there, and it's still coming! Looks like Ben's prediction was right!"

"I'm afraid it was," Gus replied between chattering teeth. "Better get back inside. The temperature's dropping."

§§§

"Wake up! Wake up, Frank!" Breach called out as he shook Lewis by the shoulder. "It's three p.m.! Damn it! We were so exhausted we slept through most of the afternoon! I just got up a few minutes ago! If we don't get in gear now, we'll lose the last day and we can't do that! I'll make some coffee, toast and eggs while you get ready. Then it's down to work!

"Oh, in case you're wondering, the radio said the total snowfall so far is seventy-four inches, but it's tapering off. Maybe the Principle of Evil figures It has us where It wants us, because Ben's weather magic isn't supposed to start until sometime tonight. The old shrink just might catch Evil off guard after all. Just thought you should know," Gus said whimsically, testing his friend's determination and nerve.

"At least that's some good news," Lewis replied sleepily. "But the way I feel, the slightest glimmer of hope would look all out of proportion. Don't worry. You and Ben are right, and I've resigned to it. For some reason the three of us were thrown in this together to try to stop this madness. I'm OK. When the time comes, this old man will show everyone what he's made of. You can count on it!"

"That's the real Frank I've seen in the clutches during our battle with NightShadow," Breach said laughingly as he turned the corner of the guest room and made his way down the stairs to the kitchen. "That's the Frank we're all going to need before this is over!"

"So what do we have here?" Breach asked Lewis later as they entered the study and picked up the documents Yakov gave them. "I see this as a three-fold process. First, the Second Consecration of the Staff. Next, the actual ritual of the Final Summoning, since that has to be done to bring the bastard back to this world. And finally, the Final Return. I think we should take them one by one and deal with any specifics that come up."

"That's about as good a plan as any," Lewis replied uneasily. He made his way over to the window and opened the curtains.

"The first thing I noticed about the Second Consecration," Breach started, "is its simplicity. All it looks like Ben has to do is trace over the circles he has painted on the Temple floor with the Magical weapon the document called the 'Knife with the Black Handle,' and then do the same for all of those names and symbols inscribed in the inner circles. But I noticed he doesn't have to trace any figures in the air as he did when he showed us the staff. Then he has to—"

"Gus," Frank whispered from his position at the window. "Gus! Come here, quick! Look there, down in your backyard. Next to the garage. Are my eyes playing tricks on me or what?"

Breach strained his eyes to peer through the sheet of falling snow. Slowly, the outline of the garage at the end of the long backyard came into focus. "Yeah, so? What's the problem?"

"Look closely. Pick a spot on the left side of the building near the back corner and fix your attention on it. Then watch what happens in the area around it."

Breach did as instructed. As he stared, his eyes adjusted to the backdrop of falling snow. "What the!"

"Then you see it too?" Lewis asked quietly, as if they were secretly spying on the motion they both saw.

"Yeeaaa," Gus replied slowly, equally quiet. "Yeah, I see it! What the hell is it? It looks like a pink, bald head peeking in and out from behind the garage. It's got to be pretty big for us to make it out at this distance and through falling snow yet!"

"Not only that," Frank replied, pointing to an area just above the garage roof. "Look up there!"

"Smoke?" Breach said loudly. "Black smoke? Some son-of-a-bitch is setting my garage on fire? In this weather? What's going on here anyway! Don't we have enough trouble on our hands? Who the hell would do something like that? Quick, let's get him!"

As Breach turned away from the window and began running toward the door, Frank's arm shot out and collared him, pulling him back to the window. "No, Gus! Look! There they are! There's two of them!"

The two bewildered men stood spellbound as they watched two pink, hunched over, hairless forms race from their positions behind the garage out into the open snow.

"How the hell can they run on top of all that snow?" Frank asked. "Why don't they sink down in it? We would!"

"Never mind that! They're carrying torches!" Gus cried out, "and they're headed this way! Goddamn it, Frank, they're gonna set the house on fire! We don't have a second to lose!"

Without further words, they raced out of the study, through the guest room and down the stairs. Breach grabbed his service revolver from its holster, pegged on a coat rack at the bottom of the steps, and darted toward the back door. Frank skirted around him, grabbed the doorknob, and pulled hard. As the door flung open, Breach burst through the doorway and onto the back porch, looking for his targets. Before he could identify the enemy's position, the sound of crashing glass fell on the two men's ears.

"Fire!" Frank yelled. "In the kitchen and living room! They threw the torches through the windows! The house is on fire!"

As Frank puffed his warning out through the cold air, Breach saw one of the creatures in the snow, standing to the left of the kitchen window. His finger froze on the trigger as he stared into the huge thing's black eyes. Its pupils were filled with a red, burning madness. For a split instant, the cop felt the mania was being directed at him personally. Its hunched back; enormous hairless head with bleeding white fangs; thin and excessively long arms with claw-like appendages for fingers—all spoke of a living hate that crawled out of Hell itself to enter the world of men.

He sensed evil flowing from the creature in waves, like some black energy being directed toward him through an unseen lens. The old cop intuitively knew this abomination was one of the legions serving the conscious Principle of Evil. But there was something in the madness. Something dark and attractive began to weave its spell over him. Breach felt his eyes grow heavy, and a profound melancholy beginning to flow through him as he lowered his weapon. When his gun arm dropped, the thing in the snow moved toward the porch and the hypnotized man.

"It's no use!" Frank screamed out as he beat the flames in the kitchen with a blanket. "It's spreading too fast! Help me, Gus! I can't handle the kitchen and the living room myself! What the hell are you doing out there! Give me a hand or—"

As Lewis dropped the blanket and turned toward Breach, he saw his friend standing motionless on the porch, the hideous beast moving up the stairs toward him. It was now only a few feet away from its prey. Without thinking, Lewis ran through the doorway, wrapped his arms around the Chief, and sent the two of them crashing through the back porch railings, face down into the snow-drift below. The creature gave out a baleful howl as its victim was wrenched from its grasp.

The impact and shock of hitting the snow full face snapped Breach out of his trance. As he rolled around onto his back, his fingers locked around his revolver, its sights falling on the head of the monstrosity coming at them. Before his first shot rang out, the creature's companion sprang out from the side of the burning house, and leapt toward them. Volley after volley cracked through the winter air. All six lead projectiles ripped through the two descending fiends. Groans of searing agony mixed with the report of the weapon rang out, as the creatures slumped to the snow, kicking out their life force amid streams of black liquid flowing from their gaping mouths and wounds.

"Frank! Frank!" Breach shouted, as he shook a motionless Lewis. "Are you all right? Snap out of it!"

"Oooh," the mortician moaned, lifting his head from the snow pile. "What happened?"

"You just saved me from those things," Breach replied, exhausted. "The damn thing had me in its power. I felt like I was mesmerized, falling into some kind of black void filled with a sick yet somehow attractive peace, if that's the word for it. I tried to snap myself out of it but couldn't. I saw the thing coming at me, but I just didn't care. If it wasn't for you, I'd be a gonner right now. Thanks, my friend. I owe you one." He patted Lewis on the back.

"And I'll take you up on it if I have to," Frank replied slowly. "But for now, I think I snapped something in my neck. It's as stiff as all get out. Help me up, will you, I've got to work it out."

"My back's none too good either," Breach said softly. "Shouldn't complain though. The fall saved my life. Here, let me help you."

Breach pulled his friend up and walked him through the snow-drifts slowly, away from the house. The entire structure was now engulfed in flames. Sounds of creaking boards and collapsing floors shot through the still, early evening air, as the two men stood by helplessly.

"It's no good now," Gus said sadly. "The volunteer fire company will never get through the snow. The house is gone. A lifetime of things that meant something to me, burning up before my eyes. No homeowner's insurance can ever replace them."

Frank did not try to soothe his friend's despair. He knew Breach was right. As he rubbed his neck he muttered, "Another price extracted by this insanity. Where the hell will it end?"

"Splat, splat, splat-splat-splat-splat," with ever increasing frequency the new sound shook them out of their depression.

"Gus! It's starting to rain! Ben did it! He actually did it! Maybe there's hope for us yet!"

As he shouted, the rain turned into a downpour, soaking them and the burning building. Thick wisps of black smoke and the sound of fizzling wood snapped through the early night air.

Breach pulled Frank by his shirtsleeve. "Let's get out of here!"

"Where to?" Frank asked, as the downpour pounded their bodies hard.

"Only one place to go," Breach shouted through the near-solid curtain of rain now separating them. "To Ben's house! He may not be expecting us until tomorrow, but that's just too damn bad! We can't do anything here, and we've got to get to shelter fast! Damn! I never knew rain could hurt like this, it's coming down so hard! Besides, from the looks of it, this snow is going to be melting fast, and we're soaked now! If we don't get dry soon, we'll catch pneumonia! Or worse, we could drown in a quick melt, and we sure in the hell don't need either of those scenarios playing themselves out! This way! Two blocks down to 622 Pine Street!"

The two exhausted and injured men supported each other as they made their way through the rising water. Huge eight-foot drifts of snow melted on all sides of them instantly, as the downpour smashed into their sparsely clad bodies. Several times one of them lost his footing and fell into the rapidly forming streams, pulling the other down with him.

"We're halfway there!" Breach yelled through the pounding rain-storm. "We've got to keep going! Hang on tight! These currents could sweep us away if we lose grip on each other!"

"We should have grabbed our coats! But with everything hap-pening so fast and the fire spreading through the house, I guess we're lucky we escaped with our lives! Let's just keep going!"

Step after painful step passed, as they continued to struggle through the rising waters.

After they passed through another half-block, Breach yelled. "The temperature! It's getting colder! Looks like Ben upped his schedule! It's just starting to get dark, and he's bringing on the freeze now! Wasn't supposed to be until the night sometime! My God, what's happening! It's freezing!"

As he finished complaining, the surface beneath their feet began to turn into a hard layer of ice. Both men lost their footing, and careened into a remaining snowdrift.

"We're almost there! Another quarter-block! Keep going!"

Crawling over the frozen ice and snow, they continued to glide along, losing their balance several times and falling face down onto the ice sheet. Bruises matching those on other parts of their bodies began forming on their worn faces and arms.

Suddenly, between chattering teeth, Breach called out. "We're here! Let's get inside as quick as we can!"

Slipping and sliding, the two friends continued to crawl on all fours until they reached the back steps of Ben's home. Using the railings for support, they pulled themselves up the stairs, threw open the screen door, and battered the back door with their shoulders until the lock sprang and the door flew open. Once inside, Gus' hand fumbled along the wall for the light switch. A second later, the warm glow of the ceiling light greeted their eyes. Waves of warmth from the furnace flowed over their water-soaked, black-and-blue bodies, as they dropped themselves onto the kitchen chairs.

"I never knew heat could feel so good," Breach wheezed out, shaking. "I'll never complain about summer heat again!"

"Me too," Lewis replied weakly. "This has turned into a hell of a situation! I don't know if we can recover by tomorrow afternoon to be of any help to Ben."

"We've got no choice," Breach answered bitterly. "We're here now, safe and sound, with nothing else to do but to tend these battered old bodies, and rest. But remember. No heavy meals! Ben's warning to keep the physical body weak so the spiritual one remains strong is our only ace in the hole, and we have to keep to it! Besides, with what we were through, I don't think I could eat much anyway."

Frank shook his head in agreement, and the two men sat quietly for a few minutes.

"You know what's strange," the old cop finally said, "even though I feel physically done in, I somehow feel strong inside. Maybe that's what Ben was talking about. Maybe our spiritual selves are taking over!"

"Funny you say that. I feel the same way. I'm hungry, but not too much, and I'm feeling whole, inside. Guess Ben does know what he's talking about!"

"Yes I do," a voice emerging from the living room darkness said softly. "You're both right. And from the looks of the two of you, it makes perfect sense. You see, your physical bodies are weak, and your spiritual natures have taken over. You're deriving your strength and energy from spirit. That is what I wanted! That is what we need! And that's why, bruised and exhausted as you are, you must keep to your fast.

"Once the spiritual components of your nature gains a firm foothold, a peculiar type of strength will flood into your bodies. Your minds will begin to see the outside world anew, and you will view events from a very unusual perspective. But more than that, hidden knowledge will enter your minds at the right moment. Knowledge neither of you possesses right now. And that, my dear friends, is what could turn the tide of battle in our favor, to end this nightmare once and for all."

"Ben!" Gus and Frank shouted together as they jumped to their feet.

"I'm sorry, but we had to come early! We had no choice! We studied the documents you gave us through Tuesday and Wednesday, right up to this afternoon when—"

"I know, Gus, and I'm terribly sorry you lost your home. I 'saw' everything while I was in the astral working with the spirits of the Elements. That's why I brought the freeze on a little earlier than I originally planned. But it's all right. I think it will work out anyway. You see, the fact that the two qlippoth who were sent to destroy you both were themselves destroyed, threw a monkey wrench into the plans of the Principle of Evil. It was a daring gamble, and one that nearly paid off. That is, if it wasn't for Frank's sharp eye when he spotted the qlippoth from the study window, and his quick thinking when the one beast had you hypnotized!"

"In the astral? Spirits of the Elements? And…qlippoth? What are you talking about?" Frank broke in.

"The astral plane is another level of existence above this one. It's where all Magic is really done and where it works, you might say. In some rituals, it's necessary for the Magician to actually leave his physical body, enter that plane, and do his Magic there directly, so the results will come quickly. Otherwise, it may take repeated rituals and much more time for the realities he creates on that plane to come down to earth, so to speak—for them to materialize here in our everyday world.

"As to the Spirits of the Elements, there are spirits governing the realms of nature. These Elements include what you normally think of as air, fire, and the rest. But in reality, they are much, much more. They are universal principles that exist throughout all Creation, because in fact, all Creation—all matter and energy—are composed of them. Physics has many exotic names for the parts of their natures, from electrons and protons to gluons and quarks. But the essence of these particles are the Five Elements, namely, Spirit, Air, Fire, Water, and Earth.

"There are intelligences inhabiting these Elements. Think of them as conscious beings, lacking a body. A sort of intelligent energy existing everywhere throughout Creation, living in these Elements. Each of these Elements has a particular intelligence. Since it is of a given Element, it knows how to manipulate that Element. If the Magician knows how to call upon those intelligences, or Elementals, and lets them know his Will—not his wish—as to what he wants accomplished, he can enlist the aid of those intelligences to carry out that Will. That's what I did. The Elementals of Air and Fire were used to raise the temperature of the atmosphere to turn the snow into rain, while I called upon the Elementals of Water and Earth to bring on what I hope will be a very big freeze.

"You asked about the qlippoth. Ah!" Yakov continued, extending his right forefinger while raising his hand in the air. "That's a serious matter! The qlippoth are terrible creatures that inhabit what are called the shells—regions below Malkuth on the Tree of Life. A kind of Hell, as it were, but not the real thing. They are malignant beings responsible for so much of the world's ills. Drug addiction, alcoholism, spousal and child abuse, and much of the violence the world has known throughout time. They feed upon the weakness in people, and in the end, hurl them down to their final destruction. They delight in the final destruction of the person, bringing it about by the vice they encourage the person to indulge in to escape the very pain the vice causes. They can take physical form, and are utterly horrible as you saw."

As he spoke, creaks and cracks began echoing throughout the home.

"What's that?! It sounds like moaning, as if someone were in torment!" Frank shouted nervously.

"Don't worry," Yakov said calmly. "The big freeze has started. This is an old house. It's beginning to contract. There will be more of those sounds as the temperature drops."

"Uh, how low of a temperature are you talking about, Ben?" Breach asked, his rain-soaked body still shaking.

"Twenty degrees below zero," Yakov replied casually.

"Have you lost your mind?! We'll never get through the four miles to Saint Alacious in temperatures like that!"

Yakov gave a slight laugh and shook his head from side to side. "That's what I figured will be necessary to freeze the remaining snow after the downpour. These are only best guesses, mind you, but I figure the rain will melt the snow down to about three feet. That's all. It will pack tight from the rain, but we'd sink in it, unless it packs even tighter. What I'm counting on is for the sub-zero temperature to freeze that three-foot of snow rock-hard beneath its surface so we don't sink too deeply into it. But it will take time to achieve.

"Remember, the snow has to freeze from the top down, not from the bottom up. So the freeze should continue through tomorrow afternoon, when—if my Magic works right—the temperature will instantly shoot up to twenty-degrees above zero. The snow will still remain frozen solid underneath. But on top, it will start to melt, and become easy to walk on. If we're lucky, we'll only sink down about six inches or so, and be able to make our way to the cemetery. Now you know my reasoning, and what I've been up to."

"Walk four miles in twenty-degree above zero weather, through a frozen bed of snow?" Frank complained loudly. "Ben, we're old men, not kids! We're not going to make it!"

"Judging from the strength in your voice, Frank," Yakov replied, "I'd say your spiritual nature is getting stronger by the minute! I don't think you're going to have as much trouble doing what we have to as you think. That is, if you correct the 'think' part. No matter how strong your spiritual self becomes, if you allow your mind to wallow in dread, you'll be of no use to yourself, and less to us! Now what's it going to be?"

Ben's shaming worked. "Ok, Ben. Ok. You're right. I've got to get this fear under control. It's so hard at times. But I'll be all right."

"Yes, you will be," Yakov replied gently, yet firmly. "There is more in you than you allow to come through, Frank. Listen to me my friend! Trust in yourself and in what you know is right! The Principle of Good will aid you when you least expect it!"

"Let me get all of this straight," Breach cut in anxiously. "This freeze will go on to about what time Saturday?"

"No. That's changed too because I had to start my weather Magic early. I'm now hoping it continues to around four p.m. tomorrow… uh, Friday."

"So we're going to do the Second Consecration tomorrow night at midnight, during the first hour of the day of Saturday, as you said, because that's the sixth day of the seven day window in which Cavendish can be destroyed. And if I remember right, it's the hour ruled by Mars?"

The psychiatrist nodded in agreement. "Yes, as I told you, he cannot be destroyed on the seventh day. The Lord's day is forbidden. So if we don't succeed before the last stroke of the clock at midnight on Saturday and it turns into the Lord's Day, NightShadow will become immortal, join up with Stannish, and the eternal nightmare for all humankind and Creation itself will begin."

Breach looked at his host grimly and said, "How long will the Second Consecration take?"

"About two hours."

"What do we do until tomorrow night at midnight," Frank asked pointedly.

"And when do we leave for the cemetery?" Breach followed up.

"We rest as best we can both before and after the consecration. The two of you will be even weaker from the energy the ritual will take from you. Even though you'll only be observers, so to speak, it will be extremely demanding, especially since both of you are pretty weak right now. So gentlemen, rest and light food is called for between now and then. But as I said, your spiritual selves will become much stronger and will carry the both of you through this infernal business.

"As to when we leave for Saint Alacious? Around five Saturday afternoon, just as the sun begins to set. A good thaw will be on by then, even at twenty-degrees above zero. I figure we should be able to cover about three-quarters of a mile an hour. So with some luck, we should be able to get there in about five hours with frequent rests, give-or-take. That will put us in the cemetery about ten at night. It will take only minutes to summon NightShadow back to his grave, and the Final Return carried out."

"Cutting it kind of close, aren't we?" Breach asked, his doubt in Yakov's timing rising in his voice.

"Can't be helped. We were dealt these conditions by the Principle of Evil. It's the best plan I could come up with."

"Well, I guess it's the best plan we're going to get," Breach said, the doubt in his voice dropping.

"I guess so," Lewis added. "But it's the twenty degrees above zero that bothers me."

"Once we begin walking, and with the warm clothes I'll supply, we'll be all right. It's like anything else. Once you start, you get use to what you're doing, and you just keep on going. It's human nature. In the meantime, you two better make your way upstairs. Take a warm, not hot, bath. Otherwise your bodies will go into cellular shock and you'll be laid up for days. Then Cavendish wins, without so much as the slightest opposition from us. Remember. Both of you were thrown into the picture for a reason. What that is, I don't know. But without both of you, I am certain I can't send Cavendish back alone. Go ahead now and clean yourselves. You'll find plenty of fresh clothing in my closets. Pick out what you like. When you are ready, rejoin me down here and we'll have a meal and relax. It's going to be a long night."

§§§

The second hand of the clock above the sink struck eight-thirty p.m. as Breach and Lewis walked hurriedly into Yakov's kitchen, drawn by the aroma of fresh cooked food.

"Man, what is that heavenly smell?" Breach roared out. "I haven't smelled anything that good in all of my sixty years! What are you cooking Ben?"

"It's amazing how the human mind reframes the simplest of things when it's under dire stress," Yakov replied, his psychiatrist's fascination with the human mind coming to the surface. "Everything is 'better.' The taste of simple food, the odor of toast, a beam of moonlight reflecting off a still pond of water—whatever the senses come into contact with. It's a return to the innocence of childhood I tell you! It never ceases to amaze me!"

"Yeah, fine," Frank added, "but what are you making for dinner? I'm starved and could eat a, a…"

"A light meal?" Yakov laughed back.

"Yeah, that's about it," the mortician answered gloomily. "For a minute I forgot."

"Well, cheer up! We have fresh garden salad, several types of dressing, scrambled and sunnyside up eggs, fried potatoes and onions, and skim milk. A feast if ever I saw one!" Yakov replied in a teasing voice. "Come and get it!"

An hour later the three men moved into the parlor. Breach patted his stomach as he and Lewis sat down in the same chairs they did two days earlier. "That was a very good dinner, Ben, thank you! I really needed it!"

"The same for me too Ben," Frank added. "It's been a very tough day."

Yakov did not sit down, but paced the center of the floor in front of his two guests.

"Is something bothering you?" Breach asked as he leaned forward in his chair.

"Something is not right," Yakov replied softly. "I'm sensing something, but I can't put my finger on it."

"What do you mean, sensing something?" Frank asked as he nervously slid across the seat of his chair.

"Magical development not only opens and evolves the spiritual faculties, but the psychic ones as well. Unless you learn how to block things out, you become like a radio receiver with a tuner set to all frequencies at once. Nothing but gibberish will result, and you'll burn out mentally and emotionally in no time flat. At other times, like now, you use the psychic faculties to 'tune in' to certain frequencies. You're actually making sense out of different impressions your senses—both physical and nonphysical—are picking up. It's another way of gaining knowledge and insight into the world around you. I'm picking up something that feels like runaway panic. And it's not coming from any of us. But there is a danger connected to the panic."

As he spoke, his eyes became transfixed, staring off into deep space, as if he was making mental contact with the source of the panic and danger. "Yeessss," he said, drawing the word out, like puffing out a ring of smoke. "Yeessss. There is more here, much, much more. There's hate. A blind, mindless hate breaking through the panic and—" He broke off in mid-sentence as he eyes refocused on his guests. "Quick! Get down to the cellar now! Into the Temple! There's not a second to—"

Yakov's last word died in midair, as wailings filled the home and furious pounding started at the front and back doors.

"Hurry!" Yakov cried, as he darted toward the small alcove leading to the basement door. Frank and Gus jumped from their chairs and ran with him. "The danger is to us! They'll be inside the house any second!"

"Who?" Frank screamed, as they made their way down the short flight of steps.

"The qlippoth! There must be hundreds of them! Their hate is as black as death, and they mean to kill us!"

Yakov paused for a split second at the Temple door, bowed his head, and made some gestures with his hands in front of it before pulling it open. As he did, the sound of hundreds of feet racing through the floors overhead fell upon the terrified men's ears.

"Get inside!" Yakov yelled. "Hurry, hurry!" he shouted as he pushed Frank and Gus into the Temple.

As the aged Magician started to pull the door of his House of Worship closed, a reddish-orange arm dripping a clear slime-like substance shot through the opening and grabbed Yakov's arm.

"Give me a hand!" Yakov shouted. "It's got me! It's trying to pull me out! After it kills me, the Temple won't be sacred any longer! Then they get to you two! Aaagghhh! It bit me!!"

Before Breach and Lewis could get to their friend's side, the fiend on the other side of the door bit again, and again, and again, making a loud chewing and slurping sound as it ate.

"Oh my God!" Yakov screamed out, "it's devouring my flesh!"

Cry after cry shot out from the Magician's twisted mouth. His tortured features threw his two allies into blind hysteria. Without thinking, Lewis tugged at Yakov's waist, pulling the malformed head of the beast through the door opening. As the head entered the doorway, Breach tore his revolver from his belt and smashed it against the qlippoth's skull as hard and as fast as he could.

"Here you little fucker!" the old cop screamed. "See how you like pain! Let's see just how thick that fucking skull of yours is!"

Breach shoved Frank out of the way, and pounded furiously on the fiend's head as others of the creature's kind poured down the stairs and began pulling at the Temple door. Finally the creature's skull split in two, exposing a green mass serving as its brain. A greenish-yellow pus-like liquid oozed from the monstrosity's open skull and dripped over Breach's revolver and hand as it squealed and fell to the floor, blocking the Temple door open. As the qlippoth kicked out its life, Yakov fell against the doorframe, unable to pull himself back into the Temple. Without thinking, Breach grabbed him by the shoulder, and with one motion flung him backward into the Temple.

"Shut the door! For God's sake, Gus, shut…the…door!" Frank screamed, the terror in his voice causing his words to trail off into nothingness.

"I can't! There's too many of them! They've got too good a grip on it!" As he yelled, several arm-like appendages of different colors with razor-sharp, ebony-like claws sliced across the door opening, poking, gouging, and ripping at Breach's body. Blow after blow fell on the right side of his body. As blood began to soak through his shirt, the Chief of Police screamed at his assailants. "Enough! You want war, you little pigs? Then that's what you got!"

To Frank's and Yakov's surprise, Breach pushed with all of his strength in the direction the qlippoth were pulling. The Temple door exploded outward, knocking its attackers backwards onto the floor and against the walls of the cellar's middle room. In an instant, Breach burst out of the Temple to face the enemy. As he emerged into the room, neither his mind nor eyes could grasp the reality he faced. Yet in some unknown way, the filth of them did not terrify him. With a grim expression, he started coldly at the fiends. Without conscious thought, Breach stretched his arms out forming a cross, and began speaking in an unknown tongue, vibrating words he did not understand.

As Frank eased the wounded psychiatrist down to the Temple floor, he whispered to Yakov. He did not want to attract the attention of the horrors Gus was now facing on the other side of the open door. "What is he doing? What are those sounds he's making?"

Yakov smiled through the searing pain shooting through his body and replied weakly, "The time has come when the fasting brings the spiritual nature to the fore. That nature will gain a firm foothold, and a peculiar type of strength will flood into your bodies, as has happened when Gus smashed through the door. His mind now sees the world differently, even accepting the horrors the eyes are beholding. To him, the outside world is new and strange, yet understandable, because he views it from a very unusual perspective. He is not just Gus Breach anymore. He has temporarily become a hybrid. He is now an angel of God existing in a mortal man's body.

"Those 'sounds' he is uttering to the beasts now locked in the room with him, are the dawning of the Hidden knowledge I told you would enter your minds at the right moment. This is knowledge neither of you possesses ordinarily, but such knowledge could turn the tide of battle in our favor. That's what is happening! Listen to him! Those are not sounds, Frank! They are words from the Enochian language. The language of the angels themselves. The language given them by God Itself."

As Yakov spoke, a horrendous wailing and screaming broke through to the two men huddled on the Temple floor.

"What is that?" Frank asked, panic rising in him.

"Gus is not simply speaking to them in the Enochian tongue. He is not aware of it, but he is pronouncing what is referred to as the 'Barbarous Words of Evocation.' Powerful, secret words that strike terror in all such things as are standing in front of him now. But it gets better. Listen to the strangeness of the words! He is now reciting to them some of the Enochian Keys. They are verses of prayers given Man by the angels themselves. Prayers that declare the power and justice of God throughout Its entire Creation, on all planes of existence. I imagine at this very moment many of the fiends are dying.

"Those prayers and Barbarous Words further divide their already divided natures, until they can no longer remain in physical form in the world of men, their pain at hearing such pronouncements is that great. You see, not only are they being reminded of God's rule over Its Creation and of their own fragmented natures, but they do not see Gus Breach, the local Chief of Police, speaking those terrible words. No. What they see is a mighty angel standing in their midst, reciting the Enochian Keys, or Calls, who is armed by God, and sent to destroy them. At least, those now cornered in that small room with the great Angel."

"You mean to tell me Gus is now some kind of angel?" Frank asked in disbelief.

"No, of course not!" Yakov snapped back. "Didn't you hear what I said? He's entered a spiritual state that cannot be mimicked, but only brought about in high ritual Magic, or else spontaneously, when the danger is great and the spiritual nature overtakes the weakened human body, a body weakened by purposeful fasting. He has become a hybrid for the moment only! Part angel, part man! It's the angel you hear out there, acting through him and commanding through his voice!"

As he spoke to Frank inside the Temple, guttural sounds mimicking human-like words begging for mercy coursed through the screams and wailing. Breach's mind had turned inside out. He was no longer an old cop whose right side and arm were bleeding badly from the attack of the qlippoth a few minutes ago. He was now looking through a glowing, white-silver sheen, with an identity he did not understand. A feeling of sanctity flowed through his veins, as an image of a terrible avenging angel rooted itself in his soul. He knew this was an angel come to destroy the living malignancies in front of him.

As the avenging angel continued to speak, the harsh voice changed its tone. Now it was a flowing, melodic voice, and ecstasy shot through the man-angel hybrid, saturating the words of power flowing from his mouth. The angel had entered into the most dreaded of all of the Keys, calling upon God Itself to destroy the evil in front of him.

The divine being took no notice of the forms the monstrosities took. It did not notice the round, fat blobs that shook like jelly as they raced from wall to wall on spindle legs, the single eye in the middle of their gross bodies popping in and out of its black socket. Nor did the angel now working through Breach's mind and body see the short, trumpet-shaped pink forms with three eyes set below rows of gnashing, yellow fangs. The angel's nature was too exalted to allow the eyes that beheld the God of Creation to acknowledge the green and yellow freaks with bloated legs and rail-thin carcasses clawing at the air with blood-soaked talons, or the gaping mouths floating through the air, their ravenous teeth biting their own lips, trying to devour themselves. The bedlam of other forms screeching, tearing at the walls, trying to claw through the stone foundation of the house to escape, all went unnoticed by the divine being.

As it continued to pronounce the Barbarous Words and Calls through the body of the Chief of Police, the two-odd-dozen qlippoth trapped in the middle room with the being of light began to die. Some reeled backward, falling to the floor, kicking and thrashing as their sick lives ended. Others screamed, making guttural noises and howling as they put their paws over their ears, hemorrhaging from the mouth and eyes before dropping to the floor, lifeless. The terrors clawing at the walls trying to escape smashed their malformed heads against the stone surface until their skulls split, their lifeless forms dropping to the cement floor, while the remaining fiends fled to the corners of the room, tearing their stomachs and throats open, killing themselves.

Suddenly a hush fell throughout the cellar and upper floors, as a bleeding Gus Breach walked slowly back into the Temple, closing the door quietly behind him. "It's over," he said to the two men sitting on the Temple floor. "All of the qlippoth that tried to break in here are dead. Are you two all right?"

"Ben is done up pretty bad, but I'm ok," Frank replied. "What about you? Are you all right, Gus?"

"I feel strange. Like I'm 'more' than me but becoming 'less,' if that makes sense," Breach said, shaking his head from side to side.

"That's normal," Yakov said weakly. "You temporarily merged with your own angel—your Guardian Angel as the Christian religion calls it—and the connection is fading. That's how it works. The fast brought it on. Now you know why I was so insistent upon our fasting. When the physical body becomes weak and the spiritual nature becomes strong and great danger arises, such an event as the one you experienced happens. But it doesn't always happen the way you experienced it.

"The declaration of your own spiritual nature can take many, many forms. This brief merging with your angel is only one such form. All we can count on is that 'something' will happen. Then it's up to us to be alert enough to feel it happening and direct it, or as in this case, just let it happen. That's the uncertainty in these things, but that's just the way it is. Do both of you understand?"

"I think so," Breach replied in a dreamy way. "But I still feel strange."

"I understand." Frank answered. "Be alert for anything from the spiritual side, and either use it as best we can, or just go along with it."

"Yes." Yakov confirmed. "Do whatever feels right when your spiritual side kicks in, and leave it at that."

"What the...?" Frank shouted, as the sound of a hundred pounding feet once more began over their heads. "They're back! The qlippoth! The ones Gus killed in the other room were only a handful! His words drove the others upstairs off, but only for a short time! They were able to escape! Do you think they know what happened to their pals down here?"

"Certainly they know!" Yakov replied. "In the spiritual realms—whether of the Principle of Good or Evil—the natures of the beings of those worlds are connected. Oh, they know all right, and the ones upstairs are glad they weren't caught down here with an avenging angel where there was no escape! But now the ones upstairs will reap havoc throughout the night. Noise-wise, I mean. That pounding, screaming, grunting, and growling will continue until the first light of day. Then they must return to the places they know best, the dark corners and shadows cast off by the light, just as they were cast off by both God and man.

"You see, when I sensed their presence and rushed us down here, I knew the attack was on. I knew we'd have to lock ourselves in the Temple. It's the only place they can't get at us, provided we seal ourselves inside."

"But they tried to pull the door open!" Frank objected. "I thought you said nothing can come into this holy place unless you invite in?"

"They weren't trying to come in here," Yakov replied. "They were trying to pull us out! They knew that if they got the door open, at least one of us would have fallen into their grasp, and the others would have followed to help him. They knew they could count on us to help each other. Let me tell you, those things up there know the ways of human nature better than most people do! They wanted to get us out there. Not to come in here. That they can never do!"

"You're very quiet, Gus," Frank said as he turned his attention from Yakov.

"I'm all right. Just give me a few minutes. I still feel kind of strange."

"Leave him alone!" Yakov snapped. "The connection between him and his angel is fading. It's a delicate time for him, psychologically and physically. Leave him be. He'll be back to himself in a little while. In the meantime I suggest we tend our wounds. Mine are worst, but those gashes on Gus' right arm and side look pretty bad. Here, Frank, help me up!"

"How are we going to clean and dress the wounds?" Frank asked. "You don't have any water or antibiotic creams or even peroxide down here, do you?"

"There is more in this Temple than you might think. Help me over to the closet."

Frank pulled the older man up gently from the floor and walked him over to the north wall of the Temple. After Yakov applied some pressure to the wall's seamless surface, a crack appeared, giving way to a narrow panel that sprung open. The Magician removed two box-like brass containers, a brass vessel shaped like an oversized bottle, a large brass basin, and a length of white cloth. He placed everything on the altar.

Removing a small knife from his pocket, Yakov turned to Lewis, handed him the knife, and pointed to the cloth. "This is clean white linen. I always keep plenty on hand because it is frequently needed in Magic. It's as close to sterile as we're going to get. Start cutting! We're going to need plenty of bandages!"

As Lewis cut the cloth into strips, Yakov used his left hand to mix powders from two of the containers, and poured fresh water from the vessel into the basin.

"What are you doing?" Breach said, breaking his self-imposed silence.

"We're about to tend our wounds. These powders are ground myrrh and frankincense. It's not generally known today, but frankincense is a powerful antiseptic, and myrrh produces a paste that tends to rapidly seal and heal open wounds. Put them together, and we have a very potent first aid concoction."

"Yeah, but what about rabies!" Frank asked nervously. "Those things out there are from some kind of Hell. Can't we get a disease from their bites and gashes?"

"The only thing those creatures can pass on to humans are moral and spiritual diseases, not physical ones," Yakov replied in a matter-of-fact tone. "More so, our actions are immune to that type of sickness. No, we're more likely to get an infection from the germs on our own skin working their way into our bloodstream through the wounds, than from the qlippoth, hence this little medical treatment of mine. It's going to hurt, though. I've used it before."

"Moral and spiritual diseases!" Frank complained. "What about almost tearing us apart! If they only cause those types of disease, how the hell come they tried to kill us outright?!"

"This is the great gambit I told you about. This game is for all of the marbles, for domination over the entire universe—over all of Creation—by the Principle of Evil. I didn't go into it when I first spoke about it because I saw no reason to. Both of you had enough to contend with just trying to accept the contents of the documents I gave you to study. But you might as well know now, after the events of this night.

"This is not the first attempt the Principle of Evil has made to gain dominion over Creation. There have been others throughout time. I discovered them in ancient manuscripts I came across in my research. All of those attempts failed. Yet in those attempts, some of the normal laws of Magic were suspended, as they are now. One of those laws is the inability of the qlippoth to kill human beings outright. Thus their attempts to destroy us tonight."

"But it's not over!" Frank yelled loudly, as the poundings on the floors above them increased, with howls, yelps, grunts and moans added. "Just listen to them! If they can't get at us in this room but they can still kill us, it doesn't take a rocket scientist to figure out all they need to do is set the house on fire like before! We'll burn to death down here! Or they could flood the cellar, and we'd drown like rats! Look you two! We've got to get out now! There must be a better way! We can't think clearly bottled up here! But once we're out and in the open, we'll be able to get our thoughts together and save ourselves for the big fight in the cemetery! It's our only chance!"

As Frank's anxiety reached panic level, he raced toward the Temple door, grabbed the handle and tried to turn it. At that instant, a strong hand closed on his right shoulder and spun him around. The wounded cop caught his panicked friend square in the jaw with his clenched left fist, sending Lewis crashing to the floor. He lay motionless for a few seconds, sobbing, his head bent toward the floor. Neither Yakov nor Breach said anything, but waited until their friend composed himself.

"I'm all right now," Frank muttered, shame forcing his words out. "I swear that's the last time I'll lose it. I'm fed up with fear and being the weak link in our small chain! Hear me! From this point on, I would rather die than let it overtake me again!"

"Now whose spiritual nature is taking over?" Yakov said kindly. "It works that way, Frank. It takes different events and different times for each individual before their God-like nature takes over. I think you'll be just fine now. Just don't beat yourself up over this! Consider it part of the process you had to pass through to reach the point you're at now. Because in truth my friend, that's the way it works! Here now! Let's get our wounds tended and dressed."

Frank helped them with the painful first aid work. After smearing the frankincense-myrrh paste into their wounds, he wrapped Ben's right arm tightly with several layers of white linen, and then did the same for Gus' right arm and side.

"You two going to be ok?" he asked, almost lightheartedly.

"The arm is stiff and will remain so for days," Yakov said in a disgusted tone of voice. "But that's the way it'll have to be. I have some flexibility in the fingers though, and that's important for the Second Consecration. I guess I should be thankful after all."

"Yes!" Frank replied with the energy of his newfound spiritual strength and courage.

"Same here," Breach said with a grunt. "This wrapping is so tight, if I didn't know better I'd think you were trying to mend a set of broken ribs!"

"Couldn't be helped. The pressure is needed to make sure the paste holds firm and the bleeding doesn't start again. Now look whose complaining!" Frank said with a laugh.

"During your panic attack you brought something up, Frank," Yakov said, cutting through Lewis' laugh. "Something I think both of you should understand a little better. As I said, under normal circumstances the qlippoth cannot physically kill a human being. Instead, they latch onto the person's weaknesses and accelerate it so that the person spirals down into moral and spiritual decay. Normally, the qlippoth cannot use the Elements to bring about destruction either. Burning the house down or drowning us is not possible, normally. But under these special circumstances—Evil trying to take control of Creation—it would be a fair question to ask if this normal inability of the qlippoth to use the Elements has changed.

"Let me put it another way. If some of the normal laws of Magic are temporarily suspended during this latest siege by the Principle of Evil, could it be the qlippoth could now use the Elements to destroy us? The answer is yes! I found this out when I was working my weather Magic on the astral plane. When I discovered this condition, I was successful in attaining an accelerated degree of my own. It is called 'Divine presence of self' on the astral plane. Just as happened to Gus, I attained union, but not with my guardian angel. It was with each of the four great Archangels ruling the Elements of Fire, Air, Water, and Earth.

"While I was in that state, something else happened that at best occurs only once in a lifetime for the fortunate few. I touched the part of the Living God within me, what the Jewish Kabbalah and the Qabalah of Western Magic calls the 'Yechidah.' In that instant of 'no time,' my will that the qlippoth not be able to use the Elements to destroy us or any other human beings was made fact again, because it was the Yechidah Itself commanding it. In other words, the normal law of Magic that the qlippoth be unable to use the Elements was re-instituted, even during this time of Evil's latest siege.

"I was not quick enough to save Gus' home. How I wish I could have. That's why the fiends were able to use ordinary fire to burn it down. They could use of the Element of Fire and the other three Elements before I united with my Yechidah. Now, all is as before. For them, the Elements will refuse their attempts to use them. For the qlippoth, Fire will not burn, Air will not move, Water will not flow, and Earth will remain fixed. Thus, they cannot set this house on fire, they can't flood it, they can't summon a hurricane to destroy it, nor can they call up an earthquake to topple it. All they can do is what they are doing now—make a lot of noise to frighten us. And of course, kill us physically if they get their hands on us. Aside from that, they have no power."

"Aside from that!" Breach said wryly. "Isn't that enough? Haven't you considered the entire picture, Ben? What if those bastards should fall on us as we attempt to get to the cemetery? You said it yourself. They can kill us! What are we going to do to kill them? We have no weapons! I expended the six rounds in my revolver killing the two that attacked Frank and me! I have no more ammo! Don't forget, we had to leave my burning house with just the clothes on our backs. I couldn't go back inside to get more munitions if I wanted to! Besides that, we have four miles of mountain paths to travel, through the remains of the biggest blizzard to ever hit these parts, not to mention the ice-over you created! Now add that we'll be trying to make our way to Saint Alacious in bitter cold weather, carrying who knows what, at our ages, and maybe you can see my point! Ben, we have a huge problem on our hands! Didn't you consider all of these things, or am I losing my courage now?"

"No, you're not losing your courage, Gus," Yakov replied calmly. "I was going to explain all of this to the both of you tomorrow when you arrived here at noontime. But seeing we had a forced change of plans thanks to those fiends up there, now's as good a time as any to answer your questions. They are completely understandable.

"I have been doing more than weather Magic over the past two days. Much more. I was preparing for the eventualities you mentioned. And yes, to prepare, I was working on the astral plane exclusively, so the results of my willed creations would manifest in our world quickly. I'll go into that in a moment. But first of all, I want you to understand you do not 'kill' a qlippoth. Not in the usual sense of the word. All you did with your revolver was to destroy the form it created to enter our world. After that form was destroyed, its essence—the malignancy that is the qlippoth—simply returned to the shells.

"Those creatures are eternal, because the vices and sickness within men are eternal. Those vices are actually universal principles that pay allegiance to the Principle of Evil, and so they can never be destroyed. Except, except for those you destroyed when you united with the angel out in the middle room. Those pieces of the evil they represented were forever removed from existence—even from their existence in the shells below Malkuth. It's like putting a hole in a container at a certain point. No matter how much new liquid, or more of that evil principle you add to the container, it will only hold what can fit below the hole. So in fact, you have deprived the very Principle of Evil of some of its power—only a tiny amount to be sure—but some of its power nevertheless, and for all time.

"The problem is, as a human being you can't remain in an exalted state of union with your angel to do more of the same. If you did—if you were able to—your body would give out, and you would die. The enormous amount of energy the body must contain during the state is so great, your physical self would literally burn up. It's as simple as that. Besides, as I told you, the declaration of your spiritual nature can and will take many forms. It won't always happen the way it did out in the other room. Even the most advanced Magician can't achieve that state. That is, not until he undergoes something which I haven't undergone yet. So where do we stand?

"When I was working on the astral and touching my own Yechidah, I contacted the Spirit of Death and questioned it. It told me many things. One of the things it told me was when the Staff of Resurrection or Return is brought to life during the Second Conse-cration, the qlippoth will flee back to the shells and remain there. Not even the conscious Principle of Evil can force them to return to our world, so great is their terror of the 'Final Death,' as they name it.

"You see, Gus, those few you destroyed in the other room underwent Final Death. It is the thing they fear the most, as does the Principle of Evil. If the Principle of Evil would force the qlippoth to enter our world again after the Staff is brought to life, the Staff's very presence in our world would instantly destroy all qlippoth for all time, and evil would lose its most valuable soldiers. In losing them, it would create an everlasting imbalance in the eternal struggle between Good and Evil, tipping the scales of the universe toward Good for all time. Evil itself would then 'die,' having literally destroyed itself. That's why it won't try to force the qlippoth back to this world after the staff is brought to life. If it did, it would be signing its own death warrant, and its very nature prevents it from doing that.

"It's a circular argument for evil. It simply can't be done. To conclude, gentlemen, the only thing those insanities above us can do throughout this night and tomorrow night is to try and terrify us with their antics. Nothing more. When the staff is brought to life on Saturday, the day of death itself, during the first hour of that day which is ruled by Mars—the god of bloodshed, war and slaughter—

those things carrying on above us now will fly back to the shells in 'no time' at all. They simply cannot endure in a world in which the Staff has been brought to life. During those times, humankind is temporarily free from those monstrosities. That's how it works."

"But what of the other staffs? The one Cavendish used to bring Stannish back, and the other one Shannon used to resurrect Cavendish?" Frank asked calmly. "Do you mean to say the qlippoth stopped bothering mankind during those times too?"

"That's a very good question, and the answer is yes. But the staff is 'alive' for only for a very short period of time, just long enough for the corpse to be resurrected or returned. After that, if you read the documents I gave you carefully, the life of the staff returns to the realm of death. Then the qlippoth that plague humans will return and begin their business all over again. It's all part of the suspension of some of the laws of Magic. Like daily life, Magic is a very complicated matter, but still, a very real one. Now I suggest we bed down as best as we can, and wait for sunrise."

"When will that be?" Gus asked. "I seemed to have lost some everyday knowledge in all of this."

"That's normal. You're still coming down to being Gus again. You'll be all right. Sunrise is around 7:30. We have a long night ahead."

The trio huddled in the southeast corner of the Temple throughout the night in total darkness. The fiends had cut the electricity off. As they listened, the roar of a hundred pounding feet above their heads continued. Moans, growls, and long howls added to the fury of the rampage, broken only by the sound of heavy thuds.

"They're tearing my home up," Yakov said gloomily at one point. "That's one thing I couldn't stop." Intermittent banging on the door of the Temple brought Gus and Frank to their feet several times, even though Yakov assured them the beasts could not break through. "It's of no matter. The Temple is sealed from all evil, as I told you before. Even if they broke through the physical door, they cannot enter this holy place."

As the hours passed, the men became use to the thundering noise above their heads, and finally dropped off to sleep. Suddenly a gentle voice and soft tap on their shoulders awakened them. "Time to get up," Yakov said softly. It's 8:00 a.m."

As Breach and Lewis stood up, the sound of complete silence in the rooms above them greeted their senses. "Are you sure it's safe to go out?" Gus asked.

"Quite sure," Yakov replied. "Besides. What are we to do? Remain in here throughout the day? No, they're gone. Back to the shadows and dark places of the earth. The light of the sun burns them as fire burns us. Let's go upstairs and evaluate the damage."

As the three men emerged from the alcove on the first floor Yakov raised his voice. "Damn it! They didn't leave much for us, did they?"

Everywhere they looked, destruction met their eyes. Furniture was slashed through and the matting pulled out and strewn throughout the house. Mirrors were shattered, tables splintered, lamps smashed into small pieces, wall ornaments pushed into the walls, while the walls themselves displayed thousands of huge claw and gouge marks.

"No, they sure didn't," Breach replied slowly. "I'm really sorry, Ben. Looks like you'll have a massive repair job on your hands when all of this is over."

"Let's send Cavendish back to his grave first," the psychiatrist replied angrily. "Then it will almost be a pleasure to deal with something like this! Let's get cleaned up. I'll see if there's any food left. If there is, we can have some breakfast."

"Look at this!" Frank said excitedly as he looked through the living room window. "It's like a palace of glass out there! By the way, Ben, can you turn up the heat? It's freezing in here! That is, if you still have a thermostat!"

"I'm afraid the thermostat is gone," Yakov replied as he joined Breach and Lewis at the window. "We'll have to make do with the temperature we have."

As he stared out the window, his sullen mood lifted. "The big freeze is working!" he said in a triumphant voice. "Look at the house over there! It's actually encased in a solid sheet of ice! One continuous sheet! Even the windows are frozen over! And look at the snowline! The downpour must have melted two-thirds of it! I'll bet there's not more than two to two-and-a-half feet of snow out there, packed down tight, frozen right through! Gentlemen, when it starts to warm up this afternoon, by tomorrow we'll have a surface to walk on, as I promised! After seeing the drop in the snow level, I'll bet you a dime to a doughnut we'll sink down a couple of inches at most, and have real traction to boot! We have a fighting chance after all!"

"But until then," Breach cut in, "how about we get cleaned up, put some more clothes on to keep warm, and get something to eat, if that's possible. God, I'm hungry!"

"You two go upstairs and tend to yourselves. I'll clean up down here and nurse my wounds. I can feel the frankincense-myrrh combination working. Then I'll see what I can find for us to eat."

When Frank and Gus rejoined Yakov in the kitchen an hour later, he was busy opening a can. Without turning to his guests he said, "This is all that's left. A loaf of bread, those three cans on the table, and this one. As you can see from the mess around here, the fiends gorged themselves on just about everything I had in the larder. They also emptied the refrigerator, and the gas lines to the stove are out too. So this will have to be a cold meal. Our 'last supper' together, you might say. By the way, the telephone is out. Not that anyone could help us, but, well, we are completely on our own."

As Breach and Lewis made their way to the kitchen table through the debris of half-eaten food, empty cans and smashed glasses scattered over the floor and ground into the walls, Frank said matter-of-factly, "We should be grateful for what we have! Imagine if they left us nothing! I'll say Grace."

Yakov and Breach looked at each other in amazement. Both men suddenly realized the transformation their friend went through in the Temple the night before was a lasting one. His fear and ignoble ways had permanently departed from him.

As the three comrades reached for the food Frank said, "Tuna, baked beans, potato slices, and pearl onions. And the bread! Not bad, men. Not bad at all!"

"Ah, come on," Breach whined, "stop that happy shit will ya Frank? This 'last supper' is not what I had in mind for what could be my last meal on this earth! Get serious!"

"Why?" Lewis replied, as a great smile broke out over his small, round face. "If this is our last supper together because some of us or all of us get killed over the next day or so, then we'd better make the most of it! Because where the three of us are headed to after this life, guys, a meal like this is going look like a feast!" Frank's lighthearted attitude shattered the cold misgivings the three shared over the upcoming events. All three started to laugh loudly, toasting each other with their paper cups filled with tap water, and began their final meal together.

"I suggest we try to get some real sleep," Yakov said when they were finished. "Find whatever is left of the beds upstairs and make yourselves as comfortable as possible. I'm going to rest down here. It's 10:30 now. I'll wake you at four p.m. Then we'll gather up what we need, go back down to the Temple, and lock ourselves inside before the sun sets. We were lucky yesterday. They came late. We won't be today! You can be sure the qlippoth will be back here when the first rays of the sun quit."

"What time will the sun set today?" Frank asked.

"A little after five," Yakov replied, "but an hour should be all we need to get prepared."

"Once we're secured inside, we'll wait for the last stroke of midnight. Then it will be Saturday, and the hour ruled by Mars will be in force. That, my friends, is when we can start the Second Consecration of the Staff."

▼

CHAPTER TEN

THE SUMMONING

"It's four o'clock!" Yakov called out from the bottom of the stairs. "Let's rise and shine, men! We've got work to do!"

"How did you two sleep?" he asked Breach and Lewis when they joined him in what remained of his parlor.

"Not very well," Breach answered surly. "Sort of off and on. I couldn't get what we have to do out of my mind. But I was pretty comfortable, Ben, so I probably rested better than I think."

"That's about the size of it for me too," Frank added. "It could have been a lot better, but still, I feel ok."

"You're both right," Yakov replied. "I have to admit, the two of you are handling the inevitable anxiety connected with our situation like champs! I keep using my knowledge of psychoanalysis to keep my anxieties in check. But you two are amazing! You're doing it without the knowledge and training! Makes me proud to be up against this problem with the two of you!"

Breach saw through Ben's attempt to make them feel special in this critical hour. Although he lacked formal training in the psychological sciences, he nevertheless understood human nature from his years on the police force. He smiled warmly to Yakov, but said nothing.

"Here!" Yakov went on, handing Breach and Lewis some soiled bread and an open tin of kippers. "I found these under the port-a-dolly in the kitchen. I ate my portion earlier. Better get it down fast, because we have to get going!"

As they gulped down their food, Yakov walked over to the window in the living room and motioned for them to join him.

"Look!" he said excitedly. "Just look! The thaw has started! The temperature is rising!"

As Gus and Frank peered out of the window through the rapidly fading sunlight, they saw the house previously covered in ice.

"Unbelievable! Look at it!" Frank said joyfully. "The ice is falling off in huge chunks! I've never seen anything like it before!"

"I have," Gus said. "Once in Pittsburgh, years ago. We had a bitter freeze, and then for some reason a really fast rise in temperature. Everything thawed out almost instantly. I forgot about it until now. I have to tell you though, I never thought I'd see anything like it again!"

"We're on target," Yakov said happily. "Let's get to work! Get three mattresses, pillows, blankets, and a couple boxes of matches. I'll get a hurricane lamp I filled with kerosene just the other day. At least we won't have to spend the time before the Second Consecration in total darkness like we did last night! Oh. I have two flashlights and some spare batteries. I'll bring them too, just in case!"

At four forty-five p.m., as the sun was sinking fast toward the western horizon, Yakov closed the Temple door and sealed it.

"We'll be ok now," he said to his two companions. "Better put the mattresses in the corner where we slept last night. It's furthest from the door. Psychologically, that may be important when they start carrying on again. I'll set up the hurricane lamp."

"What time do you have?" Breach asked Yakov a few minutes later.

"Five-fifteen. I bet it's going to start any—"

The final words of his sentence fell into silence as the madness of the previous night began to repeat itself. Screams, moans, grunts, growls, and pounding began again in the rooms over their heads.

"Damn!" Breach whispered. "It sounds like they brought every diabolical thing from their special Hell with them! Is it me, Ben, or does it sound like there are more of them up there now than there were last night?"

"I'm afraid I have to agree with you. It sounds like several hundred of the monstrosities running around up there now. Let's bed down and try to get some sleep. We've got nearly seven hours before we begin the Second Consecration. After that, those things should leave once and for all. Then it's back upstairs until five tomorrow afternoon when we leave for Saint Alacious."

"And what are we to do between the time those things up there leave and then?" Frank asked.

"Wait," Yakov replied. "And pray I haven't made any miscalculations along the way."

The three men relaxed into their mattresses, fluffed their pillows and began to wait. In minutes their physical and nervous exhaustion caught up with them. They drifted off into a sound sleep amid the nightmarish noises above them.

The old cop's eyes opened suddenly. As they focused, he became aware of the off-tan color of the Temple's ceiling and surrounding walls, and rustling noises in the north corner of the room. Breach's heart pounded wildly in his chest as he jumped to his feet, ready to engage the enemy his panic told him must have somehow invaded the Temple.

"We were just about to awaken you," Yakov said gently. "Did you have a good rest, Gus?"

Breach's heart began to slow, as he realized the sounds in the corner were coming from his allies. "I heard the two of you rustling around. I thought…" his dialogue trailed off. "But yeah, Ben, I had some of the best sleep I've had in weeks. I'm ready for anything now."

"Good!" Yakov replied slyly. "From the way you sprang to your feet, I would say you're ready to take on the qlippoth themselves!"

"Well, I wouldn't go that far old boy, but I'm ready. What are you two doing anyway?" He replied in a calm voice, paying no attention to the crazed poundings and screams in the rooms above them. Its continued presence throughout the night had made his nervous system immune to it.

"It's eleven-thirty p.m., Gus. The Second Consecration will begin in half an hour," Yakov answered. "Frank's been helping me set things up."

As Breach looked around him, his mind was catapulted into another reality, one he had sensed throughout his life, but which he never took time to explore. The Temple no longer glowed with a warm yellow hue. Instead, an intense red light filled its space. In the center of the room, the nine foot white circle with its two smaller inner circles now appeared to be black. The Hebrew characters, Latin words, and strange drawings between the inner circles glowed a fiery red. The contrast between the red and black colors stung his eyes, making him turn his gaze away from them.

In the center of the circle, the flat black, cube-like altar now displayed numerous items. A single brass candleholder with a blood red candle; a silver chalice with strange figures and words on them in a language he did not understand; a long hazel wood rod with equally strange markings; a brass container on three legs filled with sand and a small charcoal brick; a strange looking knife whose black handle was inscribed in white with other markings and characters from some long dead tongue; and leaning next to the altar, a large, broad-bladed sword whose brilliant red handle and blade were painted with curious green figures, Hebrew characters, and Latin words. Set off from these items in the center of the altar lay a white pouch with a protruding red cord.

Mesmerized by the objects in front of him, Breach moved through the circles. Without thinking, he stretched his hand toward the items on the altar. As he did, a loud voice seemed to crack out from some point above him.

"Don't touch any of those things! Keep your hands off of them! They are not for you, nor are they of your nature, Breach! If you make contact with them, you will destroy yourself and set Night-Shadow free for all time!"

Yakov's tirade snapped him back to his present reality. Ben was always kind to him. The older man's warning, coupled with calling the cop by his last name, told him the Magician was deadly serious.

"I…I'm sorry, Ben," Breach replied meekly. "I felt dazed all of a sudden, and wasn't thinking!"

"Then start!" Yakov fired back. "Keep your fingers off everything and anything unless I direct you otherwise! Those are the Magical weapons of Goetia, a 'grammar of Magic' from the eighteenth century that has its roots back in the Dark Ages! It literally means 'the book of howling'! Those weapons must never be touched by anyone other than the Magician who created and consecrated them! To do so would bring irreparable harm to the individual! You would be flung down into an abyss of suffering you cannot imagine, and would end our war with NightShadow with Cavendish being the winner for all time! Those are the tools with which I will call forth the Spirit of Death. Now you know! And be careful you don't step on the other candles! They're the only ones I have that fit the bill for this particular ritual!"

"What other candles?" Gus asked apologetically.

"Wake up before you take another step!" Yakov cautioned once more, but in a more even tone of voice. "Take a look around you!"

Breach froze to his spot, slapped his face several times, and then massaged it hard. In a minute he was fully awake, and then he took a close look around the room. All was as before except that now he noticed a brass candlestick had been set up on the floor in each of the four quarters of the room. Each bore the same blood red candle as on the altar. In the north quarter of the room where Yakov and Frank were working, Breach spotted a large equilateral triangle painted in black on the floor, around which were written three words in English. Inside of the triangle was another brass dish with sand and a charcoal brick, its three legs raising it off the surface of the triangle. Outside of the triangle, at each angle, was a large, thick, flat black candle situated on a brass plate.

"Uh, permission to join you," Breach said, asking for approval in a military fashion.

"Permission granted!" Yakov replied with a smile. "Just be careful."

"What is the triangle for? And why the red candles around the circle and on the altar, and the black ones out here?" Gus asked as he stared down at the figure in the north end of the Temple.

"Come on now, Gus!" Yakov said, concerned. "You said you and Frank spent two days going over the documents I gave you to study! The reason I gave them to you was so both of you would be familiar with the ritual and what we have to do afterward! If you don't have this part down, you'll inevitably fail us during our darkest hour and evil will win! Is that what you want? Don't you remember what you read? Think, man!"

Ashamed, Breach struggled to make his brain work properly in the altered reality he found himself in. "Uh, let me see," he said thoughtfully. "Oh yeah. The red candles correspond to Mars which rules the hour when the Second Consecration begins. It's sort of like setting the frequency in the circle for the force of Mars to home in on. Yeah, that's right! Now I remember! And the triangle? You'll put the staff in its center before we enter the circle. Then you'll light the charcoal block in the triangle and add a 'bittersweet suffumigation' or incense, the way I think of it, to the burning coals. Then you'll light the three black candles. They correspond to the nature of Saturn, which rules death, among other things. Then we get into the circles, and begin. How's that for an old man getting his memory back!"

"That's what I wanted to hear, Gus," Yakov replied with a smile. "See? It's not as hard as you thought. Remembering new things, I mean. Age has nothing to do with it. A person's laziness in getting his brain going does!"

"Give me a break," Breach answered jokingly. "I just got up! It takes time to come around!"

"Sorry," Yakov replied with a serious note in his voice. "The time for breaks is well past. What time do you have?"

Breach was surprised his lighthearted attitude was rejected, especially after Yakov paved the way for it. His law enforcement experience told him it was the tough times that called for some humor, if only to be able to get through them. "Apparently the old man doesn't see it that way," he thought. "Better not push it."

"It's eleven fifty-three," Breach replied.

"Good."

Yakov opened the closet and removed the long black velvet cloth containing the Staff of Resurrection or Return. Grasping the covered staff firmly with both hands, he removed the cloth and placed the black ebony staff in the center of the triangle next to the brass dish. The hideous Face of Death on top stared out madly at Breach and Lewis. As they fixed their sight on its protruding fangs, hollow cheeks, and gaping mouth, they sensed that the hellish vision would devour them if it could.

The mindless fury in its bulging eyes and the madness of its wooden hair streaming out in all directions, spoke of the agony and horror it endured throughout its fifty-odd years on earth. But its Trance of Resurrection no longer sent waves of panic through them. Its glow of black light and pulsating, low guttural howls no longer struck terror in them as it did only days before. Their minds were now immune to the chaos of the grave the Staff represented, having become trapped in the vortex of the moment's altered reality, a reality they now accepted as being every bit as valid as the daily existence in which they spent their normal lives.

"Prepare yourselves," Yakov said as he bent down to light the charcoal and black candles, and add the suffumigation to the burning coal. In a moment a pungent aroma arose from the brass dish in the triangle. A heavy sadness rose up from the brass dish. In a few moments, it filled the Temple air.

"The suffumigation of the Spirit of Death is lit!" he said triumphantly.

Gus and Frank closed their eyes, and began to concentrate on a small sphere of pure white light above their heads, the symbol of their own Yechidah, as the documents had explained. Each man visualized the small sphere rotating, whirling, glowing brighter and brighter. Both of them silently called upon that part of God within him to make its presence known to him, so each could establish his own divine presence of self. Yakov and his two assistants then returned to the east quarter and entered the circles. As they did, they began to recite in unison.

"In the name of the holy, blessed, and glorious Trinity, proceed we to our work in these mysteries to accomplish that which we desire. We therefore, in the names aforesaid, consecrate this piece of ground for our defense, so that no spirit whatsoever shall be able to break these boundaries, neither be able to cause injury nor detriment to any of us here assembled, but that they may be made to stand before this circle and answer truly our demands, as far as it pleaseth Him who liveth for ever and ever; and who says, I am the Alpha and Omega, the Beginning and the End, which is and which was, and which is to come, the Almighty. I am the First and the Last, who am living and was dead; and behold, I live for ever and ever, and I hold the keys of hell and of death.

"Bless, O Lord! This, thy creature of earth wherein we stand! Confirm, O God! Thy strength in us, so that neither the adversary nor any evil thing may cause us to fail, through the merits of Jesus Christ. Amen!"

As the men recited the prayer of consecration of the circle and for defense and protection, the words wove a spell about them. The hairs on their arms rose from their skins, while powerful currents of adrenalin coursed through their veins, exciting their minds to a fever pitch of religious-like devotion, and a faith in the righteousness of what they were about to do. Without their being aware of it, the destruction of the qlippoth in the rooms above ended. The living nightmares retreated into the darkest places of the earth, amid their own cries and moans of anguish and torment.

"It's midnight," Breach said softly. "It will be the last stroke of midnight right...now!"

"We begin!" Yakov cried out, his memory spiraling back through the half-century of torment the Staff and its secret life had put him through. "The hour of struggle for the redemption of mankind and of our salvation is finally at hand!"

As the three men slipped black hooded robes over their bodies and fixed the hoods on their heads, the Magician led them in the prayer designed for beginning of the ritual.

"Ancor, Amacor, Amides, Theodonias, Anitor, by the merits of thy angels, O Lord, I will put on the garments of Salvation, that this which I desire I may bring to effect; through Thee, the most holy Adonai, whose kingdom endureth forever and ever. Amen!"

Yakov picked up the white cloth from the altar and removed three, four-inch square pieces of parchment, each piece bearing figures and drawings in red and black that at its sight, fascinated his two assistants. As he placed one of them over his robe's belt and the other two around his neck, he screamed out.

"Behold! All of you who bear witness to the holy Ritual of Death and Resurrection! Behold the Magician, armed by God, without fear, who now girds himself with the Pentacle of Solomon, the Hexagram of Solomon, and the dreaded Secret Seal of Solomon, by which all shades and spirits are cast down and struck with the despair of the Pit! Take heed! Keep thee from me and those of mine who assist me here this night, and be prepared to come as you are called!"

Shivers ran up and down their spines as the Magician delivered his charge. They knew they had reached the point of no return in the Infernal Rite. Frank remained at the Magician's left side while Gus took up a position at Yakov's right hand. Facing forward, the older man picked up the knife with the black handle, moved to the east, and began tracing over the three circles on the floor with the point of the weapon. While he traced, he murmured words unintelligible to his companions. As each stroke was completed, a thin band of red flame shot up from the circles.

Working intently, the Magician completed tracing over the circles' characters, symbols and inscriptions. As before, the same thin line of fire flared up to outline each piece of writing. Taking up a long wooden match, the Magician drew three crosses above it in the air with the black handled knife, struck the timber against the side of its box, and lit the blood red candle in the brass candleholder. Holding his hands high above the candle flame he said, "I exorcise thee, O thou creature of fire, by Him through whom all things are made, that forthwith thou cast away every phantasm from thee, that it shall not be able to do any hurt in any thing. Bless O Lord, this thy creature of fire, and sanctify it, that it may be blessed to set forth the praise and glory of Thy Holy Name, so that no hurt may come to the Exorcisors or Spectators, through our Lord, Jesus Christ, who liveth and reigneth with Thee in the unity of the Holy Spirit, for ever and ever. Amen!"

Yakov was no longer aware of his assistants. His mind had united with the intent and form of the ritual. Almost bumping into Frank, he picked up the silver chalices, added some fresh water to it, and after sprinkling a small amount of powdered herb into the water, stretched his open hands over the vessel and said, "Thou shalt purge me with hyssop O Lord, and I shall be clean! Thou shalt wash me, and I shall be whiter than snow!"

After lighting the charcoal block in the brass container on the altar, the old Magician recited the same prayer over the burning cube he used to consecrate the fire of the candle. Turning his attention to some powdered herbs in a glass dish on the altar, he stretched his open hands over them and said, "The God of Abraham, God of Jacob, God of Isaac, bless here the creatures of these kinds, that they may fill up the power and virtue of their odors, so that neither the enemy nor any false imagination shall be able to enter into them. Through our Lord, Jesus Christ, who liveth with Thee forever and ever. Amen!" Then he added some of the powdered herbs to the burning charcoal.

As the smoke of the burning herbs rose, the sadness in the room vanished instantly, replaced with a fragrance that uplifted their spirits and made them slightly giddy.

Brushing past his two assistants, the Magician walked toward the east quarter of the circle with the silver chalice of water and herbs, and began sprinkling the mixture over the circles as he moved in a clockwise direction. Replacing the chalice on the altar, he took the brass dish with the burning, intoxicating herbal blend, returned to the east, and once again moving around the circle in a clockwise direction, swung the dish through the air in each quarter. As he moved around the burning red outlines of the circles on the floor, he murmured other unintelligible words, as if purifying the four corners of the world. Returning to the altar, he faced the east, bowed his head, and recited several prayers in Latin for fifteen minutes.

As he prayed, he lifted his head up addressing the heavens themselves. His voice reaching a fever pitch, as his spirit ascended to sublime heights of ecstasy. His two assistants were caught up in his rapture, as they too rose to spiritual heights neither of them had experienced before.

Without warning, Yakov picked up the hazel rod with his right hand, grabbed the sword with his left, and dashed to the northern quarter of the circle to face the Triangle of Manifestation. Pointing the rod toward the center of the triangle while lifting the sword and thrusting it at the base of the rising smoke of incense, he cried out in a voice filled with the power of his divine self.

"I do invoke and conjure thee, O Thou Spirit of Death! And being exalted above thee in the power of the Most High, I say unto thee, Obey! Hear thou me in thy hidden dwelling place in darkness, and obey my call, in the name Beralensis, Baldachiensis, Paumachia, and Apologiae Sedes, and of the mighty ones who govern spirits, Liachidae, and the ministers of the tartarean abode! And by the Chief Prince of Apologia in the Ninth Legion, I do invoke thee, and by invoking, conjure thee! And being exalted above thee in the power of the Most High, I say unto thee, Obey! In the name of Him who spake and it was, to whom all creatures and things obey.

"Moreover, I, whom God made in the likeness of God, who is the Creator according to His Living Breath, stir thee up in the Name which is the voice of wonder of the God, El, strong and unspeakable, O thou Spirit of Death! And I say unto thee, obey, in the Name of Him who spake and it was, and in every one of ye, O ye Names of God!

"Moreover, in the Names, Adonai, El, Elohim, Elohi, Ehyeh, Asher Ehyeh, Zabaoth, Elion, Iah, Tetragrammaton, Shaddai, Lord God Most High, I stir thee up, and in our strength I say, Obey! O thou Spirit of Death! Appear unto us, the servants of the Most High God in a moment, before this circle and within the Triangle of our Art of Magic, in the likeness of a shade our eyes can behold without pain, and our minds can comprehend without terror, and visit us in peace!

"And in the ineffable Name, Tetragrammaton Jehovah, I say, Obey! Whose mighty sound being exalted in power the pillars are divided, the winds of the firmament groan aloud, the fire burns not, the earth moves in earthquakes, and all things of the house of heaven and earth and the dwelling place of darkness are as earthquakes, and are thrown into torment and are confounded in thunder! Come forth, O Spirit of Death, in a moment! Let thy dwelling place be empty, apply unto us the secrets of Truth and obey my power! Come forth, visit us in peace, appear unto my eyes! Be friendly unto us! Obey the Living Breath, therefore, continually unto the end as my thoughts appear to my eyes!

"Therefore be friendly, speaking the secrets of Truth in voice and with understanding, and be ready to carry out my demands, as they are those that pleaseth the Lord God on High, for it is in his Name and by His power that I call thee forth! Come, Come now, thou Bringer of the Eternal Night of the Grave, and hearken unto all I have said unto thee!"

As Yakov delivered his command into the pungent incense smoke, his assistants shook violently, the last of their control over their fear having been ripped from them. Unable to stand by themselves, the two men butted their shoulders together in order to prop themselves up. Slowly, the red light filling the Temple began to flash, creating a strobe light effect, as black forms appeared and disappeared in the area outside of the circle. The charcoal brick in the triangle began to hiss and sputter violently, throwing hot sparks of coal and incense in every direction. As the two terrified men looked on, they rubbed their eyes trying to focus on a dark, ever-changing frame beginning to appear in the triangle's smoke.

"Hear me!" Yakov continued, his voice now sounding like claps of thunder. "By Nirraka and Gehenna, and by the Island of the Dead that floats in the Ninth Region of Hell, supported by the souls of the damned, and by the Pandemonium of the Pit itself on the First Day, when those that sinned in the Face of God were cast out by Michael the great Archangel who standeth at the right hand of God with his sword of fire, and who is ever prepared to carry out the will of the Most High by the Sword of Justice of the First Day and the Last, I call upon thee to appear unto us here!

"Hear thou me, thou Great Harbinger of Death and the Eternal Death! Come unto me here, now, and prepare to do my bidding! For behold! Behold! I am a Son of the Living God that created me and thee to carry out His Will until the Day of Doom! And by his Living Breath that fills my nostrils and His spirit that indwells within me, I call thee forth! And the horrible Sea of Glass that He has fashioned for all spirits of whatever nature that dare to challenge His will which is above all things, I call thee forth unto me, now!"

The cement walls of the Temple began to ripple, as if made of a plastic some secret wind had just discovered. Moans and shrill cries broke out throughout the Temple, issuing all around. The black forms darting throughout the spaces outside the circle took form, drawing into hideous faces without bodies, their red and green tongues wagging back and forth, in and out, gagging, as if about to vomit out some infernal sickness from the Pit itself.

As Yakov continued to recite the first conjuration in a more threatening voice, stressing the Names of God and reminding the thing forming in the smoke of the Magician's divine nature, the dark outline in the triangle's incense smoke finally took form. Breach and Lewis continued to shake violently, as the dark, ever-changing form suddenly shifted its shape into a flat, jet-black, rectangular solid. While they watched, the blackness stretched itself into a human-like shape, tossing its dense cloak of shadow around itself, giving it the appearance of a heavy robed figure like them. As the shade hovered above the burning coals, the eyes of the Face of Death sprung open, revealing a swirling mass of something streaked with dull silver-color motions.

"My God!" Lewis whispered in a cracked voice, "The eyes, Gus! What…what is that color in the staff's eyes? I…I've never seen anything like it before! It's not even black! It's, it's…"

Before Breach could answer, the robed figure in the triangle began to speak. A shrill, ringing voice seemed to come from every point in the Temple at the same time.

"Who art thee that dares to summon me before the time appointed for him has come! Answer me now, lest I sweep thee into my bosom and carry thee away to my abode of Death and Eternal Death! Answer me quickly, my time grows short!"

"No!" Yakov cried out in a powerful voice! "Thou shalt not depart from thy place before this circle until I give thee the Discharge to Depart! Thou art constrained here by the Names of the Most High, afore uttered by me, and commanded by He who lives within my Breast of Justice!"

The Staff began to vibrate and pulsate, as its black light shot out from the triangle into the Temple. The Trance of Resurrection was broken. The face atop the Staff began to twist and contort, gnashing at the air, as if to devour them. As its teeth snapped out, low guttural growls and howls leapt from its open mouth at the same time, as if it were convulsing, knowing it was about to be brought to life fully. Lifting itself up and down, it pounded the hard floor while the howls and growls increased in volume and severity. Hideous moans fell in place behind the other screams, as the staff objected to the new terror of being brought fully to life in the world of humanity.

"Silence!" Yakov yelled, as he pointed the Magic sword at the Staff, and began to recite prayers Frank recognized as being in the Enochian tongue. Then he continued, "Thou canst not return unto the world of Death until thou hast fulfilled the charge I will give thee, and thou knowest it by the Rite of Resurrection or Return that governest thee! Be silent, then, lest I deliver thee to the Twenty-First Call, which shall forever bind thee outside the world of men and the world of death, there to suffer unspeakably even beyond the Day of the Last Judgment!"

The Staff ceased rapping against the floor, but continued to groan and howl in a subdued voice. The Magician turned his attention back to the Spirit of Death, staring at it coldly.

In a victorious voice he called out, "Hear me, thou spirit from the land beyond the Fiftieth Gate! By all the aforesaid Names of the Living God, and by the Yechidah within me, I charge thee to infuse the life that rants and cries beyond the grave into this, the Staff of Resurrection or Return! Bring this creature of wood to that life fully, that it may be used by this Operator and the other two Operators as we see fit!

"Let the life of this Staff fall under my command and under our command, so that it shall carry out my bidding and our bidding, of raising the dead from their cold place in the earth, or returning the dead to that same frozen vault of sorrow, according to our pleasure! Let not this Staff have a will of its own beyond what is given it by the hidden purpose of Infernal Necromancy!

"Let it speak its secret second part of the Words of Power of the Final Summoning or the Dark Command as it is known to he who is skilled in this Art, to resurrect a dead man as we choose, so his spirit returns to its rotting corpse! Or let this Staff speak the Words of the Final Return to return that corpse to its resting place in the earth if it be our will! This is thy charge, made according to ancient writ! By He whom we both bow down to, I charge thee, fulfill my will!"

The spirit hovered in the incense smoke of the Triangle, fading in and out as the smoke thickened and thinned. Without warning, two large orbs of burning flame appeared in the emptiness of its hood. As it stared at Yakov and his two assistants through the burning flames, it spoke out. Its hollow voice seemed to echo between the Temple walls forever, as a cave without a bottom would continue to pass sounds between its never-ending walls.

"Thy will shall be done on earth as it is in Hell and in my abode of Eternal Night! But hear thou me, infernal one who dares to call me from my land of despair! There is a price to be extracted from thee and thy servants! My hand is not given without payment! Doest thou accept this, my condition?"

"Only," the Magician shot back quickly, "as it is in keeping with the Ritual of Resurrection or Return! Thou art hereby constrained not to waver from the eternal laws that govern this act, be they from this side of the grave, or thine's! So it is written in Heaven, in Hell, and in thy own abode of Eternal Night! Accept them now! This is my will, laid bare and in fact, for all the eyes of Heaven and Hell to see!"

"They are accepted!" the shade's hollow voice rang out. "See thou, the power of mine that I command at my fingertip!"

As the Spirit of Death spoke, it stretched out the right arm of its robe. An intense blackness in the form of an arm emerged slowly from the cuff. At the end of the black shaft, a single finger-like object formed. The shade first touched the face of the Staff with its finger. As Gus and Frank looked on in shock, the finger then touched the forehead of the Face of Death on the Staff, then each of its eyes and ears in turn, and finally its mouth, as if anointing them. As it moved over the face, Death called to it in words that made the two assistants feel they would faint. It called out in its hollow voice softly, but the words themselves struck such terror into the two men, their minds could barely maintain control.

"I'm going insane!" Frank cried out. "Help me Ben, please help me!"

"My God, please," Gus screamed, holding his head between his hands and shaking it violently from side to side, "save me from this terror! My God, please help me!"

Neither Yakov nor the Spirit of Death paid any attention to the horrified men. The Spirit of Death continued to move its finger over the Face of Death slowly, carefully, as if caressing one of its own kind. As it did, the howls and moans of the Staff continued, becoming even louder than before.

Bending toward the face, the Spirit of Death spoke in English once more as it looked into the Staff's eyes and said, "Accept now, my kiss! The Kiss of Death!"

As Death kissed the face on its lips, the emptiness and dull silver-colored motions in the Staff's eye sockets disappeared. Its moans and howls ceased, and calm fell over it. As the three men watched, a violet glow with red pupils began to well up in the Staff's eye sockets.

In a low, soft voice, it looked at the old Magician and said, "I am here, completed now by thy Magic. I am ready to do thy will. But I say unto thee, that after I have satisfied thy will, thee or thy assistants are to release me from this torment, so that I may return to my own place beyond the grave. Dost thou accept this condition for my aid, Abraham ben Yakov?"

"I accept thy condition gratefully," Ben replied in a hushed voice.

"And do thy two servants accept this same condition?"

"I, being the Grand Operator, hereby accept thy conditions for them. Such is given by the Rite of Infernal Necromancy, and by its secret heart of Resurrection or Return."

"Then know," the Staff continued, "that my part of the Words of Power of the Final Summoning or the Final Return of the Ritual of Resurrection or Return shall be fulfilled by me, after which thou shalt strike me hard against the stone that marks the grave of he that I bring forth or send back, while calling out in a loud and powerful voice, 'Return, by the One God over all Creation!' to release me. This thou didst not know, Abraham ben Yakov, as it is not given in the black writ, but must be delivered by me after the Second Consecration which thou hast just done, and by the Kiss of Death, which my great lord has imparted to me."

The Spirit of Death turned to Yakov and said in a still hollow, but loud voice, "My time is at hand, Magician! Give me the Discharge to Depart, for my business is now elsewhere, and I must not deter from those I must visit and take onto myself this night!"

Yakov lifted his right hand with the hazel rod, pointed it at the specter, drew three crosses in midair and said loudly, "In the Name of the Father, and of the Son, and of the Holy Ghost, depart now in peace unto your place! Go with the blessings of He whom we both adore forever and ever, and let there be peace between you and us for all time, even at the moment of thy coming for us!"

As Yakov drew three more crosses in the air with the hazel rod, the figure in the incense smoke within the triangle wavered in and out, as if evaporating. In a moment, it disappeared from sight.

"It is over!" Yakov said, the victory in his words snapping Breach and Lewis out of near mental collapse. "Say nothing, and do not move from your places! There is much yet to be done to close this ritual properly!"

Yakov moved to the east, holding the hazel rod, and began tracing pentagrams in the air, each from a different point on the five-pointed figure, while vibrating different Names of God in Hebrew as he did three days earlier when he showed Breach and Lewis the Staff for the first time. He moved clockwise around the circle continuing to trace the figures in the air, until he returned to the east. Placing the rod on the altar, he picked up the Magical sword, and repeated the process, using the sword to trace the same figures in all four quarters of the Temple.

After finishing, he leaned the sword against the altar, and went through the same motions, first with the chalice of consecrated water, and then with the brass dish of burning charcoal block and sweet suffumigation. Finally, the Magician bent down on both knees, tilted his head toward the ceiling, and with outstretched arms began to recite a long prayer in Latin. A half hour later he stood up slowly.

Turning to his two assistants he said, "We can leave the circle now, gentlemen. We have succeeded. I will cross over the circle first, just in case. All spirits should now be gone. If not—if there are any still lurking in the shadows—I will be the first to die. You two will then follow. I'm sorry, but as you know from your studies, those are the rules of evocation."

Neither Breach nor Lewis could think. Their friend's words made no sense to them as they were still recoiling from the terrors they beheld, and from the impossibility of the other reality they were leaving.

Spared the understanding of this new danger, Yakov crossed the lines of the circle and said to them, "It's all right, Frank, Gus. You can come out now. Come on, come on," he added, motioning for them to follow him. "It's time I introduced you to the Staff."

Regaining their senses, Breach and Lewis crossed over the lines of the circles and joined their friend. "Follow me, and be respectful. In all these matters, one must be completely respectful. Whether of Good or Evil, it is required. The beings of Magic are ancient, existing from the time God had Its first thought to create them. As such, they deserve the respect of man because in one way or another, they too are taking part in the grand scheme of the universe."

"You...you mean," Breach finally said, "We're supposed to honor such beings, the evil ones included?"

"I didn't say honor them!" Yakov snapped back. "I said respect them, the same way one would respect either a beautiful summer's evening under the stars, or the sight of a fierce tornado heading straight for you! You respect and admire the first. The second, you respect and fear enough to get out of its way. But you respect both of them for what they are. A creation of nature, and therefore, of God's. Do you understand now?"

Both men nodded in agreement as Yakov led them to the triangle and the awaiting Staff.

"This are my two assistant Operators," Yakov spoke as he stared into the Staff's violet eyes, the red pupils staring intently back. "You are to obey them in all matters as you would me, because they are skilled in the fashion of returning you to your place after your purpose is fulfilled."

The Staff did not answer, but blinked its eyelids in a mechanical way resembling an uneven cadence. Moving its head in a similar mechanical, choppy way, it stared at the two men and then returned its gaze to Ben.

"These are yours, they?" Its voice was low and guttural, but not unfriendly.

"They are mine," Yakov replied.

"They too shall be obeyed," the Staff replied, "as long as they are dedicated to my release after I have served thee in thy purpose.

"I have accepted your condition earlier for them and myself as you know. Do not question it!" the Magician fired back abruptly, declaring his dominance over the Staff.

"Then it is done," the Staff answered. "Take me wither thou goest now, so I may complete my task! I am needful of my place beyond the grave!"

"That time is coming soon enough," Yakov replied in a kinder tone. "Be not apprehensive, less thou force things that cannot be forced, and be imprisoned in the world of men forever, now being fully alive! Thy pain and suffering here, now, trapped in my world, would be forever lasting, and would torment thee for all time!"

"Then take me with thee as soon as thy situation allows, so I may do my work and go to my peace!"

"It shall be done," Yakov replied softly. "Fear it not! But the time has now come for thee to quit the triangle and accompany us on our journey to do what we must." Holding up the black velvet cloth he had used to conceal the Staff for a half century, the Magician said, "Tell me now, wouldst thou enjoy release from this imposed House of Darkness? For fifty years thou hast endured its false darkness, as no darkness can be as from thy land."

"No!" the Staff cried out loudly. "No! The darkness is of my nature! This, thy world, is of everlasting pain to me, for it containeth not my nature, whilst having the symbol of the Living Light, the sun, in thy heavens! Thou knowest this! Why doest thou torment me with this question? I have been trapped between my world and thine for too long, suffering continually from this world of thine! Cover me and bring me out naught except into the night of thy world when I can fulfill my work! I wish not to see the world of men nor its light, any more than I yearned to be brought into this place of suffering and torment during the first consecration by my master, Martin Cavendish!"

"I and us are thy master now!" Yakov said hurriedly, fearing the Staff was recalling its creator, and perhaps a secret allegiance to him the Magician did not uncover in his years of research.

"Never fear, old one," the Staff replied in its low, guttural voice. Its blinking eyelids and the madness remaining on its face lent it a powerful sense of other-worldliness. "My loyalty is fixed to him who giveth unto me both the First and Second Consecrations, or the last only. For so it is recorded in these things from the time the first man chose to bring back the dead into this world."

"Then it is done," Yakov replied with finality, as he placed the black cloth over the Staff, and removed it from the triangle. "I will not torture thee any longer with thoughts of the Living Light, nor its symbol in our world. Rest easy until thy appointed time has come."

"Come with me," Yakov said to his two assistants. "It is time to leave the Temple and prepare for what is to come."

The three men walked out of the Temple in silence. Yakov locked its single door, made some gestures with his hands over it the two stunned men did not recognize, and led them back to the first floor of the house. The house was beyond repair.

"The damage of the previous night can't compare to what they did tonight," Yakov said sadly. "But at least the qlippoth are gone from this world until all this is over. I guess that's something." After taking a deep breath and shaking his head momentarily, he continued. "Never mind! My house is the least of my worries now. Are you two going to be all right?"

Breach and Lewis were dazed. Free from their danger, their minds entered a state of shock. Their eyes took on the faraway look of a person caught in a daydream. Neither man could answer. Their throats had gone dry, and their hearing deadened. Their brains could not interpret sounds, and words had no meaning for them. Yakov turned over two heavy chairs and eased his friends into them.

Bending down and looking into Breach's eyes the older man asked, "Can you hear me, Gus?"

Turning to the mortician he said, "Frank, Frank! Listen to me!"

Moving backward in order to look at both of them at the same time, he snapped, "Listen to me! The two of you are not all right, but you are as good as you are going to get for quite a while! The inner concepts of reality you once used to define your daily lives have been torn away. That is to be expected from what you have just gone through!

"Every Magician, especially in his early training, goes through the same thing! Neither of you had training, but it makes no difference! What you are experiencing is the same condition I passed through many years ago! It won't harm you! It will pass in time! But I need the two of you now, such as you are, so please forgive me for what I am about to do! It is necessary!"

Yakov's disappearance into the kitchen and his return a few minutes later made no impression on the two men's senses. Nor did they see the small, box-like device the psychiatrist held in his right hand. Without speaking, he attached two small disks to the skin of Breach's shoulders near his spine, and pressed a button on the front of the device.

"Ummmwhhhaaaa!"

Breach screamed out as his body first rose up from the chair and then fell back into it. Yakov pressed the button again and again, each time sending the cop's body rising into the air and then falling back into the chair while twisting from the spasms caused by the electrical device. Finally, instead of screaming, Breach jumped up, knocked the small device from the psychiatrist's hand and shoved him against the wall.

"What are you trying to do to me—electrocute me? You ever try anything like that again, Yakov, and I'll kill you where you stand! Have you got that?"

Breach's hold on Yakov's front shirt collar began to strangle him, causing him to cough.

"Gus! Gus!" he choked out as the saliva started to flow down his windpipe, "Gus! Break your hold! You're killing me!"

In desperation, Yakov brought his open right hand forward with full force, catching the cop in the groin. With a groan, Breach loosened his hold and doubled up. Coughing violently, Yakov slowly helped Breach back to his chair.

"Are you ok?" Yakov asked cautiously.

"Yeah, yeah, I'm all right now. What the…what happened, Ben?" Breach replied in a raspy voice. "I don't feel so good!"

"I had to use a small shocking device on you to snap you out of your state of shock," the psychiatrist said in a hoarse voice. "It's harmless, but it delivers a very nasty electrical jolt. It was necessary, Gus, I assure you. I sometimes had to use it in my practice to help patients when they began to slip too deeply into states of clinical anxictics and depressions. But I have to tell you, not one of them ever tried to strangle me before!"

Slowly, Breach's mind began to put itself together. Thoughts of what he had just passed through began to order themselves in his mind. "Damn, Gus, now I remember! All of it! Was it all real?"

Pointing to the velvet cloth standing upright in the corner of the room Yakov replied, "If I take the black cloth off that staff over there my friend, you'll see just how real the entire episode was! Yes, it was all very real. But don't worry. You'll recover in time. For now, the way you are will be just fine.

"Better give me a hand with Frank. I'm afraid I have to put him through the same hell I just put you through. Given his personality type, I don't think he'll attack me, but I don't want to take any chances. The human mind's a tricky thing, especially when it's exposed to new conditions it doesn't know how to interpret. Ready?"

Breach rose from the chair, shook his arms, and twisted his body from side-to-side. After doing a few knee bends and taking several deep breaths he replied, "Yeah, Ben, I'm ready. Let's do it."

Yakov attached the electrodes to the bare skin of Frank's shoulders near his spine and pressed the button on the hand-held electrical device. Frank jumped from the chair and twisted in agony each time the high voltage jolt was delivered. After several shocks, Frank began to cry hysterically while he fell back into the chair. Yakov pulled the electrodes off of his shoulders, lifted him up, and held in his arms as he would a small child.

Patting him on the back he said softly, "You're going to be just fine, my friend! Just fine. In time all of this will wear off, and you'll be your old self again. There, there, there's nothing to worry about. Here, let me help you back to your chair. You have to relax now."

"Feeling better, Frank?" Gus asked after several minutes had passed.

"Much," Lewis replied, "but it's going to be a very long time I'm afraid, before I feel like my old self. This mess we're in is all so strange."

"Actually," Yakov replied, "I had to tell you both a little white lie to help bring you around. The mind needs all of the reassurances it can get during tough times, and so I gave you what you needed. The truth is, neither of you will ever be the same again. You couldn't be, if you think of it, simply because you have passed through experiences other people do not know exist, let alone have or will experience for themselves.

"From your battle with NightShadow in the cemetery on Monday night through the Second Consecration this night, the two of you have separated yourselves from the mass of humanity. Once done, you cannot go back. Neither of you will ever be one of them, as it were, again. Oh, you can reorient yourselves to the new or different way you now view the world because your unconscious minds will accept what you have gone through. But that's about all.

"The mystery is that you will be able to see things more clearly, and reason and think more deeply than any of your contemporaries.

In the same way, your appreciation for beauty and your awareness of the spiritual side of existence will accelerate beyond anything you have known to this point in your lives. And you will enjoy all of this! As hard as that is for you to accept, it will happen, I assure you. So I will not ask you to believe it. Just keep going, and everything I said will happen. Wait and see."

Neither Breach nor Lewis answered. For a long time, the three men sat in what was left of Yakov's parlor, pulling themselves together, and keeping their thoughts to themselves. Finally Gus spoke out.

"What time is it?"

"It's ten-to-five. Looks like it took longer than I thought for us to get through the Second Consecration and its aftermath. But still, we did very well. I'm pleased with what we accomplished."

"Listen!" Frank spoke up, his newfound confidence returning. "The Spirit of Death said 'There is a price to be extracted from thee and thy servants! Mine hand is not given without payment! Doest thou accept this, my condition?' I remember that clearly. Ben, just what did that mean? Are you holding out on us? We've come too far together for you to treat us like children. That is, if you're still trying to protect us, and I have a feeling you are. I say you should level with us, once and for all."

"That's right," Breach added. "Don't forget, you accepted terms on our behalf with both the Spirit of Death and the Staff. We have a right to know, Ben, so come clean, if there's anything to come clean about!"

"Well," Yakov began, "I wasn't sure until the Second Consecration was performed, so that's why I didn't say anything. But rest assured, after the consecration was finished, and I learned what I suspected I hadn't uncovered in my years of research, I was going to get to this before we left for the cemetery.

"The thing is, I was worried one or more of us might have to sacrifice himself in order to return Cavendish to the grave. You see, some versions of the Rite of Infernal Necromancy allude to this, but the Ritual of Resurrection or Return itself does not! At least, the version of it I put together throughout my twenty years of research, didn't mention it! Remember, only Cavendish and Stannish had the complete ritual. They had to, to be able to come as far as they have. I was sure I got most of it right, and we proved that tonight when we succeeded in the Second Consecration.

"But what puzzled me was that if Infernal Necromancy alludes to a sacrifice of one of the Operators in order to return the corpse to its grave, why doesn't its blacker counterpart, the Ritual of Resurrection or Return? Yet tonight, during the Second Consecration, the Spirit of Death said: '…hear thou me, infernal one who dares to call me from my land of despair! There is a price to be extracted from thee and thy servants! My hand is not given without payment! Doest thou accept this, my condition?' Well, now I know. Or at least, think I do.

"What the Spirit of Death actually tried to do was to get me to agree to a condition that one or all of us would be required to give our lives in order to succeed! When he tried to force this condition on me, it suddenly hit me why I didn't uncover it in my research. Those who performed this rite in ages past left this part out intentionally as a further trap for those who would meddle with it! Such attempts at coercion by spirits are found in many rituals in Magic! Even in the evocation of evil spirits called up to help the Magician! Remember the legend of Doctor Faust?"

"Just what in hell do you 'know,' Ben, after all? What are you talking about?" Breach asked impatiently.

"What I'm saying is it is possible one, or even all of us, will die trying to destroy NightShadow. But it's not a sure thing, as the Spirit of Death originally intended. That's why I answered as I did. Recall what I replied to it, if you can. 'Only as it is in keeping with the Ritual of Resurrection or Return!' I heard his bluff, and then put the final piece of the puzzle together. You see, no spirit can force a human being into a pact—which is what his bluff was, an attempt at a pact—unless the individual agrees to it! My charge constrained the spirit from acting on its own outside the limits of the ritual!

"When I told it, 'Thou art hereby constrained not to waver from the eternal laws that govern this act, be they from this side of the grave, or thine's! So it is written in Heaven, in Hell, and in thy own abode of Eternal Night! Accept them now! This is my will, laid bare and in fact, for all the eyes of Heaven and Hell to see!' I further bound it to act according to the Laws of God and nature! And what was its reply to my conditions? 'They are accepted!' In short, gentlemen, the spirit realized I knew my stuff, and finally agreed. That's how it always goes in matters of Magic.

"So now we now have a real fighting chance. Death cannot just take one of our lives or all of them in our attempt to send Night-Shadow back its world beyond the grave. Now that can only happen in one of two ways, by the Will of Divine Providence, or by some error on our parts. Because I assure you, human beings do have the gift of free will, and can carve out their own destinies!"

"Is that all you were worried about?" Frank replied in an almost causal way. "Hell, Ben, Gus and I accepted the possibility of dying in this battle after we read the documents you gave us! You were laboring over some technical point all this time?"

"Those technical points, as you call them Frank," Yakov replied abrasively, "can mean the difference between success and failure, life and death, in any major Magical ritual, let alone one of this magnitude! Yes, that was my concern, and I feel damn better I have it out now!

"While I'm making a clean breast of things," he continued, "I'd like to tell you I had no idea how the life of the Staff was to be returned to its own world. As with the matter of a human sacrifice, once again, the old Magicians who worked the Ritual made no mention about this. I can't tell you how relieved I was to find out all we have to do is strike the Staff against Cavendish's tombstone and pronounce the words out loud it gave us. That will end the entire ritual. You see, without this knowledge there would have been no end to the ritual. So even if we succeed in sending NightShadow back, the entire matter would remain an open issue. And let me tell you, in Magic you **never** leave any issues open! Ever!

"The only thing," he went on reluctantly, "is I have no idea how the Staff will produce the spiritual light and fire needed to finally end NightShadow's existence in our world. I remind both of you, it's the Staff's call of the Words of Power of the second part of the Final Return, plus the spiritual light and fire it produces that will finish him. But the Second Consecration gave me no idea how the light and fire are to be ignited. I suppose the only answer is we just have to trust and go on with what we have, because aside from this last element, we have everything else, and that makes me very happy indeed!"

"So there's still a fly in the ointment," Breach said in a heavy voice. "Guess it can't be helped."

"If you were versed in the ways of Magic, you would be grateful for all we have uncovered. It's rare indeed so much is known in any work of High Ritual or Ceremonial Magic, as it is called, before attempting the work itself. So many traps, outright lies, and deceptions are recorded in the manuscripts of the Dark Ages and Medieval times in these matters, it's pathetic. Even the Grimoires written during the Renaissance did not escape this trend. They too are littered with pitfalls for the unwary.

"Be happy we've got what we do, because I'm telling you from experience we have a great chance of destroying NightShadow and the spiritual conspiracy I firmly feel he and Stannish have concocted. I told you I had my reasons for thinking they intend to turn our world into a Black Utopia. One that will eventually overthrow the Principle of Good for all time throughout all of Creation. After the blizzard from out of nowhere, how it stalled over this region, and the attacks by the qlippoth, I'm utterly convinced my reasoning is right. Be happy we now have the position to operate from we do, because I assure you it's a strong one!"

"I think you're right," Frank said reflectively. "We're looking good. But we should rest now as best we can. We've got twelve hours ahead of us before we leave. I just wish there was something to eat!"

"Sorry," Yakov replied. "You can see from the mess the fiends made of this place there's not a morsel to be had. I could use a bit of food too. Oh well. At least your stomach growls will have company!"

"I couldn't keep a thing down," Breach replied gloomily.

"Frank is right, Gus. Let's spread out, find what's left to lie on, and try to get some sleep. When we wake up, we'll prepare for the hike to Saint Alacious cemetery.

§§§

"Did you see the thermometer on the back porch?" Frank called out to Gus and Yakov through the open back door. "It's thirty-eight degrees! At the rate the snow's melting, we'll be able to walk to the cemetery on bare ground! Ben, I gotta tell you, your 'weather magic' really worked!"

"Sure," Yakov replied with a chuckle, "it's thirty-eight degrees now! But it's only three p.m.! Wait until five, when sun is racing to the western horizon! The temperature will drop down to twenty degrees as I planned. There's just wasn't enough time to melt all of it without causing flooding problems, or worse, a bigger ice-over than the one I managed! And don't count on walking on bare ground either. We'll have a good two to two-and-a-half feet of snow under our feet. But it'll be frozen, and I'm counting on getting good traction if we sink down only a couple of inches. That's the next best thing to bare ground I could arrange, given the conditions and timeline I had to work with."

"Well, maybe things will have cleared up enough for us to drive up by the back road, or use Route 16 to get to the Heights, and then walk the last mile to the Saint Alacious!"

Yakov turned to Breach, looking for support.

"Don't count on it, Frank," Gus replied. "We haven't even heard the snow removal equipment back here on Pine Street, so there's no way they'd have time to dig out the back road to the cemetery or plow through Route 16. No doubt they're busy getting the main street cleared first. Some of the guys from the fire department probably went up early this morning looking at what's left of my house, seeing as how things have cleared up a bit. But you can count on them joining the snow removal teams after they saw there was nothing they could do."

"Do you think they're looking for you? Or for what's left of you if they think you were trapped in the house?" Yakov asked.

"No. Once they saw it was a total bust, they left. I know these people. They're very practical. First things first with them. They figured if I was caught in the fire and my body is buried somewhere in the rubble, it will keep until they have a chance to go through the debris properly. Or if Puffner told them Frank and I teamed up to follow some leads of our own, they probably figured we're off who-knows where doing who-knows-what, and will wait till we show up. Either way, they have more important work to do getting the town back on its feet.

"My only concern is Dave Barker. The kid is like a son to me and he knows it. He probably tried to convince Puffner to give him some men to help him look for me. But with things as they are, the Major wouldn't go for it. Frankly, neither would I. That probably sent Dave into a frenzy. I'm sure Puffner told the kid he needed him at the station house now more than ever before, since he's the only one there who could help his troops assist the town in a fast clean up. After a show down with Puffner, Dave would have to agree. He's like that. He'll follow orders no matter how much it hurts. He's going to make a good Chief of Police."

"So you figure, then," Yakov asked, "that as far as anyone knows, we're simply unavailable, and they're not going to bother looking for us for a while yet."

"Exactly," Breach replied. "Like I said, first things first with this town, as that's as it should be. No, my friend, we are on our own."

"Excellent!" Yakov said happily. "The one thing that's been in the back of my mind since you two arrived here was that they'd start looking for you because of the fire. But it looks like you're right. At least no one's been here so far. I checked the snow around the house when I got up, and there's not a footprint to be found. So we're safe from outside interference and can go about our work, which is another reason I want to leave around five p.m. The sun will be pretty well set, and my neighbors will be less likely to see us slip out the back door. Once we hit the field across the alley, we'll disappear into the shadows, and can be about our business."

"Sounds good to me," Breach replied. "What do you say we get to it?"

"I'm still damn hungry," Frank complained again. "Are you sure there's no food anywhere around here?"

"Wish I could help you, but when I got up, I got some things together for us and checked about food. There's not a crumb anywhere. Just as well. Our spiritual natures have to be strong and our physical bodies weak for what we have to go through. Might as well leave it at that. My suggestion is to concentrate on the upcoming job in the cemetery. Go over it in your minds so there will be as few surprises as possible when the time comes.

"All right, gentlemen," Yakov continued, changing the subject to get Frank's mind off his empty stomach. "Here's what we need to do. Follow me."

Yakov led his friends into the living room. "Here's what I salvaged from the wreck around here. First, put these warm clothes on. It's going to be colder than twenty degrees in the mountains at night I'll bet, so put on as many as you can comfortably wear and still maneuver in.

"Gus, I want you to carry this machete, just in case we run into something physical up there. It's been many years since I left this town, but I'll bet the mountains are still as wild as they were then."

"Yes, still plenty of wild bush dogs up there. They travel in packs, almost always at night. I just hope we don't run into any, especially since I'm only sporting a machete!"

"Well, that's not all I have for our defense. Here, Gus. Six for you, and Frank, six for you too," he said, handing the men six long, red cylinders with bright yellow caps. "I have six for myself as well. Nice, bright, super hot, extra-long, and extra-long life red flares. Maybe even NightShadow will get another taste of their light and fire before this is all over! And I'm sure one or two thrown at any bush dog pack will send them running away!"

"That's a guarantee," Breach said with a relieved smile. "They hate anything bright and hot! That's why they travel at night. They hate sunlight and heat, because it takes what energy they have away from them. These damn things look to be about eighteen inches long! Plenty of length to shove one in their faces and not get bit! Good for you, Ben! We can use them! Let me ask you, are you thinking what I'm thinking?"

"If you mean that since the Principle of Evil can no longer send its qlippoth to try and kill us it might try to use something more mundane—like wild dogs—you're right! But we should be ok as long as we stick close together.

"Here," Yakov said as he handed each man a long, heavy flashlight. "I put new batteries in them last week. They should last us." And finally, "Be sure to wear these heavy caps. After you're finished dressing, come back into the kitchen. I think we should have a parlay before we leave. It's 3:45 now. Time to get in gear."

A half hour later they sat down at what remained of the kitchen table. "It's been nearly a half century since I've been up in the mountains," Yakov started, "and I don't know if I remember the paths and trails there very well anymore, or if I'd even recognize them today. I take it you two are familiar with them?"

"That's Gus' department," Frank answered. "He's the hunter."

"Ben," the cop replied, "I've been here for twenty years now, and I can tell you nothing has changed. Sure, more growth in some areas, but the water company keeps the main trails and paths clear so they can service the pipeline that runs from Bear Gap to Kulpsville. So you might be surprised to find it pretty much as you remember. Nevertheless, I'll draw you a picture of the way we'll take. It has some bad spots because of mine cave-ins here and there.

"Some other places are iffy too, because old mines are slowly giving ground underneath. We have to be careful of them because with this bad weather and all the melt-off draining into those mines, what looks like solid earth could give way under your feet and you'd be gone in a second like being swallowed up by quicksand. You'd step on what looks like snow-covered ground and it'll give way and you'll go down. The slide from the sides would cover you up in an instant. But I pretty much know all those places, so I think we'll be all right. Give me that pencil and a piece of paper, and I'll draw our route."

The three men discussed the details of their hike calmly, but each could feel his heart rate increase as the minutes worn on. Finally Yakov spoke.

"Gentlemen, it's time. It's 5:10, and the darkness is growing fast. Let's get to the field while there's a trace of daylight left. We don't want to use our flashlights yet, or we'll attract attention from the neighbors."

After one final check of their gear, Yakov picked up the black velvet cloth containing the Staff. As he did, it slipped from his hands, and crashed against the kitchen wall. A low moan leaked through the cloth.

"Be silent!" Yakov said. "Your time is nearly at hand!"

The moan stopped instantly. He opened the back door and the three collaborators stepped out onto the back porch.

"What's wrong, Ben," Gus joked gently, "can't keep a hold on that thing?"

"As I told you," Yakov replied seriously, "it slipped from my hand because I expected it to weight something. Ordinary black ebony would, you know! But the laws of our universe have no meaning for it. There is no place in its nature for gravity to really take hold. Nature is defeated in this thing. It represents the energy of chaos from beyond the grave. Let's go."

"Shouldn't you lock the door?" Frank asked innocently.

"What for?" Yakov replied, as he turned his gaze toward the back steps leading to the snow-covered lawn.

The three men worked their way over the snow to the end of the backyard. Moving quickly across the narrow alley separating the yard from a large empty field, they reached a four-foot stone wall marking the edge of the field, scaled it, and began across the field as fast as they could.

"You were right," Breach puffed out in a labored breath, "this is pretty good traction. We're only sinking down about three inches! The packed snow almost feels like sand. At least we can make good time."

"Let's not count our chickens before they hatch," Yakov replied, puffing. "We have another two hundred yards to cross before we hit the edge of those trees, and from there, we move into the deep mountains. There's a lot that could happen between here and the cemetery! I just want to get out of the open so we're not spotted. Wouldn't help at all if some nosy neighbor sees us and calls the station house. Barker would hear about it and start after us. That's all we'd need!"

"Yeah, your right," Breach answered heavily. "I don't want him mixed up in this! Hell, it'll be bad enough if the three of us don't make. I don't want his death on my conscience as well!"

"Shut up you two!" Frank fired back, almost out of breath. "It's hard enough going, good traction or not, without you two scaring me more than I already am!"

"We're all scared," Breach puffed back. "Don't let it get to you."

"It's not. I got hold of myself in the Temple. Remember? I'm not about to let go now! Just don't add any more wood to the fire we already have. Ok?"

Yakov and Breach smiled to each other as the final rays of daylight ended.

"He's come a long way since you hit him in the mouth, hasn't he?" Yakov asked in a whisper.

"A hell of a long way."

"Hey!" Frank asked, his words coming more slowly between gasps of breath. "How are you two feeling anyway? I mean, your wounds? Gonna cause us any problems?"

"Are you kidding?" Breach replied to his friend who had taken the lead across the open track of snow minutes ago. "I'm too sore all over and worried about dropping dead from a heart attack to think about a few cuts and scrapes! How about you, Ben?"

"No time to think of what was. Only to think about what is and what we're heading into! I'm doing fine."

When they reached the tree line separating the field from the mountains, Yakov switched on his flashlight and looked at his wristwatch.

"What did you say about making good time, Gus? It's 6:10 already! Took us a lot longer than I figured to cross the field in this damn snow than I thought it would!"

"Yeah. I didn't think it would take this long. The four miles is starting to look a lot longer. Take five before we enter the trees. We're pretty winded."

After their break, the Gus switched on his flashlight, withdrew the machete from his coat belt, and pointed with it to a small thicket of tall brush.

"Over there. We enter there. Behind that patch of brush there's an old coal road. It will lead us to the first path that will take us to the base of the mountain. We'll only have another mile to go after that. Let's move out. And keep your eyes and ears open! We don't know what's crawling around here at night. Maybe even more than just bush dogs!"

Chills went down their spines as Breach led the way. In a few minutes, the small squad disappeared into the woods, and with them, unknown to the rest of humanity, went the world's only hope for salvation.

A wide, snow-covered road opened to them as they emerged from the other side of the tall brush.

"Look on both sides," Breach said in a low voice. "See those depressed areas that look like giant cereal bowls? They're caved-in coalholes. Even without the snow covering their surface, they can look solid. Some are. Others have false bottoms. Step on the wrong one, and down you'll go. No telling how far you'd fall. Then the slide from the walls would fill the hole you made, and no one would ever find the body.

"This road is wide enough, but from here on we go single file all the way to the cemetery. No use taking any unnecessary chances.

And another thing. Keep the conversation to a minimum, and I mean, a minimum. I want our senses alert, not caught up in needless chatter. And if you have to talk, talk softly! If there are any surprises to come, I want us doing the surprising! Not some who-knows-what lurking in the shadows!"

"You...you mean, bush dogs, right Gus?" Franks asked nervously.

"I mean anything! You know damn well there have been stories of all kinds of weird things going on in these mountains at night! Hell, you're a native here! You must have heard them! I'm here only twenty years and I heard more campfire ghost and monster stories about this place than I care to remember right now! So keep it down!"

"Yeah, yeah," Frank replied, "I heard of them, but they were just stories up until now. I mean, now they...well...sort of seem possible...as if..."

"Well, Ben?" Breach cut in. "Aren't you going to give Frank a little shrink pep talk about now?"

The psychiatrist looked at Breach grimly across the pale yellow light of his flashlight.

"Now's not the time. Besides, I don't know what's real or not around here anymore."

"I'll lead the way," Breach said. "I know these paths and trails. Now keep it down!"

The old cop made his way slowly up the slight incline of the coal road. Frank followed behind him, while Yakov brought up the rear. As they walked, Yakov noticed the gnarled and twisted limbs of the trees and undergrowth, and the black appearance they threw off into the purple-shaded night. "Like something out of Dante's Inferno," he thought, "with us headed into the Ninth Circle of Hell. Ohhh, how I wish I never heard of Martin Cavendish!"

The grinding snow beneath their boots fell from their attention as their steps took up a single rhythm. All each man was aware of was the sounds of a quiet wooded landscape. When they reached the end of the coal trail, it opened to a wider path with two trails. Breach clenched his right hand into a fist and threw it up into the air aside of his head. His tiny troop came to an immediate halt, but said nothing.

"See that path running north into that thicket?" Breach said in a voice just above a whisper. "It runs through the thicket and opens out into a wide area flanked by a lot of other low growing trees and heavy underbrush. It's the most direct route to the cemetery, but it's dangerous because of all that cover. Anything could leap out at us and be on us in no time, even when we get into the open.

"This path," Breach said pointing to a winding, snow-covered trail to the west, "is safer. There's nothing on either side except coal banks and hills, and they lie off a couple of hundred yards from the path. All the brush and undergrowth are behind them. It's safer because we'd see an enemy coming, but it'll add about a half mile to our journey. I say we take it instead of the one to the north. What do you two think?"

"I think," Yakov replied in an angry, hushed voice, "you didn't mention adding an extra half mile to our trip before!"

"Because I didn't see any need to until we saw what the conditions were up here," Breach snapped back. "And look who's complaining about revealing things a piece-at-a-time!"

"We take the north path!" the older man replied as if giving an order. "I'm worried about our time. It's 6:50 already, and we only covered about a half-mile! I say we've got to take a chance and go by the shortest possible route!"

"I'm with Gus," Frank said quietly. "I remember my son bringing me up here a long time ago. That thicket flanking the north path is pretty dense if I recall right. At least it was back then. There wasn't even any elbowroom between the path and the thicket when we walked through it in good weather. Too closed-in. And like Gus said, the open area on the other side of it is surrounded by a lot of brush and heavy undergrowth. No, no good. Let's take the west path."

"Where are you going?" Yakov called out to Breach in a subdued voice as the cop started walking toward the north trail.

"I'll check it out. If it's passable, maybe you're right and we should take it," were his last whispered words as he disappeared into the thick patch of brush and trees. Fifteen minutes later he reappeared.

"Got bad news," he said, puffing. "About fifty feet in, there's a snow wall a good seven or eight feet high. The trail is completely impassable. Looks like we're stuck with the west path."

"And the added half-mile," Yakov said gloomily. "Just great! Four-and-a-half miles to go now, instead of only four! We'd better get moving."

"One thing," Gus added, ignoring Yakov's complaint. "About a mile-and-a-half further on we're going to hit a ledge. It's about forty feet long but only two feet wide. On the left of it is a small hill. It's actually a backdrop that meets the ledge all along its length. But that's good because it gives you something to lean against. On the right is a sheer drop of about a hundred feet, what's left of an old coalhole that partially sunk in decades ago. It's not bad going in good weather, but I don't know what it'll be like now. When we reach it, we go across one at a time. I'll go first to check the footing. If anything happens to me, you two will have to try it, one at a time. Just look down at my footprints, and see what it was that tripped me up. Ok?"

"No time for any objections," Yakov replied coldly. "Thanks for telling us in advance."

They started down the wide trail, slipping, sliding, and falling intermittently over the frozen surface. It became harder for them to stand up after each fall. Their ages were beginning to show. Disgruntled, the men cursed their aging bodies, remembering the times of their youth when their feet were surer, their bodies flexible, and their stride more natural and carefree.

"I thought going downhill was going to be easier," Frank whispered as they moved along the path.

"Not in snow," Gus replied. "It's easier going uphill. You can dig in and make better time for a while, but eventually you get tired more quickly. Just keep going!"

"A lose-lose situation either way then, huh?"

"Ssshhhh! Keep quiet and keep going! I'm not enjoying this anymore than you! The path levels out a few hundred yards ahead. It'll be easier until we get to the base of the mountain!"

Continuing to slip, slide, and fall, the men slowly made their way down the path's incline. Finally the path leveled out. As Yakov picked himself and the Staff up from the snow once more, the old cop held up his right fist once again, bringing them to a halt.

"We've come about a mile-and-a-half since we left Ben's place, but the ledge is still about another half-mile away. Luckily, that next half-mile is flat. So is the mile-and-a-half to the base of the mountain. The going will be easier from now until then. But keep alert, just in case. What time do you have, Ben?"

Shining his flashlight on his wristwatch and shaking his head from side to side Yakov replied in a disgusted voice, "It's 8:30! We're not making good time at all."

"We'll get there, Ben, we'll get there. Let's keep a good thought as we plow through the rest of the damn distance!"

Slowly they crossed the open flat area, noting every night sound the mountains gave up. Taking breaks every fifteen minutes, the men felt a growing heaviness in their legs and arms, while the trunks of their bodies seemed to weigh them down even more. After what seemed to them like an eternity since they heard each other's voices, the old cop threw his right fist up once again, bringing them to a stop.

"There it is! The ledge! Well, Ben, you can relax now! We're a good two miles into our four-and-a-half mile journey! How are we doing?"

"Goddamn it!" Yakov said in a raised voice as he looked at his timepiece. "It's 9:15! We're making worse time! It took us forty-five minutes to cross the last half-mile! Overall we're only doing about a half-mile an hour since we started out! At this rate, we won't get to the cemetery until after 2:00 a.m.! NightShadow will be free! We've got to do better than this! Let's get across that ledge!"

"Calm down," Breach replied reassuringly. "The downhill part was the worst. That took a lot of extra time. You should know! You fell more than we did!" he added laughingly. "All of that sliding around didn't help time-wise, either! But from here to the base of the mountain, it's flat. And our legs should be use to the snow. We'll make it in time. Wait and see!"

In a few minutes the team was at the ledge.

"I'll go first," Breach spoke out. "But first, take a good look around. See that hundred-foot drop off to the right? The bottom of the chasm is covered with snow now, but underneath it are a lot of jagged rocks and some boulders. So be careful! Now, watch me! I'm going to snuggle up to the hill on its left as if I was engaged to it! After I get across, I'll signal you. Frank, I want you to cross next. Ben and his staff will come last. Just remember! Whatever you do, keep looking down at my footprints, walk in them only, and hug that hill! That's all you gotta do!"

He walked out onto the ledge cautiously, using his years of hunting experience and natural intuition to feel through his boots to the surface of the snow-packed cliff overhang. As his left shoulder hugged the hill, he placed one foot in front of the other, until he emerged on the other side. Waving his arms, he signaled for the next man to cross.

Frank stepped onto the ledge slowly, pressing his feet as deeply as he could into the snow as if searching for the bare ground beneath. Keeping his eyes focused on the path of Gus' footprints, he stepped cautiously into each one. Step by step he grew more self-assured as he reached the middle of the overhang.

"This isn't so bad after all," he said under his breath. "Hell, it's a breeze! And I was so worried about…" As his thought trailed off into further self-congratulations, he lifted his gaze from the tracks and smiled at Breach.

Instinctively, Gus shouted out loud, breaking his own rule of silence. "Keep your eyes on the footprints, Frank! You'll lose your balance!"

But Breach's warning came too late. As Frank lifted his eyes, the afterimage of the flashlight's beam against the snow flashed against the dark backdrop of the sky behind his friend. His balance wavered, and in a split second, his right foot slipped off the ledge and shot out into the space above the overhang. Trying to regain balance, Lewis instinctively lurched toward the small hill on his left. As he did, his full weight shifted to his left. Both of his feet slid out from under him, as he slid sideways off the overhang. As he plummeted through the open space to the bottom of the pit, he cried out the single word "Guusssss!" shattering his companions' nerves. In a few seconds, the deafening silence returned.

"Frank! Frank! Can you hear me?" Breach called out in a panicked voice as he shined his flashlight into the pit.

"It's no use," Yakov called out. "He's gone!"

"It can't be!" Breach screamed. "Frank! Frank! Get up! Get up! You can't leave us this way! Not now! Not here! We've got a job to do, and we've got to do it together! Frank, get up!"

Yakov made his way across the overhang quickly but carefully, stepping over the place where Frank lost his balance. Taking Gus' flashlight from his hands and adding its beam to his own, Ben shined the lights down into the pit.

"This is hard, Gus," he said heavily, "but you have to see it. Look down."

Breach lowered his head and followed the beams into the surrounding blackness of the chasm. At the bottom of the gorge, draped across the snow-covered outline of a large boulder, was Frank Lewis's broken body. His battered face stared up toward the heavens, as a dark liquid flowed out of his mouth and ears, dripping into the snow surrounding him. The look of terror and shock on his face reminded Breach of the trauma suffered by the spirit at the time of death as Yakov had explained to them days before.

"Sit down, Gus," Yakov said gently. "I know this is hard. It's hard for me too. I took a fancy to that man, and even thought he could study the Qabalah when all of this was over. Maybe even become a student of the Mysteries in time. He was one of a kind, and he helped us greatly. But we have to go on now without him. Frank would want it that way, and you know it."

"But what good did his death serve, Ben?" Breach sobbed out through the tears rolling down his agonized face. "If each of us had to play some part in destroying NightShadow, what good came of him dying now? Maybe if he died in a struggle with NightShadow in the cemetery, maybe then his death would have some meaning! But what good can it have now? Tell me that! You, you bastard, you and that fuck Shannon and Cavendish are to blame for all of this! I swear to you, if I had the strength right now I'd kill you myself, if for no other reason than to avenge Frank on the first fuck responsible for all of this! You, you dirty…" Breach broke his words off, jumped to his feet and turned to Yakov. Somehow, the exhausted man suddenly found the strength to carry out his threat.

Yakov jumped back, barely eluding Breach's grasp. As he regained his balance, the Magician struck the bottom of the Staff three times against the snow-covered ground while calling out in a language Breach had not heard before.

"Ooeeel Empahayy Eeehiaa Maaappp!"

Before he finished pronouncing the words, a shrill, high frequency noise shot through the night. As its volume increased, the sound drove Breach to his knees.

"Stop it!" he screamed at the top of his lungs, as though the noise in his head echoed through the night air of the mountains. "Stop it! It's killing me!"

But Yakov did not respond to his friend's plea for mercy. Instead, he waited a few more seconds until Breach fell to the ground, whimpering and clawing at his ears until they bled. Then quickly the Magician struck the bottom of the Staff against the snow three more times and said out loud, "Oooaaaaetah Baheoha Taahoobea Maaheeaatta!"

Gus stopped convulsing. For several minutes he laid silently in the snow while Yakov stood still looking at him. Finally the older man spoke out.

"Please forgive me. It was necessary. I had to stop you. Your rage was natural, but if it went unchecked, you would have killed me. You have that type of personality. Here, let me help you up. Don't worry, you didn't suffer any permanent damage."

"It's not me I'm worried about," Breach said through his sobs. "How will I ever explain this to his son?"

"Gus," Yakov said gently, "please listen to me. Frank knew the dangers just as we do. He knew he had a role in all of this. Just what that role is or was, we may never know. But where he's at now, he knows all of it, plus a lot more than any man alive. It's ok. He went through the trauma of having his spirit torn from the only vessel it ever knew, but that's all over now. He is at peace, Gus, and you've got to believe that. His suffering is over. We're still in the middle of ours, and Frank would damn well want us to carry on until we either join him in the next few hours, or succeed in destroying Night-Shadow. How about it? Are we partners again?"

Breach stared out through his tears at the aged face of his friend.

"You're right, Ben," he replied softly. "Frank would want us to get this job done. And yeah, we're partners again! I just lost it for a while. Thanks for bringing me around. No telling what I'd have done if it wasn't for you. Just what did you do, anyway?"

"The Staff has many powers you don't know about. The documents I gave you to study only covered the Second Consecration and the Final Return, so you couldn't have known its other abilities, like protecting the Magician from any physical harm another human might try to inflict. There was simply no point to you knowing about them, any more than knowing the details of the First Consecration or of the Final Summoning by which Cavendish was resurrected. It was a moot point as far as I was concerned."

"Any other moot points you might care to share with me now?" Breach asked, not knowing if he was feeling suspicious or simply curious.

"No, none," Yakov replied causally. "If you feel up to it, we'd better get a move on. We have another mile-and-a-half to cover to get to the base of the mountain, and it's nearly ten."

As they started out down the path, Gus stopped abruptly when a voice broke into his own thoughts. Yakov stopped behind him, but said nothing. Quietly, he watched as Breach began to speak out loud to some unseen agent.

The voice said *Remember what you said when I saved you from the qlippoth in your backyard, Gus? 'I owe you one!' Remember that?*

"Sure, I remember!" Gus answered out loud. "How could I forget? If it wasn't for you I'd be dead now."

And what did I say to that, huh, Gus? the voice asked gently.

"Uh, I think you said, 'And I'll take you up on it if I have to.' Right?"

That's right, my friend! And I'm taking you up on it now. I'm asking you to trust Ben. I'm here with the both of you, at least for these few moments. I want to move on to where I somehow know I have to go, but I can't just yet. I don't know if it's me that's holding myself back, or if I'm not being allowed to go yet, but here I am!

Trust our friend! There is a terrible job that lies ahead. We didn't know how terrible it would be, but it's more so than you think. But I didn't come here to scare you. Just to tell you if you trust him and yourself, things will work out. I can't see far enough ahead to know what that means, but I feel whatever the ending of this nightmare is, things will work out. Will you do that for me? I'm calling in my marker. Will you do as I ask?

Tears rolled down the old cop's face as he suddenly realized he was talking to the spirit of his dead friend.

"Sure, Frank, I'll do the best I can. That's a promise!"

The voice ended as suddenly as it began. After a few moments, Breach turned around to Yakov.

"I know you won't believe this, but Frank just paid me a visit. It was so real, as if he and I were together in some other place, I mean, really together. I didn't see him, but we were together physically. Does that make sense?"

"Yes." Yakov replied softly. "I sensed Frank hadn't moved on yet, but I couldn't be sure. Now you have confirmed it. And it was real. As real as anything can be. That's how it works sometimes. You and he met up in the mental world of imagination that lies between this one and others. It's the astral plane. The difference is, he can now move in and out of the astral and this world as he pleases. We're not that fortunate. At least, not yet," he added with a wry smile. "Can I ask," Yakov said shyly, "what he said?"

"Uh, well," Breach replied reluctantly, "He told me to…trust myself, and if we do what we have to together—as a team— everything would work out, except he didn't know how. That's all."

Yakov looked intently into Breach's face through the shades of the night. He knew he was lying. He sensed something special and secret had passed between Breach and Lewis that Gus did not want to discuss. He respected the privacy of a conversation with the other side.

"Fair enough. Shall we continue our journey?"

Alone with their thoughts of Frank, the two men made their way across the snow-covered trail. The deeper they penetrated into the woods, the more solidly frozen was the snow bed beneath their feet, lending them better traction. Their speed increased, until they seemed to be gliding effortlessly across the white surface. At other places along the trail, the snowdrifts stacked up on the sides of the path, leaving them stretches of bare ground to cross quickly. Silently they moved along, trying to divide their attention between the night sounds of the forest, and their lingering thoughts of the friend they had lost.

"We're here!" Breach said in what now seemed to Yakov to be a loud voice. "We've made it! We're at the base of the mountain! Only a half-mile to go to get to the cemetery, Ben! What time do you have?"

"It's 11:10. We did that last mile-and-a-half in seventy minutes! That's a hell of a lot better than a half mile an hour! But we still have to get to the cemetery and I have to erect the circle, and summon NightShadow. Damn it all anyway, Gus, we're still going to cut it close! Dangerously close!"

"Can't be helped, not after what happened. We're lucky we made it this far. I have to tell you after Frank died, I was thinking of turning around and heading back to town. I was going to give up. I didn't care anymore. Not about you, or humanity, or this whole frigging world. Or the fate of the universe and all the nonsense supposed to be tied up in this mess, according to you. Principle of Good, Principal of Evil, who gives a damn! That's what I was thinking. But that's when Frank's voice broke into my thoughts and he visited me. So count your blessings old boy, because at that point, as far as I was concerned, you were on your own!"

"There's more to that visit than you're telling me, isn't there?" Yakov finally asked.

Breach shrugged the question off. "If we want to make the deadline, we'd better start the final climb. We veer off here. If we continued straight on the path we're on now, it would end at the base of the mountain. There's another trail there that leads straight north to the top. But we take this side of the 'Y.' "

He motioned to the right side of the forked path. "It curves around and takes us back north right to the cemetery. This is the last half-mile and it's all uphill. It starts off slow, but gets steeper. Near the crest we're looking at a forty-five degree slope. In this snow and with that incline, we're going to get very tired very fast! I'll lead." He brushed past Yakov and began the final ascent.

"No bush dogs yet, huh Gus?" Yakov said softly as they marched along. "It's pretty close in here, like someone cut a three-foot path through the undergrowth."

"If they didn't attack us by now, I'd say those bush dogs are holed up in their burrows. This blizzard was like nothing anyone around here ever saw, and that includes them. Better keep quiet though, just in case!"

The two allies labored up the hill, digging the heels of their boots in as far as they would go with each step. Their traction became better, but they were tiring quickly.

"I don't see how we're going to get there in time," Breach said in between long, heavy puffs of breath.

"I know. We need a miracle now. Only the—"

"Look, Ben! Look! I don't believe it! We're home free!"

Fifty yards into their climb, the two men came upon the miracle they desperately needed. The shifting winds swirling through the trees and broken by the dense undergrowth had formed a sweeping motion along the narrow trail, as if a gigantic broom had simply swept the snow from the ground. As far as they could see, the trail ahead of them was clear down to the bare earth.

"What were you saying?" Breach teased.

"I was going to say only the Principle of Good could help us now, and look! It looks like it did! Remember the checks and balances I talked about?! The moves of one Principle and the counters of the other, eternally shifting back and forth, always keeping the playing field of the universe level. Looks like that's what happened here."

Without further comment, the two tired men raced up the path, puffing and panting hard with each quickened step. In what seemed like only seconds to Yakov, Breach threw his arm across the older man's moving body and said in a lowered voice, "We're here, Ben! We've made it! We're at the back of the cemetery! Quick! Up this little hill, and we'll be inside!"

The men scaled the tiny hill quickly. As they caught their breath under an enormous ancient tree, Breach pointed to a patch of trees in the north corner of the cemetery.

"There it is! Inside that thicket is Cavendish's grave!"

"I remember it from all those years ago when I visited it. Three times, as I remember. Once a few days after he was buried, a second time on the first anniversary of his death, and the final time the day before I left Kulpsville for good."

"Why? You said you were terrified of him."

"I guess…I guess I wanted to make sure he was still buried. Reassurance for a young man about to make his way in the world. At the time I thought it was closure. Looks like that piece of self-deception was just the vain wishes of a child."

"We've still got time," Yakov said as he swallowed hard, his own fear rising in his voice like a dark specter. "It's eleven thirty-five. We've got twenty-five minutes left! Let's get into the thicket fast!"

§§§

Yakov and Breach raced across the snow covered cemetery lawn as fast as they could. As they neared the entrance of the thicket, a shadow jumped out in front of them, blocking their way.

"Halt or I'll shoot!" A young voice screamed out, panicky. "Not another step, either of you! Identify yourselves!"

They stopped instantly, nearly losing their balance and falling forward. Both could hear their hearts pounding as their faces blushed a fiery red.

"Do it now!" the voice cried out from the darkness. "Who are you?"

"Dave?" Breach called out between chattering teeth. "Dave? Is that you?" He began to shake violently as his thoughts contorted. How could it be? He had taken every precaution to shield his deputy from danger. He wanted the young man to survive. Dave was his son in some way, and if this was him, now he was in the greatest danger of all.

"Gus!" the voice answered back from the shadows. "Gus! Yeah, it's me! Dave Barker! I thought—"

Breach raced toward him, grabbed him by the collar and lifted him off the ground.

"What are you doing here?!" he screamed into Barker's face. "God dammit, I told you to stay with Puffner and help him search for NightShadow! You were under orders to stick with him like glue! Why did you go against them?!"

"Gus," Barker squeaked out through Breach's grip, "let me go! You're cutting my air off! Come on, Gus, let me go!"

Yakov grabbed Breach by the back of his neck, pulled on the skin and pinched it hard. The sharp pain brought him back to the moment.

After releasing his grip, Breach said, "I want an explanation Barker, and it better be the best you ever came up with!"

"I told you Gus," Yakov cut in, "all of us drawn into this nightmare have some unknown role, and those roles are being played out. Trying to get around them won't work. Now hurry!" he ordered as he disappeared into the thicket with the Staff. "There's no time to lose!"

"We'll be there in a minute," Breach shot back angrily. "Do what you have to and we'll be right in!"

"Listen, Gus!" Barker began to explain, fear filling his voice. "I had to join you! I just had to!"

"How did you figure out we'd be up here?"

"I didn't! One of Ben's neighbors saw three men leaving his house and heading out across the field at sundown. With Night-Shadow prowling around and doing more killing since the two of you dropped out of sight, they didn't know what to think! So the neighbor called the station house and reported it. I figured it had to be you, Frank, and Ben. Who else could it be?

"Since I was in on the battle when Pete and Mike were killed, I know what's going on! It didn't take me long to figure out you three were up to something aimed at destroying it, and I figured you were headed back here. So I took off to help you."

"Oh, Dave!" Breach said in an agonized voice. "Why didn't you stay put? You shouldn't have come here. I didn't want you involved because the fact is, this is the final battle, and one we don't know we can win. The odds were against Ben, Frank, and me making it from the beginning. We all knew it. We discussed it, but we accepted them. But this is one job that's got to be done.

"Ben has his own suspicions as to what's really at the bottom of this mess, but it doesn't matter anymore if he's right or wrong as far as I'm concerned. All I know is that thing running around out there has killed eighteen people already, and it's got to be stopped, no matter what. And even if we do succeed, there's a damn good chance we'll still die. I didn't want you here. That's why I stuck you with Puffner. I didn't want you to die too. Didn't you understand that? Don't you get it?"

The young cop looked into Breach's face through their flashlight beams. Tiny tears were rolling down the old man's face. After a few moments the young cop smiled warmly.

"Yeah, Gus. Now I get it. I'm sorry. I just didn't figure it out earlier. But where's Frank?"

"He was killed on the way up at the ledge on the west path. He slipped off the overhang and fell to the bottom of the pit. Died instantly."

"I know the place. Damn, he was a good man! A lot of people are going to miss him." Barker shook his head from side to side. "It was bad getting here, was it?"

"Like nothing I ever saw before. But how did you get here? Did you take the back roads behind the high school?"

"Of course. They weren't too bad either. The winds blew the drifts to the sides of the roads. Hell, the paths were almost bare down to the ground! I left the station house at seven, and got here at nine-thirty. Then I hunkered down in the thicket by Cavendish's grave and waited for the three of you. I've been freezing ever since!"

"You'll have a lot more serious things to complain about before this is all over," Breach said grimly. "There's no more time to explain. Let's get in there and help Ben!"

As Breach turned to the path leading into the thicket, Dave grabbed his coat sleeve and pulled him back.

"Wait. You should know NightShadow broke into the station house on Thursday. It was just after night fell, about six p.m. I was on patrol with one of the military units, but the one soldier who escaped the fracas said it killed Puffner and four of his men. Tore them to shreds in seconds. Then it went for the prisoners. Gus, it ripped the bars out of the floor and ceiling and got at Rick Sadaleski, John Federoski, and Jim March. When I saw them and the others, I couldn't believe it. The attacks were more savage than the earlier ones. But that's not all. The death toll has climbed to thirty-four. After Puffner was killed, his troops went crazy. When I left, they were roaming the town, almost like looters, totally out of control. There was nothing I could do single-handedly. Just thought you should know."

Barker's report fell hard on Breach's ears. Fierce determination broke out on the old cop's face. His physical body was on the verge of collapse from starvation and exhaustion, but his spiritual nature had become powerful and took over, as Yakov had predicted. His squared jaw and tightened facial muscles told Dave the man he faced was consumed with raging hate.

"Let's join Ben, quick! It's payback time!"

As Breach and Barker broke into the opening inside the thicket, Yakov's previous words repeated in Gus' head. When the physical body becomes weak and the spiritual nature becomes strong and great danger arises…the declaration of your own spiritual nature can take many, many forms…all we can count on is that something will happen. It's up to us to be alert enough to feel it happening and direct it or just let it happen. That's the uncertainty in these things, but that's just the way it is…be alert for anything from the spiritual side, and use it as best you can or just go with the flow.

"Keep your eyes and ears open, Dave," Breach said out loud. "And above all, let your spiritual side take over!"

"What?" Barker replied with confusion. "What the hell are you talking about Chief?"

"Picture a bright white sphere above the crown of your head, and concentrate on it! I might be wrong, but it'll protect you, and maybe even help us! Right Ben?"

"That's about the best he can do now," the Magician replied. "There's no more time to prepare him! Just do as your Chief tells you, young man, and maybe, just maybe you'll come out of this alive!"

A wave of intense fear shot through the young cop as he listened to his boss's orders. Almost without thinking, he began to concentrate on a small white sphere above his head. As he focused on it, a high shrill ringing began in his ears, and gentle warmth flowed into his body and mind.

"What do we do, Ben?" Breach asked with grim determination.

"Come here! The both of you!" Yakov screamed out, holding the Staff up high in his right hand. "It's time! We only have seven minutes left!"

Breach and Barker ran to Yakov's side.

"Get into the circles! I've redrawn them next to NightShadow's grave with the Staff, as is called for! We must enter from the north, since that's the quarter ruling death. Say whatever prayers you know out loud as we cross into the circles! Now!"

As they crossed the openings Yakov left in the circles, Breach recited a Hail Mary as Barker said the Lord's Prayer. Yakov recited a prayer in Hebrew, then turned around quickly when they were inside, and with the base of the Staff sealed the openings and turned back to face the north. Barker looked on in wonder as the hideous face on top of the Staff flashed its violet eyes with red pupils at him, and sneered. The madness of its living, wooden hair streaming in all directions, the mechanical blinking of its eyelids, and the irregular, choppy motion of its head, propelled the deputy into another world. In a moment, the Staff began to howl and give off a low, guttural growl as Yakov began.

"I summon thee forth, you who escaped from the grave by the Staff of Resurrection or Return, and by the Rite of the Final Resurrection and the Final Return, you who were known in life by the name of Martin Cavendish!"

As Yakov called out into the night, the Staff began to pulsate, throwing off a black light more intense than before, its guttural growls and moans now turning into cries demanding deliverance, while Yakov strained to cry out his summoning above the Staff's wailings.

"By the Face of Death that didst summon thee forth, and by the Words of Power it uttered of the Final Resurrection, I call thee here before us, Martin Cavendish, to appear beyond this circle that I may do that which I will, as has been set down by the laws of God and the darkest part of Nature which He created, and which governs this unnatural act! Come thou forth unto us, now, thou spirit made flesh once more, and obey my will!"

When Yakov's words ended, the three men heard the sound of brush being trampled in the north, as small trees creaked and gave way beneath some unseen strain. The sounds became louder as the hidden cause behind the noises burst past the final lines of brush, out into the open.

"It's NightShadow!" Breach screamed out. "Quick, Ben, destroy it!"

Barker stood fixed to his spot, his eyes transfixed on the patch of living night standing before the circle, his mind completely blank. Before Yakov could continue, the blackness concealing Night-Shadow began to swirl and move, as if a thousand different miniature whirlwinds had started up within it. As they watched in amazement, the black currents turned inward upon the thing hiding within them. Then, as though on some signal, all of the currents suddenly converged toward their center, and in a moment were gone. Standing before them outside the circle was Martin Cavendish.

Cavendish's appearance had not changed. He was as Yakov had described. His imposing stature, shocking silver hair and steel blue eyes struck fear into the young deputy. Even Breach unknowingly took a step backward in the circle, as if preparing for physical confrontation with the man who stood on the other side of the circles. Staring at Yakov hard, Cavendish spoke out in the same melodic voice he did a half-century earlier.

"Well, Abe, looks like we finally come together for the last time! Remember how I used to call you Abe all those years ago? Of course you do! I bet you remember all those nights you and Tim spent at my house, studying the Mysteries with me! I can't tell you how disappointed I was when you broke off from me. You have no idea how much trouble you caused my Master, Seaton Stannish and me! But as you can see, we figured a way around all those nasty problems. And now, let me guess, Abe. You intend to invoke the Final Return, and send me back to the grave. Isn't that right? Isn't that why you brought those two lackeys with you? You know, I heard the other one was killed on the way here tonight. Too bad. I understand from my, uh, sources you liked him. Never fear my old friend, you and your lackeys will be joining him in a few moments!"

Cavendish's gently soft and musical voice began to lull Barker into a stupor. He slouched forward, taking up a relaxed stance.

"Snap out of it!" Breach yelled, as he jabbed the young man in the ribs with his elbow. "That's part of his game!" The pain in Barker's ribs brought him back to the unfolding drama.

"Silence!" Yakov cried out. "Thy time has come, Martin Cavendish! I will thee back to thy grave, there to suffer the torment of the damned past the end of all time, for the evil thou hast wrought upon humankind since thou arose from thy resting place! Hear thou, the Voice of Wonder, and the Words of Power of the Final Return!"

But as Yakov was about to begin, Cavendish threw up his right hand. Immediately, a huge cloak of intense blackness surrounded his hand and spread outward, trying to penetrate the circle.

"Your cloak of night cannot pierce this hallowed ground, Cavendish! See the Names of Power written within the circles' bounds! See the cry of all humanity saved by the advent of God in man which is declared in the circle, Et verbum caro factum est, Jesus autem transiens per medium! For truly, evil one, the Word has been made flesh in Jesus, and made to dwell among us!"

"Why is Ben speaking so strangely?" Barker whispered.

"Probably to concentrate on his job. He knows Cavendish is stalling for time… Oh my God, the time! Ben!" Breach called out, "Ben, the time!"

Yakov glanced down at his wristwatch. It was 11:59. Cavendish had succeeded in mesmerizing the Magician into entering a dialogue with him. In so doing, Ben had lost awareness of the last few fleeting seconds needed to destroy the evil standing before them.

"You're too late, Abe! It took thirty-four lives, but I have completely regenerated! You can't stop me now! Look at me! I am as you knew me! Strong, powerful, and in only a few seconds, I become as immortal as my Master! Then you and this filthy world will be thrown into the pit! Yes Abe, you are right! The world and this entire universe are on the edge of the abyss, and there's nothing you can do to stop it, because I know you haven't discovered the secret to ignite the light and fire from the Staff! Ah, that Final Secret! The Words of Power are not enough! It's too late, Yakov. With the final stroke of midnight, I will slaughter the three of you just for my own amusement!"

But while Cavendish savored the moment, a gentle voice rang in Yakov's head.

Remember the words you spoke to me Ben, to trust in myself? You said the Principle of Good will aid us when we least expect it. Well, you were right. I am here! It's Frank! As I entered Gus' thoughts earlier, now I'm entering yours! Listen to me, Ben! This is why my death was necessary. The Principle of Good has intervened once more! I have found the Final Secret on this side of the grave!

"Frank! Yakov shouted. "It's you!"

"What's he talking about, Gus? Is Ben going out of his mind? Oh my God, not now!"

"Shut up!" Breach shouted. "Not now! I'll explain it later!"

The spiritual light and fire of the Staff can be ignited only one way! But hurry! What you must do is…

Yakov spun around to face Breach and Barker as Cavendish prowled around the circle, laughing, waiting for the final seconds before the stroke of midnight that would mark the beginning of the Lord's Day.

"Gus, Dave, trust me!" Yakov said in a shallow voice. "You must trust me! Close your eyes!"

"Never!" Breach yelled. "You're asking too much!"

You owe me one, Gus! Frank's voice now sounded in Breach's ears. *Trust Ben! That's what we agreed on! Do it now!*

"Do it, Barker!" Breach screamed out wildly. "Trust Ben! Close your eyes!"

As the two men shut their eyes, Yakov cried out in a loud and powerful voice.

"Here thou me, Martin Cavendish! Here now the Words of Power of the Final Return! Here the Seven Words of eternal damnation for those who dare to break the law of the grave! Beeeaaatthhhaa Moreaga, Bieotooa, Toureesta Sulfookona Zeeoodoah Aaaghtteeaaa!"

As he pronounced each word, he struck the base of the Staff against the ground. When the final vowel of the seventh Word of Power ended on the Magician's lips, the Staff broke into a hideous wailing. The sound of its voice and the unknown words the Staff screamed out were so hideous and violent, the three men threw their hands over their ears, unable to endure them. As Breach pressed his hands tighter and tighter against his head, he recalled Yakov's warning about the Staff's second half of the Words of Power. "To hear them causes great terror in man, and brings about strange manifestations. Nature herself becomes horrified and revolts."

As the Staff continued to pronounce the words never written down by the ancient Magicians, the earth shook as sighs went up from Cavendish's open grave, and streaks of multicolored lights shot through the air outside of the circle. Trees creaked and fell to the earth in the forest surrounding them. Fierce winds formed and began to swirl around the circle. Cavendish himself backed away from the circle and bent his head down to his chest, as if to hide from the terrible Words being screamed out by the mad face.

"It's not enough!" Cavendish screamed through the winds. "There's less than a minute left, Yakov! Not even the Words from the Staff are enough! You know that! You need the Final Secret and you don't know it!"

"But I do, Cavendish!" Yakov screamed out, as he jumped across the circles and landed on the open ground next to NightShadow. "But I do know, now! The one slain this night as we traveled here to destroy thee revealed it to me! And this is the Final Secret!"

Breach heard the rustle of the Magician's coat as he jumped from the circle, and opened his eyes.

"Ben! Get back! Ben!" As the old cop screamed, he moved to jump from the circles to help his friend. But a powerful fist caught him on the back of his neck, sending him to his knees.

"No you don't, Gus! I'm sorry I had to hit you, but I don't want you to be killed too! I can't let that happen!" Barker cried out as he helped him to his feet. "Calm down, Chief! Ben knows what he's doing. I don't know how, but I know he knows what he's doing!"

Yakov threw his arms around Cavendish and locked them in place while holding the Staff against the enemy's back. Looking up to the heavens, the Magician cried out in a powerful but calm voice.

"Lord God of all Creation! Hear my plea! Let this staff burn with Thy spiritual light and fire needed to destroy this abomination! I offer my life in payment for the wrong I have done so many years ago aiding this beast of the fields! Bring him down, and lift me up to Thy kingdom! Let the Law of the Final Secret be fulfilled by my sacrifice!"

As Yakov's words ended, the Staff burst into a bright violet-silver flame of enormous size. In seconds, it engulfed both Cavendish and the Magician. Raging and cursing in torment, Cavendish's regenerated body began to degenerate once more. Chunks of flesh fell from his arms and face, replaced with hollow black holes. Cavendish screamed in agony and despair as Yakov struggled to pull his enemy to the edge of his grave. As he grappled with his opponent, they could hear the bells of Saint Joseph beginning to toll in the town below. Gong…gong…gong…they rang out. Cavendish lashed out with his teeth, trying to sink them in Yakov's neck. But the aged Magician butted his head against his enemy's rotting face, continuing to wrestle him to the edge of the opening.

Yakov looked into Cavendish's yellow decaying eyes and said, "Now Martin, to sleep, for both of us!" and with one final thrust, the former psychiatrist hurled the two of them into the open grave. The eleventh stroke of the bells sounded out, as Yakov and NightShadow hit the bottom of the rotting coffin, and a huge flare of violet-silver light tinged with red and blue shot upward toward the night sky. As the bells in Kulpsville struck out their twelfth chime of the final stroke of midnight, it was over.

Breach and Barker left the circle, and slowly walked over to the grave. There, in the coffin, lay the once-again decomposing corpse of Martin Cavendish. Abraham ben Yakov's left arm was still locked across the corpse's chest, as if guaranteeing NightShadow would now remain in the world beyond the grave for all time.

"So that was the Final Secret needed to send Cavendish back," Breach said softly. "Both Operators had to die. The Assistant Operator had to be sacrificed by the Principle Operator to resurrect the corpse, and the Principle Operator had to sacrifice himself if he chose to send the thing back to the grave. What a hell of a compact! And Ben never knew it until a few moments ago when Frank visited him and told him what the ancient Magicians never recorded—the Key— the Final Secret.

"If Frank didn't die, we never would have known it. Frank had to lose his life for us to find out that secret, one that could only be discovered on the other side of life. Without it, we would have failed.

"That's why Ben wanted us to close our eyes. He knew we'd try to stop him from jumping out of the circle and sacrificing himself. And if we had stopped him, the world and eventually the universe would have been lost to the Principle of Evil. The Black Utopia Cavendish and Stannish had planned to launch would have started. I finally had to trust Ben as Frank wanted, and at the eleventh hour— the most desperate time of all.

"I'll never have friends like Frank and Ben again," Breach said as his head fell forward, and tears began to flow down his frozen, cracked aging face. "But I've got to tell you, young man, I'll always remember them, and count myself as one of the luckiest men who ever lived for having had them as my friends."

"I suppose," Barker replied quietly, "you'll eventually get around to explaining to me what you just said, and you'll tell me what happened after you and Frank left me at the station house with Puffner. I'd really like to know. It's as if I was part of this somehow. As though I had to be, if that makes sense."

"Sure, son, in time I'll tell you what happened. But not for a while. It's going to take me time to sort it all and make sense of it myself. Emotional sense, I guess Ben would call it, and he'd be right.

"And as to you being part of all of this? Yes, you were. If you weren't there to hit me in the back of my neck and drop me to my knees, I would have stopped Ben. And Cavendish, Stannish, and their infernal conspiracy would have succeeded. Ben was right when he told us everyone pulled into this nightmare by Fate had some role to play. It wasn't clear to any of us at the time, but it is now."

"Give me release, back to the World of Death," the low, guttural voice cried out from behind them. "I have fulfilled my charge in the Final Return! The Words of Power of the Final Return have been uttered by me! I demand thee to now set me free as thy Master of Magic agreed!"

Breach and Barker looked down into the open grave. Lying next to Ben's left arm, aside of Cavendish's rotting corpse, was the Staff of Resurrection or Return.

"Dear Lord," Barker blurted out in disgust. "Look at its face! It's as grotesque as it was before! I can't look at it any longer, Gus!" he said turning his head away, "I thought...I thought maybe with Cavendish's death it might...I don't know...just go away somehow. Why is it still here? Still alive, if that's what it is! Why does it cry out like that? What do we do with it?"

"It's in torment, Dave. As Ben once explained, it cries out because it's being tormented by something no man can understand. It doesn't belong to our world, but to another. To the world of death, and to a life beyond the grave. Ben told us as long as it is trapped in our world, a party to this business called Infernal Necromancy, it is not just suffering. It is in unimaginable agony. That's why it cries out. It wants release!

"That hideous expression it wears is called the Face of the Second Death, since Cavendish has been destroyed. Why does it still look so horrible?" Breach continued. "Because it is symbolic of the experience of death itself. You see, after the spirit leaves its physical body at the time of death, it undergoes an agonizing trauma."

Breach caught himself, remembering Frank's and his reaction to Yakov's detailed explanation of the death experience. Wanting to spare the young man the horror behind the full explanation, he said, "But that's for another time...maybe.

"As to what to do with it? Watch."

Breach jumped down into the grave and pried the Staff from Ben's hand. Placing it on the ground next to the grave's opening, he pulled himself up to the surface, grabbed the weightless, crying piece of black ebony, and walked over to Cavendish's tombstone. Holding the Staff tightly with both of his hands, Breach lifted it in the air, swung it behind his back and over his head, and with a powerful downward motion smashed the Staff against the edge of the Cavendish's tombstone. As the Staff made contact with the cold block of stone, a loud volley like a shotgun blast broke through the still night air while Breach cried out in a loud and powerful voice.

"Return, by the One God over all Creation!"

Immediately, Breach released his grip. The Staff split in two as it fell to the ground. A second later, it burst into flames. In another few seconds it disappeared.

"As if it never existed," Breach said dryly, shaking his head from side to side. "So much pain, so much agony, so many deaths, such a world its creator, Martin Cavendish, envisioned for the world. All over. Gone, as if it never was."

"What do we do now?" Barker asked in a monotone voice. "What do we tell the town? How do we account for all of this? Frank's death? And Ben's? And all of the others? How do we deal with the military? Damn, Gus, it's going to be rough going getting ourselves out from under this mess, and getting the town back on its feet!"

"Not a fraction of the rough going the four of us have been through. Let's go, son. We have a lot of work to do."

The End

About the Author

Joseph C. Lisiewski, Ph.D. is a noted physicist involved in the study of the Relativistic Space-Time Continuum, and has published numerous nonfiction books and papers on the Occult, Magic and Alchemy. His Occult and Sci-Fi horror books, *Geometries of the Mind* and *The Altar Path* have been well-received by readers and reviewers throughout the world. *NightShadow,* his third horror novel, is his best yet.

Dr. Lisiewski combines elements of science with both Occult principles and his own experiences in these fields, which has enabled him to produce works of horror that his readers never forget—even after the lights are turned back on.

THE *Original* FALCON PRESS

Invites You to Visit Our Website:
http://originalfalcon.com

At our website you can:

- Browse the online catalog of all of our great titles
- Find out what's available and what's out of stock
- Get special discounts
- Order our titles through our secure online server
- Find products not available anywhere else including:
    - One of a kind and limited availability products
    - Special packages
    - Special pricing
- Get free gifts
- Join our email list for advance notice of New Releases and Special Offers
- Find out about book signings and author events
- Send email to our authors
- Read excerpts of many of our titles
- Find links to our authors' websites
- Discover links to other weird and wonderful sites
- And much, much more

Get online today at http://originalfalcon.com

www.ingramcontent.com/pod-product-compliance
Lightning Source LLC
Chambersburg PA
CBHW060250100726

47907CB00003B/832